Marion Zimmer Bradley's

Sword

and

Sorceress

27

Edited by

Elisabeth Waters

SWORD AND SORCERESS 27

Edited by Elisabeth Waters

Copyright © 2012 by the Marion Zimmer Bradley Literary Works Trust
Cover Design copyright © 2014 by Dave Smeds
All Rights Reserved.

Cover Painting:
"The Syracusan Bride" by Frederick Leighton, 1866.

ISBN-13: 978-1-938185-38-0
ISBN-10: 1- 938185-38-2

Trade Paperback Edition

June 12, 2014

A Publication of
The Marion Zimmer Bradley Literary Works Trust
PO Box 193473
San Francisco, CA 94119-3473
www.mzbworks.com

ACKNOWLEDGMENTS

CONTENTS

INTRODUCTION

by Elisabeth Waters

Fairy tales have made a comeback lately, from two television series: Grimm and Once Upon a Time, which started last fall, to two new movies this spring about Snow White: Mirror Mirror in March and Snow White and the Huntsman in June.

Snow White is a major character in *Once Upon a Time* and the heroine of both movies, so it's interesting to consider the various portrayals of her.

The best-know version of the original fairy tale is probably the one collected by the Brothers Grimm. In this version, after the Queen tells the huntsman to kill Snow White and he turns her loose in the forest instead, she lives with the dwarves, keeping house for them. She also manages to fall for the Queen's tricks three times (tight stay-laces, a poisoned comb, and the poisoned apple), despite the dwarves' warnings. The Disney movie of the story, which is the one I knew as a child, is very similar, except that the only trick is the poisoned apple. Snow White is still the dwarves' housekeeper.

But it seems that times may have changed. In both *Once Upon a Time* and *Mirror Mirror*, Snow White is neither passive nor particularly domestic. She may be hiding out in the forest with the dwarves, but she's using that as a base for guerilla warfare against the evil queen. She now has a sword instead of a broom, and she knows how to use it. (Even the rather passive Snow White in *Snow White and the Huntsman* manages to use a dagger by the end of the movie; the movie succeeds on its special effects much more than on plot or character development.)

I suspect that most modern viewers find it easier to identify with a Snow White who fights back. Spending years asleep in a glass coffin waiting to be awakened by "true love's kiss" is hopefully not something that girls today aspire to. We can fight for what we want, and we have a good chance of getting it.

Nowadays we use our wits instead of a sword; a good education is the best weapon we can wield. But the fight to be a queen instead of a pawn continues, and it's a cause worth fighting for. Women want and need to be people, not pawns or chattel, or—as MZB said when she started this series—"bad conduct prizes for the hero."

So let's fight on, inspired by the stories of females who do the same.

A HUNTER OF THE CELADON PLAINS

by Deborah J. Ross

This story was originally intended for a shared-world anthology. Unfortunately, however, it was a project that didn't quite make it off the drawing board. So Deborah "filed off the serial numbers" —changing the story so that it was no longer set in that world, and sent it to me. I'm glad she did, because it fits well into *Sword & Sorceress*.

Deborah J. Ross has been writing science fiction and fantasy professionally since 1982, served as Secretary of SFWA (Science Fiction/Fantasy Writers of America), and has taught writing and led writer's workshops. She's a member of the online writers' collective, Book View Café.

As Deborah Wheeler, she wrote two science fiction novels, *Jaydium* and *Northlight*, and had short stories in Asimov's, Fantasy and Science Fiction, Sisters of the Night, Star Wars: Tales from Jabba's Palace, Realms of Fantasy, and many of the *Sword & Sorceress* and Darkover anthologies. Her most recent projects include continuing the Darkover series (*The Fall Of Neskaya*, *Zandru's Forge*, *A Flame In Hali*, *The Alton Gift*, *Hastur Lord*, and *The Children Of Kings*). She's also working on an original fantasy series, *The Seven-Petaled Shield*. Two of her short stories ("Mother Africa" in Asimov's in 1997 and "The Price of Silence" in F&SF in 2009) were awarded Honorable Mention in the Year's Best SF. She's also edited several fantasy anthologies.

She lives in the redwood forests near Santa Cruz, California. In between writing, she has sojourned in France, worked as a medical assistant to a cardiologist, revived an elementary school library, studied Hebrew, classical piano, and yoga, and has been active in the women's martial arts network community.

Spring Moon Rising climbed the hill behind her village to greet
the sunrise. Below her, in every direction, stretched the Celadon
Plains. Pale green grasses, heavy with beryl-hued grain, rippled
across the land. In the distance, a herd of jade bison lifted their
horned heads. The wind tugged at her long braids. The air
smelled metallic, lightning edged with frost. In the Blue Beyond,
a rapture was gathering, a turbulence of gray and silver. The
storm was almost upon them, and it was a storm like none other.

Moon thrust the thought from her, lest it prove an evil omen.
Her own restless spirit put such dangerous thoughts into her
mind.

"Moon! There you are!" Cheeks flushed, Moon's eldest sister,
Dew On Flowers, trotted up the incline. "Why do you stand here
daydreaming, while the others are already gathered? Have you
lost your taste for meat?"

Moon turned away to hide her moment of shame. It was
irresponsible to keep the other hunters waiting once the sun was
up. She did herself and her family no honor by behaving in such
a selfish manner.

The two sisters hurried down the hill, settling their bows and
arrow-cases across their backs as they went. At the outskirts of
the village, they joined the other hunters. All together, the party
numbered a dozen, somewhat more men than women, under the
leadership of Uncle Lion Gaze. Although no longer as fleet he
once was, he was such a crafty hunter that no one questioned his
right to lead. Moon was the youngest, yet she had already killed
two bison.

Under the direction of Lion Gaze, the hunting party set out
toward the herd that Moon had seen earlier. They ran easily, at a
pace they could sustain for many hours. They carried only what
was necessary, their bows and arrow-cases, knives for
butchering, and hand axes for cutting carrying-frames.

Moon skimmed the grass-laced earth, sweating lightly, her
breath soft in her throat. Her spirits rose and the looming
darkness overhead receded from her thoughts.

Several of the young men tried to speak to her. Moon knew

they thought well of themselves, for she had seen the way the other young women of her clan looked at them, the sideways glances, the flushed cheeks. To Moon, however, they were as dull as sand. Why should she lay down her bow for someone she could outrun and out-hunt? She tossed her head, her braids flying, and refused to answer them.

"You are too picky," Dew said when they paused near the top of a hill. Below, the bison herd grazed, unaware of their presence. "Endless River or Snake Strikes could have any girl he wanted."

"Then let them!" Moon kept her eyes on the largest bison, marking him for her own. He was a massive-headed, shaggy bull, and his hide was so pale a green that he shimmered like moonlight. He would be strong and fast, so she must be stronger and faster.

Dew would not be diverted. "Think what you are doing! Do you want to end your days alone?"

"Stop worrying about me, sister. There will be time enough for marriage and children." Moon laid one hand on her sister's arm. "I know you are trying to look out for me, but I do not need a mother's scolding."

"It seems that you do, if you think a good husband will wait around for you while the long grass grows."

Moon sighed and made no answer. There was no point in arguing with Dew on the subject of husbands.

Quietly, they divided into groups and strung their bows. Moon struggled with hers, for it was new and the stiff wood resisted her. Hawk Wing made a disapproving sound.

"That's a man's bow," he commented, as if she did not already know. "It's too much for you."

Moon drew in her breath, deep into the pit of her belly, and the string slipped into place. She straightened and met his eyes. "A bow does not care who draws it, man or woman, mortal or god. It answers only to strength."

"Then it is a good thing we draw our bows with our arms and not our tongues, or you would outstrip us all." Lion Gaze came up to them. "Have you finished taunting your fellow hunters, my niece, and sowing rivalry instead of comradeship?"

Moon dipped her head. "I am ready, uncle." To Hawk Wing she said, "I am sorry for my sharp words."

"They were true ones." He turned, following the hunt leader.

They crept through the grass, keeping downwind of the herd. Not a sound betrayed their passage. One of the men startled a nest of plains sparrows that rose, crying out in the their shrill voices. An emerald-hued bison cow lifted its head, snorted, and then returned to grazing.

Dew crawled on her belly to Moon's side. "What did you say to Hawk?"

"Nothing of any importance. Look!" Moon pointed to the herd. The hunting party was close enough now to smell the warm animal musk and the scent of sweet crushed grass on the fitful breeze. The bull she had chosen stood a little apart from the others. His horns, wide and tapering, gleamed like polished bone, and the morning sun glinted on his golden eyes. Lush, curling hair covered his shoulders. He tipped his muzzle to the wind, black-rimmed nostrils flaring wide. Shaking his head, he rumbled deep in his throat.

He senses us, Moon thought. *He cannot smell us, but he knows we are here.*

Lion Gaze gave the signal. Everyone began moving, crouched down low. If they were lucky and the wind held, they might get even closer before the herd broke. This was the most difficult part of the hunt, when the possibility of discovery attended every step. No matter how well they read the temper of the beasts, no one could be sure if the herd would flee or turn and charge.

None of the hunters excelled Moon at stealth. Dew and Hawk and the two other men in her party dropped back, letting her take the lead. She slipped between the stalks of grass like a whisper from the earth itself. The smell of the bison filled her nostrils. She tasted their sweat, the dust on their hooves. The sound of their breathing vibrated along her bones.

She caught the subtle shift in that tremor, and froze. Even as she lifted her bow into position, her legs beneath her, the bull whirled and charged.

Moon surged upright. Adrenaline stung her blood. Her vision went sharp. The bull was closing fast, his head lowered, the tips of his sweeping horns aimed at the hunters. She drew the bow to its maximum tautness and held it, waiting for a target. From behind her, the others loosed a volley of arrows. One landed short and the others bounced off harmlessly. No arrow could pierce that thick hide or that massive skull.

Closer... Moon calmed herself as her arm muscles trembled under the strain. *If he turns but a little...*

"Aiee! Run!" Hawk yelled.

Moon heard their scattered flight, the cries of her sister, "Moon! Come *on!*"

The ground beneath her feet quivered like a drum. His hooves tore into the sod, throwing up clods and dust. Still she waited. At the last moment, when the bull was but a breath away from her, he swung his head to one side. One golden eye caught her in its gaze.

She loosed her arrow.

The arrow plunged deep into the bison's eye socket. He let out a fearsome cry. The reek of his blood shrilled in the air.

Moon scrambled out of the bison's path. Propelled by the momentum of his charge, he hurtled into the very place she had been standing and fell to his knees. Swiftly she drew another arrow and notched it to the bowstring.

Before she could take aim, the bull heaved himself to his feet. The shaft of her first arrow had broken off, leaving a bloody wound. He slung his head around, fixing her with his one good eye. In its molten-gold depths, she read terrible pain but also an unmistakable challenge. She lowered the tip of her arrow, fractionally releasing the tension on her bow. In that moment, the bull whirled away. She did not think an animal that size could move so nimbly. Trailing drops of crimson, the bull galloped away.

Moon watched him go. Her heart clenched. To kill one of the bison was an act of courage, of daring, and also of necessity, an act that allowed her people to survive the frozen darkness of the Ice Raven. But to wound such a noble creature, to let it suffer...

In shame, she hung her head.

"Moon!" Rushing up, Dew threw her arms around her sister. "I thought you'd be killed!"

Someone else said, "What a shot! We will sing of it to our grandsons!"

"We will do no such thing." Moon unstrung her bow and slung it across her back. Blinking back tears, she averted her face so that none of the others could see. Theirs was the glory of the hunt, the herd now galloping away. "Go!" she cried. "The hunt calls you!"

Whooping, Hawk and the other young men darted off to join the others. Only Dew stayed behind.

"I must finish what I have begun," Moon said.

"I know."

"You have no duty to come with me. Your place is with the others."

Moon thought, *This will be my last hunt. It would be a mercy for the bull to kill me, so that I do not return to my clan in dishonor.*

In answer, Dew touched Moon's arm. She seemed to be saying, *My place is here, with you.*

Moon nodded. "Stay behind me. Do not risk yourself."

~o0o~

The plains wind sang in the braids of the two women. So soft was their tread upon the earth, the grasses parted for them. From time to time, they caught sight of the bull. Once Moon saw him stumble and fall. Her heart quickened and she pushed for greater speed, but when they reached the spot, they found only a circle of flattened, blood-stained grass.

The bull led them ever farther from the hills and plains of their home territory. At first, Moon paid little heed to the changing landscape. She scarcely noticed when the countryside no longer looked familiar.

Finally, Dew called for them to stop. "We can't go on like this." Wheezing, struggling for breath, Dew bent over. With one hand she kneaded the muscles of her side. "I don't recognize this place, do you? If we continue this chase, we'll become lost."

Moon shook her head. Her braids swung heavily, damp with sweat. "The bull cannot run forever. He must stop, and then I will end his pain."

"And what then, sister? How will we find our way home?"

"You have been strong and loyal, but this is not your search. I release you from it. Go back to our people in honor."

Dew's dark brows tensed. "I will not return without you."

Moon knew better than to argue with her sister. In such a mood, Dew could be as unrelenting as rain. So they went on, more slowly now.

~oOo~

The light of the Blue Beyond shifted. Day's heat seeped from the earth, and chill gathered in the shadows. Above, the storm still had not broken. Clouds churned, heavy and oppressive. Dew, who had been trotting along silently, began to grumble. How would they track the bison in the dark? What if they met a pack of wolves or a viridine lion? What must the men think of them, to be gone so long and so far?

For a time, Moon would not listen. Twilight, pale and shimmering, washed the western horizon. The earth smelled cool and moist. She felt as if she could track the bull by the scent of his tread, the brush of his body through the grasses, and the lingering taint of animal musk.

At last, however, she relented and took heed of her sister's pleas. The ground turned rocky, rising sharply and making footing difficult. They entered a country of dense thorny brush reaching above their heads.

They found an open space and set about with their axes cutting dead branches for firewood, and living branches, thin and springy, for a shelter. They stripped off the bark to tie the branches together, and gathered moss and soft leaves for a bed. They had only a little water left, but Dew, ever resourceful, found a patch of juicy wild onions to roast.

After they had performed their evening prayers and banked the fire, the sisters retired to their shelter. Within minutes, Dew's soft breathing indicated that she was asleep. Moon lay on her back, gazing up through the opening between the roof branches.

15

The tips seemed to be reaching past the roiling clouds, toward the stars perhaps, or the faint goddess-veil. She wondered if the bull were looking up with his single remaining golden eye. If he suffered. If he hated.

Forgive me, she thought, but she did not believe he could.

~oOo~

All the next morning, they climbed. The brush here grew sparse and twisted, so dark it looked black. They scaled a pass, traversed a valley surrounded by snow-topped peaks, and climbed again. Dew said no more about turning back. They needed all their breath for climbing. Wind blew constantly, at times threatening to peel them off the rock face. Moon's leg muscles burned. Her moccasins were meant for the softer terrain of the plains, and the stones bruised her feet.

Moon wondered how the bull could have come this far, what had driven him into such barren country, and how a beast his size, with such a wound, could navigate the narrow trails. Yet every doubt was answered by fresh evidence of his passing, the print of a massive cloven hoof, or a sprinkling of blood.

The mountains rose and rose, row after distant row, ghostly white. They rested more frequently now, and drank from rushing streams. The water tasted of rock and wildness, so cold that their lips turned blue. Days passed, and in between, they slept huddled in whatever shelter they could find in the shallow, wind-sculpted caves. The storm clouds covering the Blue Beyond darkened, so that noon took on the aspect of night.

Now that they had come so far, leaving behind everything they knew, Moon still refused to give up, for fear that all their suffering would have been for nothing.

~oOo~

Moon awoke to iridescent light. She crept out from beneath the overhanging rock where she and Dew had slept, blinking in the color-drenched brightness that swept across the horizon. Her belly cramped with hunger and every joint in her body throbbed, yet she stood, for a moment oblivious to all pain, caught up in the glory above her. Red and gold, blue and green and orange

16

rippled like curtains waving in a celestial breeze. They beckoned her onward.

The trail led her upwards a short distance, then widened. For a moment, Moon thought she had reached the crest, for the lights now glimmered all around her. She breathed them in. A strange energy flowed through her.

A sound, a clink of one pebble on another, alerted her. She whirled, reaching for the knife that was not there, and realized too late that she had left her weapons behind in the shelter.

Ahead she could make out only shades of gray and shifting silver. Something moved in the brilliance. She forced herself to stand still. Whatever it was, bow or axe could not harm it. Nor, she realized, would she wish to destroy a thing of such beauty.

Do not be afraid. The words shimmered in her mind.

The next instant, the brightness faded. A man stood there, tall and well-formed. Despite the cold, his chest was bare, and as he held out one hand to her, muscles moved easily beneath his smooth skin. By his features and fringed leggings, the cut of his moccasins and the slant of his eyes, he must be one of her own people, yet she did not know him. His braids were tied with feathers of deepest blue.

Moon had never seen such a color, except in the Blue Beyond on a cloudless day. Surely, this must be a god. Trembling, she dropped to her knees and covered her face with her hands.

His touch was warm and strong as he lifted her, but she would not look directly at him. She stammered, "How shall I address you, O god of the mountains?"

"I am no god," he said. His voice was deep and as beautiful as himself. "You shall call me Bluejay. What is your name?"

Moon looked up in astonishment. Truly, a god would already know her name and her quest, and all her hidden sins. As strange and beautiful as this stranger appeared, he must be as mortal as she herself. Emboldened, she answered his questions. Who she was, her people, what she was doing so far from her home territory.

"And now I cannot go back," she concluded. "I failed to find the bull and put an end to his pain. I have shamed my people."

"The bull you sought does not suffer."

"You may not be a god, but even if you were, I would not believe you," Moon said with spirit. "I must make certain for myself."

At that, Bluejay laughed. "Since you refuse to go home, will you come with me on an even greater adventure? I have come here seeking such a hunter as yourself, one with heart as well as courage. I promise that if we succeed, and you still wish to return home, you will do so with honor."

Moon thought for a long moment. If Bluejay were not a god, perhaps he was a malicious spirit sent to entrap her. She had heard tales of such beings, songs sung around campfires in the Time of the Ice Raven. When she consulted her heart, however, she felt nothing but a surge of irrational joy.

"I will go with you, but first I must bid farewell to my sister."

Together, they went back down the trail to the overhang. Dew had made a fire, from what fuel Moon could not tell, and on that fire, a small bird roasted on a spit. Dew got to her feet and greeted the stranger, inviting him to share their meal. Politely he declined, for there was scarcely enough for one person, let alone three. He explained that he had come into this country to bring Moon back with him.

"You wish to marry her?" Dew said, eyes narrowing.

Moon began to protest, but Dew waved her to hush. If their mother had still been alive, she would have arranged the marriage contract. Dew was clearly determined to act in her stead.

Bluejay said that in his own country, the man presented the bride's family with a gift. Moon saw no possessions at hand, except possibly the feathers of startling blue tied in his hair. Yet the next moment, he was offering Dew a bison robe. It was expertly tanned, supple and sweet-smelling. As he handed it to Dew, his gaze met Moon's and she understood his words about the bull.

"This is a treasure!" Clearly, Dew was of the opinion that any man who owned such a thing must be wealthy indeed. She kissed Moon, bidding her to send word of her new life.

Moon took her bow and arrow case, her knife and hand axe. Following Bluejay, she continued back up the trail. For a long time, she was so beset with strangeness, she could not speak.

A storm came up suddenly, swirls of white and gray that grew thicker with each passing heartbeat. Moon's skin went numb with cold. Ice congealed in the pit of her belly. Still Bluejay kept on. The blizzard did not seem to affect him. Moon struggled to keep up, although she could barely make out his figure.

Suddenly Bluejay came to a halt. Although the blowing snow obscured the terrain, Moon sensed that before them lay a sharp precipice. She could feel the shape of the mountains and the solidity of rock on three sides, but in front of them lay nothing but wailing emptiness. If she stepped off that cliff, she might fall forever.

"What is this place?" she asked through chattering teeth. "It seems to me the very edge of the world."

He held out his hand. "You are right."

Moon remembered thinking that whatever happened on the search, she would never return home. She had thought she would die on the mountain face of exposure or starvation. She had not the slightest idea then of journeying past the edge of the world. In spite of this, or perhaps because of it, she took Bluejay's hand.

The moment their fingers touched, a change swept through Moon. She no longer shook with cold and fright. Something immeasurably powerful, yet gentle as feathers, caught her, held her. The whiteness of the storm fell away and in its place, across illimitable spaces, she beheld colors such as she had never dreamed. Drawn by Bluejay's sure grasp, she soared like a frost falcon.

How long the journey lasted, Moon could not say. It seemed to go on forever, and yet when she stood once more on her own feet, only the span of a single breath had passed. Too amazed to speak, she gazed at an ancient forest.

She had seen plains trees, with their misshapen, wind-scoured branches and dusty leaves. Few of them grew taller than a man's height. Now she craned her neck, straining to see the tops of the giants that rose around her. Their trunks were straight and smooth-barked, thicker than a man's outstretched arms.

Moon and Bluejay stood in a little pool of sunlight surrounded by dappled, blue-tinted shade. A jumble of lacy plants covered the forest floor. She inhaled, tasting scents that were pungent, unfamiliar, and deeply stirring.

Bluejay slipped his fingers from her grasp. "We're here."

"What is this place?"

"My home."

She stared at him for the first time. Far above, branches swayed in a wind, so that motes of light danced across his bare skin.

His eyes darkened. "You know there are many worlds, each with its own people, its own magic?"

"So our songs teach us." Her voice came in a whisper. "But I never guessed..." turning now, struggling to encompass the enormity and brightness of the forest, "...it would be like this."

"And in all these worlds," he went on, as if he had not heard, "what is the greatest danger? The most dire threat?"

"The Ice Raven, who brings dark and cold, the sleep of the soul," she answered as she had been taught. "It cannot be seen, or captured or—"

He cut her off with an impatient gesture. "The Ice Raven is a part of the natural cycle. The fallow times give the land its rest, and we take no harm from the long sleep. My people offer prayers at such times, blessing the Ice Raven."

For an instant, Moon was angry. Surely he was making fun of her, treating the beliefs of her own clan as ignorant superstitions. Then she realized he was in earnest.

"What, then?" she asked. "If you do not fear the Ice Raven, what *do* you fear?"

"Something against which my people have no defense, no power." Bluejay paused, an unreadable expression passing over his features. "But you do."

Moon wanted to laugh. What could she do and what beast could she hunt, that this strong warrior could not? He could walk between worlds! Now he truly was teasing her.

Still, his expression remained grave, and she decided that no matter how far-fetched, he took his own words seriously. "What do you want from me?"

"Do you have the courage to face that which threatens all our worlds? Do you have the will to defeat it?"

Moon lifted her chin and took her bow in hand. "I am no magician. All I have are these, my arrows. They are yours to command."

"Then come with me."

Once more, Bluejay held out his hand. This time, as she slipped her fingers through his, Moon felt a faint quivering, but she did not know if it were her own or his.

~o0o~

No blizzard rose up to blind her, no wall of whiteness, no whirl of space and light. Instead, they rose gently, following the arrow-straight trees. The air grew fresher, warmer, yet wilder. Birds passed them, not the olive-drab sparrows of the plains, but creatures adorned with extravagant rainbow plumage. They swooped through the air, their songs rising and falling. Moon cried out in delight, and Bluejay grinned.

They left the birds behind and passed the tops of the trees. The branches were so far below that Moon imagined them as a soft carpet. Clouds wafted by until only the Blue Beyond lay above them. Such a blue it was, more intense than she had ever seen.

Moon kept expecting that the next moment would bring them up against a hard blue surface, as if the Blue Beyond were the inside of a bird's egg.

We are hatchlings struggling to be born, came his voice in her mind.

The end of their upward journey came suddenly. It was not at all what she expected. One instant, they soared gently through unchanging blue. The next, a strange uneasiness hovered at the edges of her senses, like a storm front poised to break.

Bluejay looked at her with a grave expression. "This is your last chance to turn back."

"I have said I will help you," Moon retorted with a touch of heat. Did he think her so lacking in honor that she would take

21

back her word? Then she realized his words came not from any mistrust of her but from his own fears. He was tall and strong, clearly a warrior among his own people. Again she wondered what help she could give against an enemy that such a man as he dared not face.

As if reading her thoughts, he said, "Each of these wild worlds has its own form of magic. No matter how I appear to you, I have no prowess with physical fighting. My people's gift is the ability to travel between worlds. Yours—" and here he touched her chest over her fast-beating heart, "yours is courage. And you are the finest of them all. The only one who answered my call."

Before Moon could ask what he meant, he lifted his hand and under their feet stretched a wide path. One moment, it appeared to her as a beam of shimmering light, the next, a metallic cable, and still again, a twisted rope as thick as one of Bluejay's trees. Along this path, images rippled and flashed, the pale green plains of her own world, then an ocean of surging tides, beyond that, sweeping sun-kissed meadows, and in the other direction, row upon row of stone houses with glowing jewel-toned windows. The richness and beauty of the worlds captured her senses. She longed to visit them all, to walk those streets and glades and beaches.

"They are worth saving, are they not?" Bluejay asked.

Moon swallowed her answer, for no words could convey her emotion. Another breath, and she was able to say, "What threatens them?"

Bluejay pointed beyond his own world, where the visions disappeared into mist. "You will see for yourself. There."

Moon took her bow and strung it on the first attempt. Hawk had been wrong; it was not a man's bow or a woman's bow. It was a *warrior's* bow. Holding an arrow at ready, she moved toward the distant mist.

The haze began to flow and darken, like the storm on the day of the hunt. It curled around her, dampening her skin, and shutting out all other sight and sound. Something moved within the shifting currents of air and light and power. She halted, holding herself still against the hammering of her heart.

A sound reached her, a gnawing, rending noise, as if the very fibers of the world were being wrenched apart. This was no bison, no wolf or eagle or emerald-striped viper, but something far more terrible. She moved closer, step by searching step.

A shape emerged as the mist grew thin and parted to reveal a beast. It was unlike any she had ever seen, fully as huge as a bison, but long-bodied and low to the ground. Dull black scales covered its body, except for the tapering snout and the whip-like tail. A stench hung about it, the smell of rotten things, of must and slime and places best forgotten. But worse of all were its eyes, lightless pupils ringed in blood.

Hooked claws and yellowed teeth sank deep into the shining rope. The beast twisted its head, snapping threads of light, then devouring them.

Awareness shifted the beast's eyes. It rose up, froth dripping from its jaws. Rumbling sounded in its throat. It extended its head, slit nostrils flaring wide, and bared its razor teeth.

For an instant, Moon's nerve almost failed her. How could she fight such a monster? Yet if she ran away now, as every instinct urged her, what then? The beast would destroy the paths that linked the worlds together. She knew, as certainly as if Bluejay had told her aloud, that all would then fall into darkness, a night without even the Ice Raven for comfort.

The beast was already moving toward her. Whip tail lashing, it gathered itself for a leap. Moon drew her bow. Her arrow sped true, but the beast turned at the last instant. Hissing and thrashing, the monster caught the shaft between its jaws and snapped it into a dozen fragments.

Moon slipped another arrow into place. Before she took aim, however, the monster leapt, quicksilver fast.

She ducked and rolled toward the beast. The claws of its hind paws raked her as it passed overhead. Something snapped—the arrow she had drawn, not her precious bow. The creature's body cast her into shadow and flooded her nostrils with its rank odor. Then it landed heavily on the path beyond her.

Moon scrambled to her feet to face the beast. As her fingers touched her arrow case, she realized that she had only one arrow left. Only one.

Fitting it to the string, she drew the bow.

Growling, the creature took a slow, menacing step toward her. She could not see a vital target, only rows of overlapping obsidian-dark scales. Its skull was thick and she did not think even her bow could drive an arrow through its ribs head-on.

She must choose her target. One more step and the beast would be upon her.

The monster halted, as if daring her to shoot. Its tail lashed the air. She faced it, unflinching.

One arrow, only one chance.

The beast tensed its muscles for another leap. Moon crouched down on one knee and shot upwards just as its forequarters lifted. The arrow buried itself in the thin skin just to one side of the breastbone.

The beast dropped, but Moon was already rolling free. The silvery rope shuddered under the impact, then began swaying and twisting. Clutching her bow, she flattened herself on its surface. Her vision whirled sickeningly. The entire universe seemed to have come loose from its moorings, bucking and heaving like a maddened bison. Below it, or perhaps above, for in Moon's disordered sight she could not tell, yawned an enormous whirlpool, an abyss of swirling darkness.

With a great cacophonous screech as if a thousand rusted bells rang out at once, the body of the beast slid sideways and disappeared into the void.

Gradually, the path of light grew still. Moon dared to sit up. Her cheeks were slick with tears, and the air stung her eyes. She bled from four or five shallow gashes on her arms, most likely from the beast's claws, although she could not remember being struck. Her bowstring had snapped, but the bow itself seemed to be sound.

She clambered unsteadily to her feet and retraced her steps. The path felt solid, resilient, but she was trembling so badly that the slightest tremor might topple her over the side. To her surprise, she saw no sign of the frayed strands from the beast's devastation. She hoped this meant the bond between the living worlds had taken no lasting harm.

The mist closed around her as she went on, but this time she welcomed it as a friend. It stroked her torn skin, drawing out the pain. She thanked it silently. After a time, so gradually she could barely discern the change, the mist lifted. Bluejay stood there, waiting for her.

Whether the battle with the beast itself had changed her, or whether it was something in the mist or the vision of worlds strung together by a rope of light, Moon now looked on the man before her with new eyes. When she had first met him, Bluejay had appeared as a warrior, a god. Certainly, the ability to walk the worlds was a magical gift. Yet he had sought her out to do what he could not.

"It's time for truth between us," she said. "Who are you?"

The air between them wavered like heat rising from the summer plains. Bluejay's form shifted and grew more slender. He was still tall, but his shoulders were narrow, his hands graceful and soft. He wore a shirt of azure wool, touched here and there with gold, and belted over narrow leggings. Thongs of dyed leather tied a cluster of blue feathers to one of several gray braids. His face was angular, with heavy eyebrows and a long, straight nose, very different from the features of her own people. A band of cloth covered one eye; the other, golden as a hawk's, met hers steadily.

"Do you know me now?" Only his voice had not changed.

Unable to speak, she touched the cloth over his ruined eye.

"A small enough loss," he said. "Only someone brave enough to face down a charging bull, and steadfast enough to follow an injured animal so far into the wilderness, could cross the wild worlds without going mad. You see, I was right." With a small smile, he touched her cheek. "You were the one."

Moon dared not speak, dared not breathe. At first, his true appearance had seemed strange to her. Now she would not have him any other way.

Which of them, she wondered, had paid the greater price—he with his eye or she, having left behind her home, her sister, her

25

clan?

"I will take you back to your plains." Bluejay held out his hand, "if you wish it."

Moon found her voice. "I wish to go with you, but not to return to the life I had before. I wish—I wish to see all those other worlds."

To walk those beaches and meadows, to explore those cities and forests...

She felt his heart rise in his breast, even as hers did. Warm fingers closed around her own. Together, they stepped out on the luminous road.

THE MEMORY BOX

by Patricia B. Cirone

Dozens of men were trapped in a mine, and it was Amina's job to get them out. She expected the task to be difficult, but when she was deep underground, she discover a complication she had not expected at all.

Patricia B. Cirone has worked as a scientist, a teacher and a librarian, but her true love is writing. She has had a number of short stories published, including several in previous SWORD & SORCERESS anthologies and is currently working on a book. She receives frequent editorial comments on her writing from one of her cats, who considers any hand to be better employed in petting her than in typing.

"Can Onia do it?" Amina asked, turning the mug of tea around and around in her hands, and trying not to sound as if she was begging—or worse yet, whining. She kept her gaze steadfastly out the window, as if she could see something in the utter darkness outside. Utter darkness, as it would be inside the mine.

"You know that wouldn't work—she has absolutely no training," her aunt replied.

"Yes, but she is of the line. She should be able to access the box..." Amina trailed off, knowing this was all a pointless argument. It was her nerves talking, throwing up barriers between herself and what lay ahead.

"Most women of the line cannot even pluck a memory from the box the first time they try, even with some training in ordering their thoughts and working in a trance state!"

"I did." The words slipped out before she could snatch them

back from her teeth.

"Yes, and we all know how well *that* went!" her aunt said acerbically and Amina winced.

Yes, years of nightmares and waking dreams. She had not ridden that memory—it had ridden her. She had been a child, headstrong and determined; her mother vain and unwilling to spend the time to curb her willful child. Widowed young, her mother had been too busy keeping an eye out for a likely man and too proud of her ascension to the role of Memory Keeper upon the misfortune of her older sister. Amina had been jealous of the beautiful box her mother talked about so often, and was sure *she* could be just as important if she opened it and brought forth one of the memories.

She had slipped into her mother's room and sat cross-legged with the ancient box in her lap, then opened it. Somehow she had imagined it would be like walking into a fairy world, with beautiful creatures like the stories told around the fires on festival nights. Or like instantly becoming someone important, and grown up, and able to order others around. If it made her mother important simply to be the Keeper, when she hadn't actually had to use it yet, surely it would make Amina even more important if she actually had some of the memories!

Instead she had been sucked into a maelstrom of darkness pierced by cries, by odd visions floating up and vanishing before her eyes and then been grabbed and yanked violently into a world of screams and the thunder of hooves. She had stared helplessly as a horse the size of a small cabin bore down upon her and a man's face, livid with rage, had aimed a lance at her from its back. She had ducked and run, tripping over bodies of loved ones she somehow knew in this other world, and felt blood running down her face from a gash that stung and burned on her scalp. And there had been more pain and screams and people dying and then she had woke screaming in her bed. The first of many times she would wake screaming in her bed.

Her aunt had been by her bedside, not her mother. It had been her aunt who had nursed her back to a more precarious health than the robust spirits she had enjoyed before. It had been her crippled aunt who had patiently taught her to rein in her will and control her frustration and learn to separate dream from reality—both the dream that had escaped the Memory Box and taken over her mind and the dreams and self-delusions everyone wove around their lives.

A Memory Keeper needed to know herself, every wart, every failing, every blessing and every strength, before she could risk knowing others to that depth and keeping their thoughts separate from her own. Not to do so was madness, and it was only the very strength of her talent, her aunt had told her, that had preserved her from such insanity.

The strength of her talent, and the strength of her aunt's talent as well, Amina knew later. Her aunt had not just nursed her physical body back to health, but had pulled her mind back from where it was lost, entangled with the memory of that other woman, long ago. Using the skills of a Memory Keeper and a Memory Binder, she had sought and found Amina's own thoughts and somehow separated them from that other, and bound them back to her own body and her own time.

Her mother, Amina found, when she was finally well enough to ask, had left the village, abandoning her own child as the source of her own fall from grace. Stripped of her right to be the Keeper of the Memory Box, she had packed up a few belongings and moved to a town some twenty miles downriver where she took up residence with the local inn keeper with whom she had been having a mild flirtation with at local festivals and fairs over the past few years.

"But I was the one who snuck into her room and opened the box," Amina, the child, had protested. "I'm the one who should be punished, not her."

Her aunt had smiled kindly at her and stroked back the damp, fever wet hair from her brow. "It's not punishment, child, but need. The first duty of *any* Memory Keeper is to never leave a Memory Box where others can get at it—especially children. Your mother had been warned already about keeping it out where others could see it, and warned to keep it locked away from you and any other children who might come into the house.

She treated it as a piece of jewelry, for her own personal adornment, not as a powerful tool of our people."

Amina hadn't understood then, but she was too sick to protest and when she grew older, she understood what her aunt had meant, about her mother's attitude and her carelessness. Now her aunt's voice recalled her to the present. "Don't worry, it won't be like that time. You have the training to control a memory now, and just gather what bits you need to use them."

"I know," Amina answered, smiling wryly. "I've certainly worked with enough of them from the training box." She made herself sound confident; she was a grown woman now, not a child to be pampered and protected. Still, she dreaded opening that box, and working with a real memory. A memory gathered, or possibly torn, from a person who had no control over their own memories or feelings. It would not be like the training memories that Memory Keepers carefully stored; memories carefully strained of extra personal thoughts and emotions—after all, who wanted to let your innermost private thoughts and emotions be experienced by someone else, especially some child or youth who you didn't even know. And often the stored, prepared memories in the training box were of the most everyday boring events: weaving a piece of cloth, weeding a garden, cooking a meal. Those were easier to keep free of stray emotions or thoughts.

No the memories in the true Memory Box were whole—a defining moment in a person's life—or death—complete with emotions and connections and thoughts and terror.

Amina turned the now cold mug of tea around in her hands again and gazed out the window. Was that a faint bit of gray she saw lighting the darkness? The other villagers would be working through the night, trying to dig through the rubble of the cave-in, trying to free those of their own who were trapped below.

But come dawn, it would be nearly two days. Days in which any food or water the miners might have had with them would have been used up. Days in which air might be getting scarce. Days in which bodies, young and old, would have gotten weaker, injuries left unhealed, minds grown fearful with the dark and despair.

Come dawn, it would be Amina's turn to open the Memory Box and pluck a memory from it. The memory of one who had traveled the fey way into the heart of the mine and lived to tell of it. And it would be Amina's turn to try to travel that same route and hope it would connect to the trapped villagers, and lead them out.

All too soon, the knock came on the door. Since it wasn't accompanied by the sounds of rejoicing, Amina knew the attempt to dig through to the trapped miners had been unsuccessful. Not that the villagers would stop trying, but it was time for her to begin her attempt.

She went to the door and nodded her acknowledgement to the solemn faced headman. "I'll go ahead then."

"Thank you, Amina. May the Goddess be with you." He turned and walked back toward the mine entrance through the pearl grey pre-dawn light.

Amina turned toward her aunt. "Well," she said. Her aunt opened her mouth as if to speak again, then silently lifted the Memory Box to hand it to her. Amina stared at it in silence for a moment, then moved forward and took it. She refused to let her hands shake.

The last time she had held this, she had been a child. Its ornate designs and the patina of old wood still drew her, and she wondered if it was merely the beauty of its design that attracted her, or if it was somehow the memories within that were calling out to her.

Enough. She took a deep breath and slowly opened its lid, quieting her mind and seeking for the one memory she needed. The years of training, both with the quieting exercises her aunt had taught her and with the practice she had done with the training box helped, but still she felt buffeted by the voices and snatches of sight and sound that swirled around her. She mentally drew her veil across her "self" more firmly and let the memories slide past and coil back into the box until she had found... that one. She grasped it firmly and closed the box with a snap, then put it down on the table, for her aunt to put safely away.

She walked out the door and headed for the hills, letting the memory only lightly touch the surface of her mind—enough to follow it but not enough to absorb it into her being. She could follow it this way, step by step, as the memory itself had been formed, not knowing the end but only the moment. It was safer that way.

Amina found herself walking higher up into the hills than she had anticipated, but let her steps carry her, seeing differences between her sight and how things had looked to that other woman long ago—a rock grown mossy here, a thick tree that had been a sapling, a scoured fall of rock where there had been a grassy bank.

She entered a small copse of trees, their shadows deep in the now brightening skies. The air was chill here and Amina shivered. There—there at the base of a huge oak tree was a shadow darker yet. Amina pushed aside the accumulation of leaves and twigs and found a narrow twisting stairway made of roots and bits of stones descending into the darkness. She could feel the excitement flooding through the memory of the one she carried—an excitement that did not match at all the dread Amina felt. She had never liked darkness, nor small enclosed spaces. The thought of descending into that stygian blackness filled *her* with dread.

Still, taking a deep breath, she cautiously took the first step down, following the other's memory. It was too close here for the small lantern she held to do more than shine against the damp earth walls and she nearly lost her footing trying to peer down and see the next step let alone the one after that. She gave up looking down and used the other's memory to light her way. Either the stairway had been wider a century or so ago, or the other woman merely a girl and Amina felt with each footstep to find the stairs that were little more than niches.

Finally she reached flat ground and started to lift her lantern up to light her way a bit.

She stopped, astounded. Around her was a small chamber of rock, with glittering crystals growing down from the roof. Light from some crack far up above filtered down, bathing the entire chamber in a soft radiant glow. The stillness was broken by the soft sound of water trickling over stones the hues of the reds and golds of sunset.

"Beautiful, isn't it?" a bright voice enquired.

Amina spun around, startled.

No, it couldn't be. She knew it was called the fey way, but there were no such things as fairies. They were tales, spun to entertain children by the fireside.

Yet there, perched on one of the multi-hued rocks was a small figure, its skin an impossible shade of silver, with small transparent wings growing from its back. Yet for all its delicate looks, something about the face warned Amina that this small being was not of a delicate nature. Indeed, the eyes assessed her coolly, with a hint of steely determination.

"Indeed," Amina replied politely, jerking herself free of the shrouds of the memory she had been riding, and wondering which was real, the dark earthen walls of the other's memory or this place of beauty. Had she truly gone mad this time? But it made no sense; Memory madness consisted of being lost in one, not seeing something totally different!

"Looking for treasure?" the fey creature asked, her pointed chin lifting a bit, challenging Amina with her gaze.

"No," Amina replied. "Unless you count lives as treasure, which I do—but I don't think that is the treasure you were asking about."

"Lives! You think to find lives down here?" The fey creature laughed scornfully. "Seems the tales you humans tell each other have grown even larger."

"The lives of miners, villagers trapped down here after a rock fall. There is supposed to be a way through to the mine from here."

"Why do you think that?" the creature demanded.

"Because the memory I carry is from one who walked this way, and she told the village of her journey, and her memory was gathered and stored in case another would ever need to find that way. Which now, I do, to rescue those who will surely die if they are trapped much longer."

"A Memory Keeper," the creature said thoughtfully.

"Yes," Amina said firmly. "And I need to be on my way."

"She lied, you know."

"Who lied?"

"The one who gave you that memory you are carrying. She was a deceitful one. She came here looking for treasure. All she found was me. I sent her on her way. She never walked through these caverns or went into the mine."

Dismay struck Amina's heart. "No, that's not possible! There must be a way!"

She pulled up the memory of the other and, hesitating only a moment, plunged into the memory again, this time letting the wholeness wash into her. If she went mad, so be it; without this memory the other villagers, friends and kin, would die. It was her duty, her destiny, to be a Memory Keeper, to risk all for the good of others.

But she realized with dismay that the creature was right. The girl-woman whose memory she rode had lied, using her lies to gain herself attention from the other villagers in her time, to make herself important. She rode the memory to its end, to the girl fleeing from the chamber and up the narrow stairway of roots, running away from the fey creature who laughed at her, all the way to her decision to tell a fancy tale rather than admit to her panic and be laughed at by the other villagers for her pride in thinking herself strong enough to outwit the fey. For in her time they had believed in the fey creatures, and no one traveled the paths that were supposedly theirs.

And perhaps they had been right, Amina though, opening her eyes with despair. It had all been for naught. All her years of training. All her years of fear and overcoming it, in order to prepare her for a time when she was needed, for when a memory was needed.

And instead she had grasped the memory of a foolish, prideful girl, much like she herself had been that first time she opened the Memory Box. She was justly punished for that arrogance. But it was others who would pay the price. It would be the miners who would die, either suffocating or starving. Oh, no doubt she would die too—that was the price paid by those who defied the fey. But it wasn't the thought of her own death that crushed her; it was the thought of the others.

"So there is no back entrance to the mine," she said to the silvery creature, "and all this is for naught. I beg your pardon for trespassing, and will leave immediately."

"Oh, I didn't say there wasn't a way to get to your noisome mine from here," the creature replied, watching her thoughtfully.

"There is a way?!" Hope surged back up in Amina's chest. "Please, I *must* get through to them! I *must* bring them out!"

The creature stared at her for a long thoughtful moment. "I see that. You really do care about them. What would you pay for me showing you the way and letting them tramp back out through my home here?"

"Anything," Amina replied. "I will pay with my life."

"And what good would that do? Just give me a dead body down here. Bad enough all the cleaning I'll have to do after all your miners tramp their muddy boots through my home."

"Then what do you want from me?" Amina asked.

The creature stared at her cunningly. "I think I'll show you the way first—that way you will be beholden to me."

Amina felt uneasy, remembering all the tales of trickery and deception. Would this fey creature with the iridescent wings show her a way only to close it and trap the miners permanently? Or show her a false image and then claim something was owed? But what choice did she have? She would never find a hidden way into the mine, if one even existed, without the help of this creature, now that she knew the memory was false. All she could try was bargaining.

"I would rather know now, in case I would be unable to fulfill your request."

"Oh, it would be in your powers," the fey replied. "Follow me."

Before Amina could argue more, the creature had flitted off as swiftly as a darting star and stood waiting for her by the entrance to a narrow shaft cleft in the rock. *"She could be thinking to lose me in the ways of this cavern and leave me to die,"* thought Amina.

Well, she had already offered her life. If the creature was just playing games with her, she would be no worse off than she was now. Following was the only chance of finding and rescuing the miners. And if the creature demanded the impossible in payment, she would either find a way to meet her demands or find a way out of paying. She was a Memory Keeper, one whose life was given in service to her people, one who was supposed to have the courage, and the intelligence, to find ways when others couldn't. She was through with cowering before the thought of what might become; it was time to deal with what *was*.

She strode briskly after the fey, holding her lantern high. As they walked, Amina activated the light trance Keepers used for making memories; if she needed to find her way out by herself, she would be able to retrace her steps. They squeezed through narrow passageways, hurried across caverns broader than the one she had entered at the bottom of the root stairway and turned this way and that. She would think the fey was deliberately trying to trick her, but they were always moving downwards. Amina could tell that by the ache in her calves.

The cool dampness of the cave seemed to press in upon her, gradually getting heavier, as if the air itself was testing her. Still, Amina followed the flickering form of the fey creature. They left the passageways of rock and the sounds of dripping water and moved into passages that were dirt and rock. The way got harder, the passages narrower. At times Amina had to bend over, ducking her head and walking with a crabbed step. At other times she had to climb up and over piles of dirt and rocks that shifted and tumbled away beneath her feet. The air no longer smelled fresh, but close and breathless.

And then she heard a murmuring sound—more water? Air moving past an opening?

The fey stopped and slid back against a depression in the side of the passage they were in. She pointed ahead into the blackness. "Up there and down," she said.

"You can lead them out this way, but I won't let them see me.

And I won't let them see my home, either, so only you will see the way. After you lead them out, come back and I'll tell you my price."

Amina looked at her and saw something flicker in the other's eyes—something that wasn't spite or ill humor. But she didn't have time to linger and seek what it was she had seen.

"Thank you," she said to the other, sincerity ringing in her voice. She could tell now that the murmur up ahead was voices, low and muffled by the dirt and rock, but voices. "I will come back, and learn your price."

The other ducked as if avoiding her gaze, and then vanished, as if she had never been there. Amina held the lantern up, but there was no crack or crevice behind where she had been standing that she could have gone into—*fey,* Amina reminded herself with only a slight shiver.

Then she turned and started climbing up the narrow passage. It became so steep she had to hold the handle of the lantern in her mouth in order to free her hands to grasp at the rocks and pull herself up step by careful step. The passage took a sharp turn to the left and climbed a bit more and then, at what Amina thought was another turn to the right, dropped off precipitously. She gasped, scrambling backwards a bit. Below her was a section of the mine—and there, down below, slumped against rock walls and curled up against each other were the trapped miners.

She had found them.

~o0o~

It was still a matter of hours before the last of them were out of the mine. First it had taken some time for them to cut lengths of rope from the small carts used to haul ore up to the surface, and knot them together. More time still for the nimblest of the young men—of those who still had the strength to be nimble—to climb up to the small opening where Amina crouched and find a secure place to fasten the end of the rope. The best they had found was a half buried rock that neither of them trusted, so they had wound it around themselves as well, and dug their heels in, telling the lightest of the others to come up first. As more ascended, they added their hands and weight to the rope and eventually all had climbed, or been carried, up the rope.

Then Amina started the long way back, scrambling backwards down that last steep passage and then counting everyone by the now feeble light of her lantern to make sure no one got left behind. The entire journey out was like that: get through a set of passageways and turns, have a moment of rest for those who could barely walk, and for those carrying the ones that couldn't, count faces and start over again.

When they reached the end of the dirt passageways and began through those of red rock and air, Amina could see two passageways. The one she could see with her eyes and her memory, and another, just like the ones they had already battled their way through. She realized this was what the others were seeing, and wished they could rejoice in the beauty and air she could see. But she realized this was what the fey had meant; this was her home and the others would not be allowed to see it.

Indeed, Amina realized, if the villagers knew that these beautiful caves were here, they would flock to them. Folk would come from other villages to gawk and marvel. And the fey would have no home; she was right to guard it. Still, it was difficult to see the weary, desperate miners ducking to squeeze through narrow dank passages that were not there, peering to keep sight of Amina's faint lantern glow when light from above filtered through and turned damp sheens of water on the rock into glimmering mirrors and bathed the glowing rocks with beauty.

At last they reached the rooted stairway, and even that seemed to be difficult for the villagers to see. Amina wound up climbing the narrow winding way and attaching the rope they had carried with them to the bole of the tree and once again the miners had to climb up cautiously, passing the weakest of them up hand-to-hand.

The final stumbling walk down the hill was done in silence, amidst the growing dusk of a day already over, not one of them with the energy to talk until they reached the mine entrance where anxious relatives still hovered, watching the efforts of those still trying to dig through from the other side. Then the babble of voices broke out, amidst tears and hugs, and the blowing of the mine's whistle.

Amina stumbled back to her aunt's house, knowing she had to return to the cavern, but wanting just one cup of tea and to wash her face and hands. She remembered answering a few of her aunt's questions and took the mug of tea she had pushed into her hands, and woke the morning, stiff, in the chair in the corner of the room.

"Oh, no!" she cried, jumping to her feet and then stumbling forward awkwardly, on feet stiff from sleeping in a chair.

"What is it?" her aunt cried, alarmed.

"I have to go back to the cavern—umm, to the mine!"

"Why do you have to do that? All the villagers are out, dear. You did it; you got them out."

"Yes, I know, but... there's something more I need to do... Keeper work," she said finally, looking at her aunt firmly but saying nothing more.

Her aunt met her gaze and then nodded. "There often is," she said, and asked no more. She insisted Amina have something to eat—'you didn't eat a bite last night and barely sipped your tea—you need something for energy or you'll collapse like those rocks in the mine shaft, and then what can you do'—but then let Amina leave with no further questions.

Amina blessed again the fate that had brought her into her aunt's raising, for all she'd been hurt by her mother's abandonment at the time. Her aunt respected her, as well as loved her, and had raised her to be a woman, true to herself and her obligations. And now she had to fulfill one, and hope the fey was not so angry at her failure to return right away that she wreaked vengeance on the village.

Her calves, still sore from the day before, burned as she walked steadily up the hill to the copse of trees and the huge old oak that guarded the way into the cavern. She noticed with bemusement that the opening was filled with leaves and twigs and dirt as thick as if it had been undisturbed for years, instead of having been trampled by some 35 miners just yesterday.

She brushed aside the debris and climbed down the narrow, rooted stairway and into the airy cavern down below.

39

The fey sat there, watching her, waiting.

"I'm sorry," Amina said. "I meant to return right away, but I fell asleep. I came as soon as I woke up. I am ready to pay the price."

Then she swallowed hard, stood straight, and waited.

The fey smiled. "I thought you would return. You're a Memory Keeper. Even I know what that means. My price? I want memories. I want you to bring me memories."

Amina stared at her in horror—use up her people's precious store of memories to amuse a fey? She couldn't do that; she wouldn't do that.

"Those memories that we store in the boxes are for helping my people through crises. Once a Memory Keeper takes one out of the box, she is the only one who can remember it. It can never be used again. Please, is there any other way I can repay you? I can't sacrifice my people's safety."

"Oh, I don't mean *those* memories. I meant new ones—ones you could make. And then give to me. Memories like what it is like to be out under the sun. What it is like to do the things you do around the village. Maybe even memories from some of the other villagers—you can gather them, right? Little things. Celebrations, get-togethers, even regular days..."

The fey's voice drifted off, and Amina finally recognized what she had seen in the other's face in that moment at the end of the last tunnel. It had been loneliness.

"You can't go out, can you?" Amina asked softly

"I'm bound here," the fey said simply. "At least until my people come back." She clamped her teeth tightly over that second remark, as if regretting letting that slip out. Amina sensed it had been a long time since the others of her kind had been back.

"That I can do," Amina said, knowing she was committing herself to doing the one thing that she had struggled with and fought against for so long—working with, gathering and using the memories of others. But it didn't bother her now. As her aunt had said, she was a trained adult now, one with a strong gift for the task, and even when she had immersed herself into the memory of the girl who had claimed she had traveled the fey ways, she had had no problems pulling her 'self' back out and letting go of the memory.

"I will bring you memories of sunshine and harvest, of winter storytelling around the fire, of the laughter of children and the good ache of a harvest brought in. I will bring you memories of all that and more."

And she did. She went regularly to the cavern under the oak and gave not only memories but friendship to the lonely fey. And if, in later years, she seemed to grow a bit fey herself, well, she was a Memory Keeper and they always were a bit odd.

GRAVE GOLD

by Jonathan Shipley

Jenna had problems: the Church; her brother; the unquiet ghosts in the barrow; and her ability to speak with them, which could lead to accusations of witchcraft. And then, of course, there was the cursed gold. But perhaps the gold and its curse could be used to solve the problems and to get the Church to leave her and her village in peace.

This is Jonathan Shipley's third appearance in SWORD & SORCERESS after another busy year of writing and marketing short stories. Most recently, he was published in an Australian horror anthology and has several other anthologies about to make print. Although "Grave Gold" is a departure from his favorite clan, House Arburg, it revolves around one of his favorite thematic explorations: life and death and undeath. Even with so many varied presentations of undeath available to the modern reader, there is still a lot to explore. Jonathan has a web presence at www. shipleyscifi.com and lives in Fort Worth, Texas.

Looks like trouble, Jenna thought as she rooted vegetables in the garden by the inn. Down the road, a little procession was headed her direction. At first glance, it seemed to be a lord in a fine coach with a brace of riders fore and aft, but a second glance revealed that the guards' shields weren't emblazoned with family armorials, but with the crossed oak clusters of the Church. She frowned. If those four were Knights of the Holy Retribution, the occupant of the coach was a cleric of considerable rank.

Her gaze automatically flicked to the hillock with its crown of ruined towers. There was only one reason outsiders visited this desolate region on the edge of the moors—cursed gold. It drew those greedy lowlanders like a magnet. The locals had more sense. After seeing lowland visitors trek up the hill and never come down, they kept their distance. But Jenna didn't mind living right there on the doorstep, so to speak. The moors might extend all the way to hell, but the inn provided good enough employment. As a young woman without money or family, she could do far worse. Besides, her family had a way with the dead.

From her post in the garden, Jenna watched the procession roll into the inn's stable yard. So His Grandness was favoring the inn with his patronage, was he? She doubted anything good would come out of that. With a shake of her head, she gathered her vegetable baskets and headed back to the inn.

His Grandness was coming out just as she reached the door, and he was very grand indeed. It wasn't so much the silk of his robes or the heavy gold Ring of Office on his finger as the attitude of his walk and glance. Jenna had a bit of the Sight and disliked him instantly. This was a man of power who would roll over anyone who stood in his way. At least he wasn't staying.

She pushed through the door into the common room. The afternoon patronage was the usual mix of drunkards, ruffians, with the occasional honest traveler thrown in. Travelers might want a room for the night, but the rest just sat in the taproom and swilled ale through the afternoon, then moved on at sundown. The moors behind the inn had a reputation as a grim place at night, and the locals preferred a little more distance between grim and them.

Bron, the innkeep, beckoned Jenna over to the counter. "Deal with that one who just came in," he murmured, glancing at the corner where a priest in a wide-brimmed hat was drawing sour stares from around the room. "A priester is always bad for business, but he's wanting a room."

Jenna nodded. The borderlands weren't that hospitable to lowland priests, not even ones that arrived by grand carriage. Straightening her apron, she headed across the room. "This way, father," she said, pointing him toward a narrow staircase. "You'll find our rooms spare but clean."

He followed quickly, seemingly as eager to get away from the rough clientele as they were eager to be quit of him. Something prickled at the back of her mind. Did she know this priest—he felt familiar. She led him up the stairs to the room farthest away from everything. "How long will you be staying with us, father?" she asked as she ushered him into the sparsely furnished bedroom. It was small but had its own window, which was better than some.

He didn't answer, just followed her inside and closed the door.

Jenna stiffened. This was odd. And it bothered her how he kept ducking his head so that his hat obscured his face. None of that was behavior that she wanted to be alone with, though he didn't feel at all dangerous. She tensed as he stepped closer.

"Jenna," he said nervously. "It's me." And he pulled off his hat to reveal a thin face far too young to be a priest.

"Herrin?" she gasped. "What are you doing here?" Her little brother was supposed to be studying at the St. Kyre's cathedral half a kingdom away. "And why are you pretending to be a priest when you're still a seminarian?"

"I'm not pretending—people just assume when they see the robes."

"Which you encourage by hiding your face so they can't see you're just a boy," she pointed out.

He bristled. "I'm not a boy anymore, Jenna. I turned sixteen last month—old enough to be given a mission of expurgation by the Lord Bishop himself and important enough to ride with His Magnificence in his carriage."

Riding in a bishop's carriage would turn the head of a lowly seminarian rightly enough, she thought. The word "expurgation" ominously echoed in her head. "Herrin, tell me you did not come back on a fool's mission to cleanse the barrow." The reason the moors were shunned after dark had much to do with the unquiet dead up the hill.

"The Church is trying to root out all these pockets of unclean spirits," he muttered defensively. "The Lord Bishop was delighted that I know the barrow hills so well and thought I was the man for the job."

"The boy for the slaughter, you mean," Jenna sniffed. "Either your Lord Bishop is a complete idiot, or for some reason he wants to be rid of you. You grew up here. You know what happens to every gold hunter that goes up to the barrow."

Herrin gave a deep sigh. "Actually the Lord Bishop doesn't believe the barrow is all that dangerous. He says this should be an easy expurgation."

Jenna frowned. "Easy? If it were easy, Gran would have laid the dead to rest a long time ago. Remember how hard she had to work calming them down every time another gold hunter got them riled up? She knew the darkness up in the barrow better than anyone and always called it dangerous."

"I know, I know. I'm just repeating what the Lord Bishop told me. That's why I need your help. I know Gran taught you things, maybe enough to keep the dead quiet until we finish here." She stiffened. "Please, Jenna," he wheedled. "You have the Sight and Gran taught you to do up charms as well as anyone."

"Don't be making me out to be a witch, you idiot. I've never tried to bespeak the dead up there, so who knows if I have any talent at calming them. And you know as well as I do there's only one reason why any outsider, bishop or no, would be so interested in our local haunts."

Herrin fidgeted a long moment. "All right, the bishop wants the gold, but not like you think. It's part of St. Kyre's gold and needs to go south to the cathedral. The Lord Bishop is here to retrieve it. He told me his Ring of Office was blessed by the saint himself and will lead him to the missing gold, but he still needs my knowledge of the barrow. And that's why you have to spell the dead to stay quiet for a bit. Will you help me?" he added quietly.

"I'll bring you a plate of stew and a mug of ale, but beyond that"—she fixed Herrin with a stern stare—"I promise nothing."

All this was so wrong that Jenna didn't know where to start. There was no easy spell to quiet the unquiet dead for starters, and living here all her life, she'd never heard of any connection St. Kyre. The gold was cursed—everyone knew that. It would take more than the Church's blessing to make something good out of cursed gold? And the Church regularly warned people to stay clear of hauntings and call a Holy Exorcist. Why would the bishop downplay the danger of the barrow?

"First off," she told her brother, "you can't continue masquerading as a priest because priests are bad for business. If you're going to stay a while, I'll bring you some workclothes and introduce you around as my brother here on holiday. Second off, you can't be dragging me into this. Gran might have known how to help, but I'm just a barmaid with the odd charm or two at her command."

Herrin sighed. "But Gran knew everything about the barrow. I thought she might have told you before she... passed."

An awkward silence descended. Herrin hadn't come home when Gran had sickened last year. Maybe he should have been there; maybe it didn't really matter. Jenna had put it behind her. "Gran used to say that the barrow dead weren't out for vengeance and walked only because they were cursed to guard the gold. I daresay that's different from most exorcisms."

"Maybe so, though I don't think the Church differentiates. I thought I might go up and poke around this afternoon."

Jenna cringed. "Poking around? That's exactly the wrong thing to do. You stay put in your room... I'll go." Then she winced. She needed to stay out of this matter, not rush headfirst into it. But she would do it for her brother. Her gaze softened. "But it's good to see you again, Herrin. It's been too long."

~o0o~

The holding at the top of the hill had gone to ruin ages ago, but partial walls still marked the placement of the curtain wall and the main keep. It was no grand castle in the lowland sense, just the rough border holding with a barrow built into the far side of the hill.

Jenna circled the hill until she reached the low arch that served as the entrance. Was she really doing this? Apparently so. She always knew he'd have to test her talent one day. Among the clutter of notes Gran had left was a recipe for talking to the dead with some measure of protection. And if it had worked for Gran, then... well, it seemed a better plan than Herrin "poking around."

Stooping, she made her way to a central chamber lit by shafts cut in the hillside. She opened her basket and brought out a loaf of bread and thimble full of salt. These she placed on the stone plinth that stood in the middle of the chamber. "A gift for those who rest here," she intoned as she broke the loaf in half and sprinkled the salt over it. "May you look with favor on me and mine and not begrudge us our time in the sun. For night comes to all, all too quickly." Then she pulled out the kitchen knife and pricked her finger, letting one, two, three drops of blood drip down on the bread.

From deeper in the barrow she heard movement and had to plant her feet to keep from fleeing. A bit of blood freely given was supposed to grant protection, but it granted nothing against the fear she was feeling. She gritted her teeth as the clanking of metal on metal drew closer.

Shadows paused in the mouth of the tunnel leading deeper into the hill. "Why do you disturb our rest?" The words were a dry whisper that barely carried.

"We may both have the same need," Jenna said shakily. Though she had rehearsed this speech carefully, the words tumbled out chaotically. "My brother, a servant of the Church, has been sent to lay this barrow to rest, and I am blood-bound to help him."

A long exhalation issued from the shadowed figures. It sounded ominous.

"But I know from my Gran," she continued hastily, "that the dead of this barrow do not rise out of malice or vengeance, but from a curse placed upon them long ago."

"It is so. We must walk while our task remains undone." One voice seemed to answer this time.

Jenna seized on that. "Then perhaps the time has come for that task to be completed. To that end, I offer you my aid. I have no great power, but I can accomplish some small magicks. We could be allies."

Then she waited, doubt creeping over her. While all this made sense to her, how could the living know what motivated the dead? She still had the kitchen knife, but that was no real defense if the spirits turned on her.

"Perhaps so," the shadow hissed softly. "The world has turned in an unexpected way. When the moon is high, I shall come to you. Now go."

Leaving the bread and salt, Jenna retreated quickly, backing down the entrance tunnel until she reached the arch and the sunlight beyond. She took deep breaths to quiet her trembling body, then headed down the hill.

~oOo~

He arrived in full armor when the moon was as its peak. The few people in the common room noticed, but not the right things. They saw a helmeted soldier, an unwanted authority figure. They didn't see that the armor was outdated, that the crest on his breastplate was that of a long-dead clan. They didn't notice that the common room grew chill when he entered.

Jenna gathered her courage and went to meet him just inside the door. "This way, sir," she said, beckoning to a corner table where they could talk without being overheard. There were more secluded places, of course—the rooms upstairs, the stableyard, the cellar—but she didn't want to be that private with a revenant spirit. It seemed prudent to have help within easy screaming distance.

"Can you take ale?" she asked as he lowered himself into the chair. An odd question for a dead man, perhaps, but bread and salt seemed to have some appeal.

"Not really"—his voice was fuller, not longer a whisper, but surprisingly light—"but a mug before me would bring back pleasant memories."

She hurried to the counter to draw a mug and set it before him. Then, hesitantly, she took the seat opposite him. He reached up a gloved hand to loosen the strap of his helmet, and she tensed. She really didn't want to face whatever skeleton animated the armor, but there seemed no choice in the matter.

The helmet lifted, and she held her breath, expecting the moldering worst. Then she exhaled in surprise. Several surprises, actually. Not only was the face perfectly intact with piercing blue eyes and aristocratic nose, but it was also the face of a woman.

48

"You are surprised, I see," she said, shaking a cascade of dark hair.

Jenna forced a thin smile. "I was expecting more... decay. I am delighted to be wrong. This conversation just became much easier."

"You were not so wrong," the revenant said with a very human-looking shrug. "This afternoon you would have seen bare bones and rusted metal, but the moonlight allows us the semblance of what we once were. Your kind always seeks us by day, though, and so sees us at our worst."

"My kind—you mean the living?"

Another shake of her head. "Witches, sorcerers, and the like. Those who always think that the dead have power to share if the right deal can be struck."

"I'm not really a witch," she said quickly, "just a witchblood." The reference to striking a deal raised old warnings. *Trust not the dead*, the saying went, *for they will betray every bargain*. And how many times had Gran said never to bargain with the dead? Give them gifts, but never bargain. "I have no interest in striking a deal," she added, "or in power or in your gold."

"So I sense," the woman nodded. "That is one reason I am here. I believe you can be trusted."

Jenna blinked. What an odd thing to say, considering it was the dead who couldn't be trusted. "My reasons are exactly what I stated earlier. I see the curse as the adversary here, not you. I hope we can be allies."

"Refreshing." The warrior raised the mug and seemed to take a sip, though she might have only been sniffing the ale.

"How is it you are a woman?" Jenna blurted out, unable to keep the question inside any longer. "Warrioring is a man's profession."

"In my day skill with a sword was valued, whether wielded by man or woman. But your Church long ago stopped girls learning the ways of war alongside boys. Pity that. A woman has a very limited place in your world."

The statement might have been an invitation to argue, but Jenna didn't rise to the bait. She actually agreed with her guest, the more so since facing the world alone without Gran. "The world turns," she shrugged. "What about the curse? It is said to be the gold."

"It *is* the gold," the revenant said, lowering the mug again. "But not the barrow gold of local legend. Gold was stolen during the night watch from my lord's strong room. He decreed that none of the guards of my watch could rest until the lost gold returned. And so we rise each night."

"But why would your lord's decree last after death?"

"In my time, lords were also wizard-lords, and such pronouncements carried arcane weight. It is good, I think, they all killed each other off. Mine was a grim age where souls were often placed in bondage."

"Ah," Jenna nodded. It explained why there were so many of these haunted ruins. The Church exorcists would have secure jobs for decades to come. "And the exact wording of the curse?" That was important in these matters.

"Ye shall not rest by day or night 'til the gold returns—those were his exact words."

Jenna nodded, playing with interpretations of the wording a moment, then suddenly deflated. "But that was hundreds of years ago," she said slowly. "There is no chance of finding that same gold after all this time."

"But there is," the warrior insisted with a glint in her eye. "We can sense the gold that binds us. It went far to the south, beyond our reach, to the city of your kings. The thief bought a sainthood with it and they raised a cathedral to his name. There the gold remains, at least most of it. I sense a tiny bit of it has returned."

Jenna frowned. There was only one cathedral in the King's City. "St. Kyre's gold? Are you saying St. Kyre was a thief?"

"Kyre the Liar, I name him. He deceived me greatly that night."

A flawed saint—that would take some rethinking. Wait—a bit of the gold had returned? "Would a golden ring blessed by Kyre be part of this stolen gold?"

The revenant froze. "Ring?"

"Yes, the Lord Bishop of St. Kyre's has come north and intends to use his Ring of Office to find the rest of Kyre's gold."

Jenna had heard of chilly silences, but now sitting across from a dead woman, she felt the temperature physically plunge. "I didn't mean to offend, milady," she said hastily.

"I am a warrior, not a lady. I am Brechia. There you have my name."

Jenna blinked, startled. Names could be power, and it made no sense for this undead warrior to be suddenly so open. "Why—"

"To show that I trust you. You sense my anger, but it is not aimed at you. I smell anew the gold-lust of long ago, and methinks it doth royally stink. A flawed bishop of a flawed saint in the village and a traitor of your own blood much closer."

"My brother isn't a..." But Jenna fell silent as she thought about that. In a test of loyalty, would Herrin jump toward her or toward the Church? She actually didn't know. His heart was good, but he could be dense.

"It will come to a head soon," Brechia continued. "Are you still committed to help us restless dead find rest?"

"I am—but St. Kyre's gold is far away in the cathedral and short of taking the bishop prisoner and holding him for a golden ransom, I see no way of getting it. And I don't mean that seriously," Jenna added quickly because that sounded a little too much like a plan. Dealing with the dead, she couldn't afford to misspeak anything.

"Here's what we shall do," Brechia said in a low voice. "Send a message to this Lord Bishop that the barrow hoard has been found. We are willing to exchange gold for gold."

If the dead were offering a bargain, it had to be a trap... but the bishop would have Herrin in tow on any excursion to the barrow. "But you can't—" Jenna began, then fell silent. She had to avoid anything that sounded like the terms of a bargain. "I mean," she corrected, "that the bishop would never go the barrow himself. Perhaps a meeting here at the inn."

Brechia gave a quick nod. "Arrange it."

~o0o~

Jenna brought tea and porridge up to Herrin's room when dawn had scarcely broken. "Wake up. We have to talk," she said, coming through the door.

Herrin raised his head blearily from the pillow. "It's the middle of the night."

"No, it's early in the morning—that's why I brought you a nice breakfast. And we really do have to talk. I know of a way to lay the barrow dead to final rest."

That brought him fully awake. He hopped out of bed in his nightshirt and came to the table by the window where she had laid out the porridge and rudleberries. "You found something of Gran's?"

"Not directly, but..." Jenna gave a sigh. "Gran knew how to talk to the barrow dead, so I—"

"You conversed with the damned!"

"Keep your voice down," she snapped. "And yes, I talked with one of the soldiers cursed to haunt the barrow. She told me it's all about stolen gold." Deliberately she waited, knowing that should trigger a reaction in a gold hunter, if that's what her brother was.

"She?" Herrin sputtered. "A woman can't be a soldier. It's all against the natural order and..."

Jenna let him ramble on, relieved that he was reacting to gender and not gold. Finally she interrupted. "Apparently the natural order was different in her day, but that's not the point. If the gold is returned, the barrow dead can rest in peace, so they are willing to trade the barrow gold for the stolen gold that was taken south to the cathedral and—"

Herrin gave a sudden start. "St. Kyre's golden altar service? The one that sits in the cathedral vault and is brought out on High Days?"

Oh. "Then all you have to manage is"—she spoke rapidly to get the worst of it all out at once—"bringing the altar service from St. Kyre's for the exchange. I'm sure some goldsmith can create an equally wonderful altar service out of the new gold. You can even say that you need the pieces for a Church-mandated exorcism—all of which is perfectly true. How could the cathedral say no to that?"

"Probably with a sharp sword through my heart," he muttered, shaking his head. "Jenna, none of that is going to happen. The Lord Bishop would never turn over St. Kyre's altar service. He has his own plan for obtaining the barrow gold anyway."

"Which is?"

"No idea. But I know he's interested in negotiation. Where and when?"

"Tonight. Here," Jenna said. The word "negotiation" sent a chill up her spine. It was just bargaining under another name."

"And even if I had St. Kyre's gold at my beck and call," Herrin continued, "you realize, don't you, that the damned can only want a consecrated altar service for unholy reasons?"

"I doubt that," she said, but was thinking furiously. It *was* a little odd that the stolen gold just happened to be a consecrated and very famous altar service. Was she just being stupid? All she had was the word of an unquiet spirit... and she remembered what Gran said about trusting dead men. Or women.

~oOo~

As the afternoon crowd thinned out with the coming of evening, Jenna's unease grew. Brechia had a plan, the bishop had a plan, and the two were probably on a collision course. Her stomach knotted just thinking about it as she hung out freshly laundered clothes in the garden behind the inn. Then just before sunset, the Lord Bishop rolled into the stableyard with his Knights of the Holy Retribution.

Jenna kept hanging and rehanging clothes to keep from going back inside. Her instinct said to flee and leave the Church and dead to each other. But Herrin was inside. She couldn't just leave him.

Finally at dusk, she went inside, leaving laundry and basket in the garden, feeling taut as a clothesline herself. At the door of the inn, she noted a salt line across the threshold, the type intended to keep dark things out. This negotiation looked well planned on the bishop's part. Jenna whispered a quick charm as she stepped over the salt line to allow Brechia entrance. That would at least even the odds. Inside, Jenna studied the far corner where Herrin, looking edgy as a cat in a kennel, sat with the bishop. Again the man made her cringe. He might look gray-haired and dignified, but she sensed a cold darkness. As she served the meager evening crowd, Jenna noticed more salt lines at the windows.

Three Retributive Knights circulated around the perimeter of the room with swords drawn while the Knight-Commander hovered near the bishop's table. This was another man she didn't much like, Jenna realized after watching him a few minutes. Too much death on his hands... and no regrets.

Suddenly the outer door opened. A Knight stepped forward, then backed up as a verbal barrage hit him broadside. "Get out of me way, you great-assed fool! Can't you see I've got work to do and don't think I won't take it out of your hide if you put me behind!"

A launder woman pushed her way between the guards, using her basket of clothes to knock him out of her way. The scene should have roused a laugh from the inn's patrons—one of the Church's finest flummoxed by a poor launder woman, but no one was laughing, not with the Lord Bishop watching.

Jenna allowed herself the briefest of smiles, before returning to her serving. Then she stopped cold. The inn didn't employ a launder woman. Laundering was one of Jenna's many duties. Turning again, she noted the basket was filled with clothes from the clothesline in the garden, and the shabby dress and apron the woman was wearing were Jenna's own spares. The face turned toward Jenna—dark hair, aristocratic nose. One of the blue eyes winked. Brechia.

Herrin had made a point about not trusting the damned; Brechia had been equally opinioned about a traitor of Jenna's own blood. And the Lord Bishop—he might be greedy, but there was something else as well. Seeing them all in the same room like this made Jenna realize the only person she could trust was herself. Sad to say, but true.

She watched Brechia circulate among the room's customers, flirting here, haranguing there, but definitely circling the room with a purpose. Ah, breaking the salt lines, Jenna finally noticed. Did that mean that other revenants—

"This way," a rough voice muttered in her ear. "His

Magnificence wants a word with you." The Knight-Commander had her by the arm and was propelling her toward the corner table.

As she crossed the room, she gathered herself inward as Gran had taught her to look at the problem with more than her physical eyes. She had time, but only a little. What was it that needed to happen? What wish would set all this aright?

The dead needed to find final rest and haunt no more—that one was easy.

The bishop and his knights needed to go without unleashing Holy Retribution—also easy.

Then it became harder. She wanted Herrin safe from the Church, not only from foolish exorcisms and greedy bishops, but also from the mind-numbing training that was turning him into a stranger.

And for herself, she wanted... what? A life of laundering and waiting tables? It seemed not, though she had believed so only a few days ago. Now that she knew she could bespeak the dead, it seemed foolish to ignore the talent.

She dug deeper under the surface and sensed other intentions bubbling in the room. Brechia wanted rest, but also harbored anger against the greed that had condemned her to centuries of unrest. But when she concentrated on the Lord Bishop, a chill crept up her spine. He would never trade gold for gold, which left only one currency for treating with the dead—blood.

She stared at the positioning again as the Knight-Commander resumed his post, standing sword drawn behind Herrin. Her stomach clenched. The plan all along had been to offer blood-price for the gold, literally sending a boy to the slaughter. And Herrin had not a glimmer of his danger. She seated herself warily across from the bishop. At close quarters, the darkness in the man was unmistakable. She distrusted immensely whatever plan he had in motion.

The bishop focused on Jenna. "My seminarian tells me you can converse with the dead," he began.

Herrin had revealed that? Was this the betrayal Brechia had warned of? She glanced at her brother across the table and he stared back miserably. *I'm sorry*, he mouthed silently. No, this was misplaced trust, not betrayal. Herrin had no concept that a bishop's robe could hide a black heart. And now she was expected to negotiate her own brother's sacrifice. She had to do something, even something rash. "Milord Bishop," she said. "You won't be leaving here with any gold from the barrow."

The Lord Bishop flicked a cold eye her direction. "For a barmaid of no breeding," he sneered, "you seem very sure of yourself, young woman."

A sudden movement startled her. Jenna turned her head to find Brechia pulling over a chair to join them. "Having a little chat, are we now?" Brechia drawled. "I'm in for that."

"I *am* sure of myself," Jenna told the bishop, "because it would be ill if people found out that their favorite saint was a thief who stole a fortune and bought himself a sainthood... as some people hereabouts remember. And Milady Warrior of the Barrow"—there, it was out in the open—"there will be no blood-price paid here tonight because—"

"This better be convincing," Brachia commented archly.

"—because you stand within striking distance of a chance at eternal rest." It was pure bravado, just talking to forestall the worst

Brachia's expression turned unreadable.

"Ah, a revenant in mundane disguise," the bishop said, his eyes narrowing to slits. If he was disturbed by a dead presence at his table, he hid it well. "We have business to discuss. Blood for gold, that's the bargain I offer." He gestured and the Knight-Commander raised his sword to Herrin's neck.

No! Jenna pulled the kitchen knife form her apron and plunged it into the man's sword arm. With a howl, he dropped the sword, blood spurting across the tabletop.

The temperature in the room plummeted. And from the shadowy corners of the common room, figures emerged—warriors in antiquated armor. They swept across the room and were upon the Knight-Commander in two blinks. It happened so fast, he couldn't even scream as his life-force was drained by the revenants. He dropped to the floor, a withered husk.

No one moved, but the terror in the room was a palpable thing. "So you want to bargain, Milord Bishop," Brechia announced to the stone-quiet room.

"Take them all, take them all," the man wheezed, his smug façade finally shattered.

"Oh, we shall," Brechia smiled. "Starting with you."

As the dead pounced again, all Jenna could think was *trust not the dead, trust not the dead* over and over. How could she have been so stupid to start down this path?

A moment later, the bishop was a dry husk dressed in silken in robes, the suddenly shrunken flesh drawing his face into an obscene rictus smile. But on his hand, the golden Ring of Office gleamed brighter than ever. If she squinted just a little, Jenna could see threads of light stretching from the ring to the revenants, binding them all together. This was indeed part of the stolen gold.

A chance at eternal rest—that's what she had spouted in desperation a moment ago, but it might be truer than she thought. She reached across the table and slipped the ring from the withered finger just as Brechia was reaching for it. "By finder's right, I claim this ring as my own," Jenna said quickly.

Brechia gave her an ominous stare. "Enjoy it for the few minutes you have left to you."

Jenna swallowed hard. It was as if she could hear Gran whispering old warnings once again. *Beware the casual assumption, Jenna. Magic works on the exactness of words, and there are traps and opportunities within a single word.* "But this ring is your path to eternal rest. Your dead wizard-lord never said 'all the gold' must be returned, just 'the gold.'"

Brechia's eyes widened as she digested that. Then her gaze turned cold again. "And now you will use this"—she nodded at the ring—"to bargain gold for gold?"

For the briefest of moments, it was tempting. Jenna didn't want to be a serving wench all her life. Then her grandmother's whisper—*They will betray all bargains.* "No, not a bargain," Jenna blurted out quickly. "A gift freely given to send you to eternal rest."

Brechia's shuttered expression shifted to surprise. "Truly?"

Jenna nodded and placed the ring in Brechia's hand.

A long sigh emanated from every revenant in the room.

It was working, Jenna realized. From a sloppily worded curse, she had pulled a spark of hope. And once the revenants believed, anything was possible. That was also the way of magic. Already the armored warriors were drifting away, eager for their final rest. Brechia also moved toward the door, but then she turned and beckoned. "A word, if you please, Jenna."

Jenna wasn't exactly pleased but couldn't exactly refuse. She stepped away from the table with its two corpses and followed Brechia out the door.

"You're clever, I'll give you that," the revenant said when they were alone in the stable yard. "You avoided every pitfall and produced an outcome no one could imagine. And because you did it with a gift, I am obligated to repay that gift before I go to my rest."

Jenna tensed. Would she get the barrow gold after all? A gift for a gift.

"A word of advice from the grave, so to speak," Brechia continued. "You have the knack for dealing with the dead and that's a rare talent. You seem to understand that being trapped among the living after death is a curse. With all the unquiet dead scattered about this land, you could take that talent on the road and bring peace to both the living and the dead."

"I doubt the Church would want a village witchblood meddling about when it has its own exorcists."

"You misunderstand. You could become a Church exorcist."

"I hardly think—"

Brechia gave an impatient snort. "You've just saved a room full of people from the vengeful dead, Jenna. In the business of exorcism, that's all the credentials you need. And it doesn't hurt to have the backing of the Knights of the Holy Retribution, and I daresay you'll have the very full backing of those three you just saved. You can even take your dim-witted brother along as an assistant to keep him out of trouble."

Jenna mulled it over. The idea actually had merit. "And with the barrow at peace, there's no reason to stay." She gave a snort. "It might be smart to leave before word gets out and all the gold hunters arrive."

"Gold hunters?" Brechia drawled in mock surprise. "Why, whatever do you mean?"

Jenna frowned. "The gold. With no more dead guardians, the barrow will become a free-for-all."

"Ah, but there's hasn't been gold up there in centuries. Kyre stole it all."

"But—" All the gold hunters over all those years... it was all a ruse for the dead to feed off the greedy? Jenna swallowed hard, remembering how she had almost walked into that same trap a few minutes ago.

Brechia glanced up the hill toward her rest, then turned with a cryptic smile. "Last word of advice—don't ever trust the dead."

FOREVER IS A LONG TIME

by Melissa Mead

Here we have another fairy-tale creature: a selkie. Melissa is good at taking traditional fairy-tale elements and transforming them, and this story is no exception.

Melissa Mead lives in Upstate NY. Her stories have been in Sword & Sorceress 23, 24 and 26, IGMS, Daily Science Fiction, and other places. She's a member of SFWA, Codex, and the *Carpe Libris* Writers Group (http://carpelibris.wordpress.com).

The old woman everyone called Grandma Seeley stopped beheading perch and glanced out the front window. A rowboat bobbed near the opposite shore, beyond the scrap of island that hid her home from casual view.

"That's Kim's." Grandma Seeley swept the fish heads and tasty innards into a bowl for later, saving out the filets. "Whatever possessed the girl to try coming over here just when the wind's picking up?"

Grandma Seeley called to the Waters. This lake, nestled in pine-forested mountains so unlike her low, flat homeland, didn't respond to her as briskly as the sea would have, but it roused enough to carry the rowboat on a smooth path to her door.

Kim looked like she'd needed the boost. Her face was pale, and she hunched over, ankle-deep in cold lake water, as she made her boat fast to a handy stump.

"You'll ruin your shoes, child," Grandma Seeley said.

"Grandma Seeley, I really need to talk to you."

"Come in and talk, then. I've just put some fine perch on the fire." Grandma Seeley led the way to the house, and Kim followed.

Inside, the perch were just about ready. Kim looked toward the fireplace grill, then at her, wide-eyed and alarmed.

"That's an awful lot of fish. You weren't expecting me, were you? I didn't tell anybody. And Zack promised he wouldn't either."

Saying her boyfriend's name shattered Kim's carefully-held calm. Tears slid down her face. Grandma Seeley sat on the shabby plaid couch and patted the seat beside her. Kim dropped onto it, shaking.

"I'm in such trouble. I didn't mean to. Zack didn't mean to. He said he loved me. He was wearing that sweater- you know, the one I gave him last Christmas. And then... then he wasn't wearing it, and we..." Kim choked and gulped air like she was drowning. Grandma Seeley held her while she sobbed. "Dad would never forgive me. He doesn't even like us kissing. When he finds out, he'll hate me forever."

"Oh sweetheart, "forever" is a long time, even for an old lady like me. Your father loves you. Forever is too long to be without the people you love."

"But I can't go home! You have to let me stay here." When Grandma Seeley didn't respond she added "Or else I'll just take the boat and head upriver."

Grandma Seeley sighed. "Well, put on these slippers and have warm feet and a full stomach for now at least. No point in letting the fish get cold."

Kim was normally as enthusiastic about fresh perch as a seal would be, but now she shoved bits of fish about on her plate.

"Among the Selkie, wasting food like that would get you bitten," said Grandma Seeley with a gentle smile.

Kim didn't smile back. "This is no time for those old stories. This is serious."

Grandma Seeley changed tactics. "Kim, is your father really such an ogre? He never seemed so to me, back when he'd bring you here because you were too little to handle the boat by yourself."

Kim slapped herself on the forehead. "I'm so stupid! As soon as he realizes the boat's missing, this is the first place he'll come." The girl ran for the door, slippers flapping. Grandma Seeley hobbled after her, and heard a scream from the beach.

"The boat's gone! What did you do with it? This isn't funny!"

Kim ran back and forth on the empty beach, looking in vain for her rowboat. Even the rope that had tied it had vanished. Grandma Seeley looked more closely, and shivered. Hands had loosed that boat, and their owner had left no footprints.

"Kim, come inside."

"How'd you do it? You don't have a phone. You couldn't have called somebody. Where'd you put the boat?"

Grandma Seeley dipped her fingers in the lake water, grabbed hold of Kim, and traced a cross on the girl's forehead.

"Let go! What are you doing?"

"Come away from the water, child. Please. This isn't their place, they don't belong here, and I don't know why they've turned up now, but it can't mean well for us." She tried to tug Kim back to the house.

"Why, I'm here because yon fair maid cried seven tears into the sea, of course," said a male voice.

Grandma Seeley turned around slowly, with Kim clinging, white-faced, to her side. Elused bobbed chest-deep in the water, his sealskin peeled back to his waist, his human face as boyishly charming as ever.

"This is a lake, not the sea," Grandma Seeley said, marveling at the steadiness of her voice. "It's many a long mile from home, and there are no seals here, let alone selkie-folk. So if Laird Morcant sent you all this way to claim this girl, I'm afraid you've come for nothing."

Elused shook his sleek head. "I came alone, and I came for you, Feidlimid."

Grandma Seeley startled at the name. She shook her head. "Armel called me Felicienne, and he's so long dead that even that name has faded to a ghost." Heat rose to Grandma Seeley's face. "Devil take you, Elused, can't you see I'm old?"

The selkie's dark eyes filled with sorrow. "I know you had no choice but to go with that trapper, that taker of skins. But why did your daughter here never return your own skin to you, as daughters always have?"

"I'm not her daughter, buster," said Kim. Her voice was harsh, but her face was bright with wonder. "Is it really all true? About the seal-people, and having to marry guys who take your skin, and being immortal and able to change shape and all that?"

"It is," said Elused. "Feidlimid has been gone so long that the others thought her dead, perhaps killed by that trapper who stole her skin..."

"I gave Armel my skin, Elused," said Grandma Seeley, holding the sealman's hurt gaze. "I know selkie men can never be faithful, just as we selkie women must always be. It's in our blood. Armel promised to stay with me all his days, and he did. He never took any sealskin but mine, and we had no children to return it to me."

"I searched for you all his days," said Elused, with a solemnity she'd never heard in his voice, or any seal-man's. "Though the others shunned me, though I knew you must be trapped without your skin, I searched. I would have come sooner, had there been tears to call me."

Kim wiped her eyes with the back of her hand. "I'll miss you, Grandma Seeley."

"Who said I was going anywhere? Even if I had that wretched old hide, this mortal body's too far gone for me to wear it as it's meant for wearing. And you heard him: the selkie believe I wedded a butcher. Your mortal tales don't mention that selkies have sharp teeth, and bite when they're crossed. I'm dead to the tribe, and if Elused won't go back, so is he."

"You're a hypocrite," said Kim.

"What?"

"You want me to go back home, but you won't!"

"Kim, sweetheart, I wedded a trapper. A seller of hides. The others will kill me for that. Your father's a good man. He loves you. You have nothing to be afraid of."

"This guy says he loves you. What have you got to be afraid of?"

"Listen to the child, Feidlimid," said Elused.

Grandma Seeley turned her back on both of them and stormed into the house. Let Kim's father get the loan of another boat and come fetch his daughter. Kim would go home, Elused would wheedle his way back into the tribe with that eternal charm of his, and all would be as it was.

She sat rocking by the fire, listening for the chug of a motor or the splash of oars. Nothing came. She looked out the front window, and gasped. Kim stood bent-backed on the wee scrap of island, with Elused watching her intently. Grandma Seeley hurried down to the beach just as Kim straightened and shouted "Got it!" She held up a tattered brown bundle.

Elused laughed aloud. "She's daughter of your heart if not your body, Feidlimid! Guessed right off that your man would've hid your skin on this wee skerry, in his sight but not ready to your hand. Did you never think to look there?"

"Did you never think that I might not want to? That I might want to finish the life I chose?"

Elused looked wounded. "Come, put it on."

Grandma Seeley shook her head. "How'd Kim get out there? And where's her father, who should have been here long since?"

Elused shrugged. "I carried her—as tenderly as though she were a babe, don't you worry! And her father, well, I asked the waves to rock him gently for a while, so the lass could say her farewells to us."

"It's so soft," Kim said wonderingly. She unfolded Grandma Seeley's sealskin. It tumbled nearly to her ankles in folds of silvered golden-brown.

Grandma Seeley shivered. "No. It's been too long."

A glint came into Elused's dark eye. "Then the lass should wear it. A pity it should be lost because its owner died mortal."

Kim's eyes got wide. "I could? I could be a selkie like you, and be immortal and beautiful, and not have to worry about mortal stuff anymore?"

"Try it," said Elused. "Just wrap it about you and jump in the water, there where it deepens."

"No!" Grandma Seeley cried, but Kim swathed herself in the skin, closed her eyes, and jumped.

The skin tangled about her mortal limbs, as Grandma Seeley had known it would. The old woman kicked off her shoes, dove. and swam to the thrashing, choking girl's side.

"I've got you, Kim. Relax."

The dragging weight on her arms lifted. Elused was holding Kim up on the other side, and he actually looked frightened.

"I thought it would work. Truly. I meant her no harm."

"Just take Kim back to shore."

Kim wrenched away from him, throwing her arms around Grandma Seeley and nearly sinking them both. "No! I'm not letting that liar touch me again."

Grandma Seeley glared at Elused, who looked abashed. The sealskin twined about her ankles, caressing.

"For the love of the Lady! You'll all be the death of me. Kim, sweetheart, can you tread water for just a minute? When I come up, put your arms around my neck and hold on."

She dove, shedding her housedress. The sealskin wrapped itself around her, but she pushed it away from her face. Let the seal's body carry Kim to shore, but her face, her mind, herself- that would remain human.

Ah, but the water was gentle, welcoming. And in the skin's embrace, her old bones no longer ached.

She shook the alluring thoughts away and surfaced to pull Kim ashore. Elused followed, more subdued than she'd ever seen him.

"Make yourself useful," she said once Kim was shivering on the beach. "Go inside and get us both some dry clothes. I can't manage the steps in this shape, and well-mannered humans don't traipse about in the altogether."

Elused took the hint and wrapped his sealskin about his waist before he left the water. Grandma Seeley noted with envy and admiration that he was as young and spry as ever. He returned with a motley assortment of human clothing, and turned his back while Kim dressed herself in a pair of Armel's old trousers and a sweater. Grandma Seeley looked at the raincoat he'd brought her, shook her head, and wrapped her sealskin, warmer than anything a human could knit, snugly about her shoulders.

"I meant you no ill, Miss," Elused said to Kim, staring at his feet. "I only thought that if Feidlimid refused her skin it might pass to you. I've been a long time alone, and pining for company. Loneliness is a terrible thing for an immortal."

"Forever's a long time," Kim agreed, looking at Grandma Seeley.

"Elused, tell the waters to bring Kim's father here," Grandma Seeley said. "He must be nearly frantic." She pulled on her sealskin, all the way.

"Your muzzle is gray," said Elused, shocked.

The seal shook her head, and Grandma Seeley's face showed through. "Now do you see? I married a trapper, a seal-killer, and I got old. Some things can't be undone. And there's never been a selkie man on this good green earth who could think beyond his own pleasure. Now leave us both alone."

She dove, deep into the green-gold waters of the lake. Fish flashed away from her. Weeds brushed against her. Water throbbed in her ears.

No one swam to greet her, or to threaten her. Elused had spoken the truth- he was the only other selkie in these waters, so far from home. The waters were the only thing there to welcome her back to herself.

Her seal body, old though it was, felt better than her woman's body had in decades. She could swim without stopping, for miles and miles...

She surfaced, and blinked. She'd forgotten just how long a selkie could stay underwater. Kim's father was already there, on the beach. So was Kim. And so was Elused, stark naked and grinning his most suggestive grin.

Kim's father swept his daughter up in his arms and swung her into the boat. The motorboat roared away. Grandma Seeley shook off her skin and ran to Elused.

"Did you see the mortal man, Fiedlimid my love?" the selkie said, bent over with laughter. "Such a look he gave me! He'll be nothing but gentle with Kim now, for all the fault will be mine. All's well. Now, come with me. Teach me the feel of these waters."

"Do you never think?" Grandma Seeley shouted. "Now this place will be swarming with policemen, and how will we be explaining ourselves? You've turned my home into a crime scene, Elused!"

He reeled back, shocked. "But I did nothing to Kim. T'was only a trick."

"That won't matter." Grandma Seeley glared at him. "And it was a trick. A childish trick."

Elused hung his head. Every line of his sleek body expressed remorse. He probably felt it, too. For now. Something would come along to distract him. Something always did.

"You're a rogue, Elused. The same as always."

Sensing forgiveness, he raised his head and grinned.

"But I'm not the same, Elused. I'm not the selkie maid you knew. I'm Grandma Seeley too. And Felicienne."

"And Fiedlimid? Or is she truly dead?"

"She's grown up, Elused. As you never can."

"Fiedlimid, my love! Did I not swim the seas over to find you?"

"You did. But I'd be a fool to think you swam alone the whole time."

"Well, it would have done you no good to have me pining away of loneliness before I reached you, now would it?" He turned the smile she remembered on her: brilliant with a selkie male's enthralling charm. "Come back with me."

She shook her head. "This is my home now."

"Then we'll claim the waters of this place for ourselves. You and I, swimming where we please." He grinned, pulled his sealskin around himself, and slipped into the water.

Grandma Seeley looked back at her house, so carefully hidden, holding so much of her mortal life. Armel had built it to last for more decades than any human could live to see. For her. For them. Forever. How strange, that a mortal's promise could make "forever" mean more than any immortal selkie ever had.

Elused was already swimming away, a distant dot in the water. Grandma Seeley smiled, shook her head, and went to pick up her sealskin.

"Make yourself at home in my lake, old friend. But I won't be crying seven tears into it."

She stroked the soft hide. The lake called to her. But policemen would be wanting to talk to Grandma Seeley very shortly. Her seal-self would have to wait.

At least for now.

THEY THAT WATCH

by Michael Spence & Elisabeth Waters

In the introduction to last year's story we said that Michael and his wife lived with a "canine Guardian" and continued "Hmm, now what can we do with a Guardian who is a canine?" Once I had posed that question, both our minds started working on it, and thus Mika came into existence. Nobody ever said that all female mages or warriors must be human.

Elisabeth continues to juggle working on her novel, anthology editing, and writing short stories. She is currently working on a story for Mercedes Lackey's anthology *Elemental Magic: All-New Tales of the Elemental Masters* (the anthology is scheduled for December, but the story is due in three weeks) as well as her next Valdemar animal story "A Wake of Vultures." In her mundane life she spent the past tax season volunteering with the AARP Tax Aide Program, which was an educational experience and provided her with several blog entries.

Michael Spence made his audiobook debut this year with his narration of the novel *House of Zeor* by Jacqueline Lichtenberg, who called his reading "the best I've ever found in an audiobook." It's available at Audible, Amazon, and iTunes. He is now working on the audiobook versions of Marion Zimmer Bradley's books *The Brass Dragon* and *The Sword of Aldones*. Michael and Ramona have relocated to Minnesota together with Orson, a bichon-cocker mix with a tendency to rush to the front window and bark furiously—at nothing. Or so it would seem.....

The makt came to life—if one could call it that—backstage in the University of Albion's theater department's main auditorium, behind one of the eight props cabinets, and promptly began searching. It had little time in this state; it had to find something quickly to give it structure, or dissipate.

Since a makt was a variety of spell, rather than a lifeform in its own right, one would not expect it to possess all of the three classical elements of personality; it did the will of the mage who cast it, as an extension of that same will, without the distraction of accompanying passion or intellect. The mage who placed this one, however, had not had the luxury of full reconnaissance, and so had to provide for some improvisation. It therefore possessed a rudimentary intellect—again, an extension of the mage's: to scan; to observe; to choose.

And then the will would have free rein... to seek; to find.

To *possess*.

~oOo~

Melisande was in the bedroom, unpacking from her trip to the Motherhouse of the Sisters of St. Anne, when her husband came home.

"Melisande?" He seemed surprised to see her. "I thought you weren't due back until the fifteenth."

"Stephen," she said going into his arms for a hug, "today *is* the fifteenth."

"Oh."

"I'm glad to see you, too," she said pointedly.

He started. "Of course I'm glad to see you, it's just that—" he broke off abruptly, staring at the one thing that hadn't fit in her luggage. "What's that?"

"It's a dog, dear. Her name is Mika. What are you working on that's made you so absent-minded?"

The dog—a beautiful black-and-white border collie—was instantly consigned to the 'Melisande is dealing with it' category, as Stephen waxed enthusiastic about his work. "Edward and I are doing a seminar for an exchange group from the Colonies. It's incredible; their magic system is so different from ours—subtly different, but the subtleties are fascinating. There's even one girl who comes from beyond the Colonies, and we're still trying to puzzle out just what she does."

Albion's and Iberia's colonies, Melisande knew, stretched

almost halfway across North America. "You mean, beyond the Mississippi? I didn't know they had settlements there, let alone universities."

Stephen shook his head in bewilderment. "Now that you mention it, I haven't heard of any." Then he seemed to forget the question entirely. "Why do we have a dog? I thought you were at the convent to learn how to handle our daughter." He placed a possessive hand on Melisande's growing belly. "I still can't believe she's going to be a Guardian from *birth*."

"She will be, but the Paten will be kept safely at the Motherhouse until she's older and has had some training. Lady Wizard Sarras will be in charge of her training."

Melisande felt Mika rubbing against her leg. She knelt and scratched the border collie's ears. "As for Mika, we became very close at the Motherhouse. I hated leaving her. But Sister Madeleine said she just showed up one day and had lived there ever since—she was free to come home with me if she wanted to. And she *really* wanted to. Didn't you, girl?" Mika lay on her side for a tummy rub, and Melisande obliged.

"If you say so." Ordinarily Stephen loved dogs, but approaching fatherhood had so radically shifted his thoughts that the usual "academics" now coupled with "daughter" banished this dog from his mind. "I can't think of a better teacher than Sarras for our little girl," he mused.

Neither could Melisande. Lady Wizard Sarras was not only the Guardian of the Grail, to which the Paten was a companion Treasure, she was a senior member of the faculty of the University's College of Wizardry, and she had been Stephen's faculty advisor during the many, many years he had studied before finally passing his Senior Ordeal. By then, the University was home, and Stephen had slipped easily from student researcher to faculty. And now that they lived in a house, complete with a small garden, instead of the quasi-dorm used for married-student housing, Melisande was content with her life. It wasn't without its shocks, of course; discovering that she was pregnant with a Guardian was only the latest one.

Unless it wasn't... "Stephen, what did you mean by "'it's just that—'?"

"I thought you weren't due back until tomorrow, and the seminar is scheduled to meet here tonight. We've been rotating it through faculty homes to give the students a view of how we live here." He look at her anxiously. "You don't have to do anything. Edward is bringing refreshments, and we'll clean up after ourselves. You don't even have to put in an appearance—you can stay in the bedroom and rest, or you can sit in on the seminar, whichever you prefer."

It might be interesting, at that. "I'll see how I feel tonight. What time are they due?"

"Seven, and they should be gone by nine. Nine-thirty at the latest."

"Seven?!" she said in horror. "And what time is it now?"

"Uh..." He consulted his Senior Thaumaturge's sigil and gulped. "Six-forty?"

She thumped an annoyed fist on his chest. "Men! Get the chairs moved. I'll put glasses out for drinks."

~oOo~

Melisande decided to sit in on the seminar after all, but when the group arrived, she felt as if her hair stood on end. As a Sensitive, she knew this feeling well, but why now? *It could be just that Edward's here.* Edward was the Guardian of an anti-Treasure, the Sceptre of the Ungodly, and anti-Treasures could be uncomfortable things to be around. *Maybe I'm feeling things more than usual because of my pregnancy.* That was certainly possible as well.

She sat down in a comfortable chair—on the far side of the room from Edward and Stephen, and close to the fire cheerfully crackling in the fireplace, a counterpoint to the lively discussion bouncing about the living room. Mika stood vigilant at her side, scanning the students. Her head was next to Melisande's knee, so when she froze, pressing against Melisande and staring fixedly across the room, Melisande followed her stare. The girl sitting next to Edward seemed ever so slightly out of place. While all of the students' clothing was of a different style than that worn by students in Albion, this girl seemed even more out of style. Also, to Melisande's eyes, there was a sort of gray film about her, as if she were wrapped in a semi-visible shroud.

As the talk continued—tonight's session concerned Treasures and their Guardians (apparently they didn't have either in the Colonies)—Melisande realized that the girl was flirting with Edward. She looked up into his face and actually batted her eyelashes as she said, "There is a saying where I come from: *'Quis custodiet ipsos custodies?'*—and I think it would apply here. You have all of these powerful Treasures," she smiled at Edward, "and they have Guardians to watch them, but who watches the Guardians? How do you know they won't misuse the Treasures in their care?"

A reasonable question, thought Melisande, *and one I know Edward himself has considered. But look at her! The others don't appear to know that Edward is a Guardian, and they live here at the College; but* she *obviously knows. Is she a Sensitive? No, or she'd be on the other side of the room from him, like me...except that she looks as though she not only senses the Sceptre but covets it for herself.* Then the girl's eyes flicked across the room to look at Melisande, and her eyes became even more covetous. Melisande's skin crawled. *Just who—or what—is this girl?* The end of the seminar couldn't come quickly enough.

But finally everyone had gone and Melisande lay curled up in bed next to Stephen, feeling safe and cherished. She saw Mika lie down at the foot of the bed and, smiling, drifted off to sleep, happy at the thought of two individuals there who loved her. With a third on the way.

~o0o~

She was dreaming. Of course she was dreaming; she was a dog.

This wasn't the first time this had happened to her—it had started at the convent, shortly after Mika attached herself to Melisande. There the dreams had been innocent and playful: running around the convent grounds; herding the sheep and goats, whether they needed herding or not (*a dog has to keep in practice, after all*); splashing in the stream that flowed into the lake...

Now, however, play and innocence were past. Her eyes darted

from door to window and back. No sign of motion. The air smelled normal, apart from the new ashes in the fireplace. It did not do to let one's guard down. To be sure, she knew (how did she know?) that she needed to sleep for more than two-thirds of the day, something she wished weren't so but could do nothing about. At some point faith had to enter the picture; she knew that, and surely those who called her did too. Still, she must do what she could.

But just what was she watching for, and who felt this need for vigilance? Was she Melisande, her unease from the evening seeping into this dream, or was she another mind that shared Melisande's disquiet? And how could she tell?

Either way, life had suddenly lost its carefree joy, and the urge to guard was strong. But neither mind was sure exactly *what* they were guarding against.

~oOo~

After many false starts with various backstage items—ropes, sandbags, makeup brushes, potted artificial palms, a piano, and other items best left unmentioned—the final choice was perfect. Some three years previously, a student actor from the College of Wizardry, in a public performance of *Hamlet* that was attended by much of Londinium and even by the King himself on opening night, had used a carefully tuned invisibility spell to present his unrobed skeleton in the role of the late King Hamlet's ghost. The show slammed to a halt in the very first scene, unfortunately, when the Ghost appeared onstage and it became obvious that pranksters had nullified the spell, displaying the hapless thespian in all his Emperor's-new-clothes glory. The show must go on, however, and everyone tried their best to persevere...but then the actor portraying Bernardo spoke his line, *"Looks it not like the king? mark it, Horatio,"* bringing a wave of laughter from the opening-night crowd, with not a few glances toward the Royal box. For his part, Horatio valiantly tried to keep a straight face; but as he replied, *"Most like: it harrows me with fear and wonder,"* both his composure and the audience's—along with the Bard's grand tragedy—went to pieces.

After a morning's tense conversation with the Crown, the

College administration issued a tastefully-worded directive banning invisibility spells for the next three terms, along with a permanent ban on the theatrical use of any technique that risked "this or any other such wardrobe malfunction." The University's theater department regretfully constructed an oversized skeleton of wood that could be manipulated using levitation and other telekinetic spells, and the show did indeed go on.

The bone-marionette was still in its cabinet and magic-ready to boot. The makt flowed through the spaces between the door and the jamb, and a moment later those spaces shown with a ghastly violet light. With a splintering crunch the door latch burst apart. The door swung open to reveal the palely glowing skeleton, looking more than ever like the death it symbolized, rising to its feet and clumping onstage toward the footlamps and then down the steps to the orchestra. A cloaking subroutine engaged, and the skeleton vanished from the range of human sight.

With tottering steps the makt made its way up the center aisle and out the exterior doors to begin the hunt.

~o0o~

This morning Stephen had gone to meet again with the seminar, this time in its regular lecture hall. Melisande fed Mika a portion of the previous evening's dinner—pork chops with fried apples, her favorite. Stephen had fixed it for her, and she was tempted to forgive him for that evening's student invasion. After breakfast, she built up the fire in the living room and thought about doing some reading.

Mika had other plans, though. Melisande had just settled herself in the chair and picked up her book when Mika trotted up and put her front paws on the chair arm.

"Hello there. And *what* do you have in your mouth? Give it here." To her surprise, Mika dropped the tiny packet into Melisande's lap without an argument. It was a pair of Stephen's socks, still folded together. "What are you doing with this, eh?" Melisande said, scratching behind Mika's right ear and wondering whether to be angry.

Mika barked once and waited.

"I don't—oh, wait a minute. Maybe I do." With an effort Melisande levered herself out of the chair, deciding she wasn't going to do that more often than she absolutely had to until the baby came. As she picked up the sock bundle, Mika barked again and backed away toward the hallway leading to the bedroom.

"A-ha! Here we go," Melisande said, tossing the socks down the hallway. Mika swiveled around and dashed down the hallway, picked up the bundle, and brought it back. Instead of dropping it at Melisande's feet, however, she merely sat and held it up, allowing Melisande to pluck it from between her jaws. It was quite dry.

"Why, thank you, Mika," she said. "Have you done this with pregnant ladies before?" Mika only barked and darted down the hallway again.

They played fetch for a few more minutes, stopping only when Melisande paused to lean on the back of her chair and take a breath. breath. As if on cue, Mika trotted back around the chair and lay down beside it.

"My goodness," said Melisande. "If only husbands were as accommodating!" She chuckled and resumed both her seat and her book, an experimental novel about a love triangle involving a lycanthrope and—wonder of wonders!—a sympathetic hæmophage. She didn't think it had a chance, but she was willing to give it the benefit of the doubt.

She hadn't read more than five pages, however, when Mika jumped to her feet, ran to the window, and began to bark up a storm. "What in the world are you barking at?" she said, pushing herself slowly, awkwardly, to her feet and joining the dog at the window. "There's nothing out there!"

Indeed, the window showed only the empty courtyard, crisscrossed by walkways and winter-dormant grass that covered the hundred-plus yards to one of the inner castle walls of the University complex.

The border collie would not be deterred. She continued her frantic barking, her eyes focused not straight across from the window but somewhat to the left. Abruptly she stopped, bounded away from the window, and dashed leftward toward the hallway and down it toward the bedroom, barking all the way, as if seeking a better vantage point. Melisande slowly followed, calling, "Mika? What are you doing?"

Before she reached the hallway, the barking stopped.

"Finally!" she said, making her way down the hall to the bedroom. "Mika, what on God's green earth has gotten into—"

She reached the bedroom doorway and stopped. The bed was made, the rug orderly, the window closed.

The dog was gone.

She shook her head. Clearly she had gone mad. That was it. She had an absent-minded husband, a Guardian-elect child, and now a vanishing dog. She was mad, mad as the hare in March.

There was nothing for it but to make a pot of tea and go back to her book.

~o0o~

She galloped across the campus, her legs powering her past lawns, classroom buildings, offices, and the people who were normally out in the mid-morning. The sight was breathtaking, the rush of energy exhilarating. And the smells! She could smell the greenery, which surprised her, since it was still wintertime and nothing had blossomed yet. The dirt beneath her feet, the remnants of someone's breakfast from a nearby lodging, even the people walking along the walkways had their own scents.

Melisande noted that not a soul turned to look at her, which seemed strange. Normally when she strolled along those walkways people said hello, or at least smiled. But then she was also able to look them in the eye, whereas now they were looking well over her head. Her viewpoint was no higher than their knees; it was as though she were—

("—on four legs, close to the ground... Oh, I see. I'm a dog again. But it's daytime, so I wouldn't be dreaming now. Therefore I'm delusional. Of course. It only fol—")

No you're not! You're there! I'm here!

It was an actual voice, although she didn't seem to be hearing it with her ears. It was one she had never heard speak before, and she wondered why it seemed so familiar somehow. Abruptly she realized that while no one had spoken in this voice, she had heard quite a few barks of similar tone. ("Mika?")

Yes, Mellie! Me! That was the nickname a young novice had used for Melisande at the Motherhouse, and it had caught on among the nuns. It made sense that she should hear it now...unless, of course, she were imagining it too. Which could be, if in fact she had gone mad. But what if—

("I'm actually talking to you?")

Yes! Why not? You talk to me a lot!

("Well, yes...but I never really expected you to answer.")

How strange! I always answer. You must not have been listening.

Was she dreaming again? That too would make sense. She was back home—"there"—by the fire, asleep. ("The book must not have much going for it, then.")

Not much what? I don't under—

("Never mind. Where are we going?")

Bad! It's bad! Can't you smell it?

She quieted and let the impressions wash through her as Mika sailed past the Semeiotics department office, turned a corner, and headed across a courtyard toward the distant Knox Arch. ("Faintly...yes, yes, it's there! Oh my word, it *is* bad. Worse than those eggs that sat for a month before we found them...")

Yes! That's it. Bad.

("And you could smell this from the house?")

No, not in my nose... behind *my nose...all around me...that's not right, I don't know how to say—*

("No, it's fine, I understand. But now we really do smell it?")

Yes! Terrible! And it's coming.

They dashed through the archway and along a stone-floored corridor. ("Coming from where?")

Don't know. Coming to us. It wants. It wants.

("Wants what?")

It wants Dorothea. There's nothing else. It wants her.

That gave her pause. Who? The name was new to her. She knew no student named Dorothea, no teacher, no staff...

The dog leapt through one of a row of small arches bordering the corridor and out onto another swath of dormant grass. It

78

crackled under her feet, and the increased traction lengthened her stride.

Perhaps someone in town, or one of the new students. Last night there was...

Something inside her froze. *Coming to us,* Mika had said.

The baby.

~o0o~

Mika turned a corner past More Hall and saw it. The bizarre figure walked slowly but steadily beside the flagstone path in the direction that would ultimately take it to the cottage where Mellie sat dreaming, with the baby inside her. It couldn't be allowed to go past this point! Mika barked, but the thing ignored her.

Some people turned to look at her, but not at the—it seemed to be a walking stack of bones, a—what did they call it—

("Skeleton,") Mellie supplied.

That's right, a *skeleton.* No one seemed to notice it. They didn't *see* it. Even Mika could barely see it. From moment to moment flickered out of sight; one moment it was there, a dim purpley color, and then for an instant it wasn't. Was it real? *Oh yes, it's real. Unreal things don't* smell *like that!*

And indeed it did smell, enough that several of the people nearby wrinkled their noses and glanced about, puzzled. Evidently they dismissed it as either a bit of nearby magic some first-year student had botched, or something that the custodial staff would clear away soon.

Still they appeared not to see the *skeleton* thing. Maybe they *couldn't* see it! Mika knew humans could see almost all the colors she could, although they needed brighter light to do it. Perhaps this purpley color fell into the slim margin between their sight and hers. And yes, it was dimly visible... but she was fine with dim light. Mika wondered if there were a cat around. It might be interesting to find out which of them could see this thing better.

Heh. It probably thinks it's unseen. One mistake.

("Mika?")

Yes, Mellie?

("You know that I...love you very much...don't you? And...that I'm glad, so very glad you've come to stay with us?") Her voice in Mika's head held a strange quaver.

Yes! Yes, I do.

("And at the Motherhouse, I was a perfect example of a calm, serene, exceptionally rational woman? Not prone to wild emotional outbursts?")

Calm, quiet, thoughtful, yes. Very much so. Mika had no idea where this was going.

("Good.") She sounded quiet and precise even now. Dangerously so. ("Because I hope you won't be hurt if I leave you and try to sleep *without* dreaming for a while, because I'm sitting here very, very pregnant and you're telling me Hamlet's father's ghost is marching toward us and wants to do something terrible to my baby and I am *this* close to collapsing into full-on raging gibbering hysterics.") Mellie took a mental breath. ("Which won't help you either. So, if you don't mind, I'll just say Godspeed and you can tell me about it later. Okay?")

Oh. Mika supposed she was right.... *Yes. Sleep. Do speak to the King about this, will you? I will need it.*

("Uh...Lord Logas and Magistrix Judith are going to the palace this afternoon. Perhaps...oh. Okay, I will,") Mellie's voice said wearily, and fell silent. She would have been helpful, but Mika knew Mellie needed to be somewhere other than here right now.

And *here* included an oncoming bone-monster.

Did it see her? It didn't pay attention to her when she barked. Just a—a *skull*, that was right. No eyes.

She gathered her courage and charged it. She had herded sheep by nipping at their feet...but then she knew where the shepherd was and made them move towards him. Where was the shepherd for this bone-thing? Or was there one? And if so, was Mika ready to meet that shepherd?

No time for that. She knew where the skeleton-thing intended to go. *Herd it any way but there.*

Running toward its feet, she noted the placement of its left ankle. She circled around and darted toward it, her mouth opening to take a bite.

A bony arm scythed downward and swept her into the air. She landed hard on her side some thirty feet away, the wind knocked well out of her.

So much for whether it could see her. She struggled haltingly to her feet. *Ow. It thinks it's unseen. I* know *I'm not.*

The standard method was out, then, even reversed. The thing might walk slowly, but it could twist and contort itself quite nimbly. She, then, had to either move faster than it did, or do something it didn't expect.

The skeleton appeared to be articulated like that of a human being. If it actually were, then a frontal assault was worse than useless, but she might be able to hit it from the back. She'd have to be quick, though; she didn't know whether it could only see forward or it somehow sensed what was happening on all sides. If that were the case, she was in big trouble.

Nothing for it but to try. Mika approached the thing from the rear, zigging and zagging, and just when she figured it should expect her to zag, she *zigged* and launched herself toward the spot between its shoulder blades.

There was a flash of light, and then she saw nothing.

~o0o~

Darkness. Darkness and silence. Mika lay on her stomach amid absolute blackness. Had she lost consciousness? For how long? And how close was the bone-thing now to Mellie and Dorothea?

First order of business: to figure out where she was. Not on the lawn, that was certain: underneath she felt not grass and dirt but stone. The walkway? She slowly got to her feet, very carefully lest she strike her head against something above. Remembering a previous time an enemy had put her in a box, preparing to bury it and her, she shuddered.

She felt no surface above her corresponding to the floor. That was good. She eased slowly forward, and bumped her nose against a solid wall. *Box!* she thought, fighting to hold her breathing steady. *Maybe not. Turn. Do* not *panic. Turning around; good, good. Now step forward, slowly. Small steps. That thing took sight and hearing, but I can still feel.*

To her great relief she encountered, not the opposite vertical side of a box, but empty space. It was a room, then, at least thirty feet in one direction, or so she decided when she finally encountered the room's far wall.

That still left the question of her senses. What had—

WHOOMP!

Off to her right a flame burst into being underneath a boiler. She was in a basement, and someone on a floor above had decided the cold was getting to him or her and had recited the incantation that fired up this auxiliary system. Surely that was what this was, since it had lain unused until this moment. Mika blessed whoever was feeling so delicate right now.

The light from the slits in the firebox beneath the boiler shone dimly, but it was all she needed. The outlines of the basement room came into view, including a heavy wooden door off to her left.

The thing had *put* her here. It hadn't killed her. *Maybe it doesn't kill! Maybe it takes and moves.* She immediately considered what that meant for Dorothea. The thing had not come to kill her but to take her. Words like *ransom* and *changeling* crawled through Mika's mind, bringing chills in their wake.

But what would it do then? If it was alive, then there was no way to know where it would put her once it had her. That line of thought wouldn't help.

If it *wasn't* alive, however... Mika had heard long ago about spells that existed independently of the mages who cast them, like curses but with more specific orders. If this were one such spell, a *makt,* then it was mostly a simple transvection spell, with a single place to deposit its prey—here, where no one was likely to come or hear a shouting prisoner.

That gave Mika two options. On the one foot, she could stay here and wait for Mellie and the baby to be taken and then stand guard against those who would retrieve them from this place. But not only did she not know what sort of enemy or enemies she would face, she didn't know exactly what the makt would do to Mellie and the child in the process of taking them, or how soon.

She had no idea what a "hamlet's father's ghost" did, and if the makt had taken that form its actions would follow suit. She surely didn't want to find out after the fact when she could have prevented it.

That left the other foot. Mika didn't know the distance between this room and the ground outside...but the thickness of the door was a trivial matter. She gathered herself, pictured the distance in her mind, and *leapt*.

A stairway took her up one level, exiting beside the stage in what must be a theater. That made no sense, but it wasn't important. Mika had to find out where she was and get back to work.

~o0o~

Orientation was far easier once she was back outside. The makt's odor was unmistakable. Mika was dismayed to find that while she was in the boiler room the skeleton had covered fully half the distance to Mellie's house. No more pouncing attacks, then. She could not afford the time.

Something else drew her attention. The slow, shambling gait of the skeleton had become even more clumsy, if no less determined—as if the thing were somehow looser than before. A few seconds' study revealed that the thing was more poorly framed than before. It had, in fact, decreased in size by about a third. Whether the makeup of the spell had changed or it had consumed power in sending her away, it was less than it had been.

Let it transport her twice and use itself up? No, no time. The skeleton would be at Mellie's door before—

The skeleton. Mellie had recognized it as "hamlet's father's ghost." *She had seen it before.* Therefore it had been here already, and the makt simply used the skeleton so that it could stay together and move about. A framework. That meant—

Mika took off at a run. Speed was the critical factor here. If she could get in and out before it noticed her...

She jumped. Not directly at its back, but alongside it. As she passed it, her jaws closed on a rib and she wrenched it loose. She hit the ground and darted off to the side.

If you can't turn it around, take it apart.

She spat out the rib. *Not bone at all—wood!* What she would give right now for a bit of fire from that boiler room... Alas, leaping that far would exhaust her, let alone leaping back, and she dared not expend the energy. Nor did she know any fire-from-heaven spells. *Eh, well. Keep doing what works.* The ribs came off most easily, although she knew that sooner or later she—*wait. Try it now.* She circled around, came back zigging and zagging toward its left rear, chose her target, jumped, *pulled, and...there. Let's see it throw me without a hand.* The other followed soon after.

She pulled another rib off and flung it away, laughing to herself. *Normally* they *throw the sticks and* I *chase them. Something turns around after all.*

Her jaws closed on the thing's right ankle and she twisted. The foot didn't come off, but with a now-useless ankle it folded under the leg, and the skeleton crashed to the ground.

And disappeared.

That she didn't expect. Its task was to take and send away, and Mika expected it to continue working toward that end even if it had to pull itself along with what was left of its arms and legs. Like the Furies of old, a makt didn't give up.

Mika gathered her wits, did some serious if momentary reflecting, and leapt.

~oOo~

She found it in a garden. More specifically, in a maze.

Six-foot-high hedges outlined the paths of a labyrinth. Mika had no idea how large it was but presumed that one would not construct such a place without a suitably intricate puzzle to be solved. All she could see was a path that continued straight for some distance before and behind, turning behind the wall at each end, with other paths branching off at intervals.

At the end of the straight path before her was the makt, lying face down on the grass. It had taken her several leaps to find it, but find it she did. *So the wards around the College would have kept you out but not in. That suits me well. You just didn't think I could follow.*

Mika lay on the grassy path for a moment. Those leaps had nearly exhausted her, but she was undeterred. If a makt could pursue its prey like a Fury, so could she—and better. It had failed to secure its prey. She had not.

The makt was half its former size. For all she knew, it might disappear again. Let it. She would follow, after she recovered some of her strength. Slowly she got to her feet and began walking toward it.

The skeleton-thing took note of her arrival. As she approached, the skull lifted from the path, and the eyes that were not eyes regarded her. The ends of the arms moved in a peculiar dance, and something about them made Mika stop and back away.

The skull sank back upon the earth, and the makt's dim purple glow suddenly turned a bright red-orange. Mika heard a hum like an angry hornet, then two, then four, then eight, growing to fill the air around her. The brilliant glow swelled outward from the makt in all directions, a dome that burned like an expanding sun.

Mika backed away, but not far enough. With a clap of thunder the fiery dome exploded.

~o0o~

Nothing moved in the labyrinth for about a half-hour. Then, with agonizing slowness, Mika—singed but alive—again struggled to her feet. She glanced toward where the makt had been, nothing remaining but a scattering of ashes and two great charred gaps in the hedge walls. Not that they would be of much help to Mika as she trotted down the path in the other direction, seeking the exit the old-fashioned way.

She remembered that strange movement that preceded the blast. The power remaining in the makt was clearly considerable, explaining both the event and its effects; but it seemed doubtful that spell-casting would be needed to trigger it, especially since the skeleton lacked fingers to weave the spell.

No, she decided, sometimes a gesture was just a gesture. Mika suspected that had the makt still possessed hand- and finger-bones, the gesture would not have been polite.

"...and the ashes we recovered in the labyrinth match the wood pieces littering your courtyard. I think it likely, therefore, that Melisande's story is true, and this opinion will be reflected in my report." Corporal Juliana of the City Guard stood at something resembling parade rest before Magistrix Judith's desk. The hearing was only semi-formal, but one would not catch Juliana neglecting the forms. The Chancellor of the University turned her gaze to Officer Conrad of Campus Security, who echoed the City Guardsman's conclusions.

"Very well, then," she said. "Lord Llewellyn will have to submit the bill for his landscaping to someone else. In cases of of enemy action, which evidently this is, we are not liable." She turned to Melisande, seated in one of several chairs that lined the wall. Beside Melisande sat Mika, somewhat the worse for wear but upright, clear-eyed, and tail wagging. Behind Mika stood Stephen, his hand on his wife's shoulder. On her other side stood Edward.

On the wall above them someone had painted, in skillful calligraphy, a fragment of a psalm: "*My soul waits for the Lord, more than they that watch look for the morning.*" It was a favorite passage of the Chancellor's, particularly when she found herself hip-deep in the proverbial alligators and needed a reminder of the objective to drain the swamp. Today's investigation, with alligators aplenty, had taken until well past midnight; doubtless everyone, not just the Campus Security sentries, was looking eagerly for the morning.

"I thank you for your patience, Melisande and Stephen...yes, and Mika," said Magistrix Judith. "We're almost at the end here, and I believe we can get you home to bed well before the morning arrives." To Stephen she said, "Finally, Professor, please tell Lord Logas and the officers here about your seminar at midday."

"Yes, my Lady," said Stephen. "Nothing negative occurred for most of the period—indeed, we were all conducting a delightfully energetic discussion on the question '*Quis custodiet ipsos custodies?*'—until shortly before noon, when, with no apparent precursor events, one of the students suffered a violent death."

The Chancellor nodded. "The nature of that death?"

"Clearly magic-based, my Lady. The student was ignited from within, seemingly spontaneously, and almost before we knew it the combustion was complete. All that remained was the charred skeleton. And a blackened chair."

Again Magistrix Judith nodded. "Your opinion, my Lord High Wizard?"

Logas pursed his lips. "The report Senior Thaumaturge Melisande has given us, based on the rapport she enjoyed with Mika"—at whom he glanced; she looked him square in the eye—"is that Mika believes the event at Lord Llewellyn's estate to be the self-termination of a makt, a motile spell-construct existing apart from, but not utterly independent of, the wizard who casts it. Since it existed as an extension of the wizard's will, its destruction rebounded on its maker. Hence the event during the seminar, which we may term a 'magical backlash.'"

"And yet you say this was not entirely consistent with the run-of-the-mill makt, if such a thing could be said to be."

"Correct, my Lady Chancellor. It would seem that the wizard invested this makt with some degree of intellect, so that it could secure a suitable framework for its existence without supervision. This would follow if the wizard were a student with a stringent schedule. As an unforeseen result, the makt abandoned its task when faced with the improbability of success rather than, as we would put it, 'die trying.' I am considering the hypothesis that with any degree of intellect comes an instinct for self-preservation."

Magistrix Judith frowned. "Yet followed in this case by suicide. Why? And what about its behavior before destruction?"

Logas's expression didn't change, but Melisande saw his eye twinkle. "Spite."

The Chancellor harrumphed, then addressed the group as a whole. "You see the problem before us, ladies and gentlemen. This wizard was an exchange student from beyond the Colonies, which to us is *terra incognita*. And yet she held not only knowledge of our own people, procedures, and lore, but an agenda that included kidnapping—initially Lord Edward, or more likely the Sceptre of which he is Guardian, but redirected at the child of Melisande and Stephen, who will be a Guardian when she is of age. I consider the trans-Mississippi region a very credible threat, and recommend that we each give its study the benefit of our particular talents. I do not doubt that much remains to be discovered, and we will benefit from the forewarning.

"This hearing stands adjourned."

After the Guardsmen and Edward had left, Stephen and Melisande made their way out, with Mika behind them. Before she was out the door, Logas called, "Michaela!"

The dog stopped and turned to face him.

"Lady Sarras sends her greetings. She looks forward to seeing you again when she returns to campus next week."

Mika woofed brightly.

~oOo~

"You should have seen it," Stephen said enthusiastically to Melisande. Edward had joined them for supper, and now they were seated in the living room of the cottage. "Right there in the middle of the discussion she turned into a souped-up jack-o-lantern. Flames shooting out of the eyes and mouth and everything. Of course the skull was empty, burnt completely out."

Melisande decided no, thanks, she needn't have seen it. To her relief, Edward changed the subject. "If she had kidnapped me, what would that have accomplished?"

"Can't say for sure, of course, but we can imagine what the bad guys could do with the Sceptre. Not that they'd need it themselves, but consider what would happen if they planted it in the King's palace. Or the Chinese Emperor's, or the Caliph's."

"And then there's your daughter. Who I gather has a name, eh?"

"Well," said Stephen, "Mika seems to think so." He laughed. "Who am I to second-guess the family dog? Who, as it happens, rescued her and her mother from kidnapping, possible brainwashing, subversion...and the Paten with her."

Melisande chose this point to break her silence and rise to her feet, cutting off the discussion. "You two can stay up all night theorizing horrors if you want. *I'm* going to bed before I have nightmares for the next three months."

~o0o~

"Whatever Mika is, she's not an ordinary dog." Stephen held Melisande close—or as close as he could. "She's more like a guardian angel."

"Or a Guardian," Melisande murmured, already half-asleep.

She was dreaming again, the kind of dream that she now recognized and welcomed. Tonight Mika's thoughts were unusually clear: *Who guards the Guardians?* The reply was simple.

I do.

STRAW-SPUN

by Leah Cypess

This is definitely the most unusual take on the story of Rumpelstiltskin that I have ever encountered, and I love new twists on old stories.

Leah Cypess lives near Boston, MA, and used to live in New York City, where she briefly worked as a lawyer. This is her second sale to SWORD & SORCERESS. Her first, in SWORD & SORCERESS 23, was a retelling of The Lady of Shalott; she freely admits that twists on familiar tales and tropes are her favorite type of story. Her two published young adult fantasy novels, MISTWOOD and NIGHTSPELL, apply this method to shapeshifters and ghosts, respectively. You can find out more about her and her writing at www.leahcypess.com.

Alina unfolded the letter slowly and with great care: it was very old, and felt thin and fragile under her steady fingertips. Her heart was pounding in a way unfamiliar to her, and not just because of the whispers she had heard on the way to the throne room: *gold to straw* from two passing courtiers, *the end of the peace* from a duke to a lady, *Rumpelstiltskin*—she hadn't turned fast enough to see who'd said that.

She had come to the sitting room to ask her father about the whispers, but before she could say a word, he had handed her the letter. She smoothed out the last fold and focused on the ornate, flowing script so similar to her own.

The king was watching her. She composed her face and read.

~oOo~

I have four days until your third birthday, and it isn't enough

90

time. They say if you discover a goblin's true name, it gives you power over him. For the past month I have been living in the library, searching through the forbidden books, trying to figure out which one he is and if anyone knows his name. It is a fruitless, endless task. I will not lie: it is also boring. Even the fear of death doesn't change that.

Four days. I have an entire bookshelf left. Even if his name is there, which I doubt.

What will he do with you?

You need to understand: when I signed you away to him, you were nothing. Not a sigh in the wind, not a speck on the fabric of the world. You were nothing, not even a possibility of something, for though I had spoken to your father once or twice, I had never even touched his hand.

Yet you were real enough, to him, to be worth my life. My life and a roomful of gold. How could something that didn't even exist be worth that much?

If I hadn't done it, you would never have existed at all. So I told myself. I was buying not just my own life, but yours: three years of life for you. Children are happy creatures, and I swore you would be the happiest of them all, you-who-were-nothing. Three years of joy. Who wouldn't trade for that?

It seemed so easy, so simple, when you were not real.

It was lack of experience, you see, that brought me to this. I didn't know that parents love their children. Mine didn't.

The king doesn't like what I am doing. Nobody does. Whispers rise around me, suspicious and fearful. Does that make me seem like a better mother, that I am willing to risk my life for yours? Even if it's too late? How could I know, back then, what I was willing to do for a life that didn't exist?

Ah, but I lie. I always knew the whispers would come. That at first I would be their marvel, the girl who spun straw into gold, the commoner who married a king. For as long as the harvests were good and the borders at peace. But that when times turned bad, they would speak of witchcraft, and unholy bargains, and the devil.

Times are still good. But my days were always numbered. As yours were.

No, it's no good drawing similarities between us. No good rambling on when I should be straining my eyes at yet another book. Cursed sorcerers and their cursedly small writing.

I just wanted to tell you... somehow... that I failed. I love you after all, despite all I did to avoid it. Your wide dark eyes when you were drawn from my body, your tiny red fists and feet. When I realized, suddenly, that you were something. *The most important thing in the world. And that I had realized it too late.*

I know it is inadequate—even silly. But I am writing this letter to say that I love you. And that I'm sorry.

~o0o~

Alina refolded the letter slowly, until it was so small she could hide it in her palm. She looked at her father.

"Why," she said, "did you show me this?"

The king folded his hands together. They were old, crooked hands; the days when they had wielded a sword were long over. The ruby signet ring seemed too heavy for his fingers.

"Because," he said, "we were wrong about what happened. Your mother never found his name."

"Then why am I alive?" Alina asked.

She asked it calmly and precisely, the same way she asked about the progress of the negotiations with Aimar, and saw a flicker of approval in her father's eyes. The king was a very calm, measured person. He found excessive emotion distasteful, and his definition of "excessive" was stricter than that of most people.

"I don't know," he said. "But I suspect, now, that your mother managed a trade."

Alina rose from her seat and walked to the back of the sitting room. The portrait of her mother hung between two tall windows, overshadowed by their heavy sills, nearly invisible when the sun shone through. There was no good reason to display it more prominently, for there was nothing remarkable about it. Alina's mother had not been particularly beautiful, or regal, or striking. She looked like what she was, a village girl wrapped in yellow silk.

Until a few moments ago, Alina had never been told there might be anything about her to admire.

She didn't know why that made her angry, but it did; and she knew she had better not let her father see that anger. So she kept her eyes on the painting, and her back to the king, while she spoke.

"What would a goblin take for a life?" she asked—but as soon as she asked, she knew. Suddenly she was afraid as well as angry. She took several deep, steady breaths, trying to hold her shoulders still, so her father wouldn't guess.

"I don't know," her father lied to her. "The sorcerers have been working on figuring it out ever since it... happened. We know a bit about the goblin who is commonly known as Rumpelstiltskin—not his true name, of course, but it's what the commonfolk call him. He has appeared sporadically in the Western Woods for several centuries. He is evil, and loves to cause trouble for humankind. But there are no stories of his making bargains with any of us, before...."

His voice trailed off. Alina thought of the story she had been told: how her mother had discovered the goblin's true name, how in his rage he had pulled the ceiling down upon their heads and killed them both. Her father would not want to repeat the story now. Not when he was about to tell her the truth.

She could save him the trouble. But first she must compose herself. She concentrated on what she was: Princess of Ciern. Sole heiress to the kingdom. Valued adviser to her father the king.

"It will cause great difficulty with Aimar," she said evenly, "if I am no longer available to marry their prince. That is the crux of the negotiations."

No reply. She turned around and saw her father staring at her with wide, startled eyes.

"It will mean war," she said. "That is the most important thing, isn't it?" And as she said it, she truly believed it. Her responsibility to her people settled around her like a comfortable, heavy cloak.

"Yes," her father said finally. "But—"

Alina smiled. She enjoyed showing off how smart she was; people rarely expected it, when they saw her porcelain features and golden hair. It was especially fun when she managed to surprise her father, who should have known better.

"It's rather obvious," she said. The folded paper in her palm had grown damp. "What would a goblin take in exchange for a life, except another life? My mother gave him hers."

"We know little about the fae," her father said warningly.

"I'm not faulting your sorcerers, Your Majesty. They must have suspected it. But now they know." Her voice didn't even threaten to quaver. She was proud of that. "My mother was fifteen when she bore me. Eighteen when she... disappeared." She lifted her eyebrows. "I am eighteen now."

Her father leaned back, looking thoroughly impressed. Somehow it wasn't as satisfying as it usually was.

"Eighteen years for eighteen years. That must have been the bargain." She glanced once at her mother's portrait before meeting her father's eyes again. "And you know it now, because Rumpelstiltskin is back. The bargain is over, and he's come back for me."

~o0o~

It was not as simple as that, of course. It never was, with the fae.

What had happened was that gold was turning back into straw.

There were fifty bales of gold thread in the king's storeroom, left over from Alina's mother's bargain. Or rather, there had been. Until that morning, when the seneschal did his daily check and found instead a roomful of old, moldering straw.

The sorcerers were universally agreed: it was a sign of Rumpelstiltskin's return.

The advisers were universally agreed: it was an unmitigated disaster.

"The sorcerers might be correct," Alina told her maid, Rose, while her hair was being brushed for bed. "The advisers certainly are."

Rose made a sound of assent, the brush never ceasing its steady strokes. Alina caught a glimpse of the maid's expression in the mirror. Rose had a broad, pleasant face that usually bore a slightly puzzled expression. Though far less intelligent than Alina, she was the closest thing the princess had to a friend.

She also reported everything Alina said to the king. Alina didn't mind that. She had no secrets from her father.

"The real question," Alina went on, "is what has happened to the gold we've already traded. But of course we don't dare ask. If our neighbors think we tricked them on purpose, then Aimar, Mosun, and Palis could all invade at once."

"The king's cape is still gold," Rose offered, as she worked out a tangle.

Alina refrained from wincing as her hair twisted sharply against her scalp. Rose did not have a gentle hand with a brush. It was a small pain Alina chose to bear, for the sake of her only friendship. And, she often thought, as an exercise in self-discipline. A princess could not afford to let her feelings show on her face, even—especially—when those feelings were pain.

"Yes," she agreed. "Thread that has already been woven seems to have remained gold."

For now. She could only hope the goblin would tell them what he wanted before the king's cape disintegrated and covered him in straw.

Rose put the brush down at last, and Alina got to her feet and went to her window. Below her sprawled the city, lights and gray silhouettes in the night. All those thousands of people—and thousands more, beyond the city—getting their hair brushed, or brushing it on their own, getting ready for bed. Intact families, with no men gone for war, no women weeping over the deaths of soldiers.

For now.

Alina had never questioned why her father married her mother for the sake of bales of gold. Ciern was not a rich country. The gold—and her father's wisdom in using it—had helped protect these people for almost two decades. The king would not have been what a king should be, if he had spurned his responsibility to those thousands and thousands of people because he did not love a woman.

Alina knew very few of the thousands of people in the city below her. She did not love any of them. But she did not want them to suffer because she had failed them.

She sighed, turned away from the window, and allowed Rose to change her for bed.

~o0o~

That night, the empty room that had once been used for spinning was suddenly no longer empty. The sentry Alina had posted there came to let her know, and Rose shook the princess awake from a dream in which gnarled green hands pulled her down into the earth.

Alina dressed simply and swiftly, in a long white gown, and hurried through the hallway with Rose's disapproving stare burning into her back.

The west wing of the castle was dark, bare, and deserted. There had been a fire here—years after Alina's mother had died—and though it hadn't damaged the thick stone walls, a faint, ashy smell still drifted through the corridors, between the singed and crumbling tapestries and the blackened remains of carved wooden furniture. Alina had a torch, but its light was only enough to let her see her way, not to show her what was hiding in the shadows.

She knew there were things hiding in the shadows. She could hear them, brushes of wind where there should be no wind, half-heard sounds that could have been the scraping of branches or the hiss of the wind. They were the sorts of sounds that a person would think—would tell herself—she was imagining. But Alina had never been one for imagining.

When she reached the room where her mother had once spun straw into gold, she pushed it open without allowing herself to hesitate. She didn't even acknowledge to herself that she wanted to hesitate.

The torch went out as soon as she stepped into the room. All at once it was dark, so dark that when she briefly closed her eyes, it made no difference.

Alina knelt and put the torch down on the floor. She settled it carefully on its side, then straightened and said, "I am not afraid of the dark."

A moment of silence—she fancied it was startled. Then a voice said, "Perhaps it is I who am afraid of the light."

It was a female voice.

Alina stumbled forward, one step, then stopped. She whispered, "*Mother?*"

"Come no closer," the voice said. "If you see me, it will break what little protection I have."

Alina's fingers dug into the thin silk of her gown. "Protection from whom?"

"From *him*. Do you have to ask? Do you not know my story?"

As her eyes adjusted to the darkness, Alina could make out a hint of movement at the far end of the room. She was seized by a sudden, shocking hunger: a desire to see the woman hidden in the shadows, to look her in the eye. To see if she resembled her. Alina looked nothing like her father, but maybe...

She had never wanted anything so badly in her life. And at the same time, it was something she had wanted her entire life without ever really knowing it. She tried to get a grip on the sudden turmoil inside her, and she succeeded. Mostly.

"I read your letter," she said. Her voice came out clear and smooth.

"Ah," the woman said. A short sound, not much more than a breath, but Alina heard the surprise in it.

There was silence for a moment. Then her mother said, "So you know that I love you. Come to me, my daughter. The king will let you go now, because of the gold."

"It's not that simple," Alina said.

She heard her mother's indrawn breath. "It is, my daughter. It is always that simple, to choose love."

Alina stood very still. She squared her shoulders. She said, "I know the goblin's true name."

Silence—but a silence more profound, somehow, than the ones that had come before. Alina snatched up her useless torch and rushed forward, into the shadows.

It was as she had suspected. Her mother was gone.

~o0o~

That afternoon, for the first time in her life, Alina lied to her father.

She didn't know why she was doing it—another rare sensation for her. She was allowing herself to be guided by her emotions, like the silly noblewomen she had always despised. But something about hearing her mother's voice had let her emotions loose, and something else—her anger at her father, perhaps—made her not want to rein them in. Besides, she trusted her own intelligence enough to consider that there was a good reason for her distrust of the king, even if she hadn't fully figured out what it was.

So she lied.

She was very good at lying—it was another essential skill for a princess—and her father had no reason to doubt her. She explained her actions of the night before by telling of her intent to go, alone, and give herself to the goblin when he appeared. That part was true, yet it was the thing her father had the most difficulty with.

He didn't tell her the truth, either, about why he couldn't accept the obvious solution. He raged that she had no right; that she—or rather, her impending marriage and the alliance that hinged upon it—were too important to the realm.

"Not as important as the gold," Alina corrected him.

She was right, and he knew it, and yet he raged. He, too, was being controlled by his emotions now. She marveled at it. Was this part of the goblin's plan?

They said the fae were ruled entirely by emotions, that their courts were seething masses of love and hate and jealousy and desire. It had always sounded abhorrent to her, but now she thought she could see why some people were drawn to it.

It was a while before her father calmed down enough to ask the obvious question, and that was when she lied.

"He was there," she said, "but the torch went out, and I didn't see him. I told him I was there to fulfill my mother's bargain, and he just... he *laughed*." She shuddered. "It was not a human sound. I don't know how I even knew it was laughter, but it was. And then he was gone."

"The gold in the storeroom," one of the king's sorcerers reported, "is still straw." The sorcerers had been nervously silent while the king raged, and still looked nervous—as well they might, Alina thought, considering how useless they were turning out to be.

"Don't you mean the *straw* is still straw?" she asked pointedly. "It was never truly gold."

The sorcerers exchanged glances. One of them, a scrawny young man, said reluctantly, "Human magic cannot change the true substance of things. But the fae... we do not know what the fae can do."

"It seems to me," Alina said, "that there is a lot you don't know."

"Daughter," the king said warningly. The Sorcerers' League was a powerful force, not one to anger lightly. Alina knew this. The note of surprise in her father's voice made her flush. But she kept her scornful gaze on the young sorcerer's bony face.

"We know better than to go meet him on grounds of his choosing," the sorcerer snapped at her. "If you had waited, things might have turned out differently."

Alina was not surprised by the open disapproval in his eyes. She was used to it, from those who spent enough time with her to see past her beauty. People found her strange and unwomanly. The duke of Darmil, who had courted her last fall, had told her that she needed to acknowledge the passionate side of her nature—with an eye, apparently, to benefiting from that acknowledgment himself. But Alina saw the breathless romances and desperate tears of her maids, and had never seen any benefit in them. She liked being cool and calm, unaffected by emotional storms.

It didn't bother her that so many found her unnatural. Her father, too, was calm and dispassionate—and her mother, it had always been impressed on her, was not. It was a good way to rule a kingdom. Her father liked her even demeanor. He always had. And he was the only one whose approval she had ever wanted.

Until last night. Until she heard the voice of the mother who loved her, and had suffered terribly for that love. It made her wonder what it would be like to love fiercely, wildly, without regard for consequences. It made her wonder if the duke was right, and there was something she was missing.

She kept her eyes on the sorcerer, and her voice angry, as she spoke. She didn't want to look at the king, and she didn't trust herself to disguise her voice.

"They *will* turn out differently, next time," she said. "He has shown that he can be drawn into the open, by me. I can make him appear before the court. And before you."

"How?" It was the king who asked.

She had to look at him then, but years of training stood her in good stead. She met his faded blue eyes with utter calm. She even smiled.

I'm sorry, Father. But the thought didn't make it into her voice.

"By the threat of taking me out of his reach. The king of Aimar has been pressing us to announce a betrothal. Let us do it in three nights' time."

The king looked at her for a moment. She had never noticed, somehow, the depth of the wrinkles around his eyes.

Then he turned and said sharply, to the sorcerers, "Will that be enough time for you to set up a spell?"

The sorcerers assured him that it would, and the king nodded, even though they all knew that no human spell had ever captured any of the fae.

Only one human being, outside of legend, had ever held the fae to any sort of bargain. And that was Alina's mother.

~o0o~

The ball was a bit sparse, due to its being so hastily put together. All the members of the court came, of course, and the few foreign dignitaries who happened to be in attendance; but the ballroom still seemed empty, the music echoing a bit hollowly among the dancing couples. Alina took her turn among the dancers, wearing a violet gown of layered silk, her scalp aching from Rose's ministrations. The king sat on the dais, his face blank. The sorcerers stood together at his side, blue-robed and murmuring secretively.

The goblin appeared in the middle of the dance floor. He appeared quietly, with no smoke or flames, so that it was a moment before the shrieks of the dancers alerted Alina to his presence. She stood utterly still as the lords and ladies stumbled and fled, some brushing hard against her in their haste, almost knocking her over. She planted her feet wide on the marble floor.

The sorcerers drew together and cried out a spell in unison. Alina felt that brush by her, too. The jostling of the dancers had not made her stumble; the spell did. She took one step sideways, to keep her balance. But the goblin just stood there and grinned as the magic shattered against him.

He was ugly and beautiful at once. Ugly because he looked almost human and yet horribly *not*, beautiful in the wildness and magnetism that radiated from him. His skin was tinged green, his deformed features hovering between animal and human. He was short, and wide, and might have been naked. It was hard to tell if those shimmering blue-green feathers were his clothing or a part of him.

He ignored the dancers, the sorcerers, and the king. He looked at Alina, and her breath caught under the force of his gaze. It was so powerful that nothing else about his appearance seemed to matter.

"So," the goblin said. His voice was like discordant music. "You claim to know my true name?"

"I do," Alina said, her voice as cool as years of practice could make it. Only she felt the sharpness with which her fingernails dug into her palms.

"And you will call me by it? Before the court?"

He knows, she thought, and forced her fingers loose. Her palms still hurt, and she felt the sharp sting of blood. "I will."

There was an utter silence, such as had never before been heard in the court of Ciern. Even the sorcerers' robes did not rustle. They stared, seven pairs of piercing eyes. *They* did not know.

"I will," she said again.

"Then do it," the goblin commanded. "If you would have your freedom, do it."

"Wait," the king said. Alina did not dare look at him, to see if *he* knew. "What happens to her if she is wrong?"

The goblin's protruding upper lip curled, touching the tip of his long nose. "A bit late to be worrying about consequences, Your Majesty."

"Someone else will say your name," the king said. "I will do it."

"It has to be me." Alina pulled herself as high as she could. "The name is only true coming from me." She faced the goblin. "I call you Father."

If the court had been silent before, now it was a tomb. Even the king uttered not a sound—which told Alina that, if he had not known, he had at least suspected.

And had tried to protect her anyhow.

The goblin broke the silence with a laugh—a long, inhuman cackle. Alina did not flinch.

"How did you know?" her real father asked, when finally he was done.

"I never felt truly human." Though she had never realized it, either. "And my mother hinted at it, in a letter she wrote me. That was why she never expected my father to let me see the letter."

The *my father* came out of her mouth without thought, and she felt the king's flinch from halfway across the room.

"Then you will come with me," the goblin said, and she returned her attention to him, where it should have been all along.

He did not phrase it as a question, but Alina hesitated. *Tell me before the court... if you would have your freedom.* And she had it. They all knew, now, that she was not the king of Ciern's daughter, and that meant she was no longer useful. The treaty with Aimar would have to be sealed some other way.

She already had a few ideas for how that could be managed. She wanted to tell her father... but he wasn't, of course. Wasn't her father. Her father was a creature of Faerie with whom her mother had dallied and then turned to for help. Whose child she had kept from him, for as long as she could.

102

Alina wanted to help the king anyhow... but that was just something *she* wanted. He had many advisers, after all. At least half of them understood the political landscape well enough for their advice to be useful. But none of them could save her country. None of them could bargain with a goblin.

"Change the straw back," she said, in the tone she usually reserved for impertinent ambassadors.

"Come with me." He held out a hand; it was overlarge, and gnarled, and his fingernails curved like claws. "Your mother misses you. She will teach you our ways, and in a few days, you will be able to transform the straw yourself. If you still care to."

Alina swallowed hard. This, she told herself, was where she could do the most good. Unless she plunged into the life of the fae, into love and passion and madness, and no longer cared about doing the most good.

The thought terrified her, and at the same time it pulled at her. The pull seemed stronger than the fear.

That was what the goblin was counting on. *If you still care to.* He'd said it as if it was a taunt.

Her real father grinned at her, a grin wild with pure delight.

She crossed the marble floor, step by steady step, and did not flinch as she took his hand. It felt cold and scaly and very strong. She half-turned, not meaning to, and looked at the king.

Who was standing. Who was being restrained by one of the sorcerers.

"Why?" he demanded. Speaking to the goblin. "Why do you want her?"

"Which *her*?" the goblin said, and laughed. "Because I loved your queen, as you did not. And this one is my daughter. I love her too."

It was true, of course; the fae couldn't lie. And she could hear the sheer intensity in his voice when he spoke of her mother, the fierceness of his passion. If the duke of Darmil had spoken to her like that, would she have considered his offer after all?

Yet the goblin's love had not kept him from leaving her mother in a marriage with a man she didn't want, from bargaining with her for the fate of her child. The love of a fae would be possessive and selfish.

Perhaps that was what her mother had liked about it. Her mother, who had never known love. Alina wondered what it would be like to be loved that fiercely, wanted that openly.

The king shook off the high sorcerer's grip. "Alina," he said hoarsely. "Don't. The gold is not important."

He knew that wasn't true.

"I'll still care to," she assured him, calmly and surely. She smiled.

Then she turned and took the goblin's other hand.

~oOo~

Three days after Princess Alina was kidnapped by the goblin in a spurt of smoke, all the straw in the castle storage rooms turned back to gold.

Three weeks later, when the king was in his study examining a map—the map of the border between Ciern and Aimar—the door opened and the princess walked in, still wearing her heavy violet betrothal dress.

The king looked up at the first creak and went very still. He looked older than he had three weeks ago, the wrinkles around his eyes deeper, his jaw sagging lower. He was silent for a space longer than he would once have been, before he said, "They let you leave?"

"They couldn't stop me," Alina said, "once I knew their ways."

A longer silence. Then the king said, in a voice that sounded even more unsteady by contrast with hers, "And why—why did you come back? Your mother didn't want to, once she knew their ways."

The silence was momentary but vast. Alina looked at her father, and knew she would never tell him of the time she had spent in the courts of the fae. Of the overwhelming force of their loves and passions, so wild and all-consuming that the tales of humans dying for faerie love made sense to her now. Of the warmth of her mother's arms, satisfying a lack she hadn't known she had.

She would never tell him how close she had come to staying,

once she knew their ways. Until she had come across her mother's letter, and opened it, and read it again.

You were nothing. Not when her mother had chosen to love one of the fae, or to lie with him, or to bear his child. Her mother had not loved her then, could not have loved her, because she didn't yet exist.

Which was why love, for all its power, had failed her. It had come too late to make a difference. But responsibility... responsibility was something you could feel for an unborn child. For a child not yet conceived. For the possibility of a child.

Or for thousands of people she didn't know.

It is always that simple, to choose love.

But it was the king who had chosen love. Her mother had simply been swept away by it.

"Their ways are wild and fierce and free," Alina said at last, knowing her father wouldn't understand. "But our ways are real."

The king looked at her, his expression grave. She wondered, suddenly, if he did understand. If he had always known, as she now knew, what she was giving up and what she was choosing.

"Besides," Alina said after a moment, "I wanted to talk to you about Aimar. We will have to find another solution, now that I won't be marrying their prince."

"Aimar," the king said, after a long moment, "will be a problem."

"Perhaps," Alina said. "I think I know how we might deal with them."

The king nodded and moved over. Alina lifted her hem, stepped over the bench, and sat beside him. She pulled the map closer.

"I believe," she said, "that if we build a bridge over the river here...."

They bent their heads together to take a closer look, and remained that way for many hours, talking in low tones as the sky outside the window dimmed into dusk and then deepened into night.

MAHRUT'S ROAD

by Nathan Crowder

I love to read stories from non-European traditions. It's always interesting to view the world from a different viewpoint, and to see gods created for other ways of life. Mahrut may be a difficult god to belong to, but life in his service is never dull.

Currently living with his cat Shiva in the Bohemian wilds of Seattle's Greenwood neighborhood, Nathan Crowder works to create the stories that he would like to see in the world. Not content in a single genre, his published works span horror, science fiction, superheroes, clown noir, zombie westerns, urban sci-fi, and of course fantasy. "Mahrut's Road" stemmed from his belief that the landscape of heroic fantasy needed more women heroes and less Euro-centric world-building. His fondness for curry might have played a pivotal role in this decision. He has staked out a corner of the internet at www.nathancrowder.com where he rambles about writing, social justice, pop culture, and fringe candy. He is also fond of Twitter where he appears as NateCrowder at a 140 characters a shot.

As a child Siri Viraj wanted nothing more than to welcome the monsoon season with dance, to twirl in the temple courtyard with flowers in her hair. She would have been a dancer if not for the will of Mahrut, the Inside-Out God. A fever in her tenth year left the small but strong girl clinging to life and sent her on a silent journey on the Shadow Road. Siri finally awoke when the fever passed days later, reborn anew to unexplained visions and sudden fits of anger. The village elder knew the signs well. Mahrut, he of the red rage and madness, had staked his claim.

Siri had been marked as one of his chosen.

As soon as she could walk again, the young girl was sent from her parent's home to the temple of the Inside-Out God. She took her oath to Mahrut and trained for years as a priest before being released into the world for a life of service to the community.

In keeping with the tradition of the priesthood, Siri traveled Mahrut's road without clear direction. Less than a year of service took her far from home. She traveled by foot where possible, by river when necessary. For the past several months, a dugout canoe had been her chief means of travel, her twinned maces her only constant companions.

Siri stuck close to the bank whenever possible, where the currents were less chaotic. Heavy, sweet–smelling blossoms on laden goma tree boughs brushed her cheek like a baby's fist as she paddled down the slow-moving river. Siri lost herself in the sensation. Half-remembered dreams of dancing possessed her mind until the boat's wooden hull thudded against a sunken log.

The unexpected impact jostled the canoe, but months of practice navigating the swollen river kept her upright and dry. She shook a finger at the distracting blossoms. "You thought you had me there, Mahrut. I did not see through your disguise, but Siri Viraj is nimble like a dancer!"

There was a sudden explosion of movement from the bushes along the bank, and Siri reached reflexively for the twin maces at her belt, almost losing the paddle to the river in the process. A child, no more than five years old, burst from behind the verdant depths of the undergrowth, and ran downstream. Her small voice shouted, "Hurry! Hurry! A priest arrives!" Shortly, Siri heard the cries of the child echoed by other, adult voices.

Once around the river bend, she saw a small clutch of white, mud-walled huts and a humble, open-walled shrine without visible adornment. A crowd had gathered to see her approach. Siri watched as hope faded to grim acceptance once they recognized her colors and spotted the copper emblem of Mahrut around her neck. A community this size was too small to accommodate a priest of its own. They had to make do with whatever religious authority wandered through. Most of the twelve gods had traveling priests of some kind. With the exception of the temple masters in the City of Stone Faces, all of Mahrut's priests were wanderers. The children of the Inside-Out God were tolerated, revered, held as blessed, but no one wanted them in their towns for long.

Self-consciously, Siri touched the medallion against her breast, a head splitting open as a smaller face appeared within the skull. The people had gathered quickly at the sign of her approach. Their need for a priest was apparent on dozens of disappointed faces. She paddled the canoe to shore, and two young men stepped from the crowd to help drag it onto the pebbled bank.

She pitched her voice to be heard above the murmur of the few dozen villagers. "Mahrut has guided me here." It was the standard greeting of the priesthood. And it was as true a statement as she could make. No schedule, no conscious plan dictated the route Mahrut's children took as they wandered the land. They let madness and rage guide their steps, trusting their patron to take them where they were needed. "Do you have need of a priest in this village? I would exchange sacred rites for a few days of food, and can sleep upon the floor of your shrine, if you permit me."

Siri tracked the gaze of several villagers to a tall, balding man with a hawkish nose. As village leaders went, he was younger than Siri was used to seeing. Few wrinkles and no gray in his thinning hair marked him as experienced. It made her wonder what hardship might have befallen the small community to trust their leadership to one so young. The leader motioned her towards the shrine with a resigned nod. The crowd parted to let her through.

The life of a traveling priest was not an easy one. Mahrut rarely led his children to prosperous communities with their own priesthoods. Siri was accustomed to sparse accommodations, and most villages she visited maintained little more than a small shrine, open on three sides to the elements with a central fire pit to keep her warm in the frost season. This village was no different. She shrugged off her feathered cloak and left it on the worn stone to serve as her bed for later.

She offered up a quick prayer to the Inside-Out God, the mantras tumbling off her lips as rote sounds that held more ritual than meaning. She did not need to raise her voice to be heard. Mahrut rode within her, nestled in the red-hot rage and madness at her core. She let the bows and supplications stretch out the sore muscles in her arms and back, wincing at the tightness. The village leader stayed outside, stoic in the shade of the shrine's peaked roof, until Siri was done with her devotions. Once her final bow was completed, Siri turned and waited with a calm smile.

"A demon has come to our village," the elder said. This was not typically a claim one made without evidence. His voice did not shake with doubt.

"A demon?" Siri reached into a pouch at her waist and pulled out a handful of spiced seeds. She pondered the declaration while feeding the seeds onto her mouth one at a time. "Has anyone seen this demon?"

He shuffled his feet but lost none of his sincerity. "No. But every night since the new moon, he has entered our village and stolen a child in their sleep."

Siri nodded confidently. Her confidence was not echoed in the village elder. It might be a demon. It could be a man in the guise of a demon. It could be many things. But in Siri's eyes, one thing was certain—this village had convinced itself that it was incapable of solving the problem on their own. No Justicars traveled this far afield from the City of Bright Birds, and they had no local clerics. This village would have to make do with what help they could get. Even if that help came in the form of a compact, and self-described "delicate little flower" such as herself. Like it or not, they were stuck with Siri Viraj.

"Have food brought to me just before sunset," she decided. "I will slay my hunger, and when this demon of yours comes, I will slay him as well. Until then, this priest has traveled far today, and she needs her sleep."

Without waiting for acknowledgement from the elder, Siri removed her burnished copper helm, quickly ruffled the sweat from her short, dark hair. She made a bed for herself on her feathered cloak. The smooth, twined light maces lay next to her hand, her shoulder crooked to provide a crude pillow for her head. The village elder crept out of the shrine as quietly as his sandals would permit, but he needn't have bothered. The strange priest had slept in more chaotic places than the center of a small village. The madness helped. Chaos tended to reign behind her eyes, no matter what was happening around her. And her body knew it would need sleep for the task to which she had set herself.

The smell of a simple but spicy curry coaxed Siri from sleep's embrace. A young girl, reed thin and no more than eight summers old, was kneeling at the entrance to the shrine with a bowl of food. Siri rolled to a sitting position and held out her hand for the steaming bowl. The crude, clay dish contained a bed of rice covered with a pungent, yellow curry of bright vegetables and what she assumed to be bits of fish. The bowl was not much, but this was a poor village. She took what was offered and gave thanks in return.

The village girl sat on her haunches and watched Siri eat, silent until the bowl was almost empty. "Are you really a priest of Mahrut?"

Siri gazed at her visitor of the lip of the bowl. There was no fear in those young eyes, just a degree of skepticism that reminded the priest of her own youth. "What is your name? You do have one, don't you?"

"Mara," the girl said, furrowing her brow. "Are you a real priest?"

"Yes."

"Does Mahrut talk to you?"

Curious one, Siri thought. She wondered what age of children were being taken in the village, wondered if Mara might be next, wondered if Mara thought the same. "Maybe he's talking to me now," Siri said. She raised her eyebrow at the girl. She finished her meal and handed the bowl back. "The other children who have been taken—were they friends of yours?"

"The demon took away my little brother Kempur two nights

ago."

Ah, that's it, Siri thought. *It is not the madness that attracts this fledgling so much as the rage.* She should have noticed the clenched fists sooner. The young priest stood in one, smooth motion, a dancer's motion. She bent at the waist to collect her feathered cloak and fastened it around her throat. Siri looked at the sun, low in the sky above the goma trees. Sunset would be coming soon. Already long shadows covered much of the village. She tamped the copper helm with the boiled leather lining down upon her head. The twinned maces were last, their smooth, tapered heads like slumbering, bronze blossoms. "Two nights ago, you say? Take me to where you live before the daylight is gone."

Mara took off at an eager trot and Siri had to break into a jog to keep up with the little legs. The girl's family was near the edge of the village, a few huts from the river's bank. A wooden sash hung broken in one window. Siri pointed towards the window with one mace. "Your brother, Kempur, he was through there?" No sooner than she saw Mara's nod of confirmation, Siri was at the window, peering into the dim interior of the home. She could tell it was a richer family who lived there despite the small size of the home by the mud walls dividing the interior into a series of smaller rooms. Two rolled-up sleeping mats and a rattan chest occupied the cramped space, with a woven blanket covered the passage into what was likely the common living area. A similar room for the parents was likely on the other side of the house. Siri took it all in, nodded to herself, turned back to Mara.

"Did you see your brother taken?"

"No." Mara's face screwed up in a purple knot of anger. "I was learning needlework by the fire."

Siri didn't waste time trying to comfort the girl. There was nothing she could say that her parents hadn't likely already told her. Anyway, she was not that kind of priest. What could she say? That it wasn't her fault? She knew, or should know that already. She couldn't tell the child to let go of her anger over what had happened, not when rage and anger gave Mahrut strength; not when they gave Siri strength. "Sleep soundly tonight, little one," she said. "Mahrut will walk the road of dreams with you."

Night came quickly. The sweet hum of fiddler beetles gave way to the swoop and flutter of the bats which fed on them. The white-ruffed nightbirds cooed their mating calls in the rushes, while a fearful village huddled within their homes. Siri shared the wide branch of a goma tree with a family of bushy-tailed shrews, blind to their antics as she watched the river's edge below her. The soothing sound of the river against the bank threatened to pull her down into slumber, and she thanked Mahrut for the foresight of the afternoon's nap.

It was the sudden stilling of the nightbirds that alerted Siri. She sat up straighter in her perch, the clarity of madness empowering her vision as she pierced the darkness along the river. She caught motion in the rushes, not far beyond the end of the very branch she sat upon. She stood silently, eyes riveted upon the rustling of the tall reeds as something long moved through them. Sure hands unhooked the maces from her belt, leather straps secure around her wrists lest they slip. Either whatever approached the village from the water hadn't noticed her, or it didn't perceive her as a threat, as it continued on its way unabated. "Mahrut, let your rage be my rage. Let your madness guide my hand," she whispered.

With swift, dancer's steps, Siri raced down the tree branch. She felt it bend beneath her slight weight as she approached the end, her path narrowing with each step. She sprang, twisting as she sailed through the air to land near the head of the creature, facing back the way she had come. A serpent head—wide enough to swallow a pig whole—rose from the riverside reeds to meet her. The river masked the true size of the scaly threat, but Siri had seen many river snakes in her travels. This one was the mother of all of them if the head were any indication. At a guess, she figured it to be longer than a dozen men laid end to end. "What hell have you escaped from, demon?"

She hadn't really expected a response. But her life had a way of defying expectations. As a child of the Inside-Out God, she had learned to adapt.

The serpent's tongue tasted the air, two sets of eyelids blinking an assessment; a warning. "Thisssss village is mine, priesssssssst! Itssssssss people are my tribute!"

There were only a few guidelines given to the traveling priests that were the same, regardless of which god they served. Among the first was this: if you encounter a beast which speaks, kill it without hesitation. The world which had come before this had been destroyed by gods long-banished, and there was always the fear that they would return to destroy the world anew, wearing the bodies of beasts like they did in the before times.

Siri's right arm swung powerfully, seeking to crush the skull of this threat before it could strike, but her target was no longer there. The massive jaw was already in motion, and struck at her leg as she shifted. The teeth were small, but the jaw crushed with the might of a falling mountain. She cried out as she felt the bone in her shin creak near to breaking. She brought both maces to bear on the jaw of her attacker, and it was enough to win her release but nothing else.

Siri limped back several steps to reassess the situation. Every time she put her full weight on the injured leg, a jolt of searing pain shot through her body, daring her to cry out.

The serpent heaved its muscular length from the water to mass on the shore beneath the swaying head, easily halving the distance between it and Siri. Timeless yellow eyes surveyed Siri from far above her head, well out of reach of her maces. Muddy brown scales flecked with gold glistened in the starlight. "Sssssstand assssssside and you ssssssshal be ssssssspared. Oposssssssse me and your ssssssssskin sssssssshal decorate my nessssssst."

"I am a delicate little flower," she replied, shifting back and to the side while the massive head followed her every motion, "but I am no one's decoration. This village is under the protection of Mahrut. It is you who should withdraw before you taste the rage of the Inside-Out God."

The demon serpent lunged through the sultry night air. Instinctively favoring the healthy leg, Siri reacted like a dancer, and spun to the side as the powerful jaw dug a furrow in the turf where she had stood only moments before.

Siri gave herself over to the motion, surrendered to the dance as she continued to spin. The steps of a dance used to welcome back the moon flowed through her body unbidden. Arms crossed above her head, swept down and across her body, connected with the nose of the serpent as it took another swipe at her. Siri never noticed.

Mahrut moved through her, pounding through her veins, thundering in her head. She was a road and Mahrut traveled her, rode her madness, channeled rage from her every sinew. The demon serpent swung his head left, then right, unable to predict the priest's movements as twinned maces fell like thunder, striking scales from his body with every blow.

Hundreds upon hundreds of pounds of murderous muscle coiled from the water, tried to encircle Siri, tried in vain to contain her movements. But every contact sent her spinning in another direction, unpredictable as a flower on storm-tossed seas. Just when her capture seemed inevitable, muscular coils encircling her in a tightening grip, she managed to slip the grasp by running up the body of the serpent. It was like trying to grab a handful of water. The demon serpent became so obsessed with predicting her next step that he failed to realize how close she had gotten to his head.

As Siri danced upon the shifting coils of the enemy beneath her feet, she became distantly aware of the rage of the Inside-Out God moving through her, massing in the base of her spine. Power surged through her as she took two, swift steps up the scaly length of her foe. Maces held wide swung inward like the jaws of an iron trap, crushing the serpent's head where they met in the middle.

Suddenly free of Mahrut's presence, Siri was pitched to the soft mud of the riverbank with the serpent's death throes. The thrashing body destroyed a pair of canoes on the shore, hers included, before it finally came to rest. Siri was distantly aware that she had underestimated the length of the beast by the length of two villagers at least.

Around the village, shutters were thrown wide, doors cracked open to spill flickering light upon the dusty streets. Siri took a moment to catch her breath as the bravest among the farmers and fishermen made a careful approach. She stood and returned the maces to her belt. Without a word, she slid into the waters of the river and vanished beneath the languid waters before anyone could think to stop her.

She was oblivious to the nervous chatter that started up on the riverbank. She was listening to another voice, the whisper of Mahrut and the sibilant threat of a giant serpent. A nest, it has said. And a nest might mean more danger in the future.

Though her lungs burned for air, she trusted Mahrut to show her the way. Just as Siri felt she could hold her breath no more, her head broke the surface in a muddy cave somewhere on the river's far bank. She held the symbol of Mahrut aloft, muttering a short prayer to him in gasping breaths, and the copper pendant glowed with a red light. In a hollow of mud and discarded snake skins, she found dozens of smooth, black stones. No, Mahrut told her, eggs. The cave was spacious, but not spacious enough to hold more than one of the giant serpents, and of that she was thankful. She only distantly remembered defeating the first demon and doubted she could do the same again if she had to, and certainly not in this confined space.

Once her breath had been regained, Siri methodically smashed each of the eggs, killing their half-formed cargo. There was nothing else keeping her there. She took a deep breath and swam back for the shore.

When her head broke the surface, she could hear the voices coming from the village. The awestruck farmers were already spinning tale about the madwoman who had saved their village from the demon, while others argued that it was merely a large snake and nothing more. There was even one loud boast from a voice that had barely broken into manhood that claimed that he could have done the same had he but known it was a serpent. As she made her way quietly to shore under the cover of darkness, more and more the talk turned to how long the strange priest had been gone beneath the river's waters. With a conflicted mix of gratitude and regret, they sounded ready to consign her body to the river, the final victim of the great evil that plagued their small community.

"It takes more than a river to kill Siri Viraj, wielder of the snake-hammers!" she shouted, wading from the shallows just downstream from the clump of villagers.

A cry of surprise went up from those of weaker constitution, and Siri was pleased to hear that one of those was the boaster from earlier.

"It had a nest," she said wearily as she shook poured water from her copper helm. "She," Siri corrected herself, "she had a nest. Your village should be safe now."

The village elder emerged from the crowd, his wife hugging him closely, huge eyes peering from behind his shoulder. "You have done a great service to our village," he said. "If there is any way we can repay Mahrut or his servant…" he let his voice trail off. He had already told her about the village's lack of wealth. There was a nervous smile on his face as if he pondered if there were rewards beyond riches that he had not considered.

Siri licked river water from her upper lip. She looked past the villagers to the corpse of the giant serpent. Demon or not, her twinned maces had not slain anything that grand before. Its blood had blessed her weapons, baptized them in violence and madness. Mahrut whispered in her ear, and she smiled. "Does anyone in your village know leatherwork?"

A broad-shouldered young man stepped from the crowd, nodding in acknowledgement.

"Cure some of the leather from your demon," she commanded. "Wrapped around the hafts of my weapons, they shall serve as a warning to all those who cross the path of Mahrut."

She passed the maces over to the tanner. The village was safe for the now, at least. When she left the village, she would be outfitted with weapons befitting a demon slaying priest of the Inside-Out God. Until then, there would be lazy afternoons, simple curries, and if she was very fortunate, dancing.

STORM OVER TAKTSANG

by Catherine Soto

I am pleased to have another story of Lin Mei, her brother Biao Mei, and their cats. Shadow and Twilight have grown from the helpless kittens Lin Mei found into useful partners in her adventures. Given her periodic errands for the Emperor's Intelligence service, Lin Mei does lead an adventurous life.

Catherine Soto sold her first story to *Sword & Sorceress 21*, and she has been writing about Lin Mei and her brother ever since. When not writing or at the obligatory day job, Catherine hangs out at the Asian Art Museum or explores sushi bars, although this year she's been spending more time at the public library. She's also working on a novel about her characters. There's a Kindle book called *The Temple Cats*, which is a collection of her first five stories (from *Sword & Sorceress 21-25*), so she at least has a start on it.

"We have seen worse," Biao Mei said. There was a moment of silence as Narrayam Dorjhe looked at him.

"I am sure you have," he replied quietly. Lin Mei sat very still, watching closely. The lama turned his gaze to her.

"And do you have anything to add?" he asked. She shook her head ever so slightly.

"No, Rimpoche," she replied, using the honorific carefully. "I do not." He looked at her for a moment, his eyes seemingly looking at some dark interior in her soul.

"I'm sure the experience must have been upsetting to you," he commented. Was there a hint of mockery in his words? Lin Mei chose her words carefully.

"The sight would have upset the most hardened of souls," she replied. There was another moment of silence as Narrayam seemingly weighed her words.

"Of course," he said. "It was rather unsettling for all concerned." He stopped to take sip of tea. "Thank you for taking the time to talk to an old man," he said, setting the tiny teacup down. "You may go now."

They made their bows and left quietly, emerging into the shadows of the mountain looming above the temple complex.

"That was not so bad," Biao said.

"No," Lin Mei agreed, eyeing the forested heights. "It was not." Nearby, too nearby in Lin Mei's opinion, young monks were washing away the blood stains on the cobblestones. What remained of the dead monk had been taken away by the rogyapas, the body-breakers, who had taken his earthly form away to the upper reaches of the mountain, there to be dismembered and left for the elements and the carrion birds. From the main temple they could hear the sonorous droning of the monks, as the lengthy and complex funerary rituals designed to cleanse the temple complex of the defilement of death had already begun.

"I wonder why the tiger did not take the body with him," Biao mused.

"I do also," Lin Mei said quietly, eyeing the scene. "The wall is not that high. It would have been easy for a tiger to leap over, even carrying a man." On the wall was a single paw print, in the dead monk's blood, where the large cat had scrambled over. Lin Mei's eyes narrowed as she saw the print. "Let us go see to the cats," she said, striding off. Biao Mei shrugged and followed.

Shadow and Twilight were sleeping on a mat on the corner of the quarters they had been given. That was good news at least. They had been tense and nervous all night long, prowling the confines of the room. Lin Mei had probed their senses, using the bond she had developed with them. She had sensed danger, malevolent and violent, just outside the building which housed them. And in the morning, just as the droning of the conch shells called the monks to their morning meditations, the body of Kalsang Rampa had been found. Lin Mei and her brother had heard the commotion and run outside to investigate. As caravan guards they had seen more than their share of bloody scenes, and so had been called by the Abbot, Narrayam Dorjhe, to give both their testimony, and experienced opinions.

"You should attend the purification ceremony," Lin Mei observed. "It will make the monks feel better." Biao Mei nodded.

"Good idea. And you will go for a walk?"

Lin Mei smiled. "It's a cool morning. It's just right for some fresh air." She was skilled at teasing out truth from gossip. Also, as a young woman, she would not be welcome within the sacred temple confines of the monastery.

Breakfast was a mixture of tea, toasted barley flour, salt, and butter, all churned to froth in a wooden container. Lin Mei smiled wistfully as she considered the horror with which her mother would have reacted to such a barbarian repast. But she and her brother had been long out of the Empire. And even longer from their parent's home. She shut down that line of thought abruptly. She had other things to do.

Outside the monks had finished their gruesome task. The alleys between the buildings were empty. Well enough, with almost everyone at the ceremonies she could conduct her investigation without interruption.

She eyed the wall. It was high enough to provide difficulty for a man trying to climb it, but she had once seen a tiger vault over a similar wall while carrying a young water buffalo. Above and beyond the walls she could see the steep face of the mountain, dotted by scraggly evergreens that had taken root in the cracks in the rock. It would be a hard climb even for a tiger.

She eyed the narrow alley where the monk had been killed. It was paved with rounded cobblestones still wet from the night's rain as well as the efforts of the monks. On an impulse she walked down to the small building where Kalsang Rampa had labored copying sacred manuscripts. The door was unlocked and she pushed it open to find an aged monk going over yellowed scrolls.

"May the Enlightened One's understanding light your path," he greeted as she came in. "How may I assist you?" Lin Mei made a bow.

"I am Lin Mei. I express my sorrow at the loss of your fellow monk," she said. "I only met him yesterday for a short while, but I found him to be kind and gentle."

"That he was," the old man agreed. "I am Kunchen Lobsang. Would you please sit?" he asked, pointing to a yak-hair mat. She sank to the mat as he turned to lift a pot of hot water from some coals in a small hearth. "May I offer some tea?" he asked.

"That would be most kind," she replied. It would have been impolite to refuse. In moments she was holding a hot mug of black tea flavored with butter and salt. She waited for her host to drink first before taking a polite three sips.

"It is very sad that such a learned monk would be taken by a beast," she ventured.

"All is impermanent," he replied. "Even the mountains will weather away in time. Still, it is sad." He took another sip of tea.

"It was fortunate that he was able to finish copying the manuscripts for the Daci'en monastery," he added. Lin Mei put a properly sorrowful expression on her face and bowed low in acknowledgement. It also hid her face while her mind raced. She was certain it had not been an idle remark. But what did he know?

"I am certain the monks at Daci'en will be most pleased," she said. "I am also certain they will be equally sorrowful at the news of his passing." She did not add that she and her brother had no intention of returning to the Empire any time soon.

"Daci'en has a great collection of sacred texts. It is well-known to be favored by the Son of Heaven," the old man said.

"It does," Lin Mei agreed. Where was this going?

"The death of Kalsang Rampa is a great loss," the old man went on. "Not only was he an industrious copier of sacred texts, but his knowledge of languages, such as the Hind and Tifun tongues, made him even more valuable as a bridge between the kingdoms of this land."

"I was unaware of his accomplishments," Lin Mei responded. She knew this already. And the old man was sure to know that. Abruptly she drank the last of her tea in one long sip.

"I am thankful for the refreshment," she said, bowing her head low to the mat. He bowed low in return, a generous act from one such as him. With a few more pleasantries she left.

Outside, in the cool air of the mountains, her mind raced. Years of service in the Empire's Intelligence arm had made her sensitive to the slightest hints of intrigue. She wondered if she was making too much of an old man's ramblings, but dismissed the idea. Kunchen Lobsang was still alert and keen of mind. His had been no idle words.

On impulse she walked to the gate. The monastery was on a ledge that narrowed at both ends. Here it was just wide enough for the gate. There were no guards to stop her, and she wandered out on the path leading down to the plain stretching out far below. Here, where the mountains met the steppes, was the strategic Ang-Xi Corridor, only four day's ride across at this point. Beyond were the nomad lands. The mountain behind her was only the first ridge of the vast ranges that separated the steppes from the rich land of Hind to the South.

Difficult and dangerous, the mountains were home to the Tifun Empire, a warlike and barbarous realm. The Tifun Khans were masters of the mountains, and from the peaks their armies had defied all others. Those thoughts sent her mind back to the reason she and Biao Mei were there, to a meeting in Kendar weeks before.

~o0o~

"The Empire is two gourds on a vine," Ro Min had said. "The Eastern heartland is connected to the Western Protectorates by the Ang-Xi Corridor, which lies between the Tifun Empire to the south and the nomads to the north. The Empire can hold off either, but if they should unite they could cut the corridor and divide the Empire in two." She did not add that Kendar was in the west.

"There have been rumors of messages and gifts between the Tifun Khans and the nomad khans," Lin Mei had said.

"That is true," Ro Min replied. "The messages concern us most. The Empire's Ministers for the Barbarian Lands have used diplomacy and gifts to keep the nomad tribes divided and hostile to the Tifun Khans. But of late the Tifun Khans have pursued a policy of friendship between their lands and the nomads. Tifun covets the Empire's Western lands. Not only are they a source of wealth, but they control the trade routes around the mountains and down into the land of Hind. The loss of the Western Protectorates would greatly harm the Empire."

"And place the armies of Tifun on the Empire's borders," Lin Mei observed.

"That is so," Ro Min agreed. "We have a man in the Taktsang Palphug Monastery. It is on the border of Tifun and overlooks the Ang-Xi corridor. You will go and meet him, and bring back any messages he may have." She stopped to take a sip of tea.

"His task at the monastery is to copy sacred texts. Your mission, if anyone needs to know, is to bring back copies of those texts. Any messages he has for the Western Agency," she added, referring to one of the two major spy services of the Empire, "will be hidden in the texts."

Lin Mei studied her for a moment.

"This is a task that could easily be done by anyone else," she noted. "You have some other reason for sending us?" Ro Min smiled.

"I have seen how the young Prince Firuz looks at you," she said. "Even if he is an exile, he is still a prince, and attention from someone in the upper ranks can be troublesome."

Lin Mei nodded. On a prior mission to Khotan she and her brother had encountered a party of royal refugees fleeing an invading army. The young prince had been a witness to the events surrounding an attempted palace coup against the ruling Iskanderi, a coup Lin Mei and her brother, with help from their two cats, had foiled. He now had a severe case of hero worship, bordering on infatuation.

"By the time this mission is done, he should be in the Capitol," she said. Ro Min had smiled in conspiratorial agreement.

"I have spoken with his mother," she said. "Prince Firuz will be the toast of the Capitol, with many young ladies vying for his eye. She will see he is suitably distracted."

"Who is this man we shall meet?" Lin Mei asked.

"A young monk named Kalsang Rampa."

~o0o~

Kalsang Rampa was now dead. Lin Mei set her lips in a thin line. Somewhere inside her was an annoying feeling that it was no coincidence. With thoughts darker than the clouds overhead she stared off across the plain below.

Her heart stopped. Off in the distance, barely visible under the towering clouds was another cloud, dust kicked up by hooves. She eyed the cloud, noting the size. This was no caravan.

She ran back inside. "An army on the approach!" she shouted to two monks she saw just inside, pointing off in the direction of the horizon. With worried frowns they followed her outside. For a few moments they looked somberly off into the distance, before the older of the two snorted with a muffled laugh.

"No, younger sister," he said with a good-natured smile. "It is the return of Tenzin Yonten from Qartik."

"Qartik?" she asked, puzzled. She could recall no such land.

"Qartik," the monk explained. "It is the gathering of tribute." Understanding brightened her face, along with relief that it was nothing more serious. During their travels they had sometimes come across herds of livestock and caravans loaded with goods traveling toward the monasteries that dotted the mountains. It was the custom of the monasteries to send out parties to take gifts of sacred texts to the lords of other lands, and in return gather offerings of goods and livestock. Those offerings could be quite substantial, especially from the nomad khans.

The younger of the two monks had already run off into the monastery to spread the news, Lin Mei and the older man following at a more sedate pace. Up ahead she could see a crowd streaming out of the main temple. She had not expected the funerary rituals would be over so soon. She smiled. Apparently the arrival of so much wealth took precedence over propriety.

She met Biao Mei on the lane. "You have heard?" she asked. He nodded.

"Qartik," he said. "There will be feasting to strengthen the monks for the lengthy and difficult purification rituals."

"It can only help," she replied. She led him aside to a quiet alley and told him of her talk with Kunchen Lobsang.

"Kalsang Rampa's death is very convenient," he said in a low voice, "if anyone wanted to hide something. And the sudden arrival of the Qartik from the nomad lands is also suspicious."

"A good way of carrying messages," she agreed. "This may be a good time to see to our weapons." He nodded and they headed back to their quarters.

There they found Shadow and Twilight already awake and prowling the room. She tossed them strips of dried meat and went to her sword and daggers, which she had left rolled up in her bedding.

"So you do not think Kalsang Rampa's death was just an attack by a tiger?" she asked, while passing an oiled rag over her blade. He shook his head.

"Why leave so much meat behind? And if a tiger leaps onto or over a wall, why would it leave a paw print on the wall, as if it was a seal on a manuscript? And the damage done to the body was excessive. Tigers kill to eat. Once the prey is dead, why continue to slash and bite?"

"You suspect a Tiger's Claw?" she asked, referring to the multi-bladed weapon worn like a gauntlet. He nodded.

"Weapons like that are found in these lands," he said.

"Let us keep our daggers hidden under our coats," she said. He gave no argument to that.

Outside they found a commotion and an almost festive air, quite a change from the somber dread that had prevailed just a short while before. Monks streamed down the narrow road leading down from the mountainside. Others, organized into what seemed to be work gangs, ran toward the storerooms and warehouses on the upper levels of the compound. Somewhere someone rang a bronze gong in what seemed to be a joyous celebration.

"Let us ride our horses down," she suggested. "We will get there sooner."

"And if we are on horseback we can wear our swords without their appearing out of place," he added. She smiled in agreement.

124

It was almost noon before they reached the flat land below. The monks had gathered at the base of the mountain. The herd was still off in the distance, although noticeably closer than before. They set off to meet it.

As they approached they saw well-armed riders coming to meet them. Keeping their hands in sight, they slowed their mounts.

"Who are you?" the leader of the approaching horsemen called out.

"We are servants of the Son of Heaven," Biao Mei called back. "We are on a mission to Taktsang Palphug to take back copies of sacred texts for the Daci'en monastery in Chang'An. We saw your approach and rode out to meet you."

Lin Mei eyed the approaching riders warily. Swords and daggers were no match for seven lances, not to mention the short nomad bows hanging from saddles. She need not have worried. Chuluun Battar, as their leader was called, wanted to gossip. As he and Biao exchanged news they all rode back to the herd, Lin Mei taking the opportunity to examine the nomads closely. She was closer to them than she had ever wanted to be, and this was an excellent chance to assess them.

Clad in wool and hard leather armor, and armed with lances, bows, short swords and axes, they were formidable in appearance. They rode their shaggy steppe ponies with the ease of experience, and their weapons appeared well-used. But they were in a happy mood, laughing and joking, as they rode along under leaden skies.

Ahead they saw an ox-drawn cart with a silk canopy. As they approached the man seated in the rear turned to face them.

"Tenzin Yonten," the nomad leader explained. They came to a stop near the cart. Tenzin Yonten eyed them carefully, taking in every detail.

"You are from the Empire," he said.

"That is so, Rimpoche," Biao Mei replied respectfully. "We are here to take copies of sacred texts back into the Empire." Lin Mei kept her face impassive. Tenzin Yonten was obviously from the mountains to the south, with the lean build and harsh face of a Khampa, the wild nomads of the plateau. All around them were steppe nomads. Often in the past the armies of the Empire had clashed with both. From the corner of her eye Lin Mei saw only cheerful faces. But she reminded herself it might be because they were at the mercy of the riders.

"We are pleased that the wisdom of the Enlightened One will be known to the people of the Empire," the monk said. His hand flicked his fly whisk of white yak hair vaguely toward the east. Both Biao Mei and Lin Mei bowed low in the saddle toward the monk. He flicked his fly whisk again and the cart began to roll once more.

At the base of the mountain, where the narrow road met the steppe, a throng of young monks waited with a palanquin. Tenzin Yonten was transferred from the ox-cart to the palanquin without touching ground, and the procession made its way up to Taktsang Palphug. Looking down Lin Mei could see the livestock being herded toward the mouth of a valley, which led to winter grazing grounds. She realized how wealthy and powerful the monastery was. It occurred to her with a chill that the monasteries, and the monks that ran them, were the true rulers of the mountains of Tifun, and the steppe nomads, for all their wild and barbaric nature, were strong believers in their teachings. The threat of an alliance was suddenly very real.

At the monastery Tenzin Yonten alighted and strode through the gate to be met with the cheers and greetings of a returning conqueror. Behind them monks made their way up the road bearing bales of tribute to be taken to the storerooms of the monastery. No one seemed too concerned about Chuluun Battar and his party, who had now grown to about twenty armed men. Lin and Biao Mei managed to separate themselves from the throng without attracting too much attention and returned to their quarters, to be met with baleful glares from the two cats.

"Unhappy at being neglected for so long," Biao Mei observed. Lin Mei smiled and tossed Shadow another strip of dried meat before taking a seat on a yak-hair mat. Twilight curled up on her lap.

"The nomads seem well-disposed to the monks," she

observed. Biao Mei nodded, his face grim.

"Tenzin Yonten spent several months in the nomad lands, meeting with their khans," he said. "They could have discussed an alliance."

"Among other things," Lin Mei replied. "But why was Kalsang Rampa killed, and by whom?"

"There is more to this than Tenzin Yonten," Biao Mei said. Lin Mei nodded.

"We need to learn more," she said, standing and dropping Twilight on the mat. "I will go out and see if there is more to learn. Maybe you can spend some time with the nomads, and see what they may say? Take a jar of rice wine."

"Good idea," Biao Mei said. Lin Mei tossed two more strips of meat to the cats and refilled the bowl of water she had set out for them. After slipping their daggers inside their quilted coats they went out.

On an impulse Lin Mei decided to visit Kunchen Lobsang again. By now it was late afternoon and shadows slanted long down the mountain and out on the plain. The old man was brewing tea when she entered his rooms, bowing low at the doorway.

"This one seeks understanding," she greeted.

"I can offer you tea," he replied, grinning. Along with tea laced with butter and salt he offered tsampa, the barley bread of the mountains, and strips of roasted meat, which Lin Mei suspected came from some of the newly arrived livestock. He confirmed her guess.

"Not all of the tribute will stay here at Taktsang Palphug," he said. "Most we share with the people of the land, as they share what they have with us." Lin Mei nodded in understanding. It was a common practice. The monasteries gathered goods as tribute from their own lands as well as those far away, and then distributed them near and far. It was a form of trade, with the monasteries at the center of a vast network of commerce and industry.

"Has there been any more news of the tiger that killed Kalsang Rampa?" she asked after a few polite sips of tea.

"Much talk, but little real news." He smiled. "It is always that way."

"We have found it so," she agreed, biting off a piece of tsampa. She looked at him for a moment, deciding how much to share, then decided to take the risk.

"It was odd," she began, "that we heard no sound, even though we were so close to the scene. There was not even a cry."

"It must have been quick," the old man replied, taking another sip of tea, "and a surprise."

"Was he working late?" she asked. "I would imagine that he normally would have been asleep in his room at that time of night." He shook his head.

"The task of copying the scrolls for the Daci'en monastery had been finished." She looked about at the scrolls lying about. He smiled.

"I believe he had them bundled and in storage in the Norbu Pema," he said. "That is the storeroom next to the main temple." Lin Mei looked at him for a moment. Was that an invitation? She thought carefully for a moment.

"The northern nomads seem very devout," she noted. "Certainly they have been generous."

"They are followers of the path of the Enlightened One," he replied smiling, "although their faith, while strong, is simple and not fully comprehending. Still, their fervor earns them merit."

"That is also true of the people of the mountains?" she asked. He laughed softly at that.

"You speak truth," he said. "But not all in the mountains follow that path. The old religion of Bon is still strong, among all classes." Lin Mei's face stayed placid, but the words rang clear. They had been in Tifun, and had seen the power of the priests of the old religion, and of the shamans of darker magic of Bon. One of them had been an advisor to the Tifun Khan. She glanced at the small window high on the wall.

"It is getting late," she said. I must thank you for your hospitality."

"I take grace from your visit," the monk replied.

After a few more pleasantries she left.

Outside darkness had fallen. The streets and alleys were deserted, although the sound of merrymaking came from nearby buildings. It seemed as if Kalsang Rampa's rites would have to wait. That suited what she had in mind.

The cats seemed to sense her plans. They were up and prowling, eager to go out. Her brother was running a whetstone along the edge of his sword blade. She checked her own sword and daggers. They could have split a hair.

"The nomads seem happy," he told her. "This is like a holiday for them. But I notice they drank little, and kept their weapons close."

"Odd, if they are on holiday," she said. "But we'll eat first." Her brother nodded. No need to explain what she meant.

When they went out night had already fallen. They made their way down the street, silent in their felt boots, Shadow and Twilight prowling ahead. Lin Mei did not meld her senses with theirs. Not yet.

Idly she wondered about her brother. He had taken the sudden change in their mission with equanimity. She knew he was not one of those men who enjoyed fighting for its own sake, and the thrill of adventure held no appeal for him. They had lived long in the western lands, where romantic notions died sooner than men did.

She knew the speed and skill of his blade, which had brought him notoriety throughout the harsh lands they traveled. That had never seemed to matter to him—but she knew what did. Ro Min, archer and bodyguard, and master spy for the Empire, was of better than average looks. Biao Mei was completely in her thrall. Lin Mei served the Empire for a variety of reasons, but Biao Mei served his heart. She hid her smile as her knight-errant brother trod silently by her side, hand near his sword hilt.

The main temple loomed up ahead. The Norbu Pema was the building next to it, small only by comparison. It occupied the space between the temple and the sheer rock wall.

They stopped under the eaves and looked around. The street was empty. Lin Mei took a small packet from her coat, and took out a pair of small bronze hooks. It took only a few moments to open the lock. They slipped inside and closed the door behind them. Some coals still glowed in a small sand-lined hearth in the center of the room. She used them to flame a sliver of kindling and used it to light a butter lamp.

She saw a mass of treasure, piled haphazardly about. As caravan guards they had seen valuable goods, but never before in such quantity. Piled to the rafters were stacked rolls of silk, gold and silver scroll rollers, ornaments, and bullion, and boxes of exotic hardwoods inset with jade, pearls, and coral. Wrapped bundles and leather sacks hinted at even greater treasures.

"What I would give to be in on the sacking of this place," Biao Mei breathed. A sheepish look appeared on his face. "If it were not so holy," he added.

"Your piety is reassuring," she muttered. She searched the room, looking for any scrolls that might have belonged to Kalsang Rampa. She had learned to read some of the cursive writing used in the mountains but the labels on the scrolls were mostly in metaphors. Without a deeper understanding of the theology of the mountains they were meaningless. She mouthed a phrase totally inappropriate to the sanctity of the place and looked about. At a far wall the two cats were nosing about at the base of a screen. Puzzled she went over.

Behind the screen a small tapestry covered the wall. As she examined the scene, apparently depicting a battle with demons, it ruffled, as if by some breeze. She pulled it aside to reveal a dark entrance. Biao Mei had come to stand by her.

"That is interesting," he said.

"It is," she said, wondering if they should explore it. But before she could decide the two cats leaped past her and into the darkness. Muttering another colorful metaphor she followed.

Just inside they found a basket of dry wood staves suitable for torches. They lit two from the butter lamp and followed the cats down the narrow defile, apparently a crack in the rock of the mountainside. Ahead they could see the passage widen. As they stepped out into the open space they stopped, Lin Mei gasping.

If the treasure in the Norbu Pema had been a surprise, this was a shock. The cavern was large enough to hold the main temple building. And piled high within were stacks of treasure that made those in the Norbu Pema pale by comparison. Not even the treasure room of the Son of Heaven could compare. Their practiced eyes catalogued their find. Wealth from all the lands they knew about was piled high around them, and much they did not recognize.

"What is this place?" Biao Mei breathed.

"No mere monastery," Lin Mei replied in a whisper. Her mind tried to make sense of it all. Before them was wealth accumulated over centuries from the richest kingdoms of the earth, donations from the devout as well as profits of astute trading. Her earlier realization that the monks were the true rulers of these lands came back to her. Here was wealth to hire armies, bribe rulers, and upset the balance of trade across the world. All held and managed by monks who spent their days in prayer and meditation in cells bare of any comfort but a small mat to sit on. She wondered how many other monasteries held such wealth.

And power, she reminded herself. Wealth and power always went together. She wondered if the rulers of the lands knew of this, the khans, kings, Iskanderi, and assorted other lords of the temporal world. She doubted it. Not even the most devout piety would stay their greed if they knew.

With a chill she realized the implications. If the Emperor, and his advisors, learned of this, the Empire's armies would march west, under whatever pretext. The Tifun Khans would march north to defend their lands and seize the treasures of the monasteries. And the nomad khans would lead their hordes south to defend their faith and enrich themselves as well. The lands of the far west, their home and their world, would be wracked by war for generations.

A hint of danger crossed her mind. The cats, indifferent to the wealth about them, were eyeing the dark entry way behind them. Lin Mei reached out with her mind and melded her senses with theirs. She heard the sounds of men moving about, and scented the smell of unwashed bodies and rice wine.

"Nomads," she whispered. She heard a click as Biao Mei

loosened his sword in the scabbard. She looked about. The cavern was large, but the stacks of goods piled high about made narrow passageways that could be defended by two swords. Even so, if they had to fight the nomad's greater numbers would be decisive. But maybe they would not find the entrance to the cavern.

That was not to be. Lin Mei's face hardened as she heard shouts, and the sound of men coming down. She looked at her brother. He nodded and they drew their blades. Suddenly they saw a torch-bearing swordsman before them. More followed. Grins split the nomad's faces as they saw they had only Lin Mei and her brother to deal with. Lin and Biao backed toward a narrow space between stacked bales of silk where they might sell their lives more dearly. With their faces lit by the torch bearer in the lead the nomad's looked demonic as they advanced. To add to the moment the cats were hissing and spitting in agitation. Suddenly she grinned. A silent command sent them to the top of the silk bales.

"Our torches," she said. "Toss them!" As an example she sent hers over the heads of the nomads to fall on the sand behind them. In sudden comprehension Biao did also. They were now in semi-darkness. Lin Mei's mind reached out once more, pleased as she sensed that Biao had caught her intention.

She was caught in a wave of dizziness as she adjusted to what she was seeing. Part of her was still seeing their attackers as they advanced in darkness, but she was also seeing them from above, in that eerie yellowish light that accompanied the cat's sight whenever she joined with them. Then the dizziness passed, and she was clear headed once more.

"Yah!" Biao Mei yelled, advancing and thrusting with his sword into the throat of the torch-bearing nomad before them. He fell, tripping one of his companions. Lin Mei thrust her own sword at the back of his neck as he fell forward.

And suddenly they were in a savage, frenzied fight, as they fought with cat sight melded with human sight against foes fighting in darkness. In the space between the stacked bales there was little room for the nomad fighters to swing their short curved swords and axes, but Lin Mei and her brother were able to use their swords to thrust and parry. Bodies fell before them.

But more came, and Lin Mei and her brother were slowly being pushed back. Still they fought on with grim determination, but it was only a matter of time. Already they could see other nomads clambering up on the bales to try and get above and behind them. Lin Mei paused for a moment to wipe sweat from her eyes, breathing heavily. Above she saw a swarthy face leering down at them. Others joined him atop the bales.

Then a snarling roar split the darkness. Stunned, everyone stopped fighting. Above her she saw the nomads' mouths gape open in surprise.

A dark form jumped over then to land atop the bales. A swipe of a paw sent the nomads tumbling down onto their fellows, red spurting from gaping wounds. A massive head tilted down to look at Lin Mei for a moment, and then the tiger leaped forward to land among the nomads. Claws ripped men open and jaws crushed their skulls as the giant cat tore through the horde. More than faith defended Taktsang Palphug.

~o0o~

They were once more in the room where they had first met Narrayam Dorjhe, once more sitting before him. He took a sip of tea from his cup. Cups of tea were on trays before them, untouched. If he was offended by their lack of manners he gave no sign. Lin Mei eyed him carefully. They had been allowed to keep their weapons, but that gave no comfort. They were in danger, and no number of blades would help.

They knew too much. They had seen the power and wealth of the monasteries. The world would rock with war if that knowledge were to be let loose.

"Kalsang Rampa and Kunchen Lobsan served two masters," Narrayam Dorjhe said softly. "That is a bad position to be in."

"The Tifun Empire was the other one?" Lin Mei asked quietly.

"That and the Bon faith," the lama replied. "The Bon clergy resent that the teachings of Enlightenment have come into lands they once held to their own faith, and the khans distrust our ties to lands beyond their grasp."

"So he and Kunchen Lobsan were the ones who reached out the nomad khans, with promise of wealth to lure them here," Lin Mei ventured. The lama smiled thinly.

"They are together once more." Lin Mei did not ask what that meant.

"Tenzin was working for me, helping set a trap," he went on. "The sacred scrolls Kalsang Rampa and Kunchen Lobsan sent to Chuluun Battar contained a message informing him of the wealth to be found here. Chuulun Battar brought a small party disguised as an honor guard for Tenzin Yonten. He apparently felt he needed no more. To reach Taktsang Palphug they crossed the Ang-Xi Corridor. Once they learned of what they could gain by sacking the monasteries, nothing, not even their faith, would have stopped other nomad bands from coming. The Tifun Khans believe they can stop any invaders once they reach the mountains, and maybe they can, but the Son of Heaven's ties to the west would have been cut. Tifun would have what it has long desired." He tilted his head slightly to look at her. With a shock she recognized the look. She had seen it the night before looking down at her. He chuckled.

"There are some of us, here and in other places," he said.

"We have heard stories," she whispered.

"People always tell stories. Sometimes they are true."

"Tiger-men," Biao Mei said in a low voice.

"Some are wolves, among other forms," the lama said, stopping to take another sip of tea. "But I wish to discuss you. In particular, what you will report. Do not dissemble. I am aware of your true calling in the service of the Emperor."

Lin Mei looked sideways at her brother. He gave a look she knew. They had long ridden together in dangerous lands and understood each other. He would follow her lead.

"We came to meet Kalsang Rampa," she said carefully. "We met briefly when we arrived, but he was killed by a tiger before a proper meeting could take place. After investigation of the situation here we conclude that an alliance between Tifun and the nomad tribes is unlikely." The lama smiled.

"It is," he agreed. He took another sip of tea. "We keep the balance among the powers," he went on. "Carefully measured gifts appease the greed of the rulers, our wealth maintains the balance of trade, lessening want, and our teachings of peace assuage the adventuresome spirit of the young warriors. There are occasional small wars, but that is all. But tell me, what of you?"

"We are servants of the Empire," she said, carefully measuring every word. "Our reports serve the interests of the Son of Heaven, and the Empire. Peace is in the interests of the Empire." The lama nodded approvingly. He had no fear they would say too much. The monasteries had a long reach.

And with that a grim peace settled into her. They had lived most of their lives beyond the Empire's borders, holding to a belief that they would someday return to claim what had been unjustly taken from them. That had been a childish fantasy. Too much time had passed and what had happened in their childhood had been forgotten as new political realities hardened, and those in power strengthened their grip. More, they had lived too long in the western lands. Their thoughts, customs, and habits were no longer what they had been as children.

Ro Min was a loyal servant of the Son of Heaven. She would report fully what they told her—even if it meant war, the loss of the Western lands, and her own eventual death. But Lin Mei and Biao Mei had left the empire. The western lands were now their home. They might continue to undertake missions for the Empire, but it would be as hired swords.

"I will not keep you," Narrayam Dorjhe said. "And it is time for my meditation." Lin and Biao Mei bowed low and left.

Outside their horse waited, saddled and ready, along with two more pack horses with heavy bundles. The cats rode atop the packs with the ease of long experience. The monks holding the reins explained they were gifts from the abbot, in appreciation for their aid. *And for our silence*, Lin Mei thought. She thanked them and they mounted and rode out.

Outside on the road leading down she spoke to her brother. "I will make the report to Ro Min," she said. He nodded.

"You usually do," he said. "You understand matters of intrigue better than I do." She looked at him.

"I would not say that," she said. They had reached the bottom. Ahead lay paths leading east and west. "Let us go home brother," she said. They turned west and rode.

Author's Note:

I've been a big fan of the Modesty Blaise books since high school, and had read all the books, as well as the short stories, but I had never read the comic strips since they were printed in the U.K. When I found there were compilations of the strips at the local library I checked them out and began to read them. One was *The Black Pearl.*

Like my story, it takes place at the Taktsang Palphug Monastary. For the purposes of my story I invented a cave that runs deep into the mountain. The Black Pearl also has a cave that runs deep into the mountain. For the purposes of my story I included a were-tiger. In Peter O'Donnell's story the Black Pearl is a Himalayan Black Bear. I was surprised as anything when I finished the story, which I know I had never read before. While I would never compare myself with Peter O'Donnell, I was struck by the similarities. By the way, in *The Black Pearl,* the bear takes a liking to Willie Garvin, Modesty's right-hand man, which is only natural since he usually gets the girls.

AIRS ABOVE THE GROUND

by Michael H. Payne

Readers of previous volumes will be familiar with this non-human mage. Cluny is a squirrel, and her familiar Crocker is human. But there are some things that no magic can save you from, and a visit to your judgmental family is high on that list.

Michael H. Payne continues the whole library clerk /church singer-guitarist /web-cartoonist /college radio thing, and in the last year he has also sold a story to what he hopes will be the first of many anthologies devoted to the new My Little Pony phenomenon. Check hyniof.livejournal.com for details.

"No way!" Crocker crossed his arms and settled himself more firmly in his desk chair, shiny and squeaky like everything else filling their new dorm room. "And that's final!"

Cluny blinked up at him from the blotter pad, her neck fur prickling. Crocker? Acting assertive? And was she imagining it, or had his round, doughy face firmed up a bit from her first sight of him at that pre-frosh mixer eleven months ago when he'd introduced himself, the only human to do so that whole night?

Of course, with all the people who'd tried to kill them since then, she supposed it would've been even more surprising if he *hadn't* begun making some sort of progress from bewildered novice to semi-bewildered sophomore....

Still—and as much as she hated herself for having to do it— Cluny knew she couldn't let him forget who was the sorcerer here and who was the familiar. So with a sigh, she put on her 'small helpless woodland creature' expression, the one with the big eyes, her paws clasped, her tail puffing up over the tufts of her ears. "Please, Crocker?"

That made *him* blink, and she could smell him wavering, the cozy, supportive feeling she always got from his magic wrapped around hers suddenly more than a little itchy. "It'll be bad, Cluny," he said, his voice cracking. "And I mean *bad* bad."

A snort from Shtasith, the firedrake draped over Crocker's bedstead like a black and gold scaly necktie. "Should you wish a true definition of that word, Crocker, I will relate several anecdotes from my years within the Realms of Fire."

Crocker scowled at him. "Or you could just breathe on me, Teakettle! That's the worst thing *I* know!"

Flexing his nostrils, Shtasith gave a greenish puff, the rotten-egg stench making Cluny wince. Crocker groaned, leaped for the window, the tiny tornado Cluny had conjured to stir a breeze in the August Friday morning heat ruffling his black curly hair. "That!" Crocker shook a finger at Shtasith. "A weekend with my folks will stink exactly like *that!*"

Cluny flared her claws, stretched the tornado's tail into Shtasith's cloud, sucked it outside. "I'm sorry, Crocker, but if we're truly going to come together as a team, balance each other, and keep each other honest, we need to—"

"To what??" His anguish folded Cluny's ears. "Totally humiliate me??" The half-angry, half-queasy look on his face was like nothing she'd ever seen there. "My folks already thought I was a blot on the family name before I got the lowest passing marks possible on the Huxley entrance exams!" He flailed his arms. "And now I can either pretend I'm a crazy, ultra-powerful super wizard like Master Gollantz wants ev'ryone to think, or I can tell 'em the truth: that they were right all along, that I'm *not* good enough to be a wizard, that I'm nothing but the world's only human familiar!"

The regular shimmering of Shtasith's magic around Cluny became hot as flame, the firedrake leaping into the air above Crocker's bed, his translucent wings beating so fast, they looked more like smoke than anything else. "You would denigrate the noble profession to which we have both been summoned?? You would insult our mistress, the most powerful sorceress in this or any other plane of existence??"

"She's a *squirrel*!" The sudden contempt in the word hit Cluny like a physical blow, startled her back a step, Crocker's white face turning red. He focused a gaze sharp as shattered glass on Shtasith and jabbed a thumb at his own chest. "*I'm* the human here! *I'm* s'pposed to be the wizard!"

Cold gripped her like the time she'd fallen into a barely thawed stream back home, and the squeak she couldn't keep from escaping her tightening throat drew Crocker's attention, his anger vanishing, his mouth falling open, his eyes bugging out. "I...I didn't...didn't mean—!" He spun, dashed for the wall, slammed into it with a shower of sparks, and Cluny felt the surge of the teleportation spell she'd designed for him.

A whoosh, and Shtasith landed on the desk beside her. "Ungrateful simian!" His long neck snaked his head around, his eyes whirling fire directly in front of her. "Shall I hunt him down, my Cluny, and teach him the error of his—?"

"No." It took some effort to keep her voice from shaking. "We'll both go, and when we find him, *I'll* do the talking."

He nodded, and Cluny reached out, touched a paw to his shoulder, let herself slip sideways with him between the layers of existence, the bakery-hot air of their room dappling into a certain green and shady glade deep within Eldritch Park, the semi-wild woodland that sprawled through the center of the Huxley campus. Ferns sprouted between the rocks, the stream trickling behind them, a shimmery little breeze whisking around the branches above, and sitting among the roots of the old tangled willow, Crocker in his grayish robes looked more like an oversized mushroom than anything else, his legs drawn up, his arms wrapped around them, his face pressed against his knees.

Discomfort jabbed Cluny like a pawful of splintery wood. She'd always thought Crocker *liked* being her familiar...

He sighed. "I need a better hiding place."

At least he sounded more like himself. Cluny tried to keep her own voice light. "You just need one that isn't mine." A realization struck her. "Is...is that it, Crocker? Do you need your own space? One you don't share with—?"

"No!" His arms and legs shot out, and he tumbled forward, his scent spicy with panic. "We're partners, Cluny—you, me, and the Teakettle—and I don't want anything that isn't yours, too! It's just—" He waved a hand vaguely behind him. "Dad's the architect who designed Pearlhome Palace, and Mom's the dressage instructor to ev'ry high-born family between here and the Dove River! There's no *way* they'd understand what you guys mean to me!" Sighing, he subsided against the willow again.

With a gust of steam, Shtasith swooped over, hovered in front of him, his front legs folded across his narrow chest. "I still find it inconceivable that you should be related to Sir Lawrence and Lady Miranda! The only child of theirs the tabloids ever mention is Lt. Lionel Crocker, second officer aboard Her Majesty's frigate *Undaunted* and often seen keeping company with Crown Princess Alison!"

Scurrying to join her familiars, Cluny had to stop and stare. "Shtasith? You read the gossip rags?"

"Of course!" He settled across Crocker's knees. "The first lesson one learns in the Realms of Fire, my Cluny, is the vital importance of minutiae where those in power are concerned. Such knowledge impresses should you meet them in peace and can often become a weapon should you meet them in battle." He swiveled his head to glare at Crocker again. "That this simian of ours should be invited to the social event of the season, therefore, the party at which it is rumored the sovereign-designate will announce her formal courtship of Lt. Crocker—" His neck ridges folded open and closed like a tiny umbrella. "I find myself floundering in complete consternation!"

Crocker poked the firedrake's side. "How d'you think *I* feel? I mean, my folks were as glad as me when Huxley took me in so we'd never hafta see each other again. But now—"

"Crocker!" Cluny grabbed the hem of his robes and scrambled up, Shtasith scooting to his right knee so she could stand on his left. "That's a *terrible* thing to say about yourself! And about your parents, too!"

"And yet—" Shtasith made a little rumbling sound. "This

behavior corresponds to the impression of the Crockers I've gathered from the popular press: they work very hard and are very good at what they do, but their lives are focused a great deal more on appearance than on reality."

A smile touched Crocker's lips. "The phrase you're looking for, Shtasith, is 'big fat phonies.'" The sour smell of guilt wafted from him, and his smile sagged. "OK, that's not fair. It's more...more that they don't ever cut anyone any slack, not even themselves, and I just never measured up."

"But you *do!*" Cluny's fur bristled. "I mean, you were instrumental in saving the lives of everyone on this campus last semester and my whole family just last month!" And for all that she wanted to start a storm cloud brewing, wanted to stoke its lightning with the grumbling in her gut, she instead took a slow breath, let it partway out. "Fine! If they're gonna be that way about it, let's *not* go!"

He shifted against the willow. "Thanks, Cluny, but—"

"Not go??" Shtasith burst into the air, all four legs flailing. "But the princess! The pageantry! The romance!"

Cluny did some more staring, and Crocker coughed a laugh. "And don't forget the invitation! I mean, did you ever read anything more threatening in your life?"

That made Cluny laugh as well, and she sliced the air with her claws, opened a rift to their room, grabbed the note and pulled it to her, the parchment stiff and as big as a beach towel in her paws. "You mean how it says, 'Your presence is expected' rather than 'requested?'"

"Yeah." Crocker sighed. "So unless we can convince the Magisterium to declare me evil again and restrict us to campus, we...we'd better go. I mean, sure, my folks don't like me much, but I don't want them *hating* me..."

Opening her mouth to tell him it was entirely up to him, Cluny blinked at a sudden scent of roses wafting over her. Honey-colored light shimmered through the clearing, a sweet and familiar voice saying, "Well, *here* you all are!" And out onto the mossy bank of the stream stepped a golden-white unicorn, as small and delicate as a newborn gazelle. "And good morning!"

Still a little dazed around Hesper, Cluny managed to nod. One of only three unicorns active in the Mortal Realm, she was running Huxley's School of Healing Arts now since Cluny had been forced to disable the previous dean, Hesper's insane mistress. All in all, Cluny couldn't quite understand why she continued to seek out their company.

Shtasith swooshed through the air to settle in front of her, his scales suddenly gleaming. "My Lady!" he bugled. "Only your presence could make this day more radiant!"

OK, so maybe Cluny could understand *some* of it....

Hesper's smile became even more dazzling. "That's ever so kind, Shtasith. I just hope my asking a rather large favor of you all won't dampen the mood."

Despite the unicorn's breezy manner, Cluny caught the ozone scent of uneasiness about her. "Hesper? What's wrong?"

Her horn flickered, and settling back onto her haunches, she seemed to deflate a bit, her next words coming out quiet but as cutting as a pair of hedge clippers. "Perhaps you know, Sophomore Cluny, how tenuous my position is here at Huxley? How a large percentage of the faculty opposes me succeeding Evantrue as dean of Healing Arts? How the thought of a mere familiar holding authority over humanoids has caused an outbreak of apoplexy the likes of which this campus has not seen in over a century?" Hesper shook her head. "Given the way you're forced to hide *your* true nature, I mean...."

She sounded so tired, Cluny couldn't keep her ears up, couldn't think of a single thing to say; it was Crocker behind her who asked, "But Master Gollantz wants you to be in charge over there, doesn't he?"

"He does." Hesper's smile sent light rippling through the grove again, but it faded just as quickly. "Unfortunately, the academic senate is beginning to rumble in ways that even the magister magistrorum might soon be unable to ignore. Which is why—" She took a breath, closed her eyes. "I was hoping you might allow me to accompany you this weekend."

Even the trickling of the stream and the breeze in the branches overhead seemed to go silent. "Of course," Shtasith muttered. He

AIRS ABOVE THE GROUND

bowed to Hesper. "A bold move, my Lady, but more than justified under the circumstances."

"What?" Cluny heard herself asking. "I...I don't—"

"The Crown Princess." Hesper looked like a statue in someone's garden, her voice just as quiet but even harder than before. "If I can gain her patronage, these slack-jawed gray beards won't *dare* throw me out." She raised her head, her eyes shimmering. "I...it's the only way I can think of."

Cluny looked back at Crocker. He was nodding.

~oOo~

It took forty-five minutes of coaching, but Cluny finally got Crocker to cast a spell that connected to the aethercom at his parents' house. "I know I should've checked in earlier," he told the butler who answered. "But I wanted to let folks know I'll be bringing Lady Hesper as my guest."

The cloudy image of the butler floating over the desk seemed to shiver. "The unicorn, Master Terrence?"

His nod got them put on hold, Crocker muttering, "Mom's gonna kill me for this..."

But when a female human voice burst from the spell, the face blonde and sharp and exactly everything Crocker's face was not, she exclaimed, "Terrence, darling! I've been meaning to call, but with all the wonderful things we've been hearing about your progress, I didn't want to disturb your studies! You and your familiars and Magistrix Hesper will be most welcome! Dinner's at six tonight! Till then, darling!" And the clouds dispersed with an audible pop.

"Well!" Cluny cleared her throat. "She seems...perky."

Crocker nodded. "She's that way with ev'ryone but horses."

"Indeed?" Shtasith let out a chuckle. "One wonders if she will react to Lady Hesper as an equine or a non-equine?"

Cluny rolled her eyes. "We're not conducting experiments."

"I dunno, Cluny." A little color had come back into Crocker's face, but not much. "Seems to me we're trying to see how much pressure it takes to pop my head off."

And while that didn't happen, Crocker *did* spend the rest of Friday packing and repacking his suitcase while Shtasith dusted every inch of the room in preparation for Hesper stopping by. Master Gollantz appeared to issue his usual dire warnings about how much damage it would cause if anyone should learn the truth of Cluny's situation, but then he smiled thinly and hoped they would have a lovely weekend before vanishing.

For her part, Cluny spread Crocker's new sophomore robes over the desk and spent the time sewing a pocket on the front with the kit her mother had given her. She could've used magic, of course, but she needed to keep her paws busy, especially when Crocker started fretting that the robes might be too formal. "Formal is good," she told him, biting the thread instead of flying across the room to sink her teeth into his jugular vein. "Formal's likely the only way we're gonna survive this."

So Cluny was more than ready when Hesper danced out of the air just as the clock tower across campus chimed five. "I've never had a chance to see actual horses close up!" she gushed.

That made Cluny smile, and she flared her claws, sent the robes sailing across to wrap around Crocker. "Alas." Shtasith sighed a gust of steam. "I continue to hold that black leather and lace would be more in keeping with the 'powerful but insane' image we are attempting to create for our simian."

Cluny leaped to the floor. "You were outvoted, Shtasith."

"Thank the powers." Crocker grabbed his suitcase, Cluny scrambling up him to her pocket, Shtasith settling across Crocker's shoulders. "I'm not even gonna ask if I can teleport us: I already feel like I'm broken into pieces...."

A golden glow sprang from Hesper's horn. "Never fear, Sophomore Crocker. As the faculty advisor here, I shall do the honors." The light whooshed to surround them like mist, and when it cleared seconds later, Cluny almost forgot to make a note of the spell's primary characteristics, she was so taken aback by the gatehouse in front of them, the ivy-covered stone walls on either side of it stretching out to be lost in the August evening shadows of the woods they were standing in.

It wasn't that the gatehouse was huge or threatening, but it wasn't warm and inviting, either: like an old soldier or a firmly-rooted tree, it gave her a feeling of strength in repose, of solidity and competence, the sort of gatehouse that would make a guest feel comfortable and an intruder feel nervous.

Crocker's father, she realized, was a very good architect.

Movement at the gate itself drew her attention from the structure to the seven armed and armored humans lined up in front of it, the royal crest filigreed in gold over their cuirasses. One of them turned, folded his arms to display the silver chevrons along his gauntlets, and said, "I'm guessing you're the son from the wizard school and his party."

"We are, indeed!" Hesper trotted forward and literally beamed at the man, the air around her sparkling. "And thank you so much for being here to meet us, captain!"

Cluny heard a yearning sigh from one of the soldiers, and the captain smiled, bowed with a flourish, everything about him suddenly congenial. "Might I offer you an escort? Your Highness is touring Lady Crocker's stables at the moment."

Hesper tossed her mane, and Cluny almost sighed herself. No glamour spell ever devised could match a unicorn simply being a unicorn. "Quite all right, captain." She glanced at Crocker. "Surely you'll be able to guide us, Sophomore Crocker?"

Crocker's head gave a spasmodic jerk that was nearly a nod.

"Good!" Hesper bowed to the captain. "Thank you again!" She cantered toward the line of soldiers, and the way they shrank away, Cluny imagined a bunch of kids staring at a soap bubble they were afraid of popping. "Come along, sophomore!"

For an instant, Cluny thought she might have to jab a claw into Crocker's chest to shock him out of his stupor, but all at once he lurched to life and stumbled after Hesper. "Right!" he yelped. "Yes! Thanks, ev'ryone, y'know?" Then they were passing through the gate, crossing the stone floor of the gatehouse, and stepping out under the evening sky again on a tidy flagstone walkway that wound away through trees carefully tended, Cluny could tell, to look untended.

With a sigh, Crocker shook his head. "Royal guards at the front gate. I'll bet Dad's strutting around like one of Mom's horses. Speaking of which—" He pointed to a grassy knoll ahead where the path split. "We bear right here, and that'll take us back to the paddocks."

Peering from her pocket as Crocker strolled along, Shtasith on his shoulder and Hesper trotting beside him, Cluny had to smile. A few low buildings showed between the trees and hills to their left, the air soft with jasmine and hyacinth, orange blossom, honeysuckle, and lavender, and Cluny felt Crocker's jangled power smoothing, the flow of his magic more normal than it had been all day. "Ev'rything OK?" she asked quietly.

"Yeah." He sounded surprised. "I mean, my folks are great when they're able to control ev'rything and make it perfect. Like when Mom's with her horses and when Dad's doing—" He waved his hands. "Doing all this."

"And it *is* perfect." Hesper's horn glowed. "The effort that's gone into maintaining this place, it almost feels like magic." She cocked her head at Crocker. "I begin to see where you get some of your more interesting qualities, sophomore."

Crocker blushed, and they came around another hill to see several wooden corrals and a sprawling stable, the earthy scents and snorts of big animals washing over Cluny like a sudden mudslide. Hesper gasped, her head swiveling, one front hoof drawing up to her chest, and all the horse sounds coming from the stables cut off like someone had thrown a switch.

The air went slippery, Hesper flashing across the empty dirt to the nearest of the stable's open windows, and Cluny could only stare as a big black horse peered out, a little white around his eyes, his nostrils flaring. Hesper didn't make a sound, her whole body smaller than just the horse's head, but she seemed to be vibrating like a struck gong. The horse looked down, andShtasith gasped, "My Lady!"

"It's OK," Crocker said. "Wanax is number one on all Mom's teams, so he's, like, the smartest horse in the world."

Sure enough, the two just held each other's gaze while Crocker hurried to the spot, Cluny not wanting to break the strange silence. But then Hesper whispered, not looking away from Wanax, "Of all hoofed folk—the horses, the antelopes, the pegasi, the gazelles, the zebras, the hippogriffs—we unicorns alone exhibit true sapience." She stretched her neck, reached her horn up as far as she could, Wanax lowering his head—

"I will have answers, Jonah!" a female voice exclaimed inside, and Crocker froze: his mother, Cluny realized. "I've never seen them like this!" A large door a few yards away swung open, a half dozen humans stepping through. "And if I've not seen it," the whip-thin blonde woman was saying to a taller man beside her, the man looking like he wanted to be anywhere else, "then it doesn't happen to horses! So perhaps you could—!"

The two other women in the group, both of them dark-haired and younger than Crocker's mother but dressed in the same sort of crisp black, beige, and crimson riding togs, gasped together. The unmistakable power flowing around the taller of them made Cluny sure she was Beatrice Elaro, top of her class at Huxley four years ago and now the princess's personal sorceress and bodyguard. The shorter, of course, was Crown Princess Alison herself, Her Highness's eyes wide with wonder and staring straight at Hesper. "Lady Crocker?" Her Highness said. "I may have found the source of the disturbance."

Lady Crocker turned, and a smile as sudden and phony as someone slipping on a mask blossomed forth. "Terrence! Darling! You're here!"

The rest of the group was looking their way by now, the other two males bearing a slight resemblance to each other and to Crocker, the older man with gray sprinkling his dark curls, the younger tall and trim in a way Cluny couldn't imagine Crocker ever would be. A smile curled this younger man's moustache, too, and Cluny recognized the mix of humor and chagrin there: she often got that same look from her own brothers. "Always making an entrance, huh, Terry?" he asked.

Crocker shrugged. "I'm a born troublemaker." He bowed to the princess before Cluny could jab him. "Your Royal Highness, Mom, Dad, Lionel, Jonah, lady I don't know." He gestured to the unicorn, still gazing up at the horse. "This is Lady Hesper, and these are Cluny and Shtasith. Sorry about the—"

"Oh, now, Terrence!" Lady Crocker laughed like she wanted the people back at the main gate to hear it. "I'm simply overjoyed that you and Magistrix Hesper could join us!"

"Magistrix?" Mistress Elaro bristled. "Lady Crocker, Hesper is no more a magistrix than the creature she's nuzzling."

Shtasith hissed, but Hesper's laugh chimed through the air. "Quite right, Beatrice!" She did her half-trot, half-dance toward Lady Crocker. "I would certainly hate for anyone to dress me in borrowed robes, as they say." She bowed to Crocker's mother, the woman's smile becoming almost genuine. "Lord and Lady Crocker, thank you for allowing me to escort your son here. Dressage fascinates me completely!"

Lord Crocker pulled himself up straighter, the greasy scent of a self-satisfied ego humming over Cluny's whiskers. "You honor our humble abode, Lady Hesper," he said, but Cluny could hear the sentiment behind the words: his house was the finest in the realm, and Hesper was only confirming it by her visit.

"Indeed!" Lady Crocker's face lit up. "We were going for a turn before dinner, Lady Hesper, if you'd like to—" Her smile faltered. "Accompany us?"

Mistress Elaro snorted, and when Hesper laughed this time, Cluny could hear her teeth grinding. "It's true, Beatrice, that my current duties seldom allow me time to stretch out and run, but I'm fairly certain I can keep up."

"Lovely!" Lady Crocker turned to her husband. "Lawrence, you and the boys head back to the house and get Terrence and his familiars settled, then we'll see you all at dinner!" She started into the stables. " Your Highness? Magistrix Elaro? Lady Hesper? This way, please!"

The stableman trooped after her, and the princess followed, Mistress Elaro ignoring Hesper so pointedly, Cluny was surprised she didn't draw blood. The unicorn, though, fell in easily between the two and began chatting about what a lovely day it had been, the princess gazing down at her with the enraptured smile Hesper always seemed to cause.

Lord Crocker waved a hand. "Well, you heard your mother. You boys get back to the house and get ready for supper. I've a bit of landscaping I need to see to." And he moved off toward the path back to the main gate.

Crocker's brother snickered. "I'm remembering how we used

to race to the kitchen garden from here."

"*You* used to race." Crocker started along the side of the stable. "*I* used to stumble over rocks and crash into trees."

That snicker again, Lionel falling in beside Crocker, and they reached another flagstone path. The man was in his mid 20s, Cluny guessed, a good five or six years older than Crocker. Was that usual between human siblings? Or—?

"So." Lionel's eyes darted sideways, met Cluny's gaze, blinked, moved away. "I hear you saved your school from the queen of the Ifriti or something."

Shtasith's intake of breath made Cluny glance up at him, but Crocker spoke before the firedrake could: "It wasn't like that exactly." He poked his brother's arm. "I hear you're gonna marry the princess or something."

Lionel nodded. "Though I must say, if I'd known what hoops I'd have to jump through when Ali gave me my diploma and that smile of hers at the commendation ceremony..." He stopped, shook his head. "Aw, who'm I kidding? The way we clicked at the dance afterwards, no way I was letting her go, y'know?"

"Yeah," Crocker said, and Cluny felt the warmth of his magic snuggle around her. "So how's life afloat?"

"Terry?" Lionel pressed a hand to his chest. "The stories I could tell you!" He proceeded then to tell some—pretty funny ones, too—while they walked through more of the estate's wooded hills, a pool house visible through the trees at one point, a nicely-rolled tennis court at another, and Cluny found herself liking him more and more.

The path wound around one last hill, and Cluny had to gasp at the house, big and rambling as a glacial moraine, perfectly situated in the landscape but still stately enough that she felt somehow underdressed wearing just her regular old fur.

"Wait," Lionel said, interrupting his account of running across a school of flying cuttlefish. "We've got most of high society stacked up in there noshing their way through as many hors d'oeuvres as Rhys and Patrin can crank out." He nodded toward a low hedge running along some tumbled rocks that Cluny suddenly realized were a wall. "So unless you're dying to hobnob with the big-wigs..."

Crocker shook his head and moved to the hedge. "May I?"

Lionel folded his arms. "You never could before."

"That was a long time ago." Crocker flared his fingers, the pattern of pale violet fire in the air telling her he was trying a lifting spell. Not sure he knew any of those, she tucked her paws into her pocket so they wouldn't show and reached out with her spatial senses to see what Crocker was—

"Ah!" Shtasith rose from Crocker's shoulders, his wings drafting a cool breeze down over her. "A secret passage!" He sliced through the air to where the hedge began, and Cluny saw it, then: a handle in the stone work half hidden by branches.

"Froth and foam!" Lionel stared at Shtasith. "It talks??"

"'He,' not 'it.'" The strain of the casting barely touched Crocker's voice. "Cluny can talk, too, but she's kinda shy." He flicked his fingers. "Outta the way, Shtasith: that thing swings right up where you're hovering."

Cluny stifled her smile and aimed a lift spell at the door they'd so nicely pointed out to her. The false front of the rock rose silently, and Lionel gave a low whistle. "So they really *are* teaching you things at that school."

"More than I can say." He grinned. "Like how a firedrake's handy when you're heading into the dark."

The glow of Shtasith's eyes cast swirling puddles of light into the rough tunnel beyond, stairs carved unevenly into the floor. Lionel snorted. "Takes a bit of the fun out when you're not barking a shin every other damn step..."

Two solid minutes of climbing, then: "Hold up, Shtasith." Crocker pointed to a hole in the wall. "This is the library."

Lionel reached through the hole and pushed something, dusty air touching Cluny's whiskers. "The coast is clear," he said, and he pushed the wall open, Cluny again amazed at how well the seams were concealed. "You'll be in your old room upstairs, Terry, and Lady Hesper's in mine across the hall."

Crocker moved after him. "Then where're you gonna be?"

"East wing guard quarters." He waggled his eyebrows. "Just outside Ali's suite, oddly enough..."

The library was large and well-kept, the summer evening fading at the windows; peering over Crocker's shoulder, Cluny watched a portion of bookcase swinging shut. "Just like in the romance novels," she said, smiling up at Crocker.

A laugh from Lionel. "Wait. Squirrel romance novels?"

Cluny felt her ears heat up, and she slid down the front of Crocker's robes into her pocket. "No, sir." She put as much shiver into it as she could, playing the nervous little rodent. "They're just the regular human kind."

His moustache quirked sideways. "You should talk to Ali; she's addicted to the damn things."

"Tell me about it," a voice drawled from across the room: a black-and-white cat giving them a half-lidded look from a table. "My mistress can't abide the things, so I'm forced to lead Her Highness's private book group when she wishes to discuss them."

"Ah!" Lionel snapped his fingers. "Terry, this is Beatrice's familiar Lorn. Lorn, this is—"

"No need, Lt. Crocker." The cat rose in one fluid motion and bowed. "I had the privilege of attending the council session where the truth about Sophomore Crocker, his familiar, and his companion was first made known."

Blinking, Crocker bowed back, and Cluny said, "It's an honor, Lorn. You're a constant example to all of us."

Lorn's ears folded. "Yes, well, as the mistress delights in reminding me, I'd be nothing but a rat-crunching farm animal if she hadn't—" The fur sprang up all over his body, the cat suddenly on all fours, his eyes wide. "Something's upset the—"

Magic crashed over Cluny, the sloppiest transport spell she'd ever felt, and Lorn was on the carpet racing for the door. "Mistress!" he yowled, the door flying open at the touch of his spell, and he shot through into a hallway beyond.

"C'mon!" Crocker took off after the cat, Cluny grabbing the rim of her pocket, Shtasith whooshing along beside, the muffled thud-thud-thud of Lionel's boots changing to a clattering as they hit the slate floor of the hall.

Down a short flight of fern-lined stairs, and Cluny could hear raised voices echoing ahead. "The gall!" Mistress Elaro was shouting. "That you would dare suggest such a thing to Her Royal Highness! It borders on the contemptible! You should—!"

"I??" And Cluny's jaw dropped: this second voice belonged to Hesper. "*You're* the one soaking in contempt, Beatrice!"

They rounded a corner and came into a vaulted reception hall, windows looking out over the grounds, a good forty or fifty formally dressed humans in various stages of bowing at the group that Cluny could tell had just appeared beside the little bandstand at the far end of the room, Crocker's mother and Crown Princess Alison staring, Mistress Elaro pointing a shaking finger at Hesper. "I'll not have the princess spoken to in that way! Unicorn or not, you need to know your place!"

Cluny had never imagined Hesper could look frightening, but right then, her front hoofs spread and planted, her horn lowered, her anger sparking the air around her—"You miserable little snip!" she growled. "If your mind were any more closed, you'd need a warning sign on your forehead!"

Mistress Elaro blinked. "That doesn't even make sense!"

"Enough!" Princess Alison didn't raise her voice, but Cluny could feel the power of her royal privilege, saw the rest of the room reacting to it as well, Mistress Elaro and Hesper both pulling their mouths closed and snapping their heads in the princess's direction. "This is not a matter to be decided lightly or in the heat of the moment." She fixed her eyes on each of the two in turn. "Lady Hesper, I have heard your request. Mistress Elaro, I have heard your comments. Now!" She turned a smile toward Crocker's mother. "Perhaps we should get ourselves cleaned up for Lady Miranda's lovely dinner."

Crocker had stopped at the edge of the crowd, Shtasith on his shoulder, Cluny craning her neck to get a view between the milling guests, but now she saw Lionel moving through them toward the princess. Mistress Elaro stood with her arms folded, her frown as heavy as an ice storm, while Hesper whirled and started for the nearest doorway, the humans stepping aside, their fear and wonder stroking Cluny's whiskers as the unicorn passed, sparks still crackling up from her.

Giving Crocker a nod, Cluny heard him sigh; he slid along the wall, reached the doorway at the same time as Hesper. "This leads back to the billiard rooms, Lady Hesper," he murmured.

"Good!" She continued stomping through and into the hall beyond though her hoofs in the carpet didn't actually make any noise. "A pool cue to the head's sure to make me feel better!"

Cluny couldn't think of a delicate way to ask. "I take it Mistress Elaro didn't support your petition."

Hesper snorted. "Mistress Elaro can kiss my unshorn fetlocks! And now she'll be whispering nothing but poison against me to Her Highness all night!"

Shtasith drifted down to hover beside her. "Fear not, my Lady. For we, too, have an agent in Her Highness's camp."

"Lionel!" Crocker snapped his fingers. "Yeah!"

"You—" Hesper's eyes shimmered. "You'd do that?"

Laughing, Cluny spread her paws. "After everything you've done for us, how could we *not*?"

~o0o~

It proved more difficult than Cluny had thought, though. After teleporting with Hesper back to the library for Crocker's suitcase, then upstairs to their rooms, not even Crocker's status got them any closer to Lionel than a third of the way down the head table. Afterwards, too, the crowds around the happy couple proved too thick, the realm's highest and mightiest all trying to get a word with Her Highness and the young naval officer scheduled to be named her consort Sunday night.

Upstairs in the deserted library, Hesper gestured with her horn, the royal party down on the deck, the lanterns flickering in the warm night breeze. "Yes, sending Shtasith would a bad idea with Beatrice standing right there."

"Ha!" Shtasith struck a claw against his narrow chest. "I would fly swifter than the swiftest arrow!"

"Exactly." Cluny shook her head. "Firedrakes are still considered weapons, y'know." She tapped her snout. "Crocker? Does that secret passage go near where Lionel's staying?"

He blinked, then smiled. "Hey, yeah! After ev'ryone's turned in tonight, we can just head over there!"

Moods lifting, they joined the party till Cluny's face went numb from holding her 'woodland creature' look and Crocker had blushed and stammered his way out of every conversation anyone tried to strike up with him. In their room, he collapsed into snores almost immediately, and Cluny found herself being wakened she didn't know how long afterwards by Shtasith: "The house has fallen silent, my Cluny. Now is the time to strike!"

Hopping onto the bed, she poked Crocker; he sat up, nodded, was lacing his boots when he asked, "Is Hesper coming?"

Cluny blinked. "Let's see if she's awake."

Out in the hallway, moonlight drifting from the skylights, Cluny tapped Hesper's door. Hearing nothing, she extended her spatial senses, felt the cabinets, the desk, the bed, but—

"She's not in there." She looked up at Crocker, Shtasith across his shoulders, her neck fur crawling. "Did either of you actually see her after we went down to the party?"

Crocker shook his head, the worried swirl of Shtasith's eyes showing his answer. Without another word, Cluny scrambled up Crocker's robes, and they headed down to the library.

The passage opened with the manipulation of a few books, and Crocker carried them up several flights, then off through a side passage and down a similar number of steps. He stopped at a section of tunnel that looked no different from the rest to Cluny till he knelt and swung one of the stairs up to reveal a maid's cupboard beneath. Dropping into it, he listened at the door, then slipped out into a darkened hallway. A few steps brought them around a corner to another door, and Crocker nodded at it.

Taking a breath, Cluny sensed around the space beyond, her little tingle growing. "It's empty, too!"

Shtasith hissed. "I mistrust this immensely! We must—!"

Sudden vertigo swept over Cluny, a burst so violent and horrible, she had to shriek. Death magic! Somewhere nearby! Crocker cried her name, then his power was stiffening around her like a plaster cast, straightening her perceptions, Shtasith's more energetic force blasting the dizziness from her head; a much weaker shockwave—from a lock picking spell of some sort?—then the feedback of that sloppy transport spell.

"Hang on!" she shouted, and flexing her own power, she snapped them through the spaces between space to the reception hall, Beatrice Elaro collapsed panting on the carpet, her dark hair a mop, her clothes mud-stained, Lorn sprawled beside her.

The magistrix struggled onto her side, brought her hands together with a crash, and her cracking voice echoed. "Guards! To the main house! Everyone! That thrice-damned unicorn attacked me, and I think she's taken the princess!"

"What??" Cluny's fur went as rigid as toothpicks.

Mistress Elaro's wild gaze shifted in their direction. "Sophomore Crocker! We haven't a moment to lose! I think I disrupted her teleportation spell before she could get the princess away from the estate, but—"

"That's crazy!" Crocker yelled, his magic jagged as pins and needles pressing into Cluny. "Hesper wouldn't do that!"

"She appeared in my room!" Mistress Elaro pushed herself into her knees, the sound of running feet coming to Cluny's ears, Crocker's mother and father and a few guests and servants rushing into the hall. "She told me she'd curse the princess if I didn't support her ridiculous request! We fought, and as she fled, I felt her power reach into Her Highness's room!"

"Fought?" Cluny tried to shake the residual stuffiness from her head. "I've felt nothing all night till right now!"

Fear and disdain mixed over Mistress Elaro's face. "A familiar and a mere sophomore student could never hope to sense the subtle energies we true magi wield!"

Cluny stared her straight in the eye. "Subtle?? Are you kidding?? Every time you transport anywhere, it feels like someone kicking me in the head! That unlocking spell and death magic were just as blatant, too!"

The magistrix's eyes flared. "How dare you??"

A clanging started then, distant and audible, Crocker and his parents startling violently. "The stables!" Lady Crocker rushed for the glass doors overlooking the back patio. "Johan would only ring the alarm in case of fire or—"

Something rattled above them; Cluny looked up, the chandeliers quivering, a rumble in the air. "Stampede," Lady

155

Crocker finished, her face going ashen. Shapes flowed out of the moonlit trees, streamed over the low patio wall, and Cluny spun out the largest shield spell she could think of as the dozens of horses crashed into the room, the glass doors shattering. Whinnies, screams, and shrieks bounced everywhere, the stink of mud and fear and sweat plastering Cluny's whiskers.

But all she could see was Wanax, the big black horse stepping in behind those who'd led the charge, a tiny slip of white gold draped over his back, blood dripping from the several holes in Hesper's flanks.

"My Lady!" Shtasith cried, leaping into the air.

"Froth and foam!" came another voice, the wall sliding open to reveal Lionel and the princess dressed in hiking clothes.

"No!" Mistress Elaro screeched, and feeling the ragged pulse of her transport spell, Cluny prayed everyone would be looking elsewhere before blasting her strongest disruption magic right into the sorceress's chest.

~oOo~

"Thank you," Hesper murmured, lowering her head back onto the pillow. "Next time you mix this potion, however, sophomore, a little more honeysuckle." She winced. "Certain forms of magic need more sweetening than others..."

Crocker nodded, set the bowl on the nightstand beside Cluny, and she made a mental note.

Princess Alison shifted in her chair. "We can continue this later if you'd like, Lady Hesper."

"Thank you, Your Highness, but there's little more to tell. After cornering me at the party and apologizing for her earlier outburst, Beatrice asked me to meet her at the stables at 2 AM so we could discuss my petition. I arrived, and she stabbed me with an iron spike hastily ensorcelled with death magic."

Shtasith hissed from Crocker's shoulders, and Cluny wished she could manage the sound as well. "All because you wanted to become dean of Healing Arts at Huxley??" she asked instead.

Hesper fixed her gaze on Cluny. "The thought of someone she considered an animal running a school at her alma mater must've pushed Beatrice over some sort of edge."

Lionel slapped the wall he was leaning against. "I never liked how she treated poor Lorn, but, well, I suppose I thought *all* magi spoke to their familiars that way."

"Not all," Hesper said, her gaze still on Cluny's, and Cluny felt her ears heat up.

The princess leaped to her feet. "But Bea *must've* known Lionel and I were just out taking the lovely night air!"

"My guess?" Cluny couldn't keep the anger out of her voice. "She'll keep saying that she didn't know, that she was fighting Hesper in honest fear for Your Highness's life. But it was her spell that unlocked the stable doors, and the only reason to do that would be so the horses could trample Lady Hesper and cover up the stab wounds."

"Alas." Shtasith puffed black smoke. "Such plans needn't be clever to be effective."

"Yeah." Crocker sounded angry, too. "And when it's the word of Her Highness's personal sorceress against a dead and crazy familiar, who's gonna look too close?"

A knock at the door, and the guard captain leaned in. "Lord and Lady Crocker, Your Highness."

They swept through, the distress on Lady Crocker's face entirely genuine. "Oh, Lady Hesper! I can't *begin* to tell you how terrible I feel that this should happen to you here! If there's anything my veterinarians can do—"

Shtasith hissed, but Hesper panted a laugh. "Thank you, Lady Crocker, but we unicorns boast so often of our healing prowess, I'd like to find out if it's true or not. Still, once I'm up and about, I'd be honored if I could visit your stables and thank Wanax and my other cousins for their help."

Princess Alison shook her head. "Rest assured, Lady Hesper, than Beatrice will be prosecuted to the fullest extent of the law. And while I will support your proposal, there *is* a position for a sorceress that's just opened up on my staff...."

"Thank you, Your Highness." A glint came into Hesper's eye. "But might I suggest a sophomore of our mutual acquaintance? If you're still looking in three years, that is."

Lady Crocker gave a gasp and turned to her husband. "Oh,

Lawrence! How wonderful! Both our sons in the royal court!"

"Mom?" Crocker's magic went hot around her. "I'm not—"

Another hiss from Shtasith, but Crocker finished with: "Not sure that's the sort of thing I'd be interested in."

"What?" Lady Crocker's face became more pinched. "Don't be ridiculous, Terrence! Of course you'll—!"

"No." He pointed a shaking finger at her. "When I didn't have any talents at all, you didn't care about me. And now that I *do* have some talents, I'm finding I don't care about you."

"Terrence!" Lord Crocker barked. "I'll not have you—!"

"Don't care, Dad." Crocker reached a hand up to Shtasith, the other to Cluny; nearly cheering, she jumped in, scurried to her pocket. "I didn't much like the way our family worked, so, well, I got another family. And while I'll always love you guys for, y'know, whatever reason, I'd rather be with people who like the real me, not some me they think I should be." He bowed to the princess. "Now, if you'll excuse me, Your Highness, I'd like to show my friends around the grounds."

Princess Alison nodded, and for all the shaking Cluny could feel as Crocker stepped out the door, he made it most of the way down the hall before his knees buckled and she had to levitate him onto a window seat overlooking the sun-drenched woods. "Did I—?" He sucked in a breath. "Did I really just do that?"

Cluny reached up to pat his chin. "You did."

A grin curled Shtasith's snout. "And splendidly as well."

"Huh." Eyes closed, Crocker leaned against the wall.

"So!" Cluny couldn't help it; she bounced against his chest, said in her squeakiest voice, "When's the tour start??"

Crocker laughed. "How 'bout as soon as I can feel my legs again?"

NETCASTERS

by Layla Lawlor

I like to get stories from new writers—not that it's easy to find new writers these days. (The good thing about self-publishing is that anyone can do it. And the bad thing about self-publishing is that anyone can do it, regardless of their ability to write, use proper spelling and grammar, proofread, or format their book properly.) When this story arrived in the slush pile, I started reading it. And I kept reading it, all the way to the end. I don't know if Layla ever heard Marion's instructions to "grab the reader by the throat on the first page and don't let go until the end," but she certainly followed them. I didn't even notice how long this story is until I did the word count.

Layla Lawlor is a freelance artist, illustrator and writer. She lives with her husband, dogs and assorted farm animals on 11 rural acres near Fairbanks, Alaska, where winters dip to 50 below zero and summers yield 24 hours of daylight. During the short (but bright!) summer she enjoys gardening and hiking, and in the winter she makes things. This is her first professional fiction sale.

Zair was rocking by the fire, mending a fishing net, when the still night outside her window erupted in a ruckus. People shouting, dogs barking, goats bellowing—a regular set-to.

She laid down her shuttle and pegboard, the rough mass of the seine slithering from her lap to the floor. Clearly someone with sense should sort things out. Besides, truth be told, she was curious. Zair picked up her walking stick and stumped outside to see what the fuss was about.

A waxing crescent moon rode low over the marsh, throwing

down a glittering trail from tidepool to tidepool and out into the wide dark ocean. The village's hill cast a black shadow across the whispering sedge. By the slender shell of moon, Zair tapped her way around back of her house, past the middens and privies to the goat pen, where half the village had gathered.

"What are you fools doing?" Zair demanded, pushing her way through the crowd. More people trickled out of their houses, drawn by the noise. Someone said "Pirates!" in a hushed whisper, and Zair rolled her eyes. Oh, there were always tales of raiders up the coast, and there had been that one time with the smugglers in the marsh... But pirates weren't known for sneaking into goat pens.

"We caught a thief, Auntie!"

She might have known: her nephews Rig and Orrel, along with a few of their equally thickheaded friends. Someone held up a lamp, and Zair could see that the boys were sitting on somebody, a stranger to judge by the long coat of colorful patches that was spread in the mud around them. No one in the village had a coat like that.

"Let him up," Zair said.

The boys, looking disappointed, let the accused thief rise to his—no, her knees. She wiped mud off her sharp cheekbone and smiled brightly at Zair: an angular, long-legged scarecrow of a woman, with a mess of short dark hair that looked like it had been hacked off with a dull knife.

"Hello, honored mother. I'm sure we can work out this tiny misunderstanding like civilized people."

"What did she steal?" Zair asked, looking around at her neighbors and relatives.

People started pulling items from pockets and cloaks. Spoons and other silver tableware. Jewelry. Small coin pouches of worked leather. Bits and bobs, the little precious things that poor people owned.

The thief's smile dimmed. "As I said, I can explain. My uncle—"

"Cheri found her in the chicken shed." Black-haired Solya pointed at her smallest daughter, who blushed and stuck her fingers in her mouth.

"I was sleeping there," the thief said. "As I explained—"

"...with her pockets full of our stolen things."

The thief opened her mouth again. Zair interrupted. "Where did you come from?" The nearest town, Trenza, was a half-day's travel with a goatcart. A lone traveler, especially one with such long legs, could have walked much faster.

The thief offered a shy, deprecating smile, which Zair distrusted instantly. "I took shelter in your village from my cruel uncle's hired brigands, until the moon set and I could leave under the cover of darkness."

"And our silver?" Solya demanded, shaking a bag that jingled.

"I am so sorry," the thief said. Her eyes dropped contritely to her hands, the long, graceful fingers clasped on her knee. "My uncle has cut off all my means of support. I would have paid you back once I regained access to my fortune."

Zair could see sympathetic credulity building on the wide-eyed faces of her nephews, who'd never been away from the village longer than it took to go to market. "Goat crap," she said loudly. "Anybody turns up in a chicken coop with half the village's silver is no princess. I say we tie her 'til morning and then decide her punishment when we've slept."

Tired from a long day at the nets, no one argued. The thief offered a wide, warm smile and held out her hands, the bony wrists together. "Please, honored mother, I will accept whatever punishment you deem fit."

"Or maybe you plan to slip the ropes as soon as we turn our backs," Zair said. The thief gave her a look of wounded innocence. "Well, I can assure you that no one ever escapes from *my* knots."

"Of course, honored mother, I am sure they don't," the thief agreed meekly.

Everyone in the village knew Zair was best with knots, so she took a twist of cord from her pocket and looped it around the thief's wrists. The thief gave the loosely bound rope a look of surprise. Plainly she'd had no idea it would be this easy.

"Where shall we put her?" Solya asked.

"Oh, out back of your privy would prob'ly do, if you don't mind the noise." A night by the privy in the cold marsh air would do their guest some good.

The thief came quietly, making no effort to escape, although the fact that she was surrounded by two dozen annoyed and well-muscled fishermen probably had a lot to do with that. Orrel took a big knife off her, a wide-bladed thing in a battered leather sheath. "We'll give this back when you leave," he said.

"Of course," the thief agreed, and her eyes followed it as it vanished under his cloak.

The privy looked too rickety to make a decent jail, so Zair took another stout bit of twine and bound the thief's hands to the stump where Solya tied up her goats for milking. There was enough rope that the thief could stand up, stretch, and lean against the side of the privy if she wanted to.

"Good night," Zair said, dusting her hands on her trousers. "See you in the morning."

"Of course, honored mother."

As they walked away, Zair's nephew Rig said, "How long d'you think it'll take her to try to escape?"

There was a thump and a loud curse from behind them. "Not long," Zair said.

~oOo~

In the morning, after the young and the strong had departed to fish for linget in the shallow channels of the estuary, Zair gathered the rest of the village—old women, small children, and Deke One-Leg—and went to see the prisoner. As expected, the thief was right where they'd left her, although her wrists were raw, her fingernails broken, and the dirt had been scraped back from the stump to a depth of two feet. Her eyes were wild, her short hair sticking up in spikes.

"What did you *do*?"

"Tied you to the privy," Zair said.

"No, no, it's more than that." The thief held up her bound hands and shook them. "You didn't even draw it tight. I could escape from more complicated bonds when I was six years old.

And yet it won't come off!"

"Course not," Zair said. "When I tie knots, they stay tied. We couldn't make a living if our nets were always coming undone, could we?"

The thief scowled at her. "I didn't want to tell you this last night, because I had no wish to frighten you, but I work for a man who takes a third part of my earnings. If I don't deliver my take to him each night, he beats me—and if anyone stops me, he beats *them*. He will already be searching for me, so I suggest you let me go before he finds your village."

Deke One-Leg laughed, and Zair raised an eyebrow. "Really? I thought you were running from your cruel uncle."

"They are one and the same."

"You're not just a liar, but a very bad one," Zair said. "In any case, strong hands are always useful during fishing season. We'll feed you and you'll work for us 'til the dark of the moon. Then you can go free."

The thief's mouth dropped open. "But it's waxing! That's twenty days, at least!"

"Then you shouldn't have thieved from people who can tie good knots." Zair folded her arms. "Or we could take a fish-cart into Trenza and dump you on the magistrate's doorstep. The penalty for theft in Trenza, I recall, is the loss of a hand."

The thief's jaw worked. After a time, she said, "You'll feed me, you said?"

"Surely. And you can sleep in the goatshed, long as you're well-behaved."

"Oh," the thief said, "the *goatshed*. How kind."

"It's better than the privy," Zair pointed out.

"True." The thief held out her hands. "Very well, you have my word. I'll work for you until the moon is dark, and I won't try to run off."

"Kind of you to give your word." Zair slit the thief's bonds with her fish-scaling knife, and after the thief had flexed her wrists and stretched, Zair reached out an open hand, palm up. The thief stared at it.

"Now what?"

"Give me your wrist." When the thief did, reluctantly, Zair bound one-half of the cut cord around it. Then, under the thief's suspicious eyes, she tied the other half to the top rail of the goat pen, a less complicated version of the knot that kept the goats in.

"What did you do?"

Zair drew a circle in the air. "You can go to the spring, the back gardens, and the goat pen. No farther."

The thief held up her arm, where the bracelet of coarse twine swung below the bony lump of her wrist. "This will stop me?" Her voice dripped sarcasm.

Some people had to learn the hard way. "Yes," Zair said, and shooed away the onlookers. "I'll bring up breakfast. I'm sure you're hungry."

She didn't expect it would take long for the thief to try an escape. And so it was. Zair and the other old people stopped to watch as the thief broke into a swift, graceful run towards the coast road to Trenza, her long patched coat billowing behind her. Then she hit the limit of the invisible tether Zair had set on her, and flipped end-over-end in a swirl of coattails and flailing limbs.

Leaning on her walking stick, Zair strolled up as the thief scrambled to her feet, cursing loudly and brushing dirt off her trousers. Zair glimpsed a brilliant green stone on a thong around her neck before the thief stuffed it quickly down her shirt.

"Now you know how far you can go," Zair said.

The thief glared through a fringe of badly cut bangs. "You did that on purpose." She tugged futilely at the knotted bracelet.

"Of course. Care for some goat cheese with your breakfast?"

~o0o~

In the next few days, with the linget running fast and everyone from fifteen to fifty out on the nets, no one missed an opportunity to put the thief to work. Whether it was painting tar on boat-bottoms, repairing holes in a thatched roof, feeding the goats or digging weeds out of someone's garden patch, something always needed doing with never enough hands to do it. The thief couldn't work on the nets or repair the protective knots that hung from every fencepost and door lintel, but there was no shortage of drudgework to keep her busy.

Zair adjusted the tether when necessary, but kept it short enough that the thief could not reach the houses. No sense giving her ideas. They'd already caught her trying to steal eggs twice, and once attempting to hide a mattock under her coat, for all the good it would do her.

Stumping out back to dump slops, Zair found the thief in an unhappy heap next to the midden, staring glumly at a ratty pack of cards that she'd produced from somewhere about her person. "Ah, good," Zair said. "The goat pen wants raking."

The thief glared. "Look at my *hands*." She spread the long nimble fingers to display blisters and inground dirt. "My hands are my livelihood. They'll never be the same."

"You stole from us," Zair said evenly. "We are poor people, but I guess you never thought of that when you took our silver. You think this is hard? We do it every day."

"Oh, what a subtle lesson," the thief sneered, tucking the cards away.

"It's no lesson; I doubt you'd learn anyway." Zair shrugged and turned back to her house. "But I'm sure you'd rather blisters on your hands to having one cut off."

"Obnoxious old woman," the thief said. "I can't believe you haven't even had the decency to ask my name yet."

"That's because you give a different name to anyone who *does* ask." Zair pointed. "The rake is at the goatshed. Pay special attention to the nanny pen; old Liddy-goat's been sick, and it's a mess over there."

"I really hate you!" the thief shouted after her.

~o0o~

"Do you think she'll take any of this to heart?" Deke One-Leg asked Zair through a cloud of stinking smoke. The drudgery of rendering the linget for their oil had begun, and the two of them were tending a rendering fire on the long apron of sand that spread below the village hill. The moon was full tonight, its silver light competing with the fire's glow on the trampled sand. Between stirring the kettle and poking the fire, they passed back and forth a clay cup of blueberry wine.

"Don't expect her to." Zair looked up the hill. Their unwanted guest was wrapped in her coat with her back against the bottom rail of the goat pen. She'd stolen a flintstriker from somewhere, and Zair could see little flickers as she tried to set the cord around her wrist on fire. "A painted rock is still no jewel. But I don't care to see her lose a hand. And it *is* useful to have extra help around the village during the busy season."

Deke stirred the kettle of linget, testing the greasy film on top. "We should make her do this part."

"Don't want to give her that much rope."

"Prob'ly smart." He shook the jug. It sloshed in a mostly-empty way. "Yesterday she told me she's the long-lost daughter of Sudala royalty, and if I let her go, she'd see us all richly rewarded." He mimicked the thief's townie accent.

"Where in the world is Sudala?"

"No idea. After that, she told me there's a dragon after her, and that it'll destroy the village if she's not gone by the new moon."

"No such things as dragons."

"I know," Deke said.

There was a distant "Ouch!" from the goat pen, and a curse.

"Just about enough for another cup in here," Deke said thoughtfully, and looked up the hill.

Zair snorted. "You're the one who picked the berries. If you want to waste all that effort, who am I to say?"

She fed the fire and then stumped up the hill with Deke behind her.

"Come to mock?" the thief said tartly, sucking her burnt wrist. "You both stink of fish, by the way. Burnt fish."

Deke topped off the cup and set it in the mud. An interested goat lipped at it through the rails; the thief snatched the cup before the goat could get its tongue past the rim. After squinting at the wine and sniffing it suspiciously, she said, "And here I thought fish-boiling parties were the height of the local night life."

Deke laughed. "You should see the young folk dance around the bonfire at the festival after the linget run. It's enough to make an old man's heart beat fast."

"You guys have a fish festival? Somehow," the thief said, "I'm not surprised."

"What better reason?" Zair asked. "Gods just sit on their heels and collect offerings. Fish, on the other hand, are useful."

The thief blinked at her, then sampled the wine. "What should I know. I'm just a thief."

"And not a very good one," Zair said.

"Hey!"

"If you were a good thief, you wouldn't be wearing a patched coat and stealing tableware from fishing villages."

"I like my coat," the thief snapped, drawing it closer about her pointed knees. "It's stylish." After a pause, she added, "I'm very good at card games and sleight-of-hand. It's what I do. But there's not much call for that sort of thing in little coast towns like Trenza."

"So you came to a much smaller town instead?"

The thief tipped back the rest of the wine, her long throat working, and wiped her mouth. "No, if you must know, I got lost. I thought I was on the road to Bonolevi, which at least is big enough to have a night life that doesn't involve fish. Instead I found myself here, and figured I'd make the most of it."

"Your sense of direction must be terrible," Zair said, "if you thought you were going to Bonolevi and ended up here."

"I'm sure it's quite obvious to you, but to a stranger, one little muddy coast road looks much the same as another." The thief rolled the cup between her long fingers. "Does your town have a name?"

Zair looked at Deke; he looked back at her. They both thought about it. "Folks in Big Crossing sometimes call it Little Crossing, I guess," he said.

"But it isn't really," Zair explained to the thief. "And what do they know; Big Crossing's all the way to the other side of the Scarp. Can't even get there in the wet season."

"I'm sorry I asked," the thief groaned. "Er, you don't have any more of this wine, do you?"

She must be desperate. Two good things could be said of

Deke's wine: it was very strong, and (mostly) nonpoisonous. "Got another jug aging out back," Deke said. "Prob'ly ready tomorrow night, maybe the night after."

The thief gave him an incredulous look. "Your wine's vintage is measured in *days*?"

"There's a fine timing to it."

She stared at him a moment longer, then shuddered and drained the sludgy dregs in her cup. "You can call me Shadow," she said in a rush.

"Oh, really?" Zair said. "We can, can we? Does anyone else?"

"It's what I always wanted people to call me. My thief name, if you will."

Zair cleared her throat. "That'd be a 'no', then."

"But it's what you can call me in this village, if you like," the thief said, and she smiled with wine-stained lips. "I swear I'll answer to it if you do."

~o0o~

After that, the thief was less sullen and even talked to people on occasion, although some of the parents began to complain when they caught her teaching the children simple tricks with her deck of cards.

"First you complain that I keep myself apart, and now it's a problem when I try to make friends."

"The problem," Zair said, "is some of the good folk in this village think you're corrupting their children."

"In my experience, most children are born corrupted. It's only the adults who think otherwise." She took out the cards and spread them with a practiced snap of her wrist. "Would *you* like to learn a trick?"

Zair had a strong suspicion that the thief had switched from sulking and simple lies to working a longer con, but there was little to be done short of hauling her into Trenza. In any case, Zair's fingers, despite the twists of age, were strong and nimble from working with ropes. She quickly picked up the tricks that Shadow called the Conjurer's Crimp and Axti's Overhand Swap.

"Guess it's not just the children in danger of being corrupted," Zair said thoughtfully, trying a sideways shuffle and sending a card spinning into the bushes.

"Watch it, old woman, that's my only deck and it's not like I can buy more from the goats." But Shadow smiled. It softened the edges of her long, bony face.

~o0o~

The moon passed full. The summer tides ran high, the second wave of linget came in, and storms hovered on the edge of the sky, purpling the horizon. Nets frayed quickly, and tempers likewise. Zair was too busy to learn card tricks, and she kept the thief too busy to teach any.

Still, on a sultry afternoon when the promise of coming rain lay heavy across the marsh, Zair discovered Shadow waiting for her when she went to milk the goats. The thief was leaning against a fencepost and pensively studying the green stone that she wore around her neck. Zair had never gotten a good look at it, but it didn't seem to belong to anyone in the village, so she didn't bother herself about it.

Shadow dropped it down her collar as Zair approached, looking guilty.

"If you've time to woolgather, you've time to make yourself useful." Zair shoved a milking bucket into her hands.

The thief sighed, but she grabbed Liddy-goat's rope halter and dragged her to the milking stake. Zair looped the goat's tie-rope briskly around the stake, and Shadow watched with interested eyes.

"What sort of payment would you want to teach me that?"

"Milking?" Zair asked, crouching by the goat's hindquarters with a hand on her flank. "Start learning now, if you want."

"No, no—I'd like to learn to tie knots like you do."

"You don't know how to tie knots?" Zair nodded towards the woven belt around the thief's waist. "What holds up your pants, then?"

"*Magic* knots, old woman."

"You've got some things to learn about asking for favors," Zair said. "It's not magic, anyway."

"Knot magic? Cute."

"*Not* magic. It's just tying knots. We tie better knots than most people, but like I said, a fisherman has to know how."

"Whatever. It looks like a useful skill, and I may never get another opportunity to learn."

Zair looked over her shoulder, studying Shadow's suspiciously guileless expression. "I've a feeling it's not the tying you're interested in, so much as the untying."

"Fine," the thief said loftily. "Don't teach me, then. I'll find someone else to do it."

"Good luck finding someone who likes you enough."

"Really? I think a lot of people here like me." Shadow's smile darted across her homely face, quicksilver-fast but warm. "I think you like me more than you'll admit."

Zair snorted and handed her the bucket of fresh, frothing goat's milk. "Take this down to Mairna the cheesemaker."

The thief took the bucket, but made no move to leave. Instead she stood looking down at the winding channels of the marsh and the ruffled ocean beyond. "How can you build so close to the water? Don't you get storms here?"

"You'll see one soon," Zair said, unlooping Liddy-goat's tether. "There's heavy weather moving in tonight. We'll bring the nets in early."

"But—all that water." The thief waved her free arm, clutching the bucket in the other hand. "And your buildings are—no offense—somewhat substandard. What if the whole place is swept away?"

"It's not usually a problem. When really heavy weather moves in, we take the children to the caves." Zair pointed to the distant Scarp, a dark line along the northern edge of the estuary. "This is just a regular squall. We'll get through it fine."

~oOo~

As predicted, by dusk the moon was long gone behind a black wall of thunderheads. Rain lashed the side of Zair's house, and the rendering fires had been extinguished, the nets pulled in. The thief had taken refuge in the goatshed.

"Are you really going to leave her out there?" Zair's niece Linnie asked when she stopped by to drop off some damaged nets for Zair to work her talents upon.

170

"She has the goats to keep her warm. She's prob'ly better off than the rest of us."

But as the wind and rain picked up, banging the shutters and battering her small, snug house, she did feel a tug of guilt. Finally she wrapped her oiled leather slicker around her and stepped out into the slanting rain. At the goat fence, she stopped to retie the thief's knot, granting tether enough to reach the first row of houses.

The goats were huddled in the three-sided shed. Zair banged her walking stick on the side. "Alive in there?"

"Come to see if I've drowned?" the thief's sulky voice issued from somewhere behind the damp mass of goats. "Thanks for the concern."

"Well, if you'd rather stay..."

"Wait, is that an invitation? To somewhere warm and dry?" The thief tumbled out of the shed in a lanky tangle of arms and legs. The rain soaked her instantly, but at least it washed off some of the mud. She followed Zair to her usual limit and then paused.

"Come on, I've given you more rope." *Enough to hang yourself if you steal anything from me,* she thought. The thief scowled as if suspecting a trick, and took a few cautious steps forward, then lengthened her stride when nothing happened.

Inside, Zair gave her a blanket, and hung the thief's sodden coat, shirt and trousers by the fire. It was the first time she'd seen the thief undressed. Shadow had a curling tattoo all up one arm, black and red ink on the supple brown skin. She also wore a few hidden items of jewelry: a silver chain on her upper arm, a jeweled anklet, and the green pendant. None of it looked too familiar, though Zair would lay odds it was stolen from *somewhere.*

"You're being awfully nice to me," Shadow said, stretching out her skinny legs and wiggling bare, dirty toes in front of the fire. "Did tormenting the thief get boring?"

"No one's been tormenting you. You've only yourself to blame for your problems, and you know it."

The thief opened her mouth to reply, when a thunderclap

shook the house. She jumped and then squinted at the seaward wall. "Are you sure the ocean isn't about to invite itself into your living room?"

Zair rose to stir the fire. "I told you, we don't often get a storm that big. Might see one this year—the weather's been rough. But we normally have enough warning to get to high ground."

"Warning from what, the little weather birds?"

"You don't live by the ocean all your life without learning to read it." Zair frowned down at the thief. "You aren't used to the water. You must come from someplace inland."

"Very clever, sheriff," the thief said, but there was no rancor in it. "Yes; I grew up in a little dirt plot in the middle of potato fields. Nothing for miles but potatoes." She shuddered. "Sometimes I still have nightmares about sorting potatoes. Just piles of potatoes without end."

Of all the things the thief had said about her past, Zair believed this one. "You left to seek your fortune elsewhere, did you?" she asked, and the thief nodded, so Zair pushed a little. "Is this the life you wanted?"

The thief looked up, and for a moment her face was open and hurt. She really was quite young, Zair thought. Then her eyes shuttered and her mouth quirked in the familiar mocking smile. "No. I learnt I was a baron's long-lost daughter, and he sent a carriage for me. Couldn't stand the life of luxury for more than a night, though. I stole a casket of gold and my father's finest horse, and took to the road."

Zair's lips pressed to a hard line. "You wouldn't have so much trouble in life if you'd give back a little."

Nothing seemed to change in the thief's posture, and yet it was harder, somehow. "I don't know what you're talking about." She smiled thinly. "Do you want to hear about my flight from my father's captivity? The children liked this story."

"Not tonight. I'm an old woman and I have work to do in the morning." Turning away, Zair said over her shoulder, "You can sleep by the fire tonight. If you take anything of mine, you'll learn some other knots I can make. You won't like them."

"I won't steal from you," the thief said, behind her.

Zair wished she could tell substance from lies in the thief's pebble-smooth words. She lay awake for a long time as the dying fire made patterns on the ceiling, listening to Shadow's slow breathing and the rain battering the hut's walls.

~o0o~

"Hope we're not making a mistake," Deke said, leaning against Zair's wall in a precariously tipped-back chair, balancing his wine cup on his stomach while he carved a chunk of driftwood into a new shuttle for Zair's netmaking. "She's got clever fingers, and she's not stupid."

Outside, the waning half-moon illuminated the thief leaning on the goat pen, studying the knotted rope that kept the goats in. She was just looking at it, occasionally poking one of the knots gently with her long fingers.

Zair shrugged and turned a seine in her lap, checking for weak spots with sure, callused fingers. "Worst thing, she unties herself and runs off."

"No, worst thing she wrecks our village knots, and us with storm season coming. Or she comes back with five burly friends and cleans us out. You heard about those pirates up the coast, right?"

"Pirates again," Zair sighed.

"My cousin heard from my nephew, heard it in Trenza. They burned out Hammer Bay, killed half the men in town, and the less said of the women, the better." Deke twisted the knife in the water-smoothed wood a little harder than necessary. "Maybe she's got friends like that."

"I'll shore up the defensive knots tomorrow. They need checking anyway."

"Just don't let her watch you do it." He refilled Zair's wine cup and his own.

Zair squinted out the window at the thief, who had given up poking at the knot and instead reached down inside her collar for whatever she wore there. Fishing it out, the thief cupped it in her hand and studied it in the moonlight.

"What's she looking at?" Deke wanted to know, peering over

Zair's shoulder.

"Don't know. Some kind of necklace. It's hers, I think, not ours. As much as anything she's got is hers. Caught her looking at it a few times—more so lately."

"Ask her about it?"

Zair lifted a shoulder in a shrug. "Not our business, seems to me."

~o0o~

Three days before the new moon, the fall rains came, flattening the sedge and glistening on thatched roofs. Everyone was wet and testy.

The thief fell in step with Zair on her way to the vegetable patch beyond the midden. "I have a problem."

"Other than being tied to a goat pen?"

"Well... no, that's pretty much it, or at least part of it." Shadow rubbed at the twine around her wrist, a reflexive habit she'd developed. "See, I didn't think you'd actually—I mean, I thought I'd be long gone by now."

"Surprise," Zair said dryly, squatting by the turnips. "Pull some of those onions."

The thief sighed and obeyed, but continued to speak. "There's something after me, and it's getting closer. Much as it pains me to admit it, I'd really hate any of you to get caught in its path if it does find me here. Granted, I'd hate to see *me* in its path quite a lot more."

"Uh-huh," Zair said. Sorrel and lambsquarters went into a pile for the stewpot, the other weeds into a bucket for the goats. "You also said your rich uncle wants to cart you off for a wedding."

"All right, yes, granted, that one may have been slightly less than true—"

"And you have four kids about to starve without you."

The thief sighed. "Are you going to hold everything I've said against me?"

"When it's a lie, yes." Zair frowned as something nagged at her memory. "Didn't you say something to Deke about a dragon?"

"Yes!"

"There's no such thing."

"There's no such thing as knots that can't be untied, either," the thief said, tensing her narrow shoulders.

"It's just a matter of tying them properly."

"Yes, whatever. Anyway, the point is you're all in danger if you don't let me go." The thief reached down her collar and hooked the thong. Zair got a better look at the pendant this time: a stone in a roughly forged metal setting, more blue than green by daylight. The thief waved it at Zair.

"So?"

"This morning, it was green. Now look at it. There's only one thing could make it turn this color."

"Dragons?" Zair said.

"Yes!"

Zair sent her down to the goat pen with the bucket of weeds.

~oOo~

The thief grew more insistent after that. It was impossible to make her do anything useful.

"I think she really does believe something's out to get her," Deke said, helping Zair drag a fishing boat out of the mud. He paused to squint at a low dark mass of storm clouds burgeoning over the sea. The rain had stopped, but the air felt heavy, expectant. "And us," he added.

"She's a liar, Deke."

"I know. But what if she's not lying this time?"

Storm weather always made everyone tense. Today was worse than usual. They'd started putting out the gill-nets for the fall mudfish run, but they brought them in early and dragged the boats up the hill. *Going to be a bad one,* Zair thought, shading her eyes and looking down from her yard at the wind raking long sweeps through the marsh grass. The sky was the color of a bruise, lit with the clear glow of stormlight. *Maybe take the kids up to the caves if it doesn't break soon.*

Evening came early and ominous. The wind rose, banging shutters and bringing cold spatters of rain. Zair was precariously balanced on a stool, taking in the washing, when Solya barged into her yard. "You have to do something about that townie!"

175

"You young people—so polite." A sharp gust of wind almost sent Zair sprawling, and she turned her attention back to her task. "What's she done now?"

Solya planted her hands on her hips. "That thief, Shadow or whatever her name is, she's got my kids running around like headless chickens. I caught Cheri trying to steal my good fish-gutting knife for slaying dragons!"

"There's no such thing as dragons," Zair said, for the twentieth time that day.

Solya threw her arms up in the air. "I know, but try telling the kids!"

"Fine," Zair said, "fine."

After a quick stop by Orrel's house, she stumped off to the goat pen, where the thief and some of the village boys were hauling the goats into shelter. The thief kept looking up nervously at the sky and then at the coast road to Trenza. Gusts of wind flattened her patched coat against her narrow body. Zair got her attention by grabbing one bony wrist, and deftly untwisted the cord tied there. Then she threw the thief's knife at her feet.

"Go. It's only two days 'til the new moon, anyway."

The thief rubbed her bare wrist. "Is this a trick to make me fall down so that you can all laugh at me again?"

"No," Zair said. "You aren't as funny as you think, and anyway, you paid your debt. So get going. You best get under shelter before the storm breaks."

The thief stared at her for a long moment, and then looked around at the goat pen and the goggling kids. Her mouth worked as if she meant to say something else. Then, without a word, she snatched up the knife and took off running into the growing gloom, headed for Trenza.

"Did I tell you to stop working?" Zair snapped at the boys, and tromped back to her house. She kept glancing at the road, but the thief was already gone from sight.

She forced herself not to look over her shoulder for imaginary dragons.

~oOo~

As darkness fell, the storm hit the shore like a fist, driving towering waves before it. Zair listened to the roar of the high surf from behind closed shutters, her hands wrapped around a mug of tea. She could hear it through the walls, over the cheerful jabber of her nieces and nephews and their kids, all gathered in her house to wait out the long wet night.

"Sounds bad out there," her nephew Rig said, leaning against the wall. "Already washed away the east weirs when I came in. I say we take the kids up to the Scarp. Some of the families already did."

His cousin Linnie shook her head, and picked up her infant son as he began to cry. The shutters thumped in the wind. "Shoulda gone up to the caves before the storm broke, if we were gonna. And there are the goats to think of."

Deke, who had made himself at home in the corner by the fire, raised his head and snorted. "This is nothing. Gonna blow itself out by morning. Let me tell you about the storm we had back—was it the year the mudfish didn't come in? Yeah. That year, the wet season started in the month of roses, if you can believe it—"

There was a chorus of groans. "This was when Great-Auntie Korie's outhouse washed away, right?" Rig said.

"The wind was like a herd of stampeding goats," Linnie took up the familiar tale, speaking along with Deke.

"—stampeding goats—hey, I'm telling this story, aren't I?"

Through the pounding of wind, rain and surf, it took Zair a moment to realize that someone was beating on the door. She cautiously unbarred it, leaning her weight to keep it from being snatched out of her hands.

The thief tumbled through the door on a wet slap of wind, so sodden in her water-heavy coat that she looked like a pole with a rug draped over it. Zair slammed the door. The room fell silent.

"What are you doing here?" Zair asked for all of them.

"Yes. Well." The thief straightened and wrung out her ragged hair. "I wanted to return something." From under her coat, she produced a silver plate and a handful of flatware.

"Hey," Deke said. "That's my daughter's good table service,

the one her no-account husband left behind when he went back to Bonolevi."

"All I know is that it was in the last house on the way out of town," the thief said.

Zair took it, angry but unsurprised. "Do we need to shake you and see if you rattle? And why are you back? Sudden attack of conscience, I presume?"

"You presume correctly," the thief said, "but it's not just the silver. I was halfway to Trenza when—well—" She glanced in the oceanward direction. "Do you have any idea what it's doing out there? Why are you people still down here, by the water? You need to get up to those caves you talked about."

"This isn't bad. Like I told you, just a storm."

"You also told me it washes away the village sometimes! You people have to get out of here."

"And you told *me* there were dragons after you," Zair said. "What's the matter, can't they fly in this wind?"

The thief scowled at her, then gave a little half-smile. "There's no such thing as dragons."

"I know that and you know that." Zair nodded at the thong around her neck. "So what's that *really* for, and why are you back?"

Reluctantly, the thief pulled it from her collar and twirled it. The stone was vivid blue. "It was a gift," she said, and paused. "No, that's not right. When I was a kid and fresh from the potato fields, a man up Dresderi way 'prenticed me. Bought me, more like. Name of Bredon." Her words faltered, then came surer and stronger with every sentence, a rural accent slipping in. "He made each of us carry one of these so he could find us if we run off. He's got a rock like this himself, and it changes color when the stones draw close together. Me, I ran, eventually. I wasn't the only one."

Zair studied her long, earnest face. "Why do you still have it?"

"Because it works the other way, too. I can tell if he's nearby." She held up the stone and let it spin. "I always kept moving, but staying in one place—I didn't think he'd find me so quick. I almost ran into him and his gang on the road, actually. I hotfooted it back here as soon as I caught sight of them."

A low murmur of voices rose around the room. Zair just snorted. "They're coming here, in a storm like this? Ridiculous."

Shadow curled her lip. "Bredon and his bunch—they *like* working in this kind of weather. It means no one will see the smoke and come to help. They'll clean out anything valuable, burn your houses and kill anyone who complains about it. They must figure that if I'm here, there's something worth stealing—"

She stopped talking, because the cacophony of wind and rain had died with the suddenness of a handclap. In the silence, the loudest sound was the drip of water falling from the eaves.

"It does this when the wind changes direction. It'll be back soon," Zair said. "And worse. Much worse. Are you telling the truth, girl?"

"I am. I swear that I am."

Zair stared at her for a long moment. Then she turned, stabbing a finger. "Rig, Orrel, Linnie—go tell everyone. Get them ready, kids all together, everyone in position, just like when those smugglers tried to rob us back in—no, you're too young to remember, but your parents will know what to do. Get the nets, the best ones. None of Rukah's; that girl's knots never hold. Hop to it!"

Shadow seized her arm. "You can't fight them; are you crazy? You don't know what you're dealing with! You have to get everyone out of the village—"

"You," said Zair, "shut up. I'm taking a big risk believing you, girl, after all your lies. You never gave us nothing but grief, and if you brought this Bredon down on our backs, you *owe* us. Now shut up and help me get ready."

The thief opened her mouth, then closed it. She swiped her ragged, sodden hair back from her forehead with one long hand, and when she raised her head, her eyes were steady. "I still think you're all going to die, but tell me what you want me to do."

~o0o~

The village lay in wet, wracked stillness, runnels of muddy water twisting between the houses. The goats huddled in their shed, not one of them visible outside. Faint stars glimmered through the thinning clouds.

Zair could hear rough laughter and hoofbeats on the coast road. Shadow hadn't been lying after all.

"Are you sure it's not over?" the thief panted as she helped Zair wrestle the wet, reeking mass of a seine into position. "The storm, I mean."

"No. It's coming back."

As if summoned by her words, a low wind keened through the village, an advance scout for the oncoming maelstrom.

Under Zair's direction, Shadow hoisted the net so that Zair could secure it to the corner of the last house with a few deft twists of rope. Working together, the villagers had surrounded the village with a hastily erected fence of the long nets that they used to fish for linget in the marsh channels. The nets were strung between houses and privies, even around the goat pen. It wasn't a tall fence—no more than waist high on Shadow.

"This isn't going to stop determined men with swords, Zair, no matter how strong your knots are."

"That's not what it's going to stop." Zair bit off a length of twine. This was the tricky part, and she didn't have much time to do it. "You're about to find out what our knots can do, Shadow."

"Dorsag," the thief said.

Zair looked up at the bony, sharp-edged face.

"My name. The one my mother gave me, I mean. Even Bredon doesn't know it. I told him I was called Lally."

Zair jerked her head in a terse nod, and said, "We're going to kill these men, Dorsag. We have to. It's them or us. If this is another lie—if these are farmers you swindled—"

"They're not. I swear it." She paused, and added, "Kill them? Really?"

"Are you changing your story now?"

"No. But... not all of them are like Bredon. Some were my friends once."

"Then give them a chance," Zair said. "Same one you got. If they lay their weapons down, they can come in. But go, be quick about it. We're running out of time."

The wind had picked up, swirling in the space between the houses. Zair could feel the strain on the knots, feel it in her brittle old bones. This had been easier when she was young. She breathed deeply, seeking calm. It didn't do to rush knotwork, especially with this much riding on it. Kneeling in the mud, she began working on a tangled mess of wet twine.

Deke arrived, breathing hard. "Everything's ready. Linnie and Therin are waiting for your okay. What can I do?"

"Help me up," she said absently, her fingers and her mind busy with the complexity of her working. The nets hummed with tension in the night. The moon was dark, the stars gone behind looming clouds. All around her, she could feel the storm—a vast presence in the night, neither friend nor foe, slightly bemused at this tiny village on the marsh, this tiny woman who would attempt to buck its might for even a moment or two.

We only need a moment.

"The longer you hold it back..." Deke murmured into her ear as he helped her around the perimeter of the village. Tying knots. Everywhere, knots.

"I know." It was a dangerous game she played. But she had always been the best with knots, the best in generations.

The wind brought her a man's voice, a stranger's. "Lally," he said, and that voice crawled with a possessiveness that turned Zair's stomach. She risked dividing her attention, turning her head to see Shadow—Dorsag—standing just inside the net fence. There must have been thirty men and women massed on the other side, all on foot but for one mounted on a shaggy moor stallion. The big man and the horse made the thief look even more spindly than usual, despite her height.

"Bredon." The thief's wet coat slapped her legs as the wind changed direction. "I'm supposed to tell you to surrender."

Bredon laughed. "Sorry, what?"

Dorsag pointed past him. In the ever-deepening gloom, Zair could no longer pick out men and women; all she could see were the glints of weapons. "Lay down your swords and bows, and refuge is yours. Eirin, are you still with this bunch? Glester! You always had more brains than the rest of this lot put together. Any of you who trust me, come quickly. Join me. Us."

Bredon's laugh rang out again. "Join you and what? Die with these fish-eaters? You with the bow—shoot her."

More than one "you" answered his command, and Zair saw the flash of two arrows, one narrow and fletched, the other a stubby crossbow bolt. Zair's breath caught, but the net held true: the arrows twanged off the air—she felt it, a frisson across her taut nerves—and tumbled to the ground.

Silence held for an instant. Sweat trickled down Zair's face despite the night's damp chill. Her heart was racing. The tension of the knots thrummed in her.

"Surrender or these people will kill you." Dorsag's voice was so soft that it could barely be heard above the rising wind. "They know what you've done, what you're capable of."

No one moved. Then Bredon drew a long, gleaming pistol from his belt, the first real one Zair had ever seen.

Deke's hand closed over Zair's clammy one. "Enough time. We're ready. Let it go."

Zair drew a breath, enough to shout, "Now!" Her voice was a thread of sound, but Deke bellowed for her, "Linnie, Therin! Do it!"

Zair pulled the string, unraveling the complex knotted structure in her hands. She felt the pent-up strain sing through the nets. Felt the snap as it let go.

The longer you hold it back, Deke had said. And indeed, the storm's ferocity had built like water behind a dam, and it crashed down on the hill, seizing the village in its foaming embrace, picking up the men outside the nets like leaves on floodwater. Deke pushed Zair to the ground as the wave broke over them, and she dug her fingers into the mud, holding fast to the twine like the lifeline it was.

~o0o~

"I really, truly cannot believe we're alive," the thief said.

The storm had pounded the village all night, and finally spent itself on the marsh and blew back out to sea, leaving a fresh-washed morning sky behind. The apron of sand below the hill now pointed eastward like a great, sweeping hook. Down on the beach, children scurried to and fro in the morning sunshine, picking up driftwood for the cookfires and taking the opportunity to search for treasures that might have washed ashore.

The sedges of the marsh lay flat and mud-colored. The village was a wreck—thatch torn apart, shutters hanging loose, gardens ruined—but it still stood.

Nothing remained of Bredon and his men. Zair thought she saw a glint, here and there, among the shifting marsh channels, where a sword or a breastplate might be half-buried in the mud. It had been so after the smugglers came, though the villagers had called up their own storm that time, and it hadn't been so fierce.

Their deaths weighed on her. But she felt worse about the poor horse. Unlike the people, it had no choice.

"Some of those waves looked higher than this hill," Shadow said.

"Prob'ly were. The ocean respects our knots. We have an understanding."

The thief stared at her. "Are you saying the storm—what, bent *around* the village?"

Zair nodded. "Good way to put it."

"That's crazy."

"It's just a matter of—"

"Tying good knots, yes, I know." The thief shook her head. Her hair had dried in stiff spikes. "You people could take over the world."

Zair laughed. "Young people. Always trying to capture the moon. Knots are very good for a few things, it's true, but useless for all else. Besides..." She let a smile peek through. "Who *wants* to own the world? It's full of dangerous sorts, like that Bredon person."

Dorsag sighed. She pulled the cord out of her shirt and cupped the pendant in her hand. It was green as glass. "I wish at least *one* of them..."

"They made their choice."

"I know." But she looked truly despondent about it. *A thief,* Zair thought, *but not a killer.*

"They didn't believe me," Dorsag said. "And I can't blame

them; I don't think *I* would have believed me if I hadn't seen a little of what you can do."

"You can lead the goat to pasture, but can't make it graze. They made their choice. As did you." Zair slapped the thief's bony shoulder and pointed up to the roof, where a mess of loose thatch spilled over the edge. "Will you make yourself useful, or should we flap our gums 'til the next storm?"

Dorsag gripped the edge of the roof and boosted herself up with the nimbleness of one who has climbed many rooftops before. "Don't think you're getting another loop of rope around my wrist."

"I untied you fair and square." Zair tilted her head back, looking up. "And you came back of your own free will. If you want to leave, you can—though we might have to search you at the edge of the village. On t'other hand, we can always use strong backs about."

The thief stood on the wet thatch in the sunshine, looking down. "This place doesn't even have a teahouse, decent or otherwise. Or a theatre. This is why I left the potato fields."

"Thought you wanted to learn to tie knots."

Dorsag's face lit up. "You'd teach me?" Her eyes narrowed a bit. "You trust me?"

"Of course not, but I'm not getting younger, and so far no one 'round here has shown much skill for making truly secure knots. Some do decently, but I could use someone with strong fingers who's willing to work hard. Don't steal the silver and we'll get on fine, Dorsag."

"I'd really prefer Shadow, if you don't mind."

Zair shrugged. "Nothing wrong with Dorsag. Could be worse. There was a girl in my age-group named Loonwit."

"*Why?*"

"Grandmother's name."

Dorsag laughed. "While we're being honest with each other, that old winemaker is over the moon for you."

Zair raised an eyebrow. "You really think I haven't noticed?"

The corner of Dorsag's mouth quirked up. "Okay, good point. Still, I don't think I'd wait around at your age."

And she'd been doing so well... up until the last bit. Well, her heart was in the right place.

"So," Dorsag said, and a spark of eagerness leaped through her indifferent calm. "What do you want to teach me first?"

"Well, to begin," Zair said, "there are sixty-eight different knots for tying down thatch."

"You're joking."

"You wanted to learn, didn't you?"

By the time they broke for lunch, the thief had already mastered two of the sixty-eight, and the roof looked better than ever. Dorsag's long, clever fingers were bloody from the coarse twine, but she was grinning.

THE SALT MINES

by Dave Smeds

Dave always sends us wonderful stories. This one features his new characters Azure and Coil, the witch who hired them to rescue her daughter, the pirates who captured the daughter, and the daughter who, while happy to be rescued from the pirates, has goals of her own. Naturally, some of these overlapping sets of goals are going to come into conflict with each other, but that's what makes a story interesting.

Dave Smeds is the author of novels such as *The Sorcery Within* and *The Schemes of Dragons*. His short fiction has appeared in myriad anthologies, including at least a dozen previous volumes of *Sword & Sorceress*, and in such magazines as *Asimov's SF*, *Realms of Fantasy*, and *F&SF*. "The Salt Mines" introduces a pair of characters that Dave suspects he will feature in other stories in the not-too-distant future.

His most recent publication is the eBook short story collection *Raiding the Hoard of Enchantment*, a gathering of seven of his recent tales of high fantasy. See www.bookviewcafe.com for details.

"The sunsets are beautiful in the Desert of Fumes" the saying went. Now Coil knew what that meant. It wasn't that the sunsets were more spectacular to the eye. It was that with dusk came the promise the air would cool enough to breathe without pain.

In the canyon below, shade had been the rule for hours. The caravan Coil and Azure had been watching was now entirely out of the harbor gates, heading westward along the trade road, camels and slaves resigned to plodding along through the night. Back within the village, lamps were being lit. Stevedores were

186

unloading the cargo of the newly-arrived merchant vessels and filling up the soon-to-depart. They worked slowly, pausing often to wipe sweat off brows or napes of necks. Hours would have to pass before the temperature dropped enough to pick up the pace.

"Another caravan will leave tomorrow night. You'll have no trouble attaching yourself to it." Lady Sirocco spoke in Irsi so classic she must have spent years studying the scrolls, but with a peculiar sort of dungburner accent that said she had come to the language as an adult.

Coil was not looking forward to threading through these shattered hills. Everywhere he looked he saw only ridges and cliffs of banded, crumbling rock. No trees. Just a wisp, here and there, of goat brush or spine weed. The route was twisted and uneven and narrow, vulnerable to avalanche or banditry. And to think it would be the nice part of the trip.

They retreated from the cliff edge, moving back into the hollow in the mountain where Lady Sirocco had set up her pavilion. The encampment was thoroughly out of sight to anyone below. It had to be. If the Salt Pirates discovered the Witch of Sandstorms had returned to their territory, they would send as many assassins as they could gather.

The remnant of a man hung in the center of the camp like a fly caught in a spiderweb, ropes splaying him as far apart as his tendons and joints would allow—and then a little more. Scorch marks decorated his flesh here and there, puffy and livid beneath the char. A brazier of hot coals stood in front of him. A plucked-out eye and severed parts that had until recently defined him as male were turning to ash atop the embers. The other eye was intact—the better to witness what the fire was claiming, Coil supposed.

"From what I have learned from this one, you will have time enough to do things right," the sorceress said. "But not much more time than that. The lord of the pirates is keeping my daughter for his own use for now, but he will ultimately send her to the pens for his lackeys to enjoy. He will do it no matter how sweet he finds her to be, because he knows it will cause me anguish. My daughter is strong-willed, but a day or two in the pens will break her. See that you rescue her before she is removed from the tower."

"We will," Azure said. Coil was glad it was she who answered. When he did it, sometimes his confidence came across as boasting. Her soft voice transformed it to prophecy.

"Go, then," the sorceress commanded. "I will be waiting."

She put the smithy gloves back on her hands and picked up the tongs she had left on the coals.

Coil and Azure headed off down the shepherd path that would take them to the harbor. They hiked as fast as the fading light would allow. Even so the screaming began before they could pass out of hearing range.

"I really wish we could turn this job down," Coil said.

"I know how you feel," his milk sister replied.

~oOo~

About all it took to join the next night's caravan was to stride into the caravanserai, locate the underseer of supplies, and announce they were entertainers willing to work in Salt Town. The underseer did not even ask what their talents were. For the sake of form, the two sides spent half an hour bargaining about the rate at which the mine scrip would be redeemed when they got back, and how much the underseer's bribe should be. As usual, Azure handled the negotiations, but her persuasive skills were not needed. By the third cup of tea, the underseer was offering terms as good as if she had agreed to slip into the back room and serve as his wife of the hour.

All too easy. Azure didn't like it. Had they actually been entertainers going to Salt Town for no other reason than to earn a living, she would have backed out then and there. But soon the underseer was stamping his master's mark on a scrap of papyrus to confirm the rate. Coil placed the contract in his money belt.

The underseer beamed, as if pleased that his shift had included the diversion of hiring them. "If you have any silver on you now, it won't do you any good in Salt Town," he added with what seemed to be honest good will. "Buy extra water. *That* will be of value."

They did as he said, though it meant renting an extra camel.

They made sure to mark their skins and kegs well, for there were a great many camels carrying the same sort of load. Just as salt was the only export out of Salt Town, water was the main import.

Water. And slaves.

A single long train of naked men was herded into the staging yard. Coil estimated there were forty of the wretches, wrists bound behind their backs, connected to each other by chains and ankle shackles. They shuffled along, backs and buttocks and sometimes faces adorned with lash marks, reeking from a voyage spent having to sleep in their own filth. They were a mix of peoples, some bearing the slavers' brands, which implied they had been acquired at auction. Most of the rest looked to be sailors from ships the Salt Pirates had captured.

One of the handlers stalked down the line with a pole, swinging at testicles, evaluating how vigorously the owners twisted or dodged to avoid a direct hit. One poor skeleton of a fellow didn't dodge at all, just took it and then tried feebly to breathe. The handler gutted him and moved on to the next in the line. After the fallen man was done twitching, the handler's two juvenile assistants sawed off his foot to free it from the shackle and dragged the remains to the sty to fatten the pigs.

Coil muttered something under his breath. Azure's knife hand twitched.

Fortunately the worst was already over. The handlers, having apparently satisfied themselves that the remaining slaves might have a chance of surviving the two-day walk to Salt Town, unbound the wrists of their charges and threw down what appeared to be piles of dirty rags at their feet.

"Put them on," the handler growled.

The slaves stared at the piles as if unsure they were hearing correctly. But as whips cracked, they picked up what proved to be cowls and cloaks of rude handspun.

Azure was surprised. Providing slaves with clothing was an expense. She decided the investment must be worth it. No doubt even the dark-skinned natives of the Steaming Lands would not survive in open salt pits without coverings of some sort. The pale antlermen at the end of the line might not last a day.

A chain of a dozen women was prodded into a corner of the yard. Intended for indoor labor, they were left naked. Both groups of slaves, though, were given gourds of water and millet porridge served atop banana leaves. Every individual eagerly seized his or her portion, but some of the former sailors chewed as if they had forgotten what it was like to have food between their teeth.

Azure had been thinking of having some millet porridge. She ate some yoghurt and dates instead.

The sun sank. The shadow of the high ridges stretched eastward and met the sea. Eventually the dust of the inland trade road cooled enough that lizards crept out of their dens and began reconnoitering the piles of camel dung in search of insects. The master of the caravan blew his ram's horn and the company set out.

The port they were leaving was called Titan's Crack. Azure considered it well named. The rockfaces on either side of the road were rough and pitted. No ancient river had made this canyon. The caravan was journeying along a crack in the very body of the continent. The plateau had somehow split apart.

To her astonishment, Azure smelled wet rock. Whatever moisture the formation possessed emerged down here in the depths of the fissure. Azure spotted a second and then a third place where the lower cliffsides were veined with seepage. She now knew what filled the natural cistern beneath the walls of the harbor—the supply of drinking water that sustained not only Titan's Crack, but Salt Town as well.

She saw no true waterfalls. And as the camels plodded onward into the night, the impression of humidity vanished.

~o0o~

Before midnight, they smelled brimstone. By the time the caravan paused a couple of hours later to cast away a slave who had not been strong enough for the journey after all, Coil's nostrils were raw from the stench. He had mocked Azure when she had taken out a handkerchief, soaked it in perfume, and made it into a veil for her lower face, but when she prepared another for him, he took it and thanked her humbly.

"The wind will change soon," said the nearest camel drover as he rubbed liniment on the abraded ribs of one of his beasts. "That will help. A little."

The drover, a leathery, whip-thin Rhirzadi of the Ibex Hills, had laughed and called the dead slave vulture meat when he had fallen, but he seemed well-disposed toward Coil and Azure. Coil welcomed his insights. He and his milk sister had seen a thousand places in their travels, but this was as out of their element as they had ever been.

The drover was correct. Eventually the temperature of the continent dropped low enough to draw marine air inland. Soon the breeze was carrying away the worst of the acidic miasma.

Dawn was purpling the horizon behind them but stars still shone in the west when the ram's horn blew again, signalling a halt. To Coil, this seemed premature. He had expected the caravan to push on at least until sunrise, if not an hour or two into the day.

"Last good spot to camp," the drover explained.

The handlers goaded the male slaves down a channel to the right. Coil and Azure stayed with the camels and the female slaves, seeking their shelter off to the left. They soon came to a natural hollow surrounded on three sides by rock outcroppings. It was a place where there would be shade available during every part of the day as long as they rearranged themselves from time to time.

The sun was up but the air still tolerable when Coil and Azure climbed to the top of one of the outcroppings. Out to the west spread the terrain through which they were to travel the next day.

Here was the heart of the Desert of Fumes.

The trade road snaked between one hellish feature after another, bleached bones of camels and humans delineating the route. Vapors rose from the cracked landscape. Magma glowed in a pair of fissures off to the south. To the north a dozen hotsprings throbbed, the oily contents never lying still. The nearest pools were dense turquoise. Farther away they were the shade of emeralds lit from within. Both types were crusted at the edges with mineral mats—their hues of orange, blood rose, and pus yellow too vibrant to seem natural. Hardened-lava ridges thrust up out of the sands as though the mummified corpse of a giant crocodile lurked below, leaving only the sunburnt ridges of its back revealed to the surface world.

Beyond the jumbled terrain, the land descended into a vast basin. Coil was good enough at judging elevations that he knew its rim was at the same level as the tideline back at Titan's Crack. Twelve hours earlier he had stood at the gates of the caravanserai and looked east and seen the ocean—an endless expanse of water. Now he was viewing a place so dry its sea had evaporated.

Somewhere down at the bottom of the basin, lost in the sulfurous haze, was Salt Town.

~o0o~

The next night was the longest Azure could recall experiencing in her one-and-twenty years. The moonlight crafted baleful shadows out of the macabre landscape. Coarse bits of lava crunched uncomfortably beneath her sandals, the desert winds having blown them onto what should have been a track worn benign by centuries of caravan traffic.

They marched and they marched. The handlers and drovers pressed hard, cracking the lash to lengthen the gait of the slaves and camels. No shelter awaited until they reached Salt Town. Go too slow, and they would be caught in the open when next the sun climbed high.

Even though the temperature dropped steadily throughout the night, the air remained oppressive, because as they descended into the basin, they passed below the winds. The air puddled like lead in a crucible, the rim of higher terrain blocking any current that might stir the layers trapped within the bowl. The perfumed veil was not enough. Azure breathed in particles that desert air was not supposed to contain, material that burned her throat, dried her nostrils, fouled the taste of her tongue. But the worst was what it did to her eyes.

Coil bore it without comment. As always. So did she, but only because complaining would have required her to open her mouth and let in more of the foulness.

Despite a pace that made three of the slaves drop dead, they were short of their goal when dawn arrived. A crepuscular glow spread across the basin floor.

"What is *that*?" asked her milk brother.

A chaotic maze of buildings emerged from the gloom. Azure had seen oasis towns of mud-brick walls, and this had that look, but the chief building material was not clay or sandstone, but salt, as if the seafloor had grown strange blocky pustules during its final evaporative decay.

A massive tower rose high from the core of the outpost. Azure guessed it was as much as a dozen times the height of the inn where she and Coil had spent their first eight years of life. A pavilionlike canopy of stiffened leather supplied life-preserving shade to the lookout platform at the top. In silhouette the structure possessed a disturbing non-architectural aspect. It reminded Azure of the corpse toadstool she had seen a year ago when she and Coil had been forced to flee across the Fever Bogs to escape the giants—except that lethal fungus had only stood as high as her ankle.

Aside from the canopy, the tower was constructed of fine veined marble. Bringing the material here from the coast and assembling the building must have taken years and cost the lives of a thousand slaves.

"That," she murmured, "is what we came here to find."

The daylight strengthened further, revealing that though the outpost might be another half hour's walk away, the caravan had already entered the mining zone. Broad, shallow pits sprawled on either side of the road. She spotted several crews of slaves prying cakes of salt from the ground and stacking them into pyramids. Elsewhere another crew was disassembling a pyramid and loading cakes into the panniers of waiting camels. Drovers were urging fully loaded camels toward shelter.

Work ended with the sunrise. The slaves began plodding toward their blockhouses, which like the outpost were constructed of salt bricks. They seemed alive only by comparison to the piles of bones where past workers had fallen. Vultures clustered around a pair that had succumbed that very night.

193

Azure shaded her sore eyes, trying to spot the far end of the excavations. She thought she saw it, but given the distance and the haze, she couldn't be sure.

"How long have people been digging salt here?" Coil asked the drover.

"Longer than men remember," replied the Rhirzadi, blowing road grit out from between his remaining teeth. "One warlord after another fought to control this place. Seventy years ago the pirates took it from the chieftains of the Gnarled Hills. Nobody called them the Salt Pirates until then. Now they'd rather die, every last one of 'em, than let this jewel be pilfered from their hoard."

The drover jerked a thumb at the tower. "There's always a prince of the cartel up there keepin' an eye on things. They rotate out every couple of years. None of 'em want to be posted here, of course, but they don't trust underlings to run the place."

Azure had heard the tales of how rich the salt trade had made the pirates. She readily understood why they would hold tightly to their prize. What astounded her was that any person had ever been insane enough to explore this basin in the first place.

~o0o~

The first thing Coil did when he woke that evening was drink an entire flagon of water. Even that was not enough to rinse away the taste of dust. He opened one of the kegs, refilled the flagon to the brim, and set the flagon beside Azure's pallet. Returning to his own pallet, he began working on what remained in the keg.

Moonlight shone brightly through the grillwork of the window of the coop the innkeeper had rented them. As he sipped, Coil contemplated the stack of kegs in the corner—their entire supply, transferred from their camels as the last thing they accomplished before collapsing for the day. How inadequate it seemed.

Azure murmured and sat up. She, too, went straight for the flagon, taking huge, unladylike gulps.

Coil considered lighting the oil lamp, but Azure was as wilted as she had ever been aside from that time they'd been poisoned in Murk Hollow. He decided she would prefer to have whatever illusion of grace the dimness preserved.

"Will it *ever* get cooler?" she whined.

"It has to," he said. "But once that happens, patrons will start wandering in downstairs. If we're going to look around before our shift, we need to head out soon."

They put on street clothes, broke their fast on raisins and roasted locusts, and tried to stretch out the stiffness from their roadsore muscles. Then they headed out the back door of the inn and began threading through the lanes of Salt Town.

Whenever they met someone going the other way, they were forced to squeeze by. The gaps between the buildings were narrow, the better to preserve shade during the day. Given the canopies on most windows, a rat would be able to travel from one end of Salt Town to the other and never touch the ground.

They stumbled across the pens without meaning to. Coil suspected they would have found more of the same no matter which quarter of the outpost they explored. Camel drovers, mercenary guards, and slave overseers lined up at the entrance. They handed over their whore chits to the doorkeep, who let them in one by one whenever a man already inside exited a stall.

In any other town, except perhaps the desperate ports along the Kraken Sea or the hovels of Lotus City, a building such as this would be a stable for livestock. But then, in any other city one might see weavers at their looms, children running after stray chickens, maidens helping their old grandfathers to the meditation house.

They continued on to their goal. They found it at the very center of Salt Town, surrounded by a circular plaza of stone pavement, standing tall as no human-made building had a right to stand, straining for the moon like the phallus of a buried god.

Whatever lookout might be stationed at the uppermost platform had lit no lamp—the better for his night vision, Coil surmised. He and Azure made sure not to step out into the plaza where he might spot them.

Lamplight did flicker through some of the windows. The lowest of those was five times as high as Coil could reach if he stood on his toes, and none were big enough to squeeze through.

The only ways in were the grand entrance and two service portals around back. Burly guards stood at each opening, and in the absence of anyone going in and out, the grates had been lowered.

"No going in the hard way," Coil said. "The soft way it is."

"It seems so," Azure sighed.

That was unfortunate. The soft way would take time. And luck.

They made one complete circuit of the outpost so that they would have their bearings. They soon found themselves back at the inn. The window of their little room looked down on them. The first patrons were ambling into the ground-floor tavern, parting the strings of beads that hung halfway down the arched entrance.

Coil paused outside. He studied the building.

"You're thinking of home," Azure said.

"I am," he replied. "I was thinking how this could never be like Mama's." His foster mother's establishment had catered to a neverending series of overnight guests, but its kitchen and back rooms had nevertheless been a sanctuary—as good a family space as any boy could ask for. Or it had been until that one awful night.

This inn was no home. No place in Salt Town was home to any person. People came here to Salt Town to work. They came to die. No one came here to live.

~oOo~

Coil showed off his rope tricks and his knife juggling. Azure sang ribald songs of the barge wenches of Reedy River. But for most of the evening, Coil played his sevenflute while Azure danced. Around them guards and drovers and off-duty cooks drank and gambled among themselves for scrip or whore chits. Finally the right prospect turned up: A guard sat down alone at a table. By his third ale he was gazing up and down Azure's curves in a way that said he had sought his release in the pens so many times in a row he wanted to prove to himself a woman would be with him of her own accord.

Coil drew the accompaniment to a close. Azure slowed her

movements to finish her last pose just as the last languid note of the flute faded below human hearing.

Coil put away his instrument and found a seat along the wall. The innkeeper brought him an ale. He and Azure did not make eye contact.

"You and your fellow having a lover's spat?" the guard asked.

Azure glided casually across the dais toward the guard's table. "He's not my lover. He's my milk brother."

"Ah. So, are you saying he won't be jealous if you spend time with me?"

"Something like that," she responded. "But I don't show favor to just any man."

He moved to a bench near the edge of the dance dais. "I expect I'm up to your standards."

Azure tilted an eyebrow at him. "And what makes you special?"

"I'm a tower guard. You won't find me sweatin' out there in the salt fields, whippin' slaves all night."

"Mildly impressive." She propped his knees together and sat sideways across his lower thighs.

He raised his hand toward her chest. His grin faded when she stuck her talon thimble into his questing palm.

"Ow!"

"Anyone can be a tower guard," she chided. "Tell me something *interesting*."

"I can nick a bluefly off a camel's ass with my scimitar, and the camel wouldn't even feel it."

"I'll keep that in mind next time my camel needs that."

"I can out-drink any man here."

She yawned.

"I've seen the prince's new plaything. The daughter of the stormwitch."

Azure shrugged. "I don't believe she's actually in there. If she were, how would *you* see her? I'm sure the only guards with access to her are eunuchs. Oh!" She eyed his crotch. "Are you a eunuch?"

"I didn't say I *guard* her, now did I? I saw her in the cage when she was brought in. Lovely little thing, she was. Fresh into her womanhood. He's one lucky man, that admiral prince. He's having her trained in the arts of the harem. Sends her to the baths every afternoon so she's fresh for him when evening comes. Sends her to the baths again when he's done what he likes."

"There are *baths* in Salt Town? You make me laugh."

"There are in the tower. The master of Salt Town can have anything he wants. He has water brought in fresh every day. Sends the dregs off to the camel troughs and slave cisterns. If you're a pirate lord, even Salt Town has its luxuries."

She scooted a bit further up his thighs. Leaned in a little. "You really saw her?"

"With my own eyes." He put his hand on one of her knees. She let it stay there.

"The Salt Pirates are taking a risk, taunting the witch that way."

The guard snorted. "She's toothless."

"That's not what I heard."

"You know what the prince is going to do? When he's tired of the sweetling, he'll send her to the pens. Even I might have a chance at her when that happens. He'll send her to the pens like he sent the witch herself there when she was the same age. She couldn't stop him then. She won't be able to stop him this time."

Over at his table, Coil had been reading the man's lips. His eyes widened.

Azure disguised her own shock by tilting forward until her mouth was only the span of a finger away from the guard's ear. "Now that's story to stir me," she cooed. "Find me when my shift is done."

She rose. Coil began to play his sevenflute. She resumed her dancing. The guard leaned back against the table, grinning like a fool.

~oOo~

By the time their workshift ended, the fool was snoring on the floor, a little beyond drunk thanks to the dose of slumberlock Azure had slipped into his tankard.

Coil and Azure cleared out of their room. By the time dawn

came and the populace went to ground to wait out the onslaught of heat, the milk siblings were tucked into a hiding place in the warehouse caves near the plaza, where the pirate prince's barrels of water were stored.

No more inn. No more flute playing and dancing. They had found the soft way in. All they had to do was wait until late afternoon. They slept in shifts while the hours passed.

The sentries at the tower service portal were wilted and sluggish of attention in the late afternoon when Coil and Azure rolled the water cart up to the grate wearing the livery of tower servants, cowls shading their faces. The men raised the grate and waved them through. Even a brief check would have revealed the pair were not the same tandem that had left a short while earlier to fetch the load from the caves.

They were likewise ignored as they turned down a passageway, guided by the scrape marks of thousands of such deliveries, and came to the hoist. No one noticed that Coil and Azure neglected to transfer their cargo. They stepped onto the platform bringing only a backpack and the short staff Coil had hidden between the barrels.

They tugged hard on the pulley ropes. Meant for raising much heavier loads than the two of them, the elevator raced upward— faster even than they could have run up the stairs.

At the first landing, they saw larder supplies and heard the banging of pots and clatter of knives on chopping boards. An appetizing odor wafted toward them. They did not pause in their ascent.

Thirty heartbeats later the hoist reached the uppermost landing. A guard was lounging on the floor beside his bench, sucking on a pipe as long as curved as a cobra contemplating a strike. The stench of fivefold leaf, sweet as new manure, pervaded the chamber.

The guard opened his eyes. Coil burst from the lift. He got to the man before he could rise. The pipe had barely fallen out of the way when Coil plunged his dagger beneath the man's chin and twisted the blade.

Azure rushed past, her own knife held ready. She stopped at

the threshold of the next room, glance darting right and left.

"Clear," she whispered.

Coil grabbed his short staff from the lift platform. He took the lead again.

As expected, they found these upper reaches of the tower, the intimate domain of the pirate lord, were mostly empty. They ran into no further delays on their way to the baths.

Their destination was not hard to locate. The passageways virtually sang out that somewhere nearby, water was caressing air. All they had to do was trust that feeling. Two floors down Coil turned a corner and spotted an ornate double door. In front of it, a eunuch guard and a harem matron were conversing.

The guard chose the wrong move. He pulled out his scimitar. That gave Coil the chance to charge forward and plunge the end of his staff into the man's sternum. The eunuch's lungs emptied, ended his chance to shout.

Unfortunately, the matron had the sense to scream. The noise lasted only a moment before Azure body-slammed into her midsection, but it was *loud.* As was the sound of her skull hitting the door behind her.

Coil didn't even take the time to curse. Speed was the only cure. Coil knocked aside the scimitar. The eunuch, though breathless, parried Coil's first swipe at his head, but not the second. An instant later the fellow slumped over the matron's limp form.

Coil and Azure flung the doors open and burst into a gloriously appointed chamber. Sunken, tile-lined pools took up both of the far corners. Light through stained-glass windows illuminated the chamber's only occupant. She was standing thigh deep in the larger pool.

The girl had less nomad blood in her, but no one who had ever seen Lady Sirocco would doubt that this was her daughter. The difference was Lady Sirocco wore a mantle that said Step Back. This gracile beauty wore one that said Join Me.

She did not seem startled to see them.

"I'm Coil," said Coil. He almost stammered. "This is Azure. We're here to rescue you. We have to move quickly."

He tossed her the washcloth from the pool's edge. It was the only item in the whole chamber other than the girl herself. There were no towels in Salt Town.

The girl waded up the ledges of the pool, shook the excess moisture from her feet, and gestured for them to lead on.

~oOo~

Almost all of the tower sentries were stationed at the bottom. So Coil headed up, sprinting. The girl was right at his heels. Azure was slow only in the sense that she spared occasional glances behind to check for pursuers.

None yet.

She heard Coil shout as he reached the lookout platform. She leaped up the last few steps two at a time and found her milk brother squared off against a single sentry.

The defender ignored Azure, naturally assuming that Coil was the threat. He did not expect Azure's knife throw. Her blade sank deep into the side of his neck.

Reflex made the man pull the knife out. Wrong move. Blood poured from the wound. His eyes glazed over. He fell back.

The twitching was soon done. Azure retrieved her knife from the dead man's loose grip.

"Let me."

To Azure's surprise, the girl wiped the blood off Azure's blade with the washcloth. After making sure she had rubbed away every trace of crimson, she handed the weapon back to Azure and tossed the washcloth onto the corpse.

"I'm Zephyr," she said.

Azure blinked. "Puh-pleased to meet you," she stammered, composure ruined precisely because she was striving so hard to retain it.

"Please tell me you have my mother's flying carpet."

Coil pulled off his backpack. He and Azure pulled out the requested item and spread it out on the bricks, careful not to let the edge slip into the spreading blood.

The carpet was silk. Thin. It was clearly not meant as something to tread upon. Its lightness and lack of bulk meant it could be—and indeed had been—folded many times and made compact. Unfurled, it was twice as long as Coil was tall, and nearly as great in width. Its designs were lavish and intricate.

"Your mother said you would know how to make it work," Coil said.

Zephyr knelt near the center. "Sit beside me," she instructed.

No sooner had she uttered the words that the sound of heavy footfalls began reverberating ever more loudly up the stairs. Coil and Azure took their places.

Zephyr caressed the fabric just in front of her knees, her fingers tracing the outline of a roc flying over a wasteland of high dunes. "To my mother, wherever she is. Go!"

The carpet lifted them as if it were as solid as a ship deck. They glided smoothly out from beneath the cap of the toadstool, heading northeast.

No sooner had they emerged into sunlight than guards poured onto the tower platform. They shouted as they spotted the carpet and its passengers.

Two of them were carrying bows.

"Make it go faster!" Coil said.

Zephyr winced. "It always starts slow."

Coil grabbed the girl and flung her sideways with him. An arrow sped through the place where they had been, opening a slice in one of his sleeves. Azure pulled them the other way just in time to avoid the second shot.

The archers nocked again and fired. This time the arrows fell short. A pair of antlermen with their longbows would have had a chance, but the guards of Salt Town had only the short bows of the deserts, meant for firing from the backs of horses or camels.

In the streets below, other guards spotted them. One or two rushed to find bows of their own, but by the time they reached their armories, Azure and Coil and the stormwitch's waif were well past the edges of the outpost.

"You're safe now," Coil told the girl.

For the first time, the youngster trembled. She curled up against Coil. He instinctively wrapped his arms around her. It worked. Azure saw the girl's breathing ease.

Slow though the acceleration was, the carpet's speed

increased at a steady rate until they were hurtling over the landscape at a rate that would humble any migratory bird. The wind of their passage whipped at their clothes—that is to say, at Coil's and Azure's clothes—mitigating the sun's fierce kiss. Azure lay down to keep her hair from whipping around her face. She studied the way her milk brother was nestling Zephyr. She studied Zephyr being nestled.

It was the strangest thing. She didn't know which one she envied more.

~o0o~

The sun had been low in the sky when they made their escape. But so fast did they travel, the orb had barely dropped below the horizon when they passed over the eastern rim of the great basin. Below sprawled the convoluted heart of the Desert of Fumes.

That landscape, fully visible in the glow of early twilight, was *changing*.

A rumble grew. It was a sound deeper than any Coil had ever heard. His ears were not sufficient to perceive it. It smote like a thundercrack but lasted far longer. It grabbed him by the skull and spine and shook him.

Suddenly the carpet shot straight up, pummeled by a blast of air. Its magic kept it stable and none of the riders fell off, but it felt as though a Titan had swatted them. The girl screamed and pressed even harder against Coil.

"Can this be happening?" Azure squeaked.

Belatedly Coil saw what she had, and no, it did not seem possible—the plateau was tearing asunder right along the route the caravan had taken. The northern side of the canyon heaved upward, then downward, then both sides separated.

They separated all the way from the coast to the rim of the basin. Sea water rushed into the gap, heading west.

"It's my mother's doing," the girl moaned.

"She's strong enough to *split the earth*?" Coil blurted. "How does a sorceress get power like that?"

"She lay with a djinn."

"In that case," Azure commented, "she must have been *very* good in bed."

203

~oOo~

The devastation played out at a tortoise pace, if only because the scale was so tremendous. The surge of ocean water reached the basin and diffused into an ever-widening flood. Within hours it would reach the lowest point—Salt Town—and would begin restoring the sea that eons of evaporation had stolen. As yet, the denizens of the outpost might not even be aware yet of their doom, though certainly they must have felt the quake. But even if they knew, they could not save themselves—not without some fantastical means such as the carpet. No camel or man would be able to flee all the way to the rim before the water would catch up. Well before midnight this very night, the only spot in Salt Town left above the waves would be the top part of the tower. Azure could already see in her mind the desperate men storming the entrances, guards just as desperately fighting to deny them entry.

Would the pirate prince wait to be thrown from the top? Would he jump of his own volition? Or if his defenses held, would he simply wait until the waters inevitably closed over his head?

Azure struggled to feel sorrow for the soon-to-be victims. The closest she could come was pity for the slaves, but she believed every one of their number would welcome a quick end to their misery. The truth was she was not sorry they would die. She was angry that *someone had killed them.*

Coil met her glance. The light was dimming, but she read his eyes as well as she ever had, from the time they had suckled at opposite breasts to now. His thoughts were a mirror of hers:

They were part of this, but they could not fix it.

The remainder of the journey through the flight was uncomfortably quiet. Neither she nor Coil felt like speaking. After the carpet had carried them beyond the clouds of dust and steam thrown up by the upheaval, she expected Zephyr to bubble over with expressions of gratitude, or at least to sob with relief. But the girl stayed tucked against Coil, her eyes closed, brow deeply furrowed.

The carpet took them north. Only when they were well

beyond the region affected by the devastation did their speed drop. Finally they were deposited gently on a moonlit stretch of sand beside a riverbed. A riparian stand of woolwood trees showed how different an area this was. Sand and stone predominated and the river had no water at the moment, but clearly rain blessed the place often enough that trees could persist.

Tucked among the woolwoods was the stormwitch's pavilion. The flaps parted and the sorceress herself emerged.

Coil helped Zephyr to stand. He had to nudge her to get her to take a few steps forward. Azure helped her milk brother fold up the carpet while Lady Sirocco completed her approach.

She took her daughter's chin in her hand, tilted her head right and left, checked her backside for lash marks. Made sure her mouth still had teeth.

"I warned you they might catch you," she scolded.

"You did," Zephyr mumbled.

"I will speak to you later. Go dress yourself," the sorceress commanded, jerking her chin at the pavilion.

Head down, the girl did as she was bid.

Azure thought of the tears that would pour if she returned to her mother, if only her mother still lived. Lady Sirocco was not even smiling.

Her tone was brighter than normal, though, when she addressed Coil and Azure. "You have pleased me beyond my expectations. Your debt is paid. In addition, you may name a reward."

Azure was caught off guard by the generosity. Coil, fortunately, was quicker witted. He held up the carpet.

Oh! Now wouldn't that make their quest ... possible.

Lady Sirocco frowned. "I will never make another like it. I haven't the years to devote to it. Are you sure you will not take gold or jewels?"

"We've had gold and jewels before," Coil said. So true, thought Azure. And somehow each time ended up with empty purses a fortnight later.

"Very well. I am a woman of my word. In the spirit of

gratitude, I should warn you it will only fly three more times, no matter who owns it."

That was unfortunate, Azure thought, but magic always had its flaws. "How far will it take us per trip?"

"As near or as far as you request. But have a care not to fall asleep, or it may take you to lands our sun has never shone upon."

The woman shifted her gaze to the dark horizon. Her focus was beyond it. Azure knew she had taken such a journey. So— there was something that could unnerve the Witch of Storms, after all.

"We will take it anyway," Coil said. Azure nodded.

~o0o~

They did not linger by the river. Lady Sirocco gifted them with a pack camel and supplies and they set out, letting the river channel serve as their marker. Their water and feed would easily get them to the next oasis.

They could have used the carpet, of course, but they had no particular place to go. They agreed it was better to save it for journeys that required its contribution.

They did not press hard. They'd had enough of grueling marches lately. But neither did they lag, because both wanted to put some distance between them and Lady Sirocco's camp. They waited until midnight before pausing at a bend in the river where driftwood had piled high—enough wood for a cookfire, as the circles of stone and charcoal of previous visitors amply demonstrated.

Hot porridge struck them as a dose of normalcy they'd not had in many meals. They'd not had hot food in days, not having wanted anything that would make them feel warmer than they already were. They made the fire, brought water to a boil, waited for the grain to soften. It felt so familiar Coil almost was able to speak. But he did not, nor did Azure say anything more than a clipped "Here," or "Thank you," or "More?"

After the second helping was in his belly, he thought maybe he could try. But no. Instead, he lay back on the sand and stared at the stars. To the south they were occluded, but to the north they were undimmed.

He stood up suddenly, almost before he knew why he was sitting up.

Azure stood as well. "What is it?"

"A camel."

The sound of two-toed feet on sand was now unmistakable.

Too late to smother the fire. Whoever was out there had seen the light source. They palmed their knives and waited.

It was Zephyr. Her garments altered her appearance, but even in the moonlight—and then, the firelight—Azure recognized the scintillant black hair, the supple spine.

She was alone.

The girl pulled her mount to a halt in front of them. They helped her down. She was sweating and shaking, a display of jitters wholly unlike the calm fugitive who had fled with them from the tower.

"Take me with you!" she blurted.

"But...your mother," Coil said.

"I can't stay with *her*."

Now this was a road of quicksand, Azure thought. They had seen very well what sort of thing Lady Sirocco did to people who kidnapped her daughter. Not that she and Coil were kidnappers, but Lady Sirocco would make no distinction.

They would be on the run forever.

"Stay with us," Azure found herself saying. "Stay with *us*."

She turned to Coil. He looked as though the camel had just eaten his thumb.

"Please?" she said.

"Please?" repeated Zephyr.

He filled his lungs. Azure knew his answer when he did not shout, but let the breath go in one long sigh.

He strode to the pack camel and freed it from its hobbles. He swatted it on the rump to send it on its way. The girl's stolen camel clumped off in tandem.

Next he went to the pile of supplies he would under other circumstances have been loading onto the beast he'd dismissed. He pulled out the carpet, unfurled it, and let it settle to the ground.

"Death is certain, sooner or later," he said. "Why have a dull life along the way?"

Azure took Zephyr by the hand. They sat on the carpet. Coil knelt beside them. He touched the embroidered roc over the dunes and whispered a destination that only he—and the carpet—could hear. Azure wondered where he had chosen.

The carpet obeyed. Away they went.

STRENGTH, WISDOM, AND COMPASSION

by Julia H. West

One of the great things about Julia's stories is her talent for coming up with new types of magic from simple things. Her story "Soul Walls" in SWORD & SORCERESS 24 used painting, along with Hopi (Native America) culture. In this story she's using baths, something most of us probably don't consider magical. Of course, baptism can be regarded as a magical ritual—I'm an Episcopalian, living in the Diocese of California, so I can say that with fearing that my bishop will want to have a long talk with me. But we baptize by sprinkling water over a baby's forehead (or an adult's, if the adult was not baptised as a baby). Julia comes from a church that uses full immersion for baptism, which may possibly have contributed to the idea.

Julia H. West is most often found covered with cats, which makes it very difficult for her to use her keyboard. During the rare occasions she manages to evade the felines, she writes science fiction and fantasy stories, which have been published in such magazines as *Realms of Fantasy* and *Spider*, and the anthologies *Enchanted Forests* and *The Shimmering Door*, as well as two earlier volumes of *Sword & Sorceress*. Most of her previously-published stories, including the tale of a Micronesian navigating a starship through interstellar danger that won her the Grand Prize for Writers of the Future XI, are available from Callihoo Publishing. You can discover more about her writing on her website at http://juliahwest.com.

Scented steam rose from the enameled tub in the bathhouse behind the witch Hyacinth's cottage. "Renata," Hyacinth said as Queen Renata disrobed, neatly folding her clothing on a bench,

"I beg of you. Reconsider now, before it's too late."

The queen turned a serene face to the witch. "Hyacinth, I've made my decision. Everyone in Orthefell suffered when Terzo killed my husband and declared himself king. When he decided to seal that kingship by marrying me, this became necessary."

Hyacinth lowered her voice. "This is likely to be more dangerous to the child growing within you than to you, at this stage. This child is all you have left of Bhaltair."

"Both he and I will need strength to survive under Terzo's rule," Renata said, voice rough. She stepped onto the stool beside the tub and let herself down into the orange-tinged water. It rose along her body as she slid down, until she sat nearly neck deep. She ran her fingers through her long chestnut hair, unraveling its braids, letting it float on the water's surface.

Hyacinth, a plain woman who looked no more than twenty years old but was much older, sighed. It was done, and she could not call back her actions now. The queen had chosen her path.

Renata took a deep breath and slid completely beneath the water, hair slowly sinking to stick in thick clumps on her shoulders. After a long time she surfaced. Water droplets, now bereft of color and scent, ran down her pale face.

"Is it done?" she asked.

"Yes, Your Majesty," Hyacinth said.

"Don't call me 'Your Majesty'. You were my nurse long before I was Bhaltair's wife. Long before Terzo coveted our kingdom. To you, I will always be simply Renata."

Hyacinth sighed again. She shouldn't make a habit of that; people didn't like their witch sounding like a lovesick girl. "Yes, Renata. You can come out now." She steadied the queen as she stepped out of the tub, then handed her a towel so she could dry herself.

Once the queen's body was dry, Hyacinth wrapped her still-damp hair in the towel and helped her into her shift. Renata stood barefoot on the bathhouse's warm tiles while Hyacinth combed her hair and braided it expertly into all its tiny plaits, then coiled it atop Renata's head. She helped the queen into her bridal splendor—gown of gold silk and pearls, overgown of cream silk and diamonds, robe of midnight blue adorned with cream lace at throat and cuffs. Last of all, Hyacinth pinned the crown into the coil of braids so that it would not slip.

Silently, Hyacinth held the queen's train as she took the stone-paved path to the road where her carriage, her armed escort, and her attendants waited. Before Renata ascended into the carriage, Hyacinth kissed her on the cheek. "Be well, love," she said, and turned away quickly, hurrying into her house. She didn't want Renata to see the tears brimming in her eyes.

~oOo~

Hyacinth stayed in her cottage the rest of the day, mixing spells and ignoring the sounds of celebration—trumpets, drums, muskets firing into the air. Her little Renata, who had been so happy with King Bhaltair, was now married to the usurper Terzo.

Hyacinth didn't see Renata again for a month. People came to her for spells—a woman who wanted beauty, a man who craved virility, the merchant who wished for luck, the poet who desired a muse. She explained the price of each spell—both in coin and in the spell's toll on each of them. "Is not your own native talent enough?" she asked the poet. "No one can know what toll the spell will take on you. What if you lose your eyesight in payment? Or perhaps the use of your hands?"

"I'll take the risk," he answered. "When I compose poems that bewitch the ladies, that make the nobles weep and shower gold on me—what will it matter? For then I will be wealthy, and can hire a scribe to write out the gems I speak."

Thus it had been throughout Hyacinth's life. Each person who wanted a spell was determined. What matter the future? They were concerned only with the now. So, because she was a witch, and that was her talent and destiny, she mixed the ingredients, heated the water, and prepared the bath.

The merchant took his spell packet home, to use in his own bath, but those who didn't want it known they'd purchased a spell, or had no bath at home, used Hyacinth's bathhouse. She only knew what toll the spell had taken when her eyesight became sharper, her hair more luxurious, or her face in the mirror younger.

Queen Renata summoned Hyacinth to the palace on the first day of the Month of Blooming. The witch dressed in her best, and set out on the long walk to the palace.

The changes that had taken place in the city since last she had walked this way disturbed Hyacinth. Once-prosperous shops had closed, armed and uniformed men stood on nearly every corner, and citizens walked quickly, peering nervously over their shoulders.

When she arrived at the palace and was escorted by four well-armed men to the queen's rooms, she felt shabby and out of place. Renata was surrounded by beautiful women in gowns of lace and jewels, who gossiped with high fluting voices and chirped their artificial laughter. It had not been so when Renata had been married to Bhaltair. She had worn simple wool except for state occasions, and ridden through the city on her own horse, and when she laughed, it had been a hearty guffaw. She had surrounded herself with capable and intelligent companions.

"Wise Woman Hyacinth," Renata said, and the witch was glad to hear that the Queen's voice had not suddenly shot up an octave. "I am with child. In eight months, I will require someone to care for the new prince or princess, and I thought naturally of my old nurse."

Hyacinth took a deep breath. So the child had survived the spell bath, and Renata had let the doctors examine her and discover her pregnancy. "Surely, Your Majesty, there are more suitable nurses," her gaze traveled over the twittering beauties surrounding the queen, "than I."

"None of my ladies has children of her own," Renata said. She met Hyacinth's gaze and wrinkled her nose. The witch knew they had chosen to remain childless for the sake of beauty spells. "They know nothing of child care. But you raised me. None would wish to deprive me of your expertise."

"In that case, Your Majesty, I accept, and thank you for your regard."

"I will have rooms prepared for you as I lay out the nursery. When they are complete, I'm sure you'd like to go over them, to see they are to your satisfaction. I'll send for you then." Briskly,

Renata waved the lace fan she held.

Hyacinth wished she could talk to Renata without her twittering retinue. The queen had always been energetic. She had excelled at riding and hunting, and spent much of every day out of doors. But now, she had a restless energy that seemed too great for the room she occupied. Others might think it her joy in her pregnancy that put the bloom in her cheeks. Hyacinth knew better. The spell bath she had taken on the day of her marriage had not been for beauty, as her husband-to-be had been told, but for strength. If only she could know what its toll had been on the queen—and on the child she carried.

"Thank you, Your Majesty." Hyacinth curtsied and kissed the Queen's hand. As she stood, she realized Renata had slipped a scrap of paper into her hand. She didn't acknowledge it, merely left the room with her armed escort.

~o0o~

Hyacinth waited until she was in her own snug cottage to look at the note Renata had given her. "Wisdom! She wants a spell for wisdom!" Her cat, Pot Pie, raised his head from where he'd been napping in the sunshine warming her work table, thinking she was talking to him. "She knows as well as I do that the great abstracts are the hardest spells. Wisdom!"

She slumped into one of the sturdy wooden chairs and put her head in her arms on the table. "Wisdom," she said, through the tears that soaked into the sleeves of her best gown. "Oh, Renata."

A long time later, Hyacinth got up, shooed Pot Pie off her table, and began pulling books from the shelves, looking for the spell she needed. She had never prepared the spell for wisdom, and didn't know anyone else who had, either. She was certain there was one, but she was also certain the cost was immense. Could she substitute another spell—common sense, for instance? Of a certainty, a ruler could use common sense.

She found the spell in the old grimoire she'd inherited from the witch who had raised her. Poppy had written it in red ink—a sure sign that it was difficult and dangerous. Hyacinth copied it out. She didn't know how long it would take Renata to have rooms prepared for her in the palace, but she must start this spell now if she wished to have it complete by the time Renata called for her.

~oOo~

A month later, Hyacinth shooed Pot Pie away from the table where she was grinding more ingredients for the wisdom spell in her marble mortar. A vase nearby held fresh cut iris and lilies; she breathed their heady scent, but it didn't make her feel any better. She was grateful she was preparing this spell in spring, when the flowers were in bloom. Fresh flowers were so much more potent than dried ones.

She had been gathering ingredients, and brewing different parts of the spell bath, ever since the day Renata had requested it. The spell was nearly complete, and none too soon. Hyacinth had been summoned to the palace two days hence.

The flasks and tubing were purified and ready for use. She dropped flower petals and minced aloe leaves into a jar of pure almond oil, and heated them together over a flame. To the pale-green oil that dripped from the tubing she added exact amounts of four different powders—those which she had been preparing for a month—and heated it again. As the contents of the flask turned a glorious clear purple, Hyacinth removed it from the flame and carried it to the cool room.

When Hyacinth returned to the palace, she had the spell in her pocket in a bottle carved of alabaster. She hoped there would be some way to slip the bottle to Renata without anyone seeing it. Terzo would certainly not let his new wife take a spell bath while she was pregnant. Spell baths were more casually used in Vezienn, his homeland, so Hyacinth was sure Terzo knew the basics about spells and their effects. A spell bath taken by a pregnant woman endowed both mother and child with the desired quality; but both mother and child paid for the spell—and in different ways. Everyone had heard tales of deformed monsters born to women who had taken spell baths during pregnancy.

Renata had already used the spell for strength. There had been a good chance at the time that the spell would kill the barely formed child. But both mother and child were strong and healthy.

Hyacinth wondered, for the thousandth time, what toll the spell had taken on them both.

As Hyacinth walked beside Renata, going through the rooms that would be hers in the palace, she glanced sideways often. Renata's restless energy enhanced her natural beauty. That must please Terzo. More's the pity. Renata did stumble often, and once she ran into a doorjamb. It was rather too early in her pregnancy for it to affect her balance. Was Renata's clumsiness caused by the spell bath?

Renata opened the door to a small room, and as they passed through Hyacinth slipped the bottle into her hand, out of sight of the bored ladies following them. "You'll have to get rid of your companions somehow," she whispered to the queen. "This is a rather obvious purple, and has a strong—though very pleasant— odor. Anyone would guess what it is."

Renata nodded. "I'll do it if I have to get up in the darkest hour of the night and bathe in a bucket. Terzo will never know. He's too busy bedding those twittering beauties."

Hyacinth squeezed her hand. "Do take care. I still can't agree with what you're doing—"

"You live in this kingdom," came Renata's furious whisper. "Do you want Terzo and his offspring to rule you? My child must be strong enough to face whatever comes, and make a fine ruler in his own right. With strength and wisdom. . . ."

"I understand." Hyacinth's whisper was almost inaudible. She didn't remind Renata that there would be payment for the bath. The queen was fully aware of that.

~o0o~

Though she ached to know if Renata had been able to use the spell bath—and what its consequences had been—Hyacinth was not summoned to the palace again until two months before the queen's child was due. She—and Renata—knew that the child would be 'early,' but they hoped no one else suspected.

The palace was very different now than it had been during Bhaltair's rule. New tapestries on the walls, expensive carpet underfoot, and gaudy statuary and bric-a-brac cluttering the hall were probably the least of the changes.

Hyacinth was taken to the room where she had met Renata before. The queen paced awkwardly back and forth, surrounded by chattering ladies and their useless needlework. Hyacinth looked closely at the queen, trying to discover what price she had paid for wisdom. But she seemed well enough, though restless and clumsy. The child would be a large one, that was obvious.

When Hyacinth accompanied Renata to the nursery for a final check that all was well, the ladies didn't even bother to follow. What mischief could a woman who could hardly waddle get into?

"One more spell—and it must be soon," Renata told Hyacinth. "Compassion. No matter what happens to me—or you—a king with compassion *can't* be as greedy and selfish as Terzo is.

"But is this wise? The cost—"

"It doesn't matter to me what payment the spell exacts. The child is healthy and strong. He's big enough now that I could bear him today and he would thrive, so the midwife assures me."

Hyacinth closed her eyes, praying for strength. "We may not have time," she said. "I don't have that one prepared, and it takes weeks. And how will I get it to you?" Compassion was another difficult spell—although not nearly as complex as that for wisdom. Hyacinth had never made it, because few people wanted it. Why risk the inevitable loss of some other faculty to gain compassion?

"Start moving your belongings into your rooms here at the palace. You needn't come yet, but if you leave the spell somewhere, hidden but clearly labeled. . . ."

"The coffer you gave me when you were a child—the one with my initial on the lid," Hyacinth said. Ten-year-old Renata had carved the ornate 'H' into the wood herself. She would know it.

Renata gave a half smile. "Good." They passed back into the parlor, Hyacinth half supporting the queen, who was clumsier than ever. Renata said, as if continuing a conversation they had been having, "Then you will start sending your possessions to the palace in a week? The midwife says the child is so active it may come sooner than expected."

"Yes, Your Majesty."

"I'll send a cart, and porters."

"Thank you, Your Majesty."

~o0o~

The reality of her move to the palace was made all the clearer when she sent off a cartload of her books and clothing. Her friend Tamarisk would live in the cottage until the young prince—or princess—no longer needed a nurse and she could return to her private life. She was apprehensive about living in such close proximity to the new King Terzo. If he came to the nursery to visit 'his' child, she would be meek and as invisible as possible. To his sort, servants were usually invisible. Perhaps he would not remember that she was a witch.

On a cold and blustery day in the Month of Storms, a carriage came from the palace. The imposing individual who stepped down from it to tell her that the Queen requested her presence had to wait. Hyacinth fed Pot Pie and gave him a last hug, gathered a bundle of things she wanted to take, left a note for Tamarisk, and closed the door. She looked back on her cottage regretfully. She would miss it, miss the independence and ability to speak her mind. But Renata was giving up so much more, living with Terzo; Hyacinth could spare a few years of a long life to raise up the next ruler of Orthefell.

Armed men were everywhere in the streets now, and few people braved the cold and possibility of tangling with the king's troops. Hyacinth missed the laughter of children playing in the snow.

As the carriage drove through the palace's main gate, a maid scurried out to tell Hyacinth that Renata was calling for her. Hyacinth left her bundle in the carriage—either it would be taken to her rooms or not, she didn't care at this point—and hurried up the stairs to the Queen's rooms.

The lying in was attended only by women, as tradition demanded, and Renata had banned her twittering companions. The only people in the room were two stolid middle-aged maids and the midwife.

217

Renata sat, propped up with pillows, in bed. Though she was breathing quickly, she was far too still for Hyacinth's peace of mind. Where was the restless energy that had filled the queen the last time Hyacinth had seen her?

Renata looked up as Hyacinth entered, but did not smile at her until the witch was nearly at her bed. The way Renata squinted at her made Hyacinth wonder if clarity of eyesight had been the payment for one of the spells. "I'm—so glad—you're here," she panted. "He's coming early, my baby, and I wanted—you to be here."

Now that Hyacinth could see the queen with her hair down in two plaits instead of up under a veil—as it had been the last two times she'd seen her—she thought she knew what another of the payments had been. Silver glints showed among the chestnut hairs at the crown of her head. How many years had Renata lost? More than ever, it pained Hyacinth that her gain was made at the cost of the people she helped.

"Thank you for calling me, Your Majesty," she said.

"I knew—you would want—to be here. Oh!"

The midwife and maids lifted Renata onto the birthing stool. Hyacinth, though she had birthed babies before, wasn't needed. She watched, uneasy. Why had Renata been in bed? Why not walking to ease the pain of the contractions?

The birth progressed quickly after that. When the baby was delivered, and the midwife had tied off the cord, the maids gently washed Renata, then carried her back to the bed and covered her up. She didn't seem to notice; all her attention was for the child the midwife held.

"My child," she whispered.

"Your son," the midwife said. "Strong, for all he's early. I think he'll have your hair, Your Majesty." Indeed, the round head was covered with chestnut fuzz. With luck, Terzo would never suspect the child's true father.

As the midwife washed and swaddled the boy, Hyacinth studied him closely. She could see no deformities—he waved his arms and legs vigorously, and blinked big dark eyes when the midwife moved him closer to the lantern. What price had he paid

218

for his mother's spell baths? There was a patch of dark skin on one shoulder, but many babies had birthmarks similar to that.

"Show him to Terzo," Renata whispered. "Show him his son."

The woman left, carrying the baby, and the maids followed her. Renata closed her eyes and went limp against Hyacinth. "It was worth it."

"What is it, Renata? What's wrong?"

"The last bath. Ever since I took it, I've been losing the use of my legs. By this morning, I couldn't stand. By the time the contractions started, not even my toes would move. But my son—he's strong, he's healthy."

Hyacinth swallowed, tears rising in her eyes.

"I've given him everything I could. He'll be the ruler Bhaltair didn't have the chance to be. He'll have strength, wisdom, and compassion."

"We still have to raise him, to teach him. Keep him from Terzo's example."

Renata sank back against the pillows and closed her eyes. "Thank all the gods I'll have you with me. You've given me the strength and wisdom to raise him the way Bhaltair would have wanted."

In a nearby room, the King of Orthefell exulted over the birth of his son. He did not ask about the child's mother.

Hyacinth had never made a bane bath in her life. She wondered grimly if, during her time here as the new prince's nurse, she would find a need to. She would be meek, she would be obedient—but if Terzo stepped outside the bounds, he would be sorry he had offended the witch who loved the queen.

DEAD PRINCESSES

by Steve Chapman

Shada has never been anyone's idea of a proper princess: that would be her sister Sienna. Shada has always preferred straight-forward fighting to diplomacy. Fortunately, she's a very good fighter.

A lapsed musician and engineer, Steve Chapman lives with his wife and daughter at the New Jersey shore. Though he spends most days high above Times Square , in the evening he can hear the ocean. His fiction can be found in *Sword & Sorceress 25* and 26, and in the forthcoming Harrow Press anthology *Mortis Operandi.*

"It is my understanding, Master Dominic," Shada said, "That once a Scarlet Guardsman is sworn to a princess as her Shield he must do whatever she commands."

The young guardsman stiffened beside her. "This is accurate, your highness."

Shada batted her eyelashes, playing the flighty girl Dominic seemed to take her for. He was terribly earnest, unable to parse even the broadest irony. It augured poorly for their future together, a future she was desperate to avoid.

Every member of St. Navarre's royal family was assigned a Shield on his or her sixteenth birthday. The tradition was designed to foster a bond that could not be corrupted by gold or sorcery.

But Shada required no bodyguard to ensure her safety. She was afraid of nothing and had no doubt that she could beat handsome, stalwart, and dim Dominic senseless on the proving grounds. Despite her protests, the dark-haired, dark-eyed junior

Guardsman had been sworn to her in a Citadel ceremony that morning. The only possibility of escaping his constant attention that Shada could see was to make his duty intolerable. If he resigned the bond then maybe they would leave her in peace.

To this end she had led Dominic into the dim passages behind Kings Hall. The corridors were roughly hewn from obsidian stone, lit only by wall-set torches. When Shada took Dominic's hand it was moist with unease.

"We should not be here." He tried to pull away.

"Your protection excites me." Shada dropped her voice to a whisper and worked hard to suppress a snicker. "I feel a dangerous swoon approaching that can, uh, only be defeated by the touch of your lips."

Dominic flushed the red of a turnip. "I cannot."

"It *is* forbidden." Shada knew her behavior was deplorable, but felt her heart sing at the look of horror on the boy's face. "Yet you are sworn to obey me in all things."

"Enough." Shada's twin sister Sienna emerged from the shadows.

Shada sighed. She should have known there was no escaping her killjoy sister. Dominic jumped to attention, back ramrod straight, arms at his sides.

Sienna had been born just moments after Shada, yet they were nothing alike. Sienna's brown hair contrasted with Shada's streaked blond, her perfectly fitted court dress with Shada's worn combat leathers. They shared only the green of their eyes, through which they saw the world in utterly contrary ways. Because Sienna had been born second, she would not have to suffer her own Shield until the next High Day.

"I had thought myself beyond shock at your behavior, Shada." Sienna's dark hair was pulled back in a ponytail, her unadorned face starkly beautiful. "I stand corrected."

Shada threw her arms around Dominic's neck. "Just wait until you have your own dreamy Shield, sworn to answer your every need."

The guardsman's face darkened from turnip to eggplant.

"You're not amusing." Sienna said. "One day you may rue

making your Shield despise you."

The notion that she'd ever require anyone's protection burned at Shada, but she kept her tone cool. "Should Dominic ever show the poor taste to despise me I would immediately command him not to."

Sienna rolled her eyes and brushed past them, undoubtedly off to spy on someone through the many peepholes into the Hall.

Shada returned her attention to Dominic, but Sienna had effectively killed the joke. Shada no longer felt funny or justified, only tired and mean.

Down the dark corridor, Sienna screamed.

Shada broke away from Dominic and launched herself along the passage, her sword hissing from its scabbard.

"Princess, wait!" Dominic cried out behind her.

Two turns of the corridor ahead, Shada found her sister standing in a pool of yellow torchlight. Strung up beside the torch was the body of a girl in a pretty purple dress.

"Sorry," Sienna said, now all business. "I was surprised."

Fair enough, Shada thought. "Who…?"

"Jennie Fassbinder, the Coin Minister's daughter." Sienna's voice shook. "I barely recognized her."

Sienna brushed Jennie's hair back from her face. She had died from a cut across the throat, but it was her other wound that drew Shada's gaze. She'd been fond of delicate Jennie, a kind and quiet girl whose blue eyes had lit up many dark Citadel rooms.

Now she was dead, and her eyes were missing.

~o0o~

Half an hour later Shada still lingered over the body, feeling sad and helpless. She could abide neither sensation, but neither could she walk away.

Scarlet Guardsmen had cleared the courtiers from the Cathedral-like space of Kings Hall, brought in the body, and taken up positions around the empty throne. Sir Gregory, the King's white-haired First Councilor, huddled with Sienna and the Master at Arms at the foot of the enormous stone seat.

"Princess, we should let the Guard handle this." Dominic looked nervously about the Hall.

"Leave me." Shada was unable to pull her gaze from Jennie's empty face.

"I'm sworn not to," Dominic said.

The stab of shame Shada felt at her behavior towards him only inflamed her fury at his presence.

Sienna returned from her huddle. "The body was placed there to be found. Gregory believes someone is sending a message."

Shada touched the sword at her belt. "It would be my pleasure to respond." She intended to make whoever had done this very sorry they had.

"Jennie was harmless in herself and her position," Sienna said. "If this is a threat, it lacks clarity."

A Citadel Warden in gleaming armor approached. At the sight of the corpse the warrior-priest gasped. "This is Lisle's Mark."

Gregory looked over sharply. "What?"

"The Shroud Maiden." The Warden crossed himself. "This means she's coming to claim her price."

A murmur of fear spread through the Guardsmen. Shada remembered the rough contours of the old bedtime story.

The Shroud Maiden Lisle, alive beyond death for centuries untold, on rare occasions wakes from her undead slumber and calls at the gates of the world's great Kingdoms.

"Get my sister as far from here as you can," Sienna snapped at Dominic. "As fast as you can."

"Princess, I don't understand."

The Shroud Maiden announces her presence by taking the life of a highborn young woman. Lisle's Mark is a purposeful mutilation: the removal of the eyes. Shortly thereafter Lisle will appear to the Kingdom's ruler and demand the realm's firstborn girl child.

"You don't need to." Sienna's tone turned to ice. "Go now. Don't let anyone stop you. Shada's life depends on it."

Anxiety rippled across the Hall as Gregory interrogated the Warden. Men drew their weapons. Voices echoed in the high rafters.

Shada's breath came too quickly. The Shroud Maiden was just a rubbish tale made to frighten young princesses, but Sienna seemed to credit it, and her sister didn't fear storybook ghosts and goblins.

"As you say." Dominic took Shada's arm. "*Now*, your highness."

The edge of Shada's right hand struck Dominic in the throat, sent him gasping to his knees. She had tempered the blow. He would live, but he would be silent for a matter of minutes and wouldn't touch her again anytime soon.

Should Lisle be refused, she will slaughter three times thirty female children of the lesser nobility, just as she killed the first.

Shada pivoted to face her sister. "I'm not going anywhere."

"You can't fight her, Shada." Sienna appeared so tense she looked like she might shatter.

"The Shroud Maiden?" Shada snorted. "She's a myth."

"That's what they tell us when we're young."

Scarlet Guardsmen swarmed about Shada, drawing weapons. The ring of blades drew tight as the First Councilor pushed through them. Tall and rail thin, the older man towered over the red-caped guardsmen.

"This is unfair." Sienna seethed.

"It is," Gregory said. "But the kingdoms that refused the Maiden now lie in ashes, torn apart by rebellion and civil war. Allaria, Karzupel, Riasch, all have ceased to be."

Shada vaguely recalled those names from her history studies. Real places, not fairy tales...

"Our father may not agree." Sienna stepped between Shada and a dozen swords, but Gregory brushed her aside. His unblinking gaze took in Shada's torn leathers, her unruly hair, and her stunned Shield, still down on his knees. Shada steeled herself for a verbal thrashing, but Gregory threw his arms around her.

"Even the wisest ruler cannot be expected to prize the realm above his own child. Your father is three days' ride from here. He will not be told until the matter is concluded." Gregory looked Shada in the eye. "The Warden and I will attempt to thwart the Maiden, but if we fail you must yield to her."

Shada found herself unable to breathe, unable to comprehend

what was happening. If this was true her entire life, everything she ever hoped to be or do, had been taken from her in the blink of eye.

"The Shroud Maiden is coming." Sir Gregory raised his voice. "Prepare yourselves."

The air grew cooler, as if a door to the sea had been opened, great gouts of fog forming. A flood of ants swarmed over the patterned carpets. Flies darkened the air.

"There's no preparing for me, old man." The girl who stepped out of the thickening mist was physically slight, clad in a tiny, threadbare black dress that had perhaps once been beautiful. Her hair, black as ink, was hacked short. Large, dark eyes dominated an elfin face. Her skin was a strange, lustrous gray, the color of a mollusk. She appeared no older than Shada and held no weapon, but the guardsmen shrank from her nonetheless.

Shada felt the girl's power like an oppressive humidity, but she looked so delicate that a single blow might knock her down.

"How did you get in here?" Gregory demanded. "The Citadel is impregnable to dark magic."

"Such powerful wards old men have smeared into your old walls." The girl's voice was musical, almost sweet. "So I walked through your large front door."

"Our guards—"

"Are dead." She fanned both hands, displaying long black talons. "Care to join them?"

"Your presence blasphemes our Citadel." The Warden held up a thin, gleaming dagger. "I bear the named blade Angel's Kiss, which can sear the unlife from the walking corpse you wear like a mask."

"I'm always game for a kiss." A smile spread across the Maiden's face, making her pretty.

The Warden charged. Shada's heartbeat double-timed. Wardens were supposedly the greatest of the Citadel's soldiers, fearless masters of every martial art.

The Shroud Maiden turned her gaze on him. Tiny black spiders crawled between her fingers, scuttled up her forearms. Ants and maggots coated the floor at her feet.

The Warden stopped in his tracks. He screamed, turned, and ran past Shada into the passages. The guardsmen fell back around Gregory.

Gregory's face was bathed in sweat. Shada had never seen him show a hint of fear, but he now appeared terrified.

"I can kill your guardsmen, old man. I can kill you." Lisle's whisper carried into every corner of the Hall. "But I'd rather have my princess."

Two Scarlet Guardsmen broke and ran. Gregory swallowed hard.

"Bring the princess to the temple in Aeyple Forest by moonrise." Lisle strode toward him. "If the moon tops the trees and she is not present, I will return to prune your children by the dozens."

Maybe Lisle possessed dark magic and a manicure of doom, but Shada found it hard to believe that she couldn't kick this wisp of a girl's teensy ass all the way back to Tartarus.

"I'll be there," she blurted out.

The Maiden's black-eyed gaze shifted to Shada. She felt spiders and maggots crawling through her hair, down her back. The urge to run was so strong she had to stamp her feet to hold her ground. But she did. She *was not* frightened.

"You?" Lisle stared her up and down. "The clothes. That *hair*. All the fighting. I don't want you." The Maiden's glare shifted to Sienna. "I require a proper princess. The dark-haired one. Bring her before the moon rises, or bathe in the blood of your daughters."

"It will be done," Gregory muttered.

Sienna's her lower lip trembled, and then her Court mask slipped into place.

"Wait!" Shada shouted, but the Shroud Maiden evaporated into a cloud of buzzing flies.

An acid mixture of anger and embarrassment churned Shada's gut. She was first born. If someone had to be given over, it should be her. This was insane. But Gregory had made up his mind and she'd get nowhere arguing with him.

The way to save her sister was to take the argument to the

Maiden. Shada knew the way to the temple. The rough contours of a plan cascaded through her head.

All eyes were on Sienna as Shada backed toward the entrance to the passages. Only Dominic, still down on his knees, saw her go. He tried to cry out, but hadn't recovered from her blow.

In silence, Shada slipped away.

~o0o~

From her perch in the trees beside the ruined temple, Shada watched the red-caped horsemen arrive. The first of them surveyed the collapsed walls and overgrown standing stones, undoubtedly noting the same potential avenues of attack and escape Shada had cataloged when she first arrived.

Two more riders flanked Sienna. Her dress was black and simple, her face blank as she approached the temple. Sienna's mastery at keeping emotion from her face usually annoyed Shada no end, but tonight she found herself grinding well-chewed fingernails into her palms, imagining the terror her sister must be hiding.

A cool autumn breeze ruffled still-green leaves, whistled through the standing stones. Shadows cast by the ruins stretched long across the grassy outcropping. Night was falling, and then the moon would rise.

Shada was ready, having arrived an hour before. She'd tied her mount deep in the forest and stripped off her sword, boots, and leathers. In her charcoal fencing tights she was able to climb quickly and quietly through the dense trees. Once the sun set she'd be virtually invisible.

And then she'd take out the Shroud Maiden.

Shada waited, silent and still, as the guardsmen made camp beside the ruins, as the sky darkened to thick cobalt and then a brilliant, star-specked black. Then she descended from branch to branch and leapt to the ground. She strode carefully, silently, as she had been taught, passing over leaf and twig as softly as the evening breeze, the ground cool and hard beneath her stocking feet.

The campfire blazed through the trees. Shada was looping around it, intending to take up a position on the far side of the temple, when she heard a footfall close by. She stopped dead, barely breathing.

"Turn around slowly, Princess."

She barely recognized Dominic in a black peasant's cloak. He was stealthy for his size, clever enough to put aside the gaudy trappings of his rank. Perhaps she had underestimated him.

"Will you face the Shroud Maiden without armor?" Shada ignored the sword directed at her heart and focused on his dark, wounded eyes.

"I'm not here for Lisle," Dominic said. "You're coming back with me, Shada."

He said her name like a curse. Her escape from the Citadel had no doubt made him look foolish. But she couldn't let his pride cause Sienna's death.

She offered what she hoped was a distractingly sultry smile. "You missed me, my Shield?"

Shada twisted past the blade and chopped at his wrist, at the same time throwing a sidekick into his ribs. Dominic dropped the sword but managed to dodge the brunt of her blow.

Shada half-turned into another kick. He blocked it with his forearm and nearly grabbed her ankle.

She sprung backwards, putting a few feet between them. He'd almost taken her down. Her muscles twitched in the thrilling anticipation of a real fight. But she had to deal with him quickly. Dominic was a faster and smarter hand-to-hand fighter than she'd imagined, so maybe there was another way.

"You're not bad," Shada said. "Help me save my sister."

"I'm returning you to the Citadel." Dominic's face colored. "If that requires beating you senseless, so be it."

He lunged forward. Shada dodged two big, fast blows, either one of which would have put her on the ground. She had apparently *really* annoyed her Shield.

She spun about and threw a footsword kick at his head. He blocked it and chopped at her leg. She twisted away and dropped into a crouch. They faced each other, both breathing hard, both looking for an opening. Dominic was really good.

Silver light glistened between the trees. The moon was rising.

"You've succeeded in getting in my way. You've got real grit." Shada relaxed her stance just a touch. "So you're going to help me."

"Even if you free Sienna," Dominic said, "Lisle will kill your father's subjects."

Shada knew it all too well. "That's why I have to kill her."

Dominic circled her tight, trying to force an opening. "It's my understanding that the Shroud Maiden is already dead."

"I didn't say it would be easy." Shada turned with him, her eyes on his hands, ready to jump.

"It's impossible."

"Difficult." Shada slipped the dagger from her sleeve. "Not impossible."

He stopped dead. "You didn't…"

"Steal Angel's Kiss from a drooling and terrified Warden?" The blade glowed silver. "It would have been stupid to ride this far without a way to kill the Maiden. In case you didn't notice before, I was only pretending to be stupid."

Dominic stared at the dagger. "If it's really possible to destroy Lisle…"

"Then your orders are wrong." Shada was surprised at the heat with which she spat the words. "Lisle terrified Gregory. Frightened people make poor decisions."

Dominic relaxed his guard. He was listening.

"Together, we can kill the Shroud Maiden." Shada took a deep breath and swallowed her pride. "Dominic, I'm sorry. I've been unforgivably unserious with you but I am a serious girl."

"The Maiden mortifies all who look upon her." He unclenched his fists. "The Warden ran from her. If you fail and Lisle survives…"

"The Warden was afraid." Shada held Dominic's gaze. "I'm not."

~oOo~

Heads turned and steel flashed as Dominic walked Shada to the fire. Her wrists appeared to be twined behind her back. He kept a hand locked around her arm, Angel's Kiss slipped invisibly up her sleeve. The silver moon lurked just below the treetops.

229

"Got her," Dominic grunted.

"Bravo," Alaric slid his blade back in its scabbard. Shada knew all three of the Guardsmen. Castor stood behind Alaric, knife in hand. Beside him Theo held Sienna, her hands bound. As if Sienna would run from this.

Sienna glared at Shada. "Whatever you're planning, just *don't*."

Panic shot through Shada's body like lightning in the bloodstream. She hadn't the art to keep it from her face.

The guardsmen looked to Dominic, hands dropping to their weapons.

"Shada's bound and disarmed." Dominic sounded bored. "What's she going to do, bite someone?"

At his tone the others relaxed. Shada looked away from her sister, the truth of her intent plain between them.

Silver light rippled across the broken stone of the temple and reflected in Sienna's dark eyes. The moon shimmered above the treetops. Shada felt a change in the air, smelled honey and jasmine. Snatches of melody, harp and lute, whispered in the breeze. Color appeared among the temple stones, pink and purple, azure and yellow.

The splashes of color bloomed into dresses, long and sumptuous ball gowns. The girls wearing them sat at a long table visible just inside the temple entrance, sipping tea and nibbling at biscuits. Hair and ribbons and jewelry shimmered in the moonlight.

Sienna and the soldiers gasped. Shada concentrated on Angel's Kiss, cool against her skin. She was armed for whatever sorcery the Maiden could throw at her.

These must be the princesses that Lisle had collected. More of them appeared behind Alaric, Castor, and Theo, as if they'd simply soaked out of the moonlight.

The Shroud Maiden stepped from the shadows, a glittering dress of midnight coiled about her slim frame. Bone white ribbons twisted in her hair, pewter rings encircling her neck, wrists, and ankles. Shada's skin tingled. The combination of magic and a Court tea party was almost more nightmare than she could handle.

Theo pushed Sienna toward the Maiden.

Lisle's black-painted lips broke into a smile. A tiny spider, wet with spittle, climbed out of the side of her mouth.

Shada again felt the crawling unease Lisle had conjured in Kings Hall. The silver-dappled darkness was alive with movement, spiders and serpents, worms and maggots. She fought down the urge to get as far away from the Maiden as possible.

Theo and Castor threw down their swords and ran. Alaric and Dominic looked like they were thinking about it.

The Shroud Maiden traced Sienna's lips with a black nail. "You'll do nicely."

Sienna's face was blank, but the tears on her cheek glistened in the moonlight.

"I'm firstborn," Shada said, her voice not nearly as strong as she'd hoped. "Deal with me."

"The princess in motley has come to rescue her sister." Lisle turned, clicking her talons together. "How exciting."

Cottony furls of cloud passed below the moon, blocking its silver light. Shadows crept across the ruins. Where they touched the princesses' dresses, colors faded and fabric frayed. In shadow, the girls' radiant skin turned gray and corrupted, revealing pockets of white bone.

A hard knot of fear formed in Shada's stomach. The princesses were wights, walking corpses that were said to be nearly impossible to kill. The head had to be severed from the body or the brain destroyed. She wasn't facing a single undead monster, but a dozen.

She forced the thought away. If she allowed herself to feel fear she was lost.

The dead girl standing behind Alaric lunged, her teeth fastening on his throat. He tried to draw his blade, but three more wights joined her, bearing him to the ground.

Dominic held two princesses at swordspoint, but others flanked him. In a moment he'd be surrounded. He locked eyes with Shada and ran into the woods.

Shada flicked her wrist and Angel's Kiss slipped into her palm. She darted between the wights. She was nearly close enough to strike when Lisle turned, opening her black eyes wide.

Shada nearly screamed. Ants and spiders were crawling all over her. She hesitated in her attack and a hand of bone grasped her wrist, wrenching her arm backwards. She pivoted and kicked out at a taffeta-gowned princess. Ribs snapped, but the grip only tightened.

Bony fingers closed around her left arm. The wights pulled in opposite directions. Blunt pain halted Shada's momentum. She tried to throw her weight left and then right, but the hands holding her were astonishingly strong.

Shada howled in frustration. Dominic and the other Guardsmen were gone. Alaric was dead on the ground, gowned princesses hungrily stripping the flesh from his bones.

"Filthy thing." Lisle plucked Angel's Kiss from Shada's numb fingers and threw it into the weeds. "Time to die, princess in motley."

The dead girls holding Shada pulled her arms wide to either side. She gasped at the pain and set her feet, trying to angle her body to minimize the force on her shoulders.

"Wait." Shada's mind raced. "I can help you."

"You will," Lisle purred. "I'm sure your flesh will prove both delicious *and* nourishing."

"I'm heir to the throne." The burning pain between Shada's shoulders grew worse. She gasped in a mouthful of air. "I can get you…whatever you want."

The Shroud Maiden raised an eyebrow. The pressure on Shada's arms eased.

"Whatever I want?" Lisle put cold fingers to Shada's throat.

"Anything." She was playing for time. A few more minutes to live were minutes to think of a way out. But no brilliant stratagem presented itself.

"I want not to be the thing that I am," Lisle said. "Can you give me my life back?"

"The mages of the Citadel—"

Lisle slapped her across the face. "Once upon a time I was a proper princess. I was pretty and well mannered and it did me little good when the Bone Dancers came and demanded me. So many mighty warriors in our castle. So many great mages. They all bowed low and handed me over to the monsters."

"I'm sorry," Shada grunted. "But why do it to us?"

"The Bone Dancers tore out my heart and made me what I am," Lisle said, oblivious to a passing whorl of cloud stripping the flesh from half her face. "Later, they made the mistake of teaching me things. And then I destroyed them."

"Sienna and I can help you."

"There's no helping what I am." Tiny spiders scuttled across the Maiden's face. "So what I want are friends who are like me. Which Sienna will soon be."

Behind Lisle two rotting girls held Sienna while a third ripped open the front of her dress. Sienna bit her lip so hard blood coursed down her chin.

They were going to tear her heart out.

Shada thrashed and kicked and only managed to reignite the agony along her arms.

"I want Sienna to take tea with me." Lisle nodded to the swollen corpses holding Shada. "And I want you to die."

Hard fingers pulled Shada's arms still further apart. Shocks of pain arced between her shoulders. At any moment the muscle and ligament would give way and her arms would be pulled from their sockets. Her heart raced, pulverizing her ribs.

She couldn't save Sienna. She couldn't save herself. She had failed. Her throat tightened and her stomach convulsed, as if terror was a physical malady overwhelming her body.

"Shada!" A dark figure bounded into the circle of princesses and dove into the weeds.

"Dominic!" Shada yelled. "Help Sienna!"

As the wights fell on him Dominic grabbed Angel's Kiss and whipped it sidearm at Shada.

She flinched as the blade sank hilt-deep into the eye of the girl holding her. And then she understood what he had done. The point of the knife sunk deep into her brain, the now truly dead girl released Shada's aching arm.

Shada pulled the dagger free with her right hand and drove it into the eye of the wight on her left.

The corpses collapsed. She was free.

Shada leapt at Lisle, her kick spinning the Maiden around. She shoved Sienna clear as Lisle opened her black eyes wide.

The Maiden's annihilating gaze stopped Shada cold. Spiders coated her right hand. She struggled against the impulse to throw the disgusting dagger into the dirt. Maggots crawled through her hair, wriggled beneath her tights. Her limbs grew heavy with the weight of them.

"You can't fight me." Lisle moved closer, talons clicking. "I'm the thousand little mouths that can't wait for your heart to stop beating so we can devour the dead meat you're about to become. The terror of me paralyzes you. I am your death, Princess. And I am eternal."

And Shada was not. She had imagined herself fearless, but she was mortal, and weak, and frightened. Just like everybody else.

She drove the blade under Lisle's ribs, through her stomach, and up into her chest.

Fear itself didn't paralyze nearly so much as the exhausting denial of it. Accepting her terror, Shada found she could step past it and let her body do what it did better than everybody else.

Stab things.

Lisle gasped. "You *hurt* me."

Shada threw an arm around the Maiden's shoulder and pulled her close, shoving the blade in deeper. Gray flesh smoked and bubbled in Shada's brutal embrace. Lisle's features moistened and dissolved, the writhing body collapsing into a pile of oily bones.

One by one the princesses fell to the ground, now only corpses, long dead.

~o0o~

The next morning Shada woke certain that something was wrong. She wandered as if in a dream through deserted Citadel corridors in the hushed minutes before dawn, the far horizon glowing blue as a robin's egg.

The vast space of King's Hall was empty but for a lone figure standing before the throne.

"Dominic." She realized what was wrong. Her Shield of a single day wasn't by her side. He had saved her life. She'd been blessed with a bodyguard of exceptional intelligence and bravery and she wanted him to know that she knew it.

The figure turned. It wasn't Dominic. Sienna looked nothing like him, and like she hadn't slept at all. "He's gone."

"Gone where?"

"He was relieved of his cloak when you fled the Citadel. He's finished in the Scarlet Guard."

Shada felt as if she'd been punched in the gut. "But he came for me last night."

"That was his decision." Sienna looked away. "The Guard is done with him."

Shada remembered the shame and fury in his eyes when they'd fought. This was why he'd been so angry. She felt a faint shame of her own.

"It was stupid," Sienna said. "Your gambit could have destroyed us all."

"You're welcome." Darts of anger pricked Shada's skin.

"Thank you. Of course." Sienna sounded vastly annoyed that Shada had saved her life. "But you're not invincible. You have to learn to *think*."

"If I was as thoughtful as Gregory you'd be criticizing me with a big hole in your chest." But Shada understood what she meant. Frightened people made poor decisions, but so did those too stubborn to be afraid. Fortunately Dominic had been frightened enough for both of them and acted accordingly. Without his fear, neither she nor Sienna would be seeing this sunrise.

"Fair enough," Sienna whispered.

Fear as an ally would take some getting used to. At this moment Shada's great fear was that she might ever again behave as stupidly as she had with Dominic. She wondered if battling wights was the easy part, that to prove worthy of this throne the truly frightening task was making sense of all the endlessly confusing people orbiting it.

Her heart beating loudly, Shada set off for the proving grounds, eager to find something to hit.

THE RISING

by Pauline J. Alama

As anyone who has ever tried to bake bread from scratch knows, yeast can be temperamental. But in this story, yeast is truly—and literally—powerful.

Pauline J. Alama is the author of the quest fantasy *The Eye of Night* (Bantam Spectra, 2002). Her short fiction has appeared in volumes 18, 23, 25, and 26 of *Sword & Sorceress* as well as in *Penumbra*, *Realms of Fantasy*, and *Abyss & Apex*. When not spinning tales, she can be found writing grant proposals, avoiding housework, singing, fooling around with a guitar, sharing books with her son, spoiling her cats, or fuming about politics.

"We won't be caught," Nash told Nima. "And even if we are, what have we got to lose? You can't afford to starve—especially with the baby coming." He knotted a handful of grain in his head-cloth, then tied the cloth back over his curly hair. "See? It's easy."

"I don't know," Nima said. "The overseer's so suspicious this year. *Ssh*! Someone's coming."

They went back to their harvesting, bending their weary backs to cut the sheaves and bundle them. It was well timed, because Haxal the overseer came striding between the rows of wheat. "Make haste," he said. "Lord Gessig wants his full harvest in the silos by tomorrow."

"Sir," Nima piped up, "when may his lordship's humble workers glean for our own use?" It was late in the harvest, and the fields were nearly stripped; she had begun to whether anything would be left for the gleaning time.

Haxal did not meet her eyes. "Day laborers who take their wages in coin will not be paid in crops as well. The gleanings will only be for those who belong to Lord Gessig for life."

"But grain costs so much this year! We're starving on our wages."

"Then take the iron ring of siavery, and get your meals from the lord's hall every day. There's no shame in belonging to a great house," said Haxal.

Nima followed Haxal's gaze downward. Sure enough, the overseer himself now wore an iron ring about his ankle: lighter and more ornate than a common field slave's ring, it nonetheless marked him as Lord Gessig's chattel, merely a higher form of property than those he commanded.

There always seemed to be a depth of misery below the one where she stood, Nima reflected. Her parents had owned their little plot of land till debt swallowed it. She had gone to work for Lord Gessig in the hope of buying back her parents' farm. Now, it seemed, she could not even afford to own herself, much less the land she stood upon. Should she bow to necessity and become a slave? Would it buy her, at least, food and safety? Or would she bear her child into slavery only to starve anyway when she had nothing left to sell—not even herself?

"Great God preserve me from that." She bent again to her task, harvesting fine wheat that she would not taste.

Luck was with them: Nima found a few edible weeds among the rows of grain. Their roots were deep in the ground, a chore to grub out, but thick and meaty, well worth the effort. They came out caked in dirt but she dared not stop work long enough to clean them.

"You have them," Nash said. "I'm not so hungry."

She suspected he was lying, but gobbled them eagerly anyway, glad for something to fill her stomach.

When the sun sank low and the field hands at last were free to leave, Nima and Nash lined up to collect the day's wage. She was surprised to see bare shoulders ahead of her in line: it was hot work harvesting, but with autumn advancing, a cold wind blew over the fields at day's end. It was not until they came within clear sight of the overseer that they realized what was going on.

"Strip," ordered Haxal.

"What?"

"You heard me. Take off your clothes: let me see that you're not taking anything with you that isn't yours."

Trembling, she removed her head cloth, grateful that she hadn't had time to take Nash's advice and stow grain there.

"Go on," Haxal said stolidly.

She fingered the neck of her robe. "Must I? It seems so shameless."

"No shame in doing what every honest field hand has done. No shame in proving you're not a thief."

She moved with deliberate slowness, hoping she might give Nash time for some last cunning dodge. But the only idea he had left was to run.

"THIEF!" With a quickness that belied his size, Haxal slung a stone at the fleeing man.

Struck by the stone, the head-cloth burst open, spilling the precious grain that was to have saved them from starvation. Nash fell to earth and did not rise. Nima ran to him and tried to raise him, but his head gushed like a pierced melon, and the breath was gone from his body.

"You killed him!" she shrieked at the overseer. "For a handful of wheat, you killed him." Reckless with grief, she pulled off her robe and brandished her nakedness at him like a war-charm. "There! Are you satisfied? Great God curse you! May you see your mother like this!"

~o0o~

Grief was a stone in Nima's heart, but it was a stone she could carry, as she had carried so many burdens before. Widowed, penniless, grieving, unpaid for her hard day's labor, but free, she walked the path of the market-carts that she had never followed before, the road to the City.

The City was a new world to her, a wonder of thick stone walls and pointed arches, looming tall houses with more than one story to them, prophets and charlatans clamoring for attention, horses clattering down stone streets that bruised her bare feet. But one thing about it was familiar: it was as hungry as the countryside.

Whole families went begging from door to door. Nima scoffed at them at first—surely that man, that woman could work for their living—and went to offer herself for hire at all the shops in the town. But no one wanted an apprentice; no one wanted a maid-of-all-work; no one wanted an under-gardener; no one wanted a pot-scrubber or a stable-mucker or a ditch-digger. "What do you think I can hire you with?" a potter said with a mirthless laugh. "In this cursed season, you think anyone's buying a bowl to remember wine by, or a dish with no bread on it?"

And so Nima joined the beggars in the streets, only to meet new disappointment. "We hardly have enough to feed ourselves," one housewife told her. Another said, "*We* ate nothing today." Even shops were starting to close, the craftsmen packing carts with their tools to travel out of the City. Nima wondered where they would go: back where she had come from, to bind themselves in slavery for a meager promise of being fed?

All her life, Nima had heard that the City was rich, that while the country people ate coarse barley and wild greens, the City people got the best wheat grown in the countryside, and the olives and grapes and apricots besides. But it almost seemed the City was poorer than the country in this year of unnatural disasters: thunder that brought no rain, labor that brought no livelihood. It was like finding the sun had no more light, the ocean no more water. In the country, the barley crop had been disappointing, but there was wheat for those who could afford it, weeds and wild roots for those who could not. Nima pulled a few unfamiliar weeds from between the cobbles of the street. Not even the most desperate of the beggars fought her for them. Were they poisonous? Too starving to care, she ate them. They were so stringy she could hardly gag them down, but she didn't die, and they quieted her empty stomach a while.

Toward sunset, she smelled something tantalizingly like bread. Following her nose to a little shop made of sun-baked mud and timber, she slipped in without knocking or asking permission. "Blessings upon your hands and head, neighbor," she said hastily, hoping no one would dare turn a blessing out of their door.

"Blessings upon you, little girl," said the woman within. She had broad shoulders, a rounded nose like a knob of dough, and streaky gray-brown hair so like her dough-smeared apron that she almost seemed to have grown in one piece out of the shop floor, apron and all. "But my bakery is closed, child, and likely to stay so for longer than I care to think."

"I haven't come to buy," Nima said. "That is, not for money—but maybe for work? Even an old stale crust would be such a godsend!"

The baker shook her head. "There's nothing left. Not even a crust."

"If I clean your shop tonight, will you give me a loaf of your next baking?'

"If I were a thief and a fraud, I'd take you at your word," said the baker with a sardonic twist of her mouth. "Even the miller had no flour to sell me today. He said only the great lords have any, and they're not selling. Here, take this for what it's worth." She placed some coins in the Nima's hand—more money than Nima had ever owned!—and tenderly wrapped the young woman's fingers over them. "If anyone will sell you wheat for that, let me know. I sometimes think the only way I'll get something to bake will be if I go out to the country and harvest it myself."

"They'd never let you," Nima said. "We harvested all day in the scorching sun, and before we could go home, they stripped us naked to make sure we hadn't taken anything away with us."

"Then there *is* a harvest? People are saying it failed."

"The barley was poor this year, but there's plenty of wheat, the finest I ever saw, all stacked away in Lord Gessig's granary. My man Nash tried to take a handful—grain that we planted, and tended, and harvested—and they killed him for it." The tears she had been too numb to shed sprang to her eyes. "I ran away to the City, hoping I could earn a living here. But it almost seems there's no food in the City."

"What's your name, neighbor?"

"Nima."

"I am Selah the Baker—or I was, while I had something to bake. What's a baker in famine-time? But I never imagined that even those that gather the harvest don't dare taste it. How does His Lordship expect to keep enough hands to plant next year's crop?"

"He pays us, but the wage isn't enough to buy the grain we harvest. The overseer says if we can't make ends meet on our wages, we can be paid in food if we sell ourselves into slavery. More and more do."

"But you didn't," Selah observed.

"I don't want my child born into slavery. But if I don't eat, there may not be enough of me to bear a child." Lifting her head, she drew a deep, savoring draft of air. "I was sure I smelled food—something brewing, at least, if not baking."

"No, there's nothing to drink either," Selah said, but her tone sounded so guarded, Nima felt certain she was hiding something.

With the boldness of desperation, Nima slipped around to the back room of the shop. "What of that dough there?"

"Don't touch that." Selah grabbed her wrist.

"When will that be baked?"

"Neighbor, the day I bake that, I might as well add my heart's blood to it, for I'll be finished. That's the rising."

"Rising?"

"Some call it the yeast, but that's not quite right. Yeast is the spirit within it. Whenever I bake, I leave aside a bit of the dough so the yeast will survive. Then a piece of it is the rising for the next batch: I work it into the dough, and it mingles the yeast in every part of it, changing it, making it rise. I brought it with me from our village when I moved to the City, and fed it new flour and honey when we settled in this new shop. If I bake the whole of it, I may get a new rising from another baker, or from the yeasts in the air, but it won't be the same one I inherited, and my baking will never be the same."

"Where did it come from?" Nima asked.

"I inherited the rising from my mother, who inherited it from her mother, and so on, and so on."

"There must have been a beginning," Nima said.

"There was a beginning of everything, neighbor," said Selah, "and yeast has been in the world since its beginning. The Great God spat into the churning mist of chaos and infected it with the spirit of growth. And the seas grew foamy like beer, and the hills of the land rose like loaves, and the herbs and the woods rose out of them. The Great God spat again on the new lands, and there the yeast of Her mouth caused new life to spring up: beasts in the fields and birds in the trees. And then from Her mouth came a word rich with the spirit of life, and it brought forth speaking creatures, women and men that have in their own mouths the fragments of that first great word.

"And while the spirit of growth was still rich and active in the dough of the world, the first baker made a barm of broken grain and water to hold that yeast and feed it. And bakers have fed the rising ever afterward. Generations of us have lived and died, yet the invisible life of the yeast remains. But now it will die unless I have something to feed it."

Nima said, "Lord Gessig has grain. Why isn't there any in the City?"

The baker thought. "You say he has fine wheat in plenty, but less of the common barley than last year?"

"Yes."

"The wheat he can sell to sea-traders who ship it to the islands, far dearer than he can sell it close to home," Selah mused. "Or maybe he simply thinks to drive the price higher by withholding it."

"If all the grain we grow is being sent to the islands, maybe I could stow away on a ship," Nima said. "But even if I could, it's still all wrong. Why should a few men hoard what many sowed and harrowed and harvested? What will happen to everyone here, if they keep on?"

"We'll have to shake lose some of their hoard," Selah said.

"How?" Nima demanded. "What can we do?"

"Maybe nothing. And yet. . ." The baker hesitated. She looked into Nima's face as if appraising her. "When my mother taught me baking, she also taught me certain secrets. No one thinks of bakers as powerful, but every day we hold in our hands the force that grew the world." She laid a hand on Nima's abdomen. "You hold the spirit of growth, too. Maybe between the two of us, we can raise more than bread."

~o0o~

At moonrise they stood in the back garden between the bakery and the ovens. It was too hot and arid to grow much there, but Selah had nursed along a few herbs, mint and basil and rosemary.

"Place your hand on the rosemary, but gently," Selah commanded. "Don't pluck it. Feel the living stem between your fingers."

Nima did as she bade. For a sower of seeds and reaper of grain, it was familiar, yet unfamiliar: she was used to handling growing things, but unused to standing still, doing nothing to them, neither gathering nor pruning nor weeding nor mulching. The stem between her fingers was like a cord binding her to earth.

Reverently, Selah placed one hand on the dough and let it sink slowly in, the springy mixture pillowing between her fingers. Then she dipped the tip of one finger of the other hand into the yeasty mix, carrying away a little of it. She touched it to Nima's head and lips, and then to her own. Finally, she rested her hand, still bearing a trace of the rising, on Nima's belly. She breathed in slowly, and Nima felt her own breath fall into rhythm with Selah's.

"Source of life, source of growth,
Source of the yeast that raises us,
Breathe into us the lightness to rise,
Culture us with the yeast of your mouth,
Revive our dry earth with the rains of growth,
Sprout us like barley. Raise us like wheat.
Grind us like grain for our neighbors' need.
Try our hearts in the heat of your ovens.
Our people hunger for bread. Here we are:

Leaven us. Let us arise for them."

~oOo~

As Selah chanted, Nima felt the stirring inside her, the child fluttering in her womb, more active than ever before. She felt the blood rushing in her veins, the milk flooding her newly swollen breasts. She ceased to be hungry, as if she drew sustenance directly from the earth.

Something seemed to bubble up within her from the ground, through her bare feet, through her legs and hips, through her womb, through her heart, through her throat, till she had to speak, though the words were nothing she had ever thought of, though the voice that issued from her lips was not her own: "Daughter of yeast, kneader of dough, baker of bread, I know you. From your first beginning in your mother's womb I know you. From the soles of your feet to the crown of your head, from the inmost marrow of your bones to your outmost lock of hair, from your soul to your flesh, I know you. I hear you. I have come for you."

"Thank you," Selah breathed huskily. "Oh, thank you."

"Do you know what you undertake?"

"To be yeast," the baker said.

"You shall be yeast, if you can bear it," the voice spoke through Nima.

"I will bear it."

"Then rise, Daughters of Yeast. Rise, Kneader of Bread. Rise, Sower of Seeds. Rise, Reaper of Grain. Rise, my children, and leaven the world.

Nima felt thin threads of living matter flow through her from the lips that spoke these words up into her brain, down into her womb. They flowed through her feet, down into the earth like roots, like runners connecting her to Selah. She felt, as if it were her own, the strength of the baker's hands, her fingers that worked the dough, her arms that shifted the heavy baking-stones, her broad shoulders. The tiny threads of life grew and multiplied, and she felt herself grow and rise bigger and bigger until it did not shock her to find she could step over the little mud-and-timber bakeshop—as, indeed, she must, for the garden was too small for herself and the baker to stand together.

"I'll raise the people in the streets," Selah told her. The baker, too, had risen up tall as the proudest house in the City.

"I'll go back to Lord Gessig's fields. My people are there," Nima said.

The road from the fields to the City that she had trudged painfully all night long, she now retraced in a swift series of leaps. Wherever her feet struck the ground, she could feel the spirit of increase working its way through the soil, spreading and multiplying.

She came to a granary where Lord Gessig stored his harvest. With a touch of her hands, the grain within it swelled and burst its wooden sides open. Wheat fountained up out of the earth like a spring, more than the greatest barn could hold.

With glad shouts, the field hands left their evening chores and ran to catch the sudden bounty.

An overseer and a guard came running to restore order. "You dogs! That's Lord Gessig's wheat. Don't think of taking a grain of it for yourselves! Help us contain it." They seemed not to see her: as large as she had grown, Nima found, she was as invisible as yeast in a loaf.

She bent down and took the overseer and guard each in one of her gigantic hands. She spoke to the grain in their bellies, and it swelled and rose inside them till they doubled over with cramps. The overseer dropped his whip, the guard his spear; Nima picked up their weapons and broke them before moving to aid the field hands.

She did not know all of them, but she recognized Elishua, an old friend of her parents. Here was someone she could trust. "Rise, Sower of Seed, Daughter of Yeast," she murmured, touching Elishua's hand.

The old woman grew to match Nima's stature. "What must I do, young prophet?"

Nima's heart quaked at the title Elishua gave her, but there was no time to argue about something so unimportant as a name. "You and I must raise the people in the fields. I'll go north."

"Then I'll go south," said Elishua. They moved through the

lands of Lord Gessig, swelling the grain in the silos, bursting the locks of strongholds, raising up more and more companions to join the Rising.

She reached the wheat field she had once worked. There was Haxal the Overseer, holding the bag of wages and ordering the workers each in turn to strip for inspection before he doled out their daily pay. She bent to him, unseen, wondering if she might make the marrow in his skull swell up until his head burst, like poor Nash's. But the thought put a bitter taste in her mouth: that was not how the spirit within her wished to work. Instead, she touched the sack of wages; the coins swelled until the sack burst, spilling coppers everywhere. While Haxal scrambled to gather them up again, she took the hands of two of her old companions, Rush and Mara, and raised them up. "Children of Yeast, Sowers of Seed, arise and help me. Raise the land."

When they came to the barley field, Nima found she could sense in her feet the seeds that had not sprouted. The spirit of growth in her stirred them, and they rose: a late crop to save her people. But it would not save them if Lord Gessig were free to hoard it to make it dearer, or ship it far off for profit, leaving none for them.

A knot of field hands stared at the miraculously growing barley in wonder. This time, when Nima took the hand of a bent-backed laborer, the yeast found its way into his heart. Instead of raising him up a giant, it swelled his soul, banishing fear. He began to speak to the others in urgent tones. Nima did not stay to hear him, but hastened to other knots of workers, raising the spirit within them. Soon, throughout the estates, slaves were striking off each others' iron rings, and a growing army of field hands advanced on the lord's hall.

Nima walked by their side, gigantic but unseen, her feet leaving no prints in the earth. When they reached the hall, a guard stood in the doorway, refusing to let the workers pass. Nima's invisible hands thrust the guardsman aside, so the crowd poured into the stronghold.

"Who are you? What are you doing in my hall?" Lord Gessig demanded of the advancing crowd.

One whose heart the yeast had raised, a woman called Lem, faced the lord boldly. "Don't you know us? We feed you every day. We built this hall of yours. We are the workers in your fields, and we are tired of starving. We want our fair share of what we harvest."

"Guards!" Lord Gessig shouted. "Seize these unruly peasants."

The guards plied whips and fists, but the field hands were so used to blows and beatings that they could not be daunted. One of them raised a spear against the field hands; Nima found a spot of mold on its shaft and let the spirit of growth spread the decay until the weapon shattered.

"See?" Lem said. "The Great God shatters the weapons of your henchmen so you will hear us."

Another guardsman looked beseechingly at his commander, as if he longed to break off the fight, and only sought permission. Nima reached out with the touch of the rising, and the spirit within him grew. He lowered his sword. "I will not stand against the Great God."

The lord glowered at him, but behind the mask of anger, he was trembling. Nima saw her former master as she had never seen him before: a coward who even at the height of power feared the people he commanded, and even at the height of wealth desperately feared becoming poor. Nima reached a hand toward the lord. If the yeast grew within him, might he not grow big-souled enough to give of his abundance? Or would he only grow bolder in greed, and send his people away hungry?

Whatever the risk, she had to give the yeast what it needed: a chance to breed and grow within another human soul. She loosed the spirit of growth to find its subtle path into Lord Gessig's heart. But, as if an iron ring closed around it, his soul would not stretch and grow. She watched in dread and awe as the lord's face turned red, then gray, then blue, as a heart that could not grow choked and died.

Yeast breeds, yeast grows, yeast dies.

~o0o~

In the morning, Nima found herself shrinking back down like

dough well kneaded, returning to human form again. But with the power of the rising still in her veins, she sprang along the road with strength, all the way to the City, to the baker's shop.

"Selah!" she cried. "Selah, the famine is over, the lord is dead, everything is new!"

"Everything is new," said a weak and weary voice.

The baker lay in her back garden, too spent to care that her head was on stone. Nima ran to her, cradled her head: it was hot as a loaf just taken from the oven.

"You're fevered," she said. "Let me find you a healer."

Selah shook her head. "No use. Yeast grows, but yeast dies to make bread for others. I knew that when I asked to become yeast."

Nima's heart lurched. "I touched people and made them rise. And now, will they die of what I have done?"

"Never fear," Selah said. "Some die, but some remain and breed, like the rising left for the next baking. So it must always be: but without the rising, many would have died of hunger before long. This time, I will pay the price of the rising; you and the others will live and breed and grow. And you, Nima, will keep this shop, and tend the rising, in my place."

"Me! I'm not a baker."

"You will be," Selah said. "Did not the spirit of yeast whisper its secrets to you in the night?"

Nima opened her mouth to deny it, but realized that Selah was right: though she remembered no teaching, she knew what to do with the dough just as she knew how to breathe and the child within her womb knew how to grow. "Yes," she said. "I will keep the rising alive."

GHOST PYRES

by Jonathan Moeller

Here is another of Jonathan Moeller's stories about Caina, one of the Emperor's Ghosts. In this case, the ghosts are still alive; they're the spies and Intelligence corps. Caina has been a Ghost for nearly two decades, yet she still encounters new and different magical threats to deal with. At least her life is never borning.

Jonathan Moeller is pleased (and astonished) to return to *Sword & Sorceress* for a sixth time with "Ghost Pyres." He is also the author of the sword-and-sorcery novel *Demonsouled*, which was published by Gale/Five Star in 2005, and is now available as a free eBook in all major eBook formats.

Visit him on the web at www.jonathanmoeller.com, where you can find, among other things, five years of interviews with *Sword & Sorceress* contributors, and *Child of the Ghosts*, a free full-length novel set in the world of "Ghost Pyres."

Caina doubled over and threw up.

A cramp shot through her limbs, and her skin prickled as if she had been stabbed with needles. Caina grabbed at the wall for support, and felt Lucan Maraeus's strong hands close around her shoulders. Which was just as well—she didn't want to fall on her face in the street. They had come here hunting spies from Anub-Kha, and collapsing in public was hardly a good way to remain inconspicuous.

After a long moment the nausea and the pain faded.

But the tingling sensation remained.

"Are you ill?" said Lucan. He was a lean man in his middle thirties, and with his fine clothes and ready smile affected the manner of a wealthy, idle lord of the Empire. Yet now the smile had vanished, and his right hand twitched toward his sword hilt.

"No," said Caina, wiping her mouth. "No. Not sickness. Worse."

His grim expression darkened. "Sorcery?"

Caina nodded.

When she was eleven, a sorcerer's spell had slain her father and left her scarred. Ever since, she had possessed the ability to sense to presence of sorcery. With seventeen years of practice, she could now sense the distance and intensity of arcane spells. It had come in handy, more than once.

"Someone just cast a spell nearby," said Caina, looking around. She and Lucan stood in one of the main dockside streets of Caer Belaen, a small town southwest of the Imperial capital. A few passing sailors cast odd looks at the nobleman and his indisposed companion, but no one stopped to offer help.

Sailors had a good eye for trouble.

"You're sure?" said Lucan.

"Aye," said Caina. "A powerful one, too." Another wave of sharp prickles crawled over her skin. "And it's still active."

"No magi live in Caer Belaen," said Lucan.

Caina nodded. "Then we investigate."

She would have investigated anyway, even if an entire chapter of the magi lived in the town. She was a Ghost circlemaster, one of the leaders of the Emperor's spies, and she had sworn to defend the people of the Empire from those who preyed upon them. And very often, magi and sorcerers were the predators.

Gods, how she hated them.

"This way," said Caina. Caer Belaen was half-abandoned, most of the merchant ships preferring the larger harbors at Caer Marist and Malarae. So abandoned warehouses lined the streets of the dockside districts, crumbling and dilapidated. The tingles grew sharper as Caina approached one of the abandoned warehouses.

She stopped, frowning.

"Do you smell that?" she said.

Lucan blinked. "Is that...burned meat?"

Caina saw red light leaking through the boards of the abandoned warehouse's doors.

"I don't think that's pork," she said.

She took a deep breath, drew a dagger from her belt, and pushed open the door.

A gruesome scene met her eyes.

The abandoned warehouse was empty, but strange, swirling symbols and odd glyphs had been painted across the walls. A heap of coals stood in the center of the room, glowing with eerie light. The flames burned too bright to be natural, and Caina felt waves of sorcerous force rolling off the fire.

A burned corpse lay atop the coals. To judge from the half-melted jewelry clinging to the blackened fingers and neck, Caina suspected the corpse had once been a woman. Fury burned through her, almost as hot as the sorcerous flames. Yet another life torn apart by sorcery, another victim murdered by a spell.

The world would be a better place if every last sorcerer perished.

And whoever had done this would pay.

"Gods," said Lucan, taking a step forward.

"No!" Caina grabbed his arm. "Don't touch it. I don't think it's safe. Let me have a look."

She took a cautious step, examining the strange designs painted on the walls. A ring of the sigils had been painted on the floor, encircling the pyre. Caina knew far more about sorcery than she wished, and she recognized many of the symbols.

"Pyromancy," said Lucan. "Sorcery that draws its power from flame."

"It also tends to drive its practitioners mad," said Caina, voice quiet. "Literally burns away their sanity."

"Those symbols," said Lucan. "I think they're designed to summon and focus the power."

"You're right." Caina gazed at one of the glyphs. It showed a stylized flame encased within a heptagon, the seven points marked with stars.

"Damn it," she whispered.

"What?" said Lucan.

"This spell," said Caina. "I recognize it. It's called the Sevenfold Pyre. It's a ritual to pull the spirit of a slain pyromancer into the world of the living. The caster burns seven victims alive, using their lives as fuel to summon up the dead pyromancer."

"But pyromancy is extinct," said Lucan.

"Not quite," said Caina. "The Ghosts killed a pyromancer in Caer Belaen decades ago, a murderer named Ravodan. He burned his victims alive to fuel his power. I think whoever did this is trying to summon up Ravodan's spirit and learn his secrets."

"Seven victims?" said Lucan. "You mean seven people have been slain like this?"

Caina blinked as the realization came to her.

"No. Not yet. The Sevenfold Pyre burns its victims one after another, in sequence." Her mind raced, her hands closing into fists. "If we can find the others, we can stop the summoner."

"How?" said Lucan.

Caina pointed at the heptagon glyph. "Do you see that? It's not just a glyph. It's also a map. The stars on the points of the heptagon..."

"Represent the victims," said Lucan. "Who will be arranged in this pattern within Caer Belaen."

"Yes," said Caina, scrutinizing the glyphs around the pyre and the dead woman. "And these symbols around the heptagon...these symbols point to the other stars. The other victims." She stared at them for a moment, and then pointed. "There. The next point on the heptagon will be five or six hundred yards north of us, if I've read this right."

"Why not go right to the center?" said Lucan. "The sorcerer behind this is probably waiting there."

"No," said Caina. "The actual summoning itself can take place anywhere within the heptagon. We'll make our way along the edges. If we hasten, we might catch the sorcerer."

And save his victims.

Lucan nodded. "Lead the way."

Caina looked once more at the twisted corpse atop the coals.

That someone would dare to commit such atrocities in the name of power filled her with a fury like a storm. She would find who had done this and make him pay...

A flicker of motion caught her eye.

A man in a hooded cloak stood in the doorway to the street, beckoning to her.

Caina hissed in alarm and drew her daggers.

"What?" said Lucan, raising his sword. "What is it?"

The doorway was empty.

Caina hurried though the doorway. The street was deserted. She saw no trace of anyone, and certainly no one in a hooded cloak.

"I...don't know," said Caina. "I thought I saw someone."

"The smoke, perhaps," said Lucan. He sighed. "I shall smell that poor woman for days."

The rage shivered in Caina's mind.

"Aye," she said. "Let's go."

They hurried north.

~oOo~

Due north took Caina and Lucan to a neighborhood of mid-sized houses, no doubt owned by merchants rich enough to live away from their shops. But like the rest of Caer Belaen, the houses looked run-down. Were their inhabitants desperate enough to use sorcery to restore their fortunes? To summon up the shade of a long-dead pyromancer?

"You should go back," said Caina. "This is dangerous."

Lucan lifted an eyebrow. "Of course this is dangerous. And I have hunted down rogue sorcerers before."

He had. And he would have hunted this pyromancer, with or without Caina's help. But that wasn't why he was here now. She saw it in his face, in the way he watched her.

He was in love with her. It was going to get him killed. And she did not need his help. She had been taking care of herself for a long time. But only a fool turned away help in the face of dangerous enemies.

And she did not want to send him away...

"Here," said Caina, pushing aside her doubts. "I think the next pyre will be here." She pointed at one of the larger houses, its whitewashed walls topped with a roof of red clay tiles. The small garden ringing the house made it look more prosperous than the others.

"That one?" said Lucan. "I know the fellow who lives there. A minor noble named Mauldron. He has a sinecure overseeing the harbor. He hardly seems the sort to meddle with pyromancy."

"No offense, my lord Lucan," said Caina, "but I've known nobles of the Empire who murdered their children for political advantage."

"Then you've met my father. Do you feel any sorcery here?"

"No," said Caina. She stepped closer to Mauldron's house. Could she have been mistaken? If she had misread the glyphs, the other pyres might lie elsewhere within the town. And innocent people would die because of her mistake...

A faint tingle brushed against her skin.

Caina cursed. "It's starting. Someone's casting a spell in that house. Go!"

Lucan raced forward, Caina following. They reached the house's front door, only to find it locked. Caina reached for the lockpicks hidden in her belt, but Lucan solved that problem by putting his boot to the door. It splintered and swung open.

Only a fool turned away help.

She flashed him a quick grin and ran into the house, dagger in hand.

They entered a deserted atrium, the floor paved with elaborate mosaics of the Empire's history. Beyond was a dining room with a long table, statues standing in niches along the wall. There was no trace of anyone, whether nobles or servants.

Yet the tingling grew stronger.

"It's here," said Caina. "I'm sure of it. We..."

She heard a scream.

"The cellars," said Lucan.

They raced into the kitchen. The door to the cellar stood half-open, a red glow shining from within. Caina hurried down the stairs and into the cellar. A forest of squat brick pillars supported the vaulted ceiling. Five men in ceremonial black and red robes stood around a pile of firewood, their arms raised, chanting in low voices. A young woman in the dress of a washerwoman lay upon the wood, her wrists and ankles tied, a gag stuffed into her mouth.

Good. They were not too late. They...

One of the men shouted and clapped his hands, and Caina's skin crawled with the presence of powerful sorcery.

The heaped wood erupted in sorcerous flames, the roar of the fire drowning out the woman's screams.

A red mist fell over Caina's vision.

The man who had clapped his hands looked at her, eyes glinting within his crimson hood. "Intruders! Kill them!"

Caina's free hand dipped into her belt, came up holding a throwing knife. She stepped forward, her arm plunging back, and flung the blade, her entire body snapping like a bowstring. The knife hurtled through the air and buried itself in the throat of the nearest robed man. He fell, choking.

The others drew swords from beneath their robes and charged.

Lucan met them, his sword a blur of steel. The robed men converged on him, seeing him as the greater threat, which gave Caina all the opportunity she needed to act. A second throwing knife buried itself in the calf of the nearest enemy. He stumbled, and Lucan finished him with a quick slash. Another man turned towards Caina, robes billowing, and launched a thrust for her head. She ducked, sidestepped, and stabbed for his side. The man dodged, sword coming back for a swing.

Only to stumble when he found Caina's boot pinning the hem of his robe. As impressive as the crimson and black robes looked, only an idiot would try to fight in one, which Caina proved when she drove her dagger into his throat.

The fight was over moments later, with four men dead, and one survivor trying to crawl away, Caina's knife embedded in his calf. Lucan flipped the survivor onto his back, and Caina saw the face of the man who had clapped his hands to finish the spell.

Burning that woman alive.

"Lord Mauldron," said Lucan to the wounded man. Mauldron was in his fifties, his face grizzled and jowly, eyes bright with pain and terror. "You're keeping disreputable company these days."

"Lord Lucan?" said Mauldron. "Did...did your father send you?"

"The Ghosts sent me," said Lucan.

Mauldron wheezed a laugh. "The Ghosts? The Emperor's mythical spies? There are no Ghosts, only shadows and stories."

"Shadows," said Caina, voice low, "that carry knives."

"You," gasped Mauldron. "I heard of you! The Ghost Countess. But you were a story..."

"Shut up and listen to me," said Caina, surprised at how calm her voice remained. "I know about the Sevenfold Pyre. I know you're trying to resurrect Ravodan. And I know that you are part of a group—a cult or a secret society. You couldn't pull this off on your own. You're going to tell me who your leader is and where I can find him."

Mauldron sneered. "I don't need to tell you anything. The Master will summon the spirit of Ravodan, and take the spirit's powers for his own. The Master will bestow great rewards on his followers, and..."

Caina stooped and twisted the knife in his calf, and Mauldron shrieked.

"Who is this Master?" said Caina.

"Your death," said Mauldron.

Again Caina twisted the knife, and Mauldron screamed.

Lucan frowned.

"Not good enough," said Caina. "Tell me his name."

"No," said Mauldron, sweat dripping down his face.

Caina drew another knife and pinned Mauldron's right hand to the floor. His scream echoed off the ceiling, much as the woman's had done.

"Tell me," repeated Caina, "his name."

"No," sputtered Mauldron, "no, I won't..."

Caina pinned his other hand to the floor.

"Stop this," said Lucan.

Caina ignored him. "Tell me about the Master," she said when Mauldron's screams died down, "or I'll start cutting things off."

"Kuroz," said Mauldron, shuddering. "The Master's name is Kuroz."

"I know him," said Lucan, still frowning at Caina. "He's an Ulkaari shaman. He makes money scamming weak-minded nobles, impressing them with parlor tricks and mummery."

Caina pointed at the pyre. "That's no mummery."

"He has some arcane talent," said Lucan, "and sometimes summons up creatures from the netherworld. One of them must have told him about the Sevenfold Pyre."

"Yes," whispered Mauldron. "The Master has power. And when he claims Ravodan's power, he will be even stronger. And we shall be richly rewarded."

"I'm sure," said Caina. "Where is he?"

Mauldron hesitated.

Caina seized the knives buried in Mauldron's hands and twisted.

"The temple of Elerion!" said Mauldron, once he stopped screaming. An abandoned temple to Elerion, the old Caerish god of the sun, stood in the center of the town. And well within the heptagon of the Sevenfold Pyre, if Caina's calculations were correct. "He will summon Ravodan's spirit there! I swear it! Please, please, no more!"

"No more," agreed Caina, and opened his throat.

She straightened up, saw Lucan staring at her.

"What?" she said.

"You went too far," said Lucan.

Caina scowled. "I did what was necessary."

"You've come to deal out pain far too casually."

Caina gave him an incredulous look. "You saw what he did to that woman."

"Mauldron deserved his fate," said Lucan. "I don't care what happened to him. I care about what it will do to you. Your hatred of sorcery is upsetting your judgment. You've told me about some of the nightmares you have. What..."

"Enough!" said Caina, her temper fraying. "I have seen too many people killed by sorcery. I will stop it from happening again!" Her hands balled into fists. "If I have to kill every magus in the Empire, if I have to butcher every last sorcerer in the world, I will do it, I will..."

Her voice cut off.

The man in the hooded cloak she had seen at the warehouse stood behind Lucan, beckoning. She snatched one of her throwing knives from Mauldron and flung it. The blade struck a pillar and clattered to the floor.

There was no one behind Lucan.

"What is it?" said Lucan, sword raised in guard.

"Nothing," said Caina, blinking. "I...thought I saw someone. Again." What was wrong with her? Had the presence of powerful sorcery unhinged her mind?

Or perhaps Lucan was right, and her hatred of sorcery had deranged her...

She pushed the thought aside. Now was not the time to worry about it.

"We should go," said Caina. "If we don't stop Kuroz now, more people than these women will die."

"You're right," said Lucan. "But we should talk more later."

Caina started to disagree, then remembered the strange vision of the hooded man.

"Maybe you're right," she said. "But later."

She retrieved her knives, and they left the cellar.

~o0o~

The temple of Elerion, like the rest of Caer Belaen, had fallen into disrepair. Once it had been a stately edifice of white marble, with columns lining the central sanctuary. Now the half the roof had fallen in, and broken columns ringed the temple like jagged teeth.

Within the sanctuary, Caina saw the flickering glow of flames.

"Kuroz is already here," muttered Caina.

"Fortunately," said Lucan, "that rubble offers plenty of cover."

They crept from fallen column to fallen column, and soon reached the edge of the sanctuary. A half-dozen men stood near the weathered altar. Five wore the red-and-crimson robes Caina had seen earlier. The sixth wore the ragged leathers and furs of an Ulkaari shaman, his pale arms and head marked with elaborate ritual scars. Kuroz himself, no doubt. Lucan had said that Kuroz made his coin scamming foolish nobles, yet Caina felt the presence of powerful sorcery as she looked at him.

Kuroz might have been a charlatan, but his powers were no fraud.

A heptagon had been painted on the sanctuary's stone floor, a black candle resting upon each of the seven points. Three of the candles had been lit, while the other four remained dark. Even as Caina watched, one of the candles burst into flame.

Her mouth thinned into a hard line. Kuroz's acolytes had just murdered another victim.

"Master!" said one of the robed acolytes. "Another candle!"

"Yes," said Kuroz, his voice rich and deep. "Soon, my friends, we shall have the power to return Ravodan's shade to the mortal world. His powers shall be ours, and you will be rewarded."

Caina felt her mouth twist. No doubt Kuroz intended to reward his followers with a quick death. Sorcerers never shared power voluntarily.

Lucan crouched next to her, his lips close to her ear.

"Those acolytes," he whispered. "They look like merchants, or minor nobles. I doubt they'll be any threat."

Caina nodded. "Kuroz is the dangerous one. If we take him down, the others will flee."

A fifth candle blazed to light. Caina shivered with rage.

"I'll distract them," said Lucan. "Once I have their attention, you take Kuroz."

"It is almost done," said Kuroz, raising his arms with a showman's flair. "I will pull Ravodan into this world once more, and we shall be numbered among the great!"

"Go," said Caina, slipping a knife into her hand. "Before he kills anyone else."

"Prepare yourselves!" said Kuroz, beckoning to his followers. "Soon you shall see me transformed, and..."

Lucan strolled into the ruined sanctuary, sword in hand.

Kuroz's speech trailed off, a frown coming over his scarred face, and the acolytes gaped at Lucan.

"Gentlemen!" said Lucan. "I wish to join your little cult. I, too, enjoy setting things on fire."

"You mock us?" said one of the acolytes. "We shall rule the world, and you dare to mock us?"

Caina circled around the base of a ruined column. If she could just get a little closer to Kuroz, she could put a knife into the shaman's throat before he could react.

"Rule the world?" said Lucan with a laugh. "You're a collection of failed merchants who burn helpless women. And when you're done, Kuroz will kill you all anyway. So, yes, I dare to mock you. Though it really doesn't take much daring."

Caina moved past the broken column. She was in plain sight now, but Kuroz and his acolytes remained fixed on Lucan. Kuroz's fingers started to move in the beginnings of a spell. He, unlike his followers, was no fool.

"Kill him," said Kuroz.

The sixth candle burst into flame.

"I'll give you one chance," said Lucan, pointing with his sword. "Leave, now, and I'll let you live." Caina blinked in surprise. She would never have considered offering mercy to the acolytes.

Perhaps Lucan had been right.

The acolytes pulled daggers from their belts and charged Lucan, screaming.

Apparently the acolytes felt no need for mercy.

Kuroz began muttering a spell under his breath, gesturing. Caina straightened up, took a quick step forward, and flung the knife in one smooth motion.

The blade slammed into Kuroz's throat.

Or it would have, had it not disintegrated into glowing splinters an inch from his neck.

He had warded himself against steel weapons.

Kuroz whirled to face Caina, his spell interrupted. On the other side of the heptagon, Lucan battled the acolytes, his sword flashing in the glow of the candles. A grunt, the clang of blade on blade, and one of the acolytes fell dead, his blood pooling on the flagstones.

"Who are you?" said Kuroz.

Caina slipped another knife into her hand. "I know about the Sevenfold Pyre, and I know you want to resurrect Ravodan."

Kuroz laughed, his eyes glinting. "Ravodan was a fool! Else the Ghosts would not have slain him. Yet his power remains in the netherworld, waiting for anyone strong enough to claim it! You are a Ghost, yes? One of those meddlers and schemers?" Another acolyte fell dead. They were unskilled and unaccustomed to fighting, while Lucan was neither. "Another fool poking into things she does not understand."

"You would know," said Caina, taking a cautious step closer. Kuroz might have warded himself from steel, but she doubted he possessed the foresight to shield himself from stone. If she picked up a piece of rubble, she might be able to brain him. Or if she got close enough, she could simply strangle him. "Pyromancy drives its wielders mad."

"I thought as much, once," said Kuroz. "But then I discovered the secrets of fire sorcery. Now I see the world clearly. All the world is fuel, fuel I will burn to enhance my power."

Shouts rang out, and another acolyte fell.

"You will not," said Caina. "You will murder no more innocents."

"Oh," said Kuroz. "I will."

He thrust out his palm, flames crackling around his fingers. Caina threw herself to the left as a blast of flame erupted from his hand. The fire missed, but the heat of it struck Caina across the face. She scrambled back to her feet at Kuroz began another spell, fresh fire shimmering in his hand, his eyes lit up with madness.

And as she did, the seventh candle ignited.

Arcane power thrummed in the air, and the ground trembled beneath Caina's boots. A beam of crimson light erupted from the heptagon, stabbing into the sky. Darkness writhed and swirled within the light, and Caina felt a sense of distance as she looked into it.

As if the darkness was a portal to another place.

A scream rang out, and the final acolyte crumpled to the floor. Lucan stepped over the bodies, blood dripping from his sword.

"Splendid," said Kuroz, flexing his fingers. "You've saved me the trouble of killing them later." He pointed at Lucan, fiery light glimmering around his hand.

Caina ducked, seized a fist-sized chunk of stone, and threw it. It smacked into Kuroz's jaw with enough force to send teeth flying, and the shaman stumbled to one knee with a cry of pain. As she suspected, he had failed to ward himself against stone. She raced forward, but Kuroz was faster. He flung out his hands with a snarl, and a sheet of fire erupted from the ground. Caina skidded to a stop and veered right, but the fire spread in front of her.

A heartbeat later she found herself trapped within a ring of fire. The heat made sweat pour off her face and drip down her neck. Through the roaring flames she glimpsed another burning ring, Lucan trapped within it.

"That rather hurt," muttered Kuroz, spitting out a mouthful of blood. "I should kill you both. Listen to you scream as I roast the flesh right off your bones." He lifted his hand, and the light of madness brightened in his eyes once more. "Or...yes. I'll make you watch first. You will see me claim Ravodan's power for myself. You'll know that you failed, Ghosts. And then, and only then, will I kill you."

He nodded to himself and turned to face the pulsing column of darkness and crimson light. Caina edged towards the flames, but the sheer heat drove her back. Kuroz had his back to her, and it would be so easy to take him down. But first she had to find a way through his sorcerous ring of fire.

One of the pillars leaned close. Could she reach up and seize it? No, it was too high, though if she knocked the pillar over, it might provide a safe path through the flames.

Kuroz began to chant, the column of light pulsing in time to his spell.

Caina's frown deepened.

Fire needed fuel. Yet Kuroz's sorcerous flames burned upon

the barren stone floor nonetheless. Or, more specifically, upon the stone flagstones covering the floor.

So what would happened if Caina tipped over one of those flagstones?

She yanked a dagger from its sheath, knelt, and began to pry up the flagstone. For a moment it did not move as her muscles trembled with strain. Then it rose up an inch or so. Caina seized the lip of the flagstone with both hands and stood, trying to bear the load with her legs. Straining, she forced the stone up, and then pushed it into the flames.

It landed with a terrific crash, opening a gap in the fire.

Kuroz spun in surprise as Caina raced through the gap in the ring of fire. He drew back his hand, flames glimmering in his fingers, but Caina was faster. She seized his wrist, spun past him, and planted her boot in the small of his back. Kuroz lurched forward, losing his balance.

Right into the broken ring of fire.

His ragged clothes ignited at once, and his scream drowned out even the roar of the flames. Kuroz staggered towards her, reaching for her with burning arms, but Caina dodged. Her hand closed around a broken chunk of rock, and she stepped as close as she dared and hammered it against Kuroz's head.

The shaman fell, wreathed in flame.

A moment later the rings of fire disappeared, though the column of crimson light still rose from the heptagon.

Lucan hurried towards her. "Are you injured?"

Caina let out a deep breath. "I'm fine." She looked at Kuroz's burning corpse. He had gotten the same death he had dealt out to his victims. He deserved to suffer. He deserved more pain than Caina had inflicted on him.

He deserved to scream.

The intensity of her hatred unsettled her.

"No. Do not be frightened of it."

A man's voice. But not Lucan's.

Caina turned, a throwing knife in hand.

The man in the hooded cloak stood near the glowing heptagon. As Caina watched, he reached up and drew back his hood, revealing a gray-bearded face with deep wrinkles and glittering eyes.

"Who are you?" said Caina. "One of Kuroz's disciples? Speak!"

Lucan looked back and forth, frowning.

The cloaked man laughed. "Kuroz was a fool with no vision. He deserved his fate. "

"Yes," said Caina.

Lucan's frown deepened.

"But Kuroz was not the only one," said the cloaked man, his eyes reflecting the pulsing column of fiery light. "You've slain so many sorcerers, so many corrupt magi. So many innocents you have avenged. But there are always more, aren't there? More magi spilling the blood of innocents to fuel their power. More sorcerers using their spells to terrorize and enslave."

Caina nodded.

"You can't kill them all," said the cloaked man. "You can't make them burn they way they deserve to burn."

"I can't," said Caina.

"You can't do what?" said Lucan.

"I tried to do it," said the cloaked man, shaking his head. "I tried to cleanse the world in fire, to transform the wicked into torches to light the path of the righteous. But I failed. I was not strong enough." His eyes, glimmering like coals in the darkness, met Caina's. "But you are strong enough. You have the will, the determination. You can hunt down every last sorcerer, every last necromancer. You can make them burn."

That sounded so very tempting. But some part of Caina's mind screamed warning, and she hesitated.

"Take my hand," said the cloaked man. "Take my hand, and I will give you the power. You will burn away the wickedness of the world, and reforge it strong and new and clean."

"Yes," whispered Caina. "They deserve to burn, don't they?"

"Caina!"

Lucan's voice struck her like a splash of cold water.

"Who the devil are you talking to?" said Lucan, looking back and forth, sword raised in guard.

Caina blinked, looked at the cloaked man, and then back at Lucan. "You...you don't see him?"

"See who?" said Lucan. "There's no one here but us."

Caina frowned. Behind the cloaked man the column of light stabbed into the sky, darkness writhing in its core. Darkness that seemed like a portal to elsewhere.

A doorway, perhaps, for something to enter this world?

The realization struck Caina.

"You," she said. "You're Ravodan."

"Yes," said the cloaked man. "The Ghosts did not understand. The world must be cleansed in fire, and the wicked shall be burn. We shall make them burn. Kuroz, too, was weak. You are far stronger. Become my host. Our purpose is one. Join with me, and my powers shall be yours. Together, we will make the wicked burn."

"No!" said Caina. "I know what you did. You murdered dozens here. The Ghosts brought you down for it!"

"They did not understand," said Ravodan's shade, beckoning to her. "And we are more alike than you know. Join with me, now."

Caina hesitated. Ravodan had been a murderer, a monster who used his sorcerous power for evil. Yet she had seen so much suffering, so much death. With Ravodan's power, could she have prevented it? Could she prevent more suffering and torment and death?

If she could, didn't she have an obligation to take the power?

She wavered, her hand starting to rise...

"Caina!" Lucan stepped closer. "Whatever it's telling you, don't listen. Remember what Kuroz did. Remember those women on the pyres!"

Caina flinched, remembering the burned corpses.

Ravodan's lips peeled back from his teeth in a snarl.

"You are mine!" he hissed. "And if you will not give yourself to me, then I will take you..."

"Go burn," said Caina.

She flung the knife in her hand, knocking one of the candles into the heptagon. Ravodan shrieked in sudden agony, the pillar of bloody light flickering. Caina flung another knife, and then another, the candles winking out, and the column of light vanished. Ravodan shuddered once, seeming to ripple and distort, and then disappeared.

And the tingling presence of sorcery against Caina's skin vanished.

~oOo~

"You were right," said Caina the next morning.

They stood outside Mauldron's house, watching Caer Belaen's militia hurry back and forth. Kuroz and his chief followers were dead, but Caina had located a list of the cult's members in Mauldron's study, and passed it on to the local magistrates. Numerous wealthy merchants suddenly found themselves under arrest for murder and illicit sorcery, and would face the headsman's block soon enough.

It was still a kinder fate than they had dealt their victims.

"About what?" said Lucan. "The weather, you mean? It is a lovely morning. Though I expected more clouds, to be honest..."

"No," said Caina. "About me. I have been too ready to deal out pain and death to those I think deserve it." She took a deep breath. "And because of that, I listened to Ravodan's shade."

"You turned him down," said Lucan.

"I did," said Caina. "But I considered it. His words were sweet. I would like to see the magi burn. I know it was a mad dream. I know that kind of power would lead only to ruin. But I wanted it nonetheless."

"I understand better than you think," said Lucan. "I told you the magi slew my wife, years ago." He looked away for a moment. "And for a long time, I wanted to kill them all. I still fight them. But that kind of hatred will devour you. You cannot live on vengeance alone."

"That's all I've known for so long," said Caina. "What else is there?"

He hesitated, and then took her hand.

"Love, perhaps?" said Lucan.

Caina hesitated, and then took his other hand.

"Yes," she said. "I think so."

JACK IN BLACK

by Linda A. B. Davis

People can do things on Halloween that they can't do the rest of the year. Unfortunately, so can other things.

Linda A. B. Davis lives in Pensacola, Florida, just ten miles from the Alabama line, where she spends much of her time swatting mosquitoes and dodging hurricanes. Her house is crazy full with a husband, three dogs, three cats, and her daughter and son-in-law who hang out a lot with their own cat. She prefers it that way and isn't sure she can write under any other circumstances.

Linda holds a master's degree in Communication Arts from the University of West Florida. She's discovered that she enjoys writing fiction as well, but specifically science fiction and fantasy. Her speculative fiction as been published in two DAW Books anthologies and other genre venues. This is her first sale to the *Sword & Sorceress* series, and she's quite stoked about her work appearing with the wonderful stories included here.

Linda also markets individual stories digitally, and you can read more about them at www.lindaabdavis.com. You may read a free story there, too.

The Halloween night sky dripped magic. It covered Kiki with an almost invisible sheen of bugaboo induced anticipation. The clouds crossed the black above in shades of gray, sometimes allowing a flicker of moonlight through. A crisp breeze cut through the stillness with abandon.

Kiki sniffed the air with purpose. The scent of dark magic slammed her, sending a shot of adrenaline through her system. She shivered once before getting a hold on the immediate sense of dread.

She didn't understand it. The Halloween magic of previous years had possessed a carefree air about it and spread easily so as to add to the fun. Everyone loved that magic.

This darker magic was different. Kiki felt the malice riding the winds. She shivered again, realizing it was taking advantage of the one day it claimed free access to the world above. Her world.

Kiki gathered herself and stepped back into her tiny kitchen to see her daughter, Bennita, talking to her best friend, Jaz. They were both already dressed for Halloween. Bennita had put together an adorable pirate princess costume, and Jaz was a neon clown, quite bright.

"She might," Jaz said.

"I'll try, but I bet not."

"Might what?" Kiki asked. "What might I do?"

Bennita huffed. "Let us go trick or treating without you."

"You were right. Not, it is. Sorry, girls. We don't know everyone who lives here and we might only think we know the others."

"We're ten years old, Mom. That's plenty old enough to go in this neighborhood. And we'll be with the other kids," Bennita said. "The kids who get to go by themselves."

Kiki looked at Bennita, knowing she was right. Lots of kids their age went by themselves, but those other mothers didn't know of the black magic whipping about their own suburban neighborhood at this very moment.

Jaz jumped in. "My mom said it was okay with her if it was okay with you. You can call her at work if you want."

"No, I don't want to bother her." Jaz's mom was a single mother and needed her job.

"Our friends will just make fun of us tomorrow for being such babies." Bennita sat down with a deflated plop.

Kiki was quiet for a moment. She studied Bennita, whom she knew was desperate to fit in. Some of her friends were already starting to snub her, knowing she was different somehow. Her rich golden eyes stood out against her soft brown skin and her crow-colored hair which curled just the slightest bit. Being kids, they assumed it was just her beauty that set her apart, not knowing enough to pay more attention.

They couldn't know what lived just below Bennita's skin, but Kiki could smell it. It was magic, just like the sort that lived within her. That magic would take over Bennita's life one day, throwing her into a maelstrom of confusion until she learned to fit her special ability into the everyday routine of life.

Kiki planned on telling Bennita everything in a couple of years, before the onset of puberty, but after she'd been afforded a childhood. She would help her daughter navigate that time with knowledge and training, something she hadn't received.

Kiki and her American parents knew nothing about the origin of her ability. They'd adopted her out of Haiti when she was five after she'd been orphaned in an earthquake. Kiki had been too afraid to tell them what she could do, afraid they'd be sorry for taking her in. She now realized the fault in her logic, but after thirty years, it was too late. It was best kept to herself and her husband, Jerome.

Kiki took a breath and leaned against the table, knowing she would somehow, certainly, be sorry for what she was about to do. She comforted herself with the knowledge that at least she could be present to keep them safe. The girls would never know she was there.

"Fine," Kiki said. "You're right. You guys are getting older, and it's time for you to start taking care of yourselves some."

The girls grinned and jumped up, immediately ready to go. Bennita kissed Kiki on her cheek. "Thanks, Mom. We'll be safe."

"Yeah, Miss Kiki," Jaz said. "All we'll get tonight is candy." She grabbed their little pumpkin bags, both pristine now but guaranteed to be grubby and torn upon return.

Kiki hugged each one and sent them on their way. She stood still for a moment, centering herself. She went to the kitchen and drank a full glass of orange juice. She'd found that some serious sugar before a shift made it easier. Liquid was the fastest way to get it.

She then went to a closet, grabbed a twin-sized sheet, and cut it in half with a couple of holes for eyes. It was cliché, but what else was she going to do on short notice? She had to hurry.

Kiki stripped and lay on her bed. She drew in deep breaths, filling her lungs and then slowly blowing the air out. This was the best way to do it. She could start the shift without preparations, but the side effects were more intense. Kiki preferred to avoid the pain.

A small, yellow glow appeared in the middle of the blotchy shadows behind her eyelids. She kept its growth to her own comfortable schedule. Only sometimes, during times of stress, did she lose control and pay the price with an uncontrolled shift. The blinding and enveloping light, accompanied by an internal shrill, screaming sound, brought on a mother of a migraine. It usually put her down for several hours. By taking her time, she just needed a few moments afterwards to gather her wits.

Kiki envisioned herself at age ten. She couldn't go forward, but she could choose any age that she'd already been. She wanted to be about the size of the girls so she could blend in. The sheet would hide her face, and her voice would change with her age.

Kiki had read fantasy stories about shifters having great pain during their shifts. Her biggest discomfort during a controlled shift was when her body felt like rubber. She could feel her muscles, tissues, bones and skin stretch to the breaking point and then resettle when everything slipped back into place.

When done, Kiki sat up and held her head in her hands, regaining her equilibrium. She stood up and studied her reflection in the mirror. Yep, it was her at ten—skinny, plaited hair, and slightly crooked teeth. Her eyes were the only caveat as they never changed. It didn't cause her many problems, but every now and again, someone remarked how much older she seemed to be when shifted young.

Kiki grabbed underclothes, jeans and a shirt that she kept in a special drawer with girls' clothes of various sizes. She shimmied into them hastily, slipped her feet into some tennis shoes, and threw the sheet over her head. She wiggled the sheet around until the holes aligned with her eyes.

Kiki glanced at the clock. Bennita and Jaz had fifteen minutes' head start on her. That probably accounted for a few houses, a checking of the bags for goodies, and talking with their friends.

She stepped outside and lifted her face to the moon again. The bad magic was still there, laying heavily over the Halloween magic. And there. Kiki caught a whiff of Bennita's magic. She hurried on.

Children charged through the streets shouting in their excitement. Kiki visually sorted through fairies, cowboys, superheroes, ballerinas and so many truly original costumes. Her favorite had to be the zombie majorette, shiny baton and all.

There! She spotted the neon green of Jaz's clown hair half a street down. She ran to catch up, cinching her sheet with her hand so it didn't get tangled in her legs. They were with a loosely grouped bunch of other kids going from house to house.

"Did you see the Muellers' house?" she heard Jaz ask Bennita. "They had a cauldron full of candy that their mom was stirring. She looked disgusting in her witch outfit."

"Yeah," Bennita responded. "We'll hit that one on the way back up. I heard the Porters are giving away doughnuts this year."

"Maybe chocolate glazed, huh?"

Kiki tried to lag behind them to stay unnoticed. She didn't need to be part of the group, but she wanted to stay close. The stench of a rot drifted by every few seconds, and she knew the source was somewhere nigh.

The kids ran to a house and Kiki started up the steps until she realized she'd forgotten a bag. Crap! Well, she'd just have to hide her arms so people would assume she had one under the sheet. She hung back on the street and watched the shadows while the kids collected their mini-Snickers and Tootsie Rolls.

Kiki wrinkled her nose. She let her eyes wander lazily over the surrounding homes, trusting her subconscious to tell her what was wrong. Her gaze rested on some bushes at the corner of the Johnston house. She sidled over while everyone was busy, and confirmed her suspicions. This was the source of the dark magic invading her neighborhood, endangering them all.

The thing was black, blacker than any black Kiki had ever seen. A chill seeped from it to permeate quite a distance beyond its reach. It had a defined edge to its shape which quivered slightly as she neared. What truly scared her though was to find herself feeling evaluated, appraised, assessed.

"What are you?" she asked.

It's Halloween. What do you think?

The words came to her covered in oil. And her magic told her what it was. It might manifest itself in many different forms, but this was evil in its truest, visible form. This is what powered the monsters of the world. Lucifer. Jack. Adolf. Pol.

And it was in her world, her neighborhood. "What do you want?" she asked.

Be honest now. You really want to know how to get rid of me. You can't. Not until I've gotten what I came for. Tasty, little morsels of magic. Your magic.

"You can't have it," Kiki said.

And you can't stop me.

A vision of red, a tiny Valentine's Day heart, bumped her as it ran by. "Sorry, Ghost!"

Of course, their magic is tempting, too. The magic of youth. Sweet, like the treats they collect.

Kiki glanced back and saw Bennita's group headed this way, taking a shortcut through the bushes to the Dos Santos house. She jumped in front of them, waving her arms and "wooing" like a ghost. "Go around. Go to the street," she said in a spooky voice, hoping they would be amused and move on.

"What's this kid's deal?" asked a pimply, massacre victim drenched in pretend blood.

"Just go around him," another voice said.

"Move him," said another.

Kiki could feel the darkness tense, tempted to spring. She needed to get these kids gone before it lost patience.

"Fine," Kiki said to Blood-Is-Us. "Step in the dog poop. It's all over in the bushes there. You don't smell it?"

Bennita spoke up. "I do, guys. It reeks."
She must be yours. Her magic has the same flavor. Nibble, nibble.
Kiki put her hands on her hips. There was no way this thing was getting its hands on Bennita.
"Just go around," she said to the trick or treaters.
"God, you're weird," said a blonde, little elf girl. "Who are you anyway?"
"Who cares?" said Blood-Is-Us. "Let's go."
They began walking around her, except for Bennita, who was lagging behind and stepped too close to the darkness. The monster shot out an oily tendril and grabbed her leg. She froze.
It was rather a blur to Kiki after that, but this *thing* had her daughter. In immediate response, she called a shift. The shift itself wasn't important, but the light that came with it was tantamount. Jerome always talked about how bright the shifting light was on the outside, too. The presence was darkness incarnate, and darkness abhorred light.
Uncontrolled, the light burst into being, overwhelming Kiki with an unholy pain ripping through her head. She barely heard the internal screaming or saw the light as she crumpled to the ground. Her body began to melt, or so it seemed, as everything stretched and pulled. Kiki had never called her power like this, and she wasn't sure she would survive it. Even if she didn't, she hoped to take the blackness with her.
She came to with Bennita shaking her, trying to wake her up. Kiki huddled on the ground, reveling in the coolness of the earth beneath her. Her skin felt like it was on fire, and she was nauseous. She struggled to her hands and knees to retch.
"Mom, are you okay?"
"Hey, Miss Kiki, do you need a drink?" Jaz asked. "Someone gave us a juice box."
"That was gnarly." Kiki recognized the irritating voice of Blood-Is-Us. His whine didn't help her migraine, upping the pain level to just short of unbearable.
Kiki emptied her stomach and wiped her mouth when she was done. "Is that thing gone?"

She realized her clothes had ripped off of her during the change, but she still had the sheet. Bennita had wrapped it around her like a towel, and it covered her to mid-thigh.

"That gross, black thing? Yeah, when the big light exploded, it got sucked into the ground. Boy, did it stink!" Jaz emphasized by holding her nose.

"Here," Kiki said. "Help me up. Then help me get home. And I will take that juice."

"What was that, Mom? And how did you get here? Where did the other kid go?"

"First, Jaz, I'm going to lie down until I can dump this migraine. Then I'll talk to Benny, and she can tell you." They'd have to create a good cover story for Jaz.

As she sat sucking the fruit punch flavored juice out of the tiny, square box, Kiki wondered what she would tell Bennita. This was ahead of schedule, and she hadn't prepared anything yet. She hoped it would come to her like it had always done before.

The real question was how to get home in a sheet with so many parents on the road. Oh, well, she thought with a sigh. It *was* Halloween.

ABOUT SWORD AND SORCERESS

by Elisabeth Waters

The *Sword and Sorceress* anthology series started in 1983, when Marion Zimmer Bradley, complaining that she was sick and tired of sword & sorcery stories where the female character was "a bad-conduct prize" for the male protagonist, persuaded Donald A. Wollheim of DAW Books to buy an anthology of sword & sorcery with strong female characters. The book was published in 1984.

The original title, *Swords and Sorceresses*, was changed during the production process when it was discovered that nobody could pronounce it in a conversation. So the first book was titled simply *Sword and Sorceress*. It was a success, so the following year we got *Sword and Sorceress II*.

It is my personal belief that if either Marion or Don had realized how successful this series was going to be, they would not have used Roman numerals, but they did, and DAW published the series through *Sword and Sorceress XXI*. (That's #21, for the non-Romans among us.)

Norilana Books picked up the series with volume 22, and because Marion was no longer alive to edit it, Vera entitled the book *Marion Zimmer Bradley's Sword and Sorceress XXII*. This led to five titles that were listed on the royalty reports as "Marion Zimmer Bradley's" with the only thing different being the ISBN.

So, we are now reissuing volumes 22 through 27 as *Sword and Sorceress 22* through *Sword and Sorceress 27*. We hope that our readers will find this less confusing. We know that we will.

ABOUT THE MARION ZIMMER BRADLEY LITERARY WORKS TRUST

The Marion Zimmer Bradley Literary Works Trust was created by Mrs. Bradley during her lifetime to hold her copyrights and administer her estate. It is now the owner of all of her copyrights, and it is reissuing her backlist and continuing the series she started: Avalon; Darkover; and Sword & Sorceress.

It is the publisher for the following Sword & Sorceress volumes:

SWORD AND SORCERESS 22, 2007
SWORD AND SORCERESS 23, 2008
SWORD AND SORCERESS 24, 2009
SWORD AND SORCERESS 25, 2010
SWORD AND SORCERESS 26, 2011
SWORD AND SORCERESS 27, 2012
SWORD AND SORCERESS 28, 2013

For more information, see our website: www.mzbworks.com.

Made in the USA
Lexington, KY
22 February 2016